Midsummer's Eve

Midsummer's Eve

— ❧ —

PHILIPPA CARR

G. P. PUTNAM'S SONS/NEW YORK

G. P. Putnam's Sons
Publishers Since 1838
200 Madison Avenue
New York, NY 10016

Library of Congress Cataloging-in-Publication Data

Plaidy, Jean, date.
Midsummer's eve.

I. Title.
PR6015.I3M5   1986   823'.914   86-650
ISBN 0-399-13148-5

Printed in the United States of America
2 3 4 5 6 7 8 9 10

Contents

The Witch in the Woods
9

Scandal in High Places
76

On the High Seas
135

Outback
161

A Visitor from Australia
224

Discoveries
276

The Witch
in the Woods

I was not quite nine years old on that Midsummer's Eve, but I shall never forget it because, after what happened on that memorable night, I ceased to be the innocent girl I had been up to that time.

My comfortable home, my easy life and my adored parents had given me no indication that such things could be. We lived amicably in what was more like a castle than a house. It had been the family home of the Cadorsons for generations. Cador meant "warrior" in the Cornish language, so our earliest ancestor must have been a great fighter. I could well believe that. The house stood on a cliff, so that from the windows we could look out on the sea. Built of grey stone, it looked forbidding. It was like a fortress. It probably had been at one time. There were two turrets and a path along the battlements from one to the other. It was known simply as Cador. My father was proud of it—my mother, too, although I sometimes thought she was a little nostalgic for her home on the other side of England—the south east corner. We were in the south west so when we visited my grandparents, or they came to us, it meant travelling the breadth of England.

When I was younger the grandparents used to come to us fairly often. Now we had to go to them for they were getting old, particularly Grandpapa Dickon.

Cador was situated about a quarter of a mile from the little town of West Poldorey, which was divided from East Poldorey by the river which cut through the wooded hills to flow into the sea. The two towns were connected by a bridge which had stood up to the weather for five hundred years and looked as if it would last as many more. Old men liked to congregate there and lean over the stone parapets contemplating life and the river. A great number of those men were fishermen and there were always boats lying in the little harbour.

I loved to be there when the fishing boats came in and to watch all the activity on the quay, which was always accompanied by the cry of the seagulls as they flew low watching for any of the fish which would be thrown back into the river.

The Cadors had for generations been lords of the manor whose unspoken duty it was to make sure of the prosperity of the two towns and the outlying neighbourhood. Consequently my brother and I were always treated with respect by the townsfolk. It was a very happy, cosy existence until I was brought face to face with another aspect of life on that Midsummer's Eve.

There was a family house in London, too. We used to meet there for it was not so very far for the grandparents to come—though it was a long journey for us. I loved travelling. As we went along through the narrow winding lanes my father often told us stories about highwaymen who held up coaches and demanded money. My mother would cry: "Stop it, Jake. You're frightening the children." That was true; but like most children we enjoyed being frightened while we felt perfectly safe in the company of our parents.

I loved them both dearly. I was sure they were the best parents in the world; but I did have a special feeling for my father and I think he had for me. Jacco was my mother's favourite—not so much because he was a boy but because she knew I was my father's, and she felt it necessary to adjust the balance.

My father was one of the two most exciting men I knew. The other was Rolf Hanson. My father was very tall and dark; he had very bright sparkling eyes which gave the impression that he was amused by life, although he could be serious sometimes. He had had an adventurous life and often talked about it. He had lived with the gypsies at one time; he had killed a man and been sent to Australia as a punishment and stayed there for nine years. My mother was beautiful with dark eyes and hair. It was small wonder that I was dark-haired; but I had inherited Grandmother Lottie's blue eyes which, as my mother said, turned up now and then in her family. I was on good terms with my brother Jacco though we had our differences

[10]

now and then. Jacco was named after our father so he was Jake really. When he had been a baby he was known as Little Jake but it became confusing to have two Jakes in the family so he was called Jacco and that name stayed with him.

It was wonderful to live near the sea. On hot days Jacco and I would take off our shoes and stockings and paddle in the cove just below Cador. Sometimes we would get one of the fishermen to take us out and we went sailing out of the harbour and along the coast towards Plymouth Sound. Sometimes we caught shrimps and baby crabs and we hunted for semi-precious stones like topaz and amethyst along the shore. We often saw the poor people down on the beach collecting limpets which they used for some sort of dish, and perhaps buying the last of the fish which the fishermen had brought in and which had failed to find buyers among the more monied folk. I liked to go down with Isaacs our butler and listen to him bargaining for fish. He was a very stately gentleman and even Jacco was a little in awe of him. When Isaacs took the fish back to the house Mrs. Penlock, the cook, would examine it carefully and if it were not to her liking she would show her disapproval in her usual forceful manner. She was a very garrulous woman. Many times I heard her complain: "Is this the best you could do, Mr. Isaacs? My patience me, what am I expected to do with this? Couldn't you find me some nice plaice or some sizable John Dorys?" Mr. Isaacs always had the power to subdue any of his staff. He would sternly retort, "It is God who decides what goes into the sea and what comes out of it, Mrs. Penlock." That would silence her. She was very superstitious and afraid to question the matter when put like that.

It was at the quayside that I first noticed Digory. Lean, lively, his skin tanned to a deep brown by the weather, his black hair a mass of curls, his small dark eyes alert and cunning, his trousers ragged and his feet bare, he darted among the tubs and creels with the slippery ease of an eel and the cunning of a monkey.

He had sidled up to a tub of pilchards while fisherman Jack Gort was arguing with Isaacs about the price of hake and had his back to us. I gasped, for Digory had thrust his hand into the tub and picked up a handful of fish which, with a skill which must have come from long training, he slipped into a bag.

I opened my mouth to call Jack Gort's attention to the theft but Digory was looking straight at me. He put his finger to his mouth as

[11]

though commanding silence; and oddly enough I *was* silent. Then, almost mockingly, he took another handful of fish which went into the bag, conveniently there for this purpose. He grinned at me before he darted away from the quayside.

I was too astounded to speak, and when Jack Gort had finished his conference with Isaacs, I said nothing. I watched anxiously while Jack surveyed the tub but apparently he did not notice that some of his stock had vanished, for he said nothing.

I believe Digory thought that because I had witnessed his villainy and not reported it, I had more or less connived at it; and that gave us a special understanding.

Shortly afterwards when I was walking in the woods, I saw him again. He was lying on the bank throwing stones into the river.

"Hi there," he said as I drew level with him.

I was about to walk haughtily past. That was not the way in which humble people spoke to our family and I thought he could not know who I was.

He seemed to read my thoughts for he said again: "Hi there, Cadorson girl."

"So . . . you know me?"

"'Course I know 'ee. Everyone knows Cadorsons. Didn't I see 'ee down at the fish market?"

"I saw you steal fish," I said.

"Did 'ee and all."

"Stealing is wrong. You'll get punished for it."

"I don't," he said. "I be smart."

"Then wait till you get to Heaven. It's all recorded."

"I be too smart for 'em," he repeated.

"Not for the angels."

He looked surprised. He picked up a stone and threw it into the river.

"Bet 'ee can't throw as far."

For answer I showed him that I could, whereupon he picked up another stone and in a few seconds we were standing side by side throwing stones into the water.

He turned to me suddenly and said: "'Tweren't stealing. All fish in the sea belongs to everybody. 'Tis anybody's for the taking."

"Then why don't *you* go and fish for it like Jack Gort?"

"Why should I when he does it for me?"

"I think you're a very wicked boy."

He grinned at me. "Cos why?" he asked.

"Because you stole Jack Gort's fish."

"Telling on me?" he asked.

I hesitated and he came closer to me. "Don't 'ee dare," he said.

"What if I did?"

"Do you know my granny?"

I shook my head.

"She'd cast a spell on 'ee. Then you'd wither right away and die."

"Who says so?"

He came closer to me, narrowed his eyes and said in a whisper: "Cos she's a . . ."

"A what?"

He shook his head. "Not telling. You be careful or it'll be the worse for 'ee, Cadorson girl."

With that he leaped into the air, and catching a branch of a tree, he swung on it for a few seconds, looking more than ever like a clever monkey. Then he dropped to the ground and ran off.

I felt the impulse to run after him and it was irresistible. We came to the cottage which was almost hidden by the thick shrubs which grew all round it. I was not far behind him. I watched him run through the jungle of shrubs to the small dwelling with its cob walls and thatched roof. The door was open and a black cat sat on the doorstep.

The boy turned to look back. He stood in the doorway and I knew he was daring me to follow him. I hesitated. Then he grimaced and disappeared into the cottage.

The cat remained on the doorstep watching me and its green eyes seemed malevolent.

I turned and ran home as fast as I could.

I knew he was, in Mrs. Penlock's words, "That varmint of Mother Ginny's." And I trembled with fear and amazement that I had stood on the threshold of Mother Ginny's evil abode and had really been on the point of going in.

I thought about the boy a great deal and I began to learn something about him, although Mother Ginny and her Varmint were evidently not a subject to be discussed in front of the young. Often when I entered the kitchen the conversation stopped. It was usually about girls having babies when they shouldn't or some misdemeanour which had been committed—and now, of course, Mother Ginny.

I knew that she lived in her lonely cottage in the woods with her cat and she had been quite alone until the coming of the Varmint, which had been only some months before. "That," said Mrs. Penlock to the company seated at the table, which included most of the staff, for they were having their midmorning refreshment—hot sweet tea and oat biscuits, "was something to set the cat among the pigeons. Who would have thought of Mother Ginny having a family! You'd have thought she'd been begot by the Devil. That Varmint is said to be her grandson so she must have had a husband or at least a son or daughter. And now she has this boy . . . Digory."

He had come to her by stealth, I discovered. One day he hadn't been there and the next he was. The story went that he had been brought to his grandmother because he was now an orphan.

It was apparently not long before he had made his presence known. Even before I discovered him at the fish market people were aware of him—and watchful. "Such another as his Granny," they said.

Now more than ever I wanted to hear about Mother Ginny and the place where she and her grandson lived.

I learned by degrees. It was a pity the servants knew that Mother Ginny was not a subject my parents would wish to be discussed before me. They were therefore wary; but Mother Ginny and her grandson were irresistible topics of conversation, and I had a habit of making myself unobtrusive. I would sit curled up in a corner of the kitchen—even sometimes pretending to be asleep—while I listened to the chatter; and if I could remain really quiet and manage to fade into the kitchen landscape I could glean a good deal.

Mrs. Penlock was a great talker. She ruled the kitchen with rigid conventionality; she knew the procedure for every occasion—her rights and everyone else's rights; she was a great upholder of rights; she was determined that these should not be diminished or exceeded; and woe betide anyone who tried to prevent her from receiving her due.

She knew the habits of all the maids and I was sure they would find it very difficult to hide any transgression from her. She reckoned that she knew her place and she expected everyone else to know his or hers.

"Mother Ginny," I heard her say, "oh, I wouldn't like to get round the wrong side of that one. It would be more than your life was worth . . . and I mean that. You girls can laugh but witches is witches and no matter if they do give you something to get you out of your little bits of trouble . . . you'd be fools to get caught up with the likes of them. I've heard talk of folks as got real pisky-mazed cos they would wander in them woods after dark and go near Mother Ginny's place. Wander round and round they do, not knowing where they be to and the piskies all out there . . . though you couldn't see 'em . . . laughing at 'em . . . And not to be right again till that Mother Ginny have took off the spell. It ain't no laughing matter, young 'Tilda. You go wandering out in them woods with Stableman John and you'll see what happens to 'ee. Then you'll be to Mother Ginny to see if she can give you something to help 'ee out. Wouldn't catch me being caught with the likes of Mother Ginny . . . no matter what."

So Mother Ginny was a witch. I gathered little bits of information about her. Her clients usually went to consult her after dark because what they wanted to ask her about was a secret between her and themselves. When the servants passed her cottage they would cross their fingers; and some of them carried garlic with them because that was said to have special powers against evil. Few would venture past the cottage after dark. And that boy Digory actually lived there!

He and Mother Ginny had become of great interest to me.

When I wanted to learn something I asked my father. He and I often went riding together. He was proud of my skill on a horse and I was constantly trying to impress him with my excellence. The manner in which he always treated me as an adult endeared him to me, for he always listened to what I had to say and gave me a sensible answer.

It was autumn, I remember, and the leaves were just beginning to turn bronze. Many of them had already fallen and made a rich carpet beneath us. There was a dampness in the air, and mist, although it was midmorning, touched the trees with a greyish blue which made them look very mysterious.

We came to the beaten track which led to Mother Ginny's cottage and I said: "Papa, why are people afraid of Mother Ginny?"

He answered at once: "Because she is different from themselves. Many people would like us all to be made in the same mould. They fear what they do not understand."

"Why don't they understand Mother Ginny?"

"Because she dabbles in mysteries."

"Do you know what they are?"

He shook his head.

"Are *you* afraid of her?"

He burst out laughing. "I am not one of those people who wish everyone to conform. I think variety makes life more interesting. Besides, I'm rather odd myself. Do you know anyone else who is like me?"

"No," I said. "I certainly do not. There is only one of you. But that is different from being Mother Ginny."

"Why?"

"Because you are rich and important."

"Oh, there you have hit the nail right on the head. I can afford to be eccentric. I can do the strangest things and people dare not question."

"They would be afraid to."

"Because their well-being depends on me to some extent. That is why they respect me. They do not depend on Mother Ginny in that way but they think she has powers which come from the unknown and they are afraid of her."

"It is a good thing to have people afraid of you."

"If you are strong, perhaps. But the poor and the humble . . . they must beware."

I continued to think of Mother Ginny. I was fascinated by everything connected with her—and that included Digory. I used to lie in wait for him and talk to him. We would sit on the banks of the river throwing stones into the water—a favourite occupation of his—listening to the plop as they dropped and seeing who could throw the farthest.

He asked me questions about the Big House, "That Cador" he called it. I described it in detail: the hall with its refectory table set with pewter plates and goblets; the coat of arms on the wall among the weaponry; helmets and halberds; the Elizabethan pole-arm, swords and shields; the drawing room with its tapestries depicting the Wars of the Roses; the fine linen-fold panelling; the punch room where the men took their punch and port wine; the chairs with their backs exquisitely embroidered in Queen Anne's tatting; the room where King Charles had slept when he was fleeing from the Roundheads—a very special room this, which must never be altered. I told him how I used to climb onto the bed in which the King had lain listening for the approach of his enemies and wondering how long it would be before they hunted him out.

Digory would listen intently. He used to call out: "Go on. Go on. Tell me some more."

And I would romance a little, making up stories of how the great Cador—the Warrior—had saved the King from capture; but reverence for the history learned from my governess, Miss Caster, made me add hastily: "But he was caught in the end."

I told him about the solarium, the old kitchens and the chapel with its stone floor and squint through which the lepers used to look because, on account of their disease, they were not allowed to come in where ordinary folks were.

He was fascinated by the squint. I told him that there were two other peepholes in the house. These we called peeps. One of them looked down on the hall so that people could see who their visitors were without being seen themselves. This was in the solarium; the other was in another room. This looked down on the chapel. It was in an alcove where ladies could sit and enjoy the service from above on those occasions when there were guests in the house with whom it would be unseemly for them to mix.

In exchange he told me a little about his home which he was at pains to make me believe was more impressive than my own. In a way it was because it was so strangely mysterious. Cador was a magnificent house but there were many such houses in England; and according to Digory there were no cottages in the world like Mother Ginny's.

Digory had a natural eloquence which even a lack of conventional education could not stem. He made me see the room which was like a cavern from another world. Jars and bottles stood on the shelves—all containing some mysterious brew. Drying herbs hung on the rafters; a fire always burned in the grate and it was like no other fire; the flames were blue and red and pictures formed in them. Battles were fought; the Devil himself appeared once with red eyes and a red coat and black horns in his head. By the fire sat the cat which was no ordinary cat; she had red eyes and when the firelight shone on them they were the colour of the Devil's eyes, which showed she was one of his creatures. There was a black cauldron on the fire, always bubbling, and in the steam which rose from it spirits danced. Sometimes Digory could see the face of some inhabitant of the neighbourhood; and that meant something important. He was always discovering something fresh. There were two rooms in of the cottage—one leading from the other. The one at the back was where he and his grandmother slept—she on the truckle bed with a red cover, and the black cat always slept at the foot of her bed. Digory's place was on the talfat—a board placed immediately below the ceiling which I was able to visualize because I had seen it in some of the labourers' cottages. There was a stone-paved yard at the back and in this was an outhouse in which Mother Ginny stored her concoctions—a source of income to her and which could cure anything from a cold in the head to a stone in the kidney. She was very clever; she could get babies for people who wanted them and get rid of them for people who didn't want them. She was as clever as God.

"She couldn't be a god," I told him. "She would have to be a goddess. Of course she is rather ugly for one of them, but I suppose some of them might have been ugly. There were the Gorgons and Medusa. Fancy having snakes for hair. Can your grandmother make her hair into snakes?"

"Of course," said Digory.

I was very over-awed and longed to see inside Mother Ginny's cottage though I feared to.

The harvest had been bad that year. I heard my father talking very seriously to my mother about it. He said the farmers would be tightening their belts. Last year's had not been too bad; but this one was really alarming.

Jacco and I used to ride round the estate with him quite frequently. He wanted us to show an interest in it.

"The most important thing for a landowner is to be proud of his estate," he told us. "He has to care for it as he would for a person."

He always listened with sympathy to what the tenants had to say. It was said that having had to "rough it" himself, he had a special understanding of their troubles, unlike some squires who had been accustomed to soft living all their lives. My father was much loved for this quality as well as respected.

Following on the bad summer came the hard winter. I awoke most mornings to see a frosty pattern on the windows; there was tobogganing down the hill and skating on the river. The gales were so strong that the fishermen could not go out. During most mornings people went down to the beach to collect driftwood. Fires were needed all through the day and night to keep the house reasonably warm.

We were all longing for the spring.

And what a pleasure it was when it came—at last to see the buds appearing on the trees and in due course to hear the first cuckoo. I remember a spring morning when I went riding with my father. It was a holiday so I was free from my desk and my father had suggested I go with him on his rounds.

We called at the Tregorrans' farm and sat talking in the kitchen where Mrs. Tregorran brought forth a batch of currant buns from the oven and my father and I tasted one each and drank a glass of the Tregorran cider.

Mr. Tregorran was a somewhat morose man; his wife was melancholy too. So gloom pervaded the house. Mr. Tregorran talked with habitual pessimism of the effect the weather had had on crops and livestock. His mare Jemima was in foal. He hoped luck would not run against him and that she would bring forth a healthy animal, though he doubted this, due to the conditions of the last months.

"Poor Tregorran," said my father as we rode away. "But he really enjoys bad luck so perhaps we should not pity him too much. Never look on the black side, Annora, or you can be sure fate will find a way of turning that side towards you. Now let's call on the Cherrys and get the other side of the picture right away. I always like to do those two together."

Mrs. Cherry, the mother of six, was once again pregnant. It was a perpetual state with her. As soon as she was delivered of one child, another was on the way. But in spite of her constant disability, Mrs. Cherry was perpetually cheerful; she had a loud booming laugh which seemed to accompany all her remarks—funny or not. Her body, made larger by her state, continually shook with merriment, for no one appreciated her mirth as wholeheartedly as she did herself. George Cherry, her husband, was a little man, not much above his wife's shoulder, and he seemed to get smaller as her bulk increased. He walked in his wife's shadow and his almost sycophantic titter never failed to follow her hearty laughter.

Soon after that visit two disasters struck the place.

Mrs. Cherry had milked the cows. "I always believe in keeping going till me times comes," was a favourite saying of hers. "Never was one to believe in lying up too early like some." So she kept to those farm duties which she could perform and halfway across the yard from the cowsheds she saw a riderless horse galloping past the house.

She went to the gate and out to the path. By that time the horse had turned back and was coming towards her. She saw it was the Tregorran mare which was in foal. She shouted, but she was too late to get out of its path and as it galloped past her she was knocked back into the hedge.

Her shouts had brought out the workmen.

She was, we were told, "in a state." And that night her child was born dead.

Meanwhile Tregorran's mare, attempting to leap over a fence, had broken a leg so it had to be destroyed.

The neighbourhood discussed the matter at length.

I went with my mother to call on Mrs. Cherry when she had recovered a little. It was about a week after the incident. Her fat face had lost most of its colour, leaving behind a network of tiny veins. She shook like a jelly when she talked; and for once did not seem to find life such a joke.

My mother sat by her bed and tried to cheer her.

"You'll soon be well, Mrs. Cherry, and there'll be another on the way."

Mrs. Cherry shook her head. "I'd be that feared," she said. "With the likes of some about us who knows what'll happen next."

My mother looked surprised.

"You see, me lady," said Mrs. Cherry conspiratorially, "I knows just how it happened."

"Yes, we all do," replied my mother. "Tregorran's mare went mad. They say it sometimes happens. Unfortunately there was the foal. Poor Tregorran."

"'Tweren't nothing to do with the horse, me lady. It was *her*. You know who."

"No," said my mother. "I don't know who."

"I was standing at the gate when she passed me. She said to me, 'Your time won't be long now.' Well, I never did like to as much as speak to her, but I was civil-like and I said yes it was close now. Then she said to me, 'I'll give 'ee a little drink made of herbs and all that's good from the earth. You'll find it'll give you an easy time, missus, and it'll cost you so little you won't notice it.' I turned away. I wouldn't take nothing from her. That was when it happened. She went off muttering, but not before she'd given me a look. Oh, it was a special sort of look, it were. I didn't know then that it was for my baby."

"You really don't think Mother Ginny ill-wished you?"

"That I do and all, my lady. And not only me. I heard she had a bit of a back-and-forther with Jim Tregorran."

"Oh no," said my mother.

"'Tis so, me lady. I know she have cured some warts and such like but when there's trouble around 'ee don't have to look too far to see where it do come from."

My mother was very disturbed.

As we walked home she said: "I hope they are not going to work up a case against Mother Ginny just because Tregorran's mare ran amok and Mrs. Cherry stood in her path."

My father was coming out of the house and with him was Mr. Hanson, our lawyer, and his son Rolf. I was delighted as I always was when Rolf came. I loved Rolf. He was so clever and he had a special way with me. I believe he liked me as much as I liked him. He never let me know that he considered me too young to be noticed. He was eight years older than I but was never superior about it as Jacco was, and Jacco was only two years older than I.

Rolf was very tall and towered over his father, who was rather portly. Rolf was not often in Poldorey because he was completing his education and was away for long periods. I thought he was very handsome, but I heard my mother say that although he was not good-looking he had an air of distinction. He was certainly good-looking in my eyes, but then everything about Rolf was perfect as far as I was concerned. His father was always telling us how clever he was and so, even on those occasions when he did not accompany his father, he was often discussed.

Rolf had travelled a good deal. He had done what they used to call the Grand Tour and he could talk fascinatingly about places like Rome, Paris, Venice and Florence. He loved art treasures and the costumes of long ago. He was always collecting something and he was passionately interested in the past.

I used to listen to him enraptured but I was not sure whether it was what he was telling me or just that I simply loved to be with Rolf.

When I was very young I told my mother that when I was grown up I should marry either Rolf or my father.

She had said very seriously: "I should settle for Rolf if I were you. There is a law against marrying fathers and in any case he already has a wife. But I'm sure he'll be flattered by the suggestion. I'll tell him."

And after that I would think that I would without question marry Rolf.

As soon as he saw me he came to me and took both my hands. He always did that. Then he would stretch back, still holding them and looking at me to see how much I had grown since our last meeting. His smile was so warm and loving.

I cried: "Oh Rolf, it's lovely to see you." I added hastily: "And you too, Mr. Hanson."

Mr. Hanson smiled benignly. Any appreciation for Rolf delighted him.

"How long are you here for?" I asked.

"Only a week or so," Rolf told me.

I pouted. "You should come more often."

"I'd like to. But I have to work, you know. But I'll be back in June for a few weeks . . . round about Midsummer."

"Would you believe it," said Mr. Hanson admiringly, "he's interested in land now. He'll be trying to pick your brains, Sir Jake."

"He's welcome," said my father. "How's the Manor coming along?"

"Not bad . . . not bad at all."

"Well, are you coming in?" said my mother. "You'll stay to luncheon. Now, no excuses. We expect you to." My mother smiled at me. "Don't we, Annora?"

My attachment to Rolf always amused them.

"You must stay," I said, looking at Rolf.

"That," said Rolf, "is a royal command, and one which I personally am delighted to obey."

My mother was still bursting with indignation about Mrs. Cherry's remarks and mentioned what she had said.

"I hear," said Mr. Hanson, "that Tregorran is talking freely about the woman's ill-wishing his horse."

"Superstitious nonsense," said my father. "It will pass."

"Let's hope so," added Rolf. "When things like this happen people work themselves up into a superstitious fever of excitement.

[22]

Civilization drops from them. They blame the forces of evil for their misfortunes."

"If Tregorran had looked after his mare properly she would not have been able to get out," said my father. "And Mrs. Cherry should know by now that it is unwise to stand in the path of a bolting horse."

"Exactly," agreed Rolf. "They know they are in the wrong but knowing makes them all the more determined to blame someone else. And in this case it is the supernatural in the form of Mother Ginny."

"I know," said my mother, "but it does make me uneasy."

"It'll pass," put in my father. "Witch hunting went out of fashion years ago. What about luncheon?"

Over the meal the subject of Mother Ginny came up again. Rolf was very knowledgeable on the subject.

"There was a period during the seventeenth century," he told us, "when the fear of witchcraft was rife throughout the country. The diabolical witch finders sprang up everywhere . . . men whose task it was to go hunting for witches."

"Horrible!" cried my mother. "Thank Heaven that is done with."

"People haven't changed much," Rolf reminded her. "There is a trait in some human beings which leads to an obsession with persecution. Culture . . . civilized behaviour is with some just a veneer. It cracks very easily."

"I am glad people are a little more enlightened now," said my mother.

"A belief in witchcraft is hard to eradicate," said Rolf. "It can be revived with an old crone like Mother Ginny living in that place in the woods." He looked at his father. "I remember one of the Mid-summer's Eve bonfires a few years ago when they were leaping over the flame because they thought that gave them a protection against witches."

"Yes, that's so," added my father. "I stopped it after someone nearly got burned to death."

"It makes gruesome reading—what went on in the past," said Rolf.

"He's been interested in these old customs for a long time," his father told us. "But I think more so since last year. Tell them about last year, Rolf?"

"I was at Stonehenge," Rolf explained. "A fellow from my college lives nearby. I went with him. There was quite a ceremony. It was impressive and really eerie. I learned quite a lot about what they surmised was the secret of the stones. But of course it is all wrapped up in mystery. That is what makes it all the more fascinating."

"He even had some sort of robe to wear," said his father.

"Yes," agreed Rolf. "A long greyish habit. I look a little like one of the Inquisitors in it. It is rather like a monk's robe but the hood almost completely hides the face."

I was listening enraptured as I always did to Rolf.

"I should love to see it," I said.

"Well, come over tomorrow."

"What about you, Jacco?" asked my mother. "You'll want to see it too."

Jacco said yes he would but he was going out with John Gort tomorrow. They were going for pilchards. John Gort said there was a glut and they'd fill the nets in a few hours.

"Well some other time for you, Jacco," said Rolf.

"But I'll come tomorrow," I cried. "I can't wait to see it."

"I'll look for you in the afternoon," Rolf told me.

"You ought to come over, Sir Jake," said Mr. Hanson. "I want you to see the new copse we're planting."

"So you are acquiring more and more land," said my father. "I can see you will soon be rivalling Cador."

"We have a long way to go before we do that," said Rolf regretfully. "In any case we could never rival Cador. Cador is unique. Ours is just an Elizabethan Manor House."

"It's delightful," my mother assured him. "It's cosier than Cador."

"They are not to be compared," said Rolf with a smile. "Still we are very satisfied with our little place."

"Oh it's not so little," said his father.

"How are you getting on with your pheasants?" asked mine.

"Very well. Luke Tregern is proving a good man."

"You're lucky to have found him."

"Yes," agreed the lawyer. "That was a stroke of luck. He has come from the Lizard way . . . looking for work. Rolf's got an eye for people and he felt he was the right sort. Good-looking, well-spoken

[24]

and above all keen to make good. He comes up with ideas for the land. You must remember, Sir Jake, we are novices at the game."

"You're doing very well all the same," said my father.

Rolf was smiling at me.

"Tomorrow then?" he said.

The Hansons' place was called Dorey Manor and was on the edge of the wood which bordered the river. They had bought it some ten years before when it had been in a state of dilapidation. The lawyer and his wife—Mrs. Hanson had been alive then—had set about restoring it in a leisurely way; it was when Rolf began to take an interest that developments proceeded at a rapid pace. Now they were constantly acquiring more land.

My father used to say jokingly: "Rolf Hanson wants to outdo Cador. He's an ambitious young man and he's attempting the impossible."

"He is making the Manor and its lands into a sizable property," added my mother.

There was not doubt that Rolf was proud of Dorey Manor. He was so interested in everything, and being with him made one interested too. I always felt more alive with Rolf than with anyone else.

He was waiting for me in the stables. He lifted me down from my horse, holding me for a few moments and looking up at me, smiling.

"You're growing," he said. "Every time I see you you are bigger than you were last time."

"Do you think I am going to be a giantess?"

"Just a fine upstanding girl. Come on. I'm going to show you the copse first."

"I long to see the robe."

"I know. But waiting will make it more interesting. So . . . the copse first."

Luke Tregern was working there.

"This is Luke Tregern," Rolf said to me. "Luke, this is our neighbour, Miss Annora Cadorson."

Luke Tregern bowed his head in greeting. He was tall, olive-skinned, dark-haired and handsome.

"Good day, Miss Cadorson," he said.

"Good day," I replied.

[25]

His dark eyes were fixed intently on me.

"There's a healthy look about these trees, sir," he said. "They're taking well."

"So I thought," replied Rolf. "We're just going to wander round and take a look."

Rolf seemed to know a great deal about trees as he did about everything else.

He said: "I'm teasing you with all this talk of trees. You are longing to see the robe. What a patient girl you are."

"No I'm not. I just like to be here with you. I really am enjoying the copse."

He took my arm and we went towards the house. "I'll tell you something," he said. "You are the nicest little girl I ever knew."

I was in a daze of happiness.

The house was small compared with Cador. It was built in the Tudor style—black-beamed with white plaster panels in between and each storey projecting beyond the one below. It was picturesque and charming with an old-fashioned garden where honeysuckle decorated the arches and the display of Tudor roses was magnificent especially when they were all in bloom, which they were almost till December.

"Come on in," said Rolf.

We went into his library—a long room with linen-fold panelling and a moulded ceiling. The room was lined with books. I glanced at the subjects: law, archaeology; ancient religions, customs, witchcraft.

"Oh Rolf," I cried, "how clever you are!"

He laughed and suddenly took my chin in his hands and looked into my face.

"Don't have too high an opinion of me, Annora," he said. "That could be very unwise."

"Why should it be?"

"I might not be able to live up to it."

"But of course you would," I declared vehemently. "Tell me about that strange ceremony."

"I've only just skimmed the surface of all these mysteries. I'm just interested in a dilettante way."

I refused to believe he did not know a great deal. "Do let me see the robe," I cried.

"Here it is." He opened a drawer and took it out.

"Put it on," I commanded.

He did. A shiver ran through me as he stood there. I could only describe his appearance as sinister. It was like a monk's robe—greyish white. The hood was big. It came right over his head and he peered out through the narrow opening in the front. It was only when the hood fell back that his face could be seen.

"There is something frightening about it," I said.

He pulled back the hood so that it fell right back, and I laughed with relief.

"That's better. You look like yourself now. In that . . . with your face hidden you are like a different person."

"Imagine the effect with several of us dressed like this. Midnight . . . and those historic stones all around us. Then you get the real atmosphere."

I said: "It reminds me of the Inquisitors who tortured those they called heretics. Miss Caster and I have been 'doing' the Spanish Inquisition. It's really frightening."

"I think that is the object. These are not quite so bad as those with pointed tops with slits for eyes. They are really quite spine-chilling. I shall show you some pictures of them."

"May I try it on?"

"It's far too big for you. It is made for a tall man."

"Nevertheless I want to."

I put it on. It trailed to the floor. Rolf laughed at me.

"Do you know what you've done?" he said. "You've robbed it of its sinister quality. Annora, you'll have to grow up." He looked at me with a tender exasperation. "You're taking such a long time to do it."

"I'm taking just the same time as everyone else."

He put his hands on my shoulders. "It seems a long time," he said.

He took the robe from me and put it back in the drawer.

"Tell me about Stonehenge," I said.

I sat at the table with him and he brought books from the shelves to show me. He talked glowingly about the gigantic stones in the midst of the barrows of the Bronze Age. I found it fascinating and it was wonderful to sit beside Rolf at the table while he talked.

That was a very happy afternoon.

* * *

There was a great deal of talk about the tragedies. The servants discussed them constantly. When I met Digory in the woods he seemed extremely proud.

"Did your granny kill Jemima and Mrs. Cherry's baby?" I asked him.

He just pursed his lips and looked secretive.

"She can do anything," he boasted.

"My father says people shouldn't say such things."

He just swung himself up onto a tree and sat there laughing at me. He put his two forefingers to the side of his head, pretending he had horns.

I could not stop thinking of poor Mrs. Cherry and the mare which had to be shot. I ran home as quickly as I could.

Talk went on about Mother Ginny and then it ceased to be the main topic of conversation and I forgot about it.

One morning when I went down to breakfast I knew something had happened. My parents were in deep conversation.

"I must go at once," my mother was saying. "You do see that, Jake."

"Yes, yes," said my father.

"Even now I may not be in time. I know it's hard for you to get away just now."

"You don't think I'd let you go alone."

"I didn't think so. But I ought to leave today."

"Why not?"

"Oh Jake . . . thank you."

I cried: "What's happening? What are you talking about?"

"It's your Grandfather Dickon," my mother explained. "He's very ill. They think . . ."

"You mean . . . he's dying . . ."

My mother turned away. I knew she had been especially fond of her father, as I was of mine.

My father took my arm. "He's very old, you know," he said. "It had to come. The miracle is that he has lived so long. Your mother and I will be leaving today."

"I'll come with you."

"No. You and Jacco will stay behind. We have to get there without delay."

"Well, we won't delay you."

"No," he said firmly. "Your mother and I are going alone. We shall be back before you've had time to realize we have gone."

I tried to persuade them to take me with them, but they were quite firm. They were going alone and later that day they left.

A few days after they had gone, the rain started—just a gentle shower at first and then it went on and on.

"Seems like there's no stopping it," said Mrs. Penlock. "It be like a curse on us, that it do. My kitchen garden be that sodden everything in it will be well nigh drowned."

There were floods in the fields; the rain found the weak spots in cottage roofs. Every day there was some fresh tale of woe.

Then the rumours started.

"You know who be doing this, don't 'ee, my dear." A whispered word. A look. "It be her no less."

Jenny Bordon's warts which had been cured by Mother Ginny a year before came back. The Jennings' baby caught the whooping cough and it spread like wildfire. Tom Cooper, doing a bit of thatching, fell off a ladder and broke his leg.

Something was wrong in the neighbourhood and the general idea was growing that we did not have to look far to discover the source of these misfortunes.

In the inns where the men sat over their pints of ale, among the women at their cottage doors or in their kitchens, the main topic of conversation was Mother Ginny.

Digory did not help matters. When Jenny Bordon—suffering from her new crop of warts—called after him "Witch's Varmint," he just stuck out his tongue and put his forefingers to his head in a gesture of which I knew he was very fond and declared he would put a spell on her.

"You can't," she called back. "You're only the Varmint."

"My Granny can," was his retort.

Yes, agreed the people, so she could; and so she had. She had put an evil curse on them all.

I was aware of mounting tension. I spoke to Jacco about it but he was too full of his own affairs to give much thought to what I was saying. On the other hand I was beginning to experience a certain alarm because of all I overheard. One of the men said: "Something's got to be done."

I tried to discuss it with Miss Caster but she was uncommunicative, though even she must have been aware of the rising animosity against Mother Ginny. She did not believe in spells. She was far too educated for that, and she certainly thought the Wars of the Roses were more important than bad weather and the mishaps which had befallen the neighbourhood.

"They are getting so angry about it, Miss Caster," I insisted. "They talk of nothing else."

"These people have nothing better to think about. We have. Let us get back to the Temple gardens where the red and white roses were growing."

"I wish my father were here. He would talk to them. I do wonder what is happening at Eversleigh. I wish they had taken me with them. I can't understand why they wouldn't."

"Your parents know what is best," was Miss Caster's comment.

The weeks passed and there was no news from my parents. Grandfather was taking a long time to die. He must be very ill or they would come home.

June had arrived. The rain stopped and summer burst upon us. At first it was warmly welcomed but as we woke up each morning to a brilliant sun which showed itself all day, and the temperature soared into the eighties, there were more complaints from the farmers.

My father used to say: "Farmers are never content. Give them sun and they want rain, and when the rain comes they complain of the floods. You can't please a farmer weatherwise." So it was only natural that now they complained.

I enjoyed the heat. I liked to lie in the garden in a shady spot listening to the grasshoppers and the bees. That seemed to me utter contentment. Moreover Miss Caster was a little lethargic and never wanted to prolong lessons—a habit she had in cooler weather. I think Jacco rejoiced in the same state of affairs at the vicarage where Mr. Belling, the curate, attended to his scholastic education.

We rode together—galloping along the beach. We went out onto the moors where we would tether our horses and lie in the long grass looking down on the tin mine which was a source of income to so many people thereabouts. Our community consisted mostly of miners or fishermen and those farmers on the Cador estate.

So one long summer day passed into another and the sun seemed to shine more brightly every day.

People grew irritable.

"Get out of my kitchen, Miss Annora," said Mrs. Penlock. "You be forever under my feet, that you do." And I was never given a cake or a scone fresh from the oven as I'd been accustomed to. It was too hot for baking in any case.

I hated to be banished from the kitchen because there was more talk than ever at this time about Mother Ginny.

We were approaching Midsummer's Eve. This was always a special occasion. Rolf, who had been away, returned from visiting one of his college friends in Bodmin who shared his interest in antiquity. He talked to me enthusiastically about some stones they had discovered on Bodmin Moor. I mentioned to him that there was a growing feeling in the community against Mother Ginny.

"It's natural," he said. "The Cornish are very superstitious. They cling to old customs more than is done in other parts of the country. It is probably the Celtic streak. The Celts are certainly different from the Anglo Saxons who inhabit the main part of our island."

"I suppose I'm only part Celtic through my father."

"And I pure Anglo Saxon if you can call such a mixture pure."

"I knew, of course, that Rolf's parents had come to Cornwall when he was five years old. He had been born in the Midlands. But he knew a great deal more about the Cornish than they seemed to themselves; and perhaps he was able to study them more dispassionately because he was not really one of them.

There were fascinating talks about old customs. He told me how most cottagers even now crossed the firehook and prong on their hearths when they went out, which was supposed to keep evil spirits away during their absence, and how the miners left what they called a didjan—a piece of their lunch—for the knackers in the mines. The knackers were supposed to be the spirits of those who had crucified Christ. "Though how there could have been enough people at the Crucifixion to populate all the mines of Cornwall, I can't imagine," said Rolf. There were the black dogs and white hares which were supposed to appear at the mineheads when there was to be a disaster. No fisherman would mention a rabbit or hare when at sea; and if they saw a parson on their way to the boats they would turn back and not go to sea that day. If they had to mention church they could call it the Cleeta, which meant a bell house—to say the word "church" being unlucky.

"How do these things come about?" I asked.

"I suppose something unfortunate happens after they have seen dogs or hares or have met a parson when they were setting out for the boats. Then it becomes a superstition."

"How very foolish."

"People often are foolish," he told me with a smile. "Of course there are a good many customs they practise which go back to pre-Christian days. Midsummer's Eve activities for instance."

"I know. Mrs. Penlock would say, '"Tas always been done and reckon it always will be.'"

I loved to listen when he talked of these Cornish customs.

For as long as I could remember we had always been taken by our parents to see the bonfire on the moors. My father would drive us out, and Jacco and I, with our parents, would watch the fires spring up, for if it was a clear night we could see them for miles along the coast.

For days before, the preparations would be made. Barrels were tarred and thrown onto the pile of wood and shavings, and a thrill of anticipation ran through the neighbourhood. There would be dancing, singing and general rejoicing.

Rolf had told me that it was said to be St. John's Festival but it really had its origins in the old pagan days; and people practised the rites without knowing what the original intentions had been.

Dancing round the fire, he said, was a precaution against witchcraft; and it was something to do with fertility rites which people often practised in the old days. To leap through the fire and get one's clothes singed meant that one was immune from the evil eye for a whole year, when, I presumed, the act must be performed again. There had been accidents and there had been one girl who had been badly burned. That was said to be a triumph for witchcraft; and it was after that when my father had said there was to be no more leaping over the flames.

It had always been a great treat for Jacco and me to stay up late and set out for the moors with our parents, my father driving the two big greys. I still remember the thrill when the torch was flung into the piled-up wood and the cry of triumph which went up as the flames burst forth.

We used to watch people dancing round the fire. No one attempted to leap over while we were there. I sometimes wondered whether they did when my father was no longer watching.

About half an hour after midnight we would drive home.

"I hope they'll be home for Midsummer's Eve," I said to Jacco.

We had ridden out to the moors and were lying in the rough grass sheltered by a boulder.

He put on his bravado look. "If not we'll go by ourselves. We can ride out."

"What! At midnight!"

"Afraid?"

"Of course not."

"Then why not?"

I realized that he had just thought of that and no doubt said it hastily; now his jaw was set and that indicated determination.

"We're not supposed to," I reminded him.

"Who said so?"

"Mama . . . Papa . . ."

"They're not here to say. We haven't been *told* not to."

"No. Because nobody thought of it."

"If you're afraid to come I'll go by myself."

"If you go I'm going with you."

He plucked a blade of grass and started to chew on it. I could see he was already making plans for Midsummer's Eve.

Thinking of it brought Mother Ginny to mind. I said: "Jacco, do you believe Mother Ginny is a real witch?"

"I expect so."

"Do you think she is ill-wishing people here?"

"She could be."

"There was the mare and Mrs. Cherry's baby and everything going wrong. I'd like to know."

He agreed that he would too.

"They are all getting scared," he said. "I heard Bob Gill telling young Jack Barker not to forget to leave a didjan for the knackers before he went down the mine. It's Jack's first week there and he looked really scared."

"Rolf says they're scared because theirs is a dangerous job. Like the fishermen. They never know when something awful will happen underground or when the sea will turn rough."

Jacco was silent, still brooding on our coming adventure. "We'll have to be careful," he said. "You don't want Miss Caster to interfere."

I nodded. Then I said: "It's time for tea."

"Let's go."

We mounted our horses and left the moor behind us. As we came down to the harbour we were immediately aware that there was more than the usual activity.

People all seemed to be talking at once.

"What's happened?" called Jacco.

I was always interested in the manner in which the people treated Jacco. He was only a boy—two years older than I was in fact—but he was the heir of Cador and would be the squire one day. They wavered between contempt for his youth and respect for the power which would one day be his.

Some of them looked away but Jeff Mills said to him: "There be trouble with one of the boats, Master Jacco."

"What trouble?"

"Her started letting in water seemingly. They had to rescue her crew."

"Are they all safe?"

"Aye. But boat be lost. This will be real bad luck for the Poldeans."

"My father will be home soon."

"Oh aye. Reckon he'll see to it. That's what I do tell Jim Poldean."

Jacco turned to me. "Come on. There's nothing we can do."

"It's odd," I said. "We were talking about the dangers of the sea only a little while ago."

"Just think. They've lost their boat. That's their living."

"But our father will help them to get a new one," I said complacently. I was very proud of him and especially at times like this when I saw how much people relied on him.

We were late for tea which did not please Miss Caster or Mrs. Penlock.

"These lardy cakes should be eaten hot from the oven," said Mrs. Penlock.

I explained that we were late because when we had come to the quay there were crowds there.

"That were a terrible thing for the Poldeans," said Mrs. Penlock.

I looked at Jacco as though to say, Trust her to know all about it.

"And," she went on, "we do know how it come about."

"There must have been something wrong with the boat," said Jacco. "The sea's like a lake today."

"Boat been tampered with most like."

"How could that be?"

"Don't 'ee ask me. There be ways and means. There be people who has powers . . . and not living very far from here neither. I could tell you something."

"Oh yes, Mrs. Penlock, what?" I asked.

"Well . . . I did hear that when Jim Poldean was setting out, who should have been there watching him but Mother Ginny. She did shout something to him . . . something about Parson having caught a hare in the church."

"Well," I asked, "what of that?"

"My patience me! Don't 'ee know nothing, Miss Annora? 'Tis terrible unlucky to talk of parsons, churches and wild animals to a man just putting out to sea. It's something that never be done . . . if it can be helped."

"But *why?*"

"There b'aint no whys and wherefores. 'Tis just so. If you have to mention the church, any fool knows 'tis to be called the Cleeta."

I remembered something Rolf had told me about this not so long ago.

"It be clear as daylight," went on Mrs. Penlock. "And this has to be stopped . . . stopped I say before we are all took sick or murdered in our beds."

Jacco and I gave ourselves up to the succulent joy of lardy cakes, which no one could make quite like Mrs. Penlock.

"They're gorgeous," said Jacco.

"Should have been eaten ten minutes ago," grumbled Mrs. Penlock, not ill-pleased.

Later that day there was a letter from my mother.

Grandfather Dickon had died. They were staying at Eversleigh for a week or so to comfort my grandmother and then they would return home. They were trying to persuade her to come back with them, but she did not seem to want to leave Eversleigh. Helena and Peterkin were there with Amaryllis—and of course Claudine and David. We should all be going for a visit soon.

Jacco and I were sad thinking of our grandfather. We had not seen a great deal of him, but when we had he had made a deep impression on us. He had been a very powerful figure and my mother had told us many stories about him. In her eyes he was a giant among men; he had rescued Grandmother Lottie from the mob during the French Revolution. We had all thought him superhuman and it was a shock to learn that he was not immortal after all.

They would not be home for Midsummer's Eve. I guessed that Jacco was not altogether displeased by this as he was longing to put his plan into action.

The proposed adventure was absorbing his thoughts. I had to admit that I was looking forward to it, too.

On the night before Midsummer's Eve, I was awakened suddenly in alarm.

Someone was in my room. I sat up.

"Sh!" said Jacco.

"Jacco, what are you doing here?"

He came to the side of my bed and whispered: "Something's going on."

"Where?"

He glanced towards Miss Caster's room, which was next to mine, and put his fingers to his lips.

"I'm going to see. Want to come?"

"Where?" I repeated.

"Out. Listen. Can you hear?"

I strained my ears. Faintly, from some way off, I heard the sound of voices.

"If you want to come, get dressed. Riding things. We're taking the horses. If you don't, keep quiet. I'm going."

"Of course I'm coming."

"Come to the stables," he said, "and whatever you do, don't make a noise."

He crept out, and trembling with excitement, I dressed. I had a premonition that something terrible was about to happen . . . but something which I must not miss.

He was waiting impatiently at the stables.

"Thought you were never coming."

"Where are we going?"

"I don't know quite. Somewhere in the woods."

I saddled my chestnut mare and we rode out.

I could see that Jacco was enjoying this. I followed him. We came to the river and went into the woods.

I said: "It's near Mother Ginny's cottage. Do you think. . . ?"

"It's been blowing up for weeks," he said. "Poldean's boat has brought it to a head."

We were making our way through the trees to the clearing. The woods had always been mysterious to me. It was only recently that I had been allowed to enter them alone. There had always been fears of our falling into the river, which was fairly wide at this spot where it was about to enter the sea.

I said: "What's the time?"

"Just on midnight."

I could now see the light of torches among the trees.

Jacco said: "Be careful. They mustn't see us."

We were close to the clearing now and the trees were thinning out. I could see a crowd of people; they were all dancing round a cart and in this cart was a figure. No, it couldn't be! Mother Ginny!

I gasped.

"It's not real," whispered Jacco. "It's a thing made to look like her."

There were people I knew there but they looked different in the light of the torches.

"We've come just at the right moment," said Jacco.

"What are they going to do?"

"Watch."

They had lighted a bonfire in the middle of the clearing and were dancing round it. Then someone took the effigy from the cart and fixed it on the end of a pole.

I gasped in amazement as they dipped the pole into the flames. A cry went up. The figure was lifted high. Its clothes were alight. They chanted; they danced; they screamed. They seemed to be in a frenzy.

I felt sick. I did not want to see any more.

I turned to Jacco and said: "I want to go."

"Oh, all right," he replied, pretending to placate me, but I knew that he, too, was sickened by what he had seen.

We rode back cautiously, taking our horses to the stables and then creeping into the house.

Neither of us spoke.

I lay sleepless through the night.

Midsummer's Eve! There had always been an aura of excitement on this day. Even the young children were allowed to sit up and were taken to the moors to see the lighting of the bonfires.

"'Tis something as has been done in these parts since the beginning of time," said Mrs. Penlock, "and I see no reason why we should ever stop what's been done by them as has gone before."

Nobody else saw any reason why either. The usual excitement was there but something more besides. There was a feverish expectation in the kitchen and it mounted throughout the day. I could hardly wait for the evening to come and on the other hand I was filled with an inexplicable apprehension.

I was up early and went down to the harbour. I saw Betty Poldean there. There was a wild light in her eyes.

"Good day to 'ee, Miss Annora," she said.

"Good day, Betty," I replied. I hesitated. I wanted to say something about her father's boat but I did not know how to. Instead I tried to comfort her with a reference to my parents' return, which would be soon now. "My father will want to know all that has been happening while he has been away," I added significantly.

"Oh . . . aye," she said; but I could see her thoughts were on the coming night. She did not look so far ahead as my parents' return.

Children were collecting wood and furse to take to the moors for the bonfire. But there would be plenty going on down here on the quay. Some of the fishermen were setting up tarred barrels on poles and they would be lighted and make an impressive sight all along the harbour. Children were being taken out for trips on the water.

"Hey there, Miss Annora," called Thomas Lewis, "what about taking a pennorth of sea?"

It was an invitation to take a little trip with him. I declined with thanks and said I was going to see how the piles were building up on the moor.

I rode home thoughtfully. Miss Caster had not said anything about the evening and I was anxious that she should not. I was determined to go with Jacco to the moor that night and I did not want to disobey her unless it was absolutely necessary.

I was thankful for the heat, which she did not like at all; she was always ready, during these exhausting days, to retire to her bedroom at an early hour.

Jacco said we would meet just after eleven o'clock at the stables. There would be no one about, as almost everyone else—if they weren't in bed—would be down at the harbour or on the moor.

I was there on time. The heat during the day had been great and the night was warm still. The sky was clear and there seemed to be more stars than usual for there was only a faint light from the waning moon's slim crescent.

By the time we reached the moor it was a few minutes after midnight and the bonfires were already being lighted. I could see others springing up in the distance. It was a thrilling sight. Several of the people were there wearing costumes of an early age . . . clothes which they must have found in trunks and attics. Some of the farmers had old straw hats and smocks and leggings which must have belonged to their grandfathers. It was difficult to recognize some of them in the dim light. They seemed like different people. I saw Jack Gort with some sort of helmet on his head. He was tall and did not look so much like the man from whom we bought our fish on the quay as some marauding Viking. Several of the young men carried torches which they swung round their heads in a circular movement to indicate the movement of the sun in the heavens. The moors looked different; people looked different; the night had imbued them with a certain mysterious quality.

I saw several of the servants from Cador with Isaacs.

"Keep well back," warned Jacco.

I obeyed, realizing that we must not be seen for if we were, we should probably be sent back.

I thought, as I watched that scene, that this was how it must have been centuries ago. The people who had danced round the bonfire must have looked a little different, but the ceremony was the same. They said nowadays that the purpose was to bring a blessing on the crops; in the old days it had been—so Rolf had told us—what was called a fertility rite which concerned all living things, including people, and when they had worked themselves up into a frenzy with their dancing, they crept off together to make love.

One of the women started chanting and the others joined in. It was a song which had come down through the ages. I could not understand the words, for they were in the Cornish language.

Then I saw a tall figure who stood out among all the others. He looked like a monk in the grey robe which enveloped him.

I knew that robe. Rolf! I thought.

People clustered round him. It was as though they were making him master of the ceremonies.

Up to that time it had been like many another Midsummer's Eve which I had watched from my parents' carriage—the only difference being that on this night Jacco and I were here alone and in secret. But I was sure that if my parents had thought of it they would have ordered one of the grooms to bring us here to see the bonfire.

And then suddenly it ceased to be like any other Midsummer's Eve.

The robed figure moved apart from the crowd; he approached the bonfire, and clutching his robe about him, he leaped high in the air . . . right over the bonfire. There was a deep silence as the flames appeared to lick his robe. Then he was clear on the other side.

A shout went up: "Bravo! Bravo!"

"'Ee be free of the witches for a year," cried someone.

"The fire didn't touch 'un."

"He did jump right clear."

I saw one of the barmaids from the Fisherman's Rest run up to the fire. She threw up her arms and attempted to leap over it.

I heard her scream as she fell into the flames.

Jack Gort was close by; he immediately dragged her out; her dress was on fire. I watched in shocked silence while they beat out the flames.

"How . . . crazy!" said Jacco.

"Papa forbade them to do it," I said.

People crowded round the barmaid, who was lying on the grass.

"I wonder if she's badly hurt," I whispered.

"They'll blame the witches," said Jacco.

"But she did it herself."

"That man started it. It wasn't so risky for him. If that thing he is wearing had caught fire he could easily have thrown it off."

The barmaid was now standing up and I was relieved to see that she was not badly hurt. I felt I wanted to go. I could not understand why Rolf—who knew my father had forbidden it—should have leaped over the fire. I did not want him to see us here.

"Better take her back to the Rest," someone said. "Here . . . you, Jim. You take her. You and she is said to be sweethearts."

"I think we ought to go," I said quietly to Jacco. "There won't be much dancing and singing."

"Wait a bit."

I saw the man they had called Jim put the barmaid on his horse. They moved away. Jack Gort had rescued her in time and she was more shocked than anything.

Someone started to sing but the others did not take it up. The mood had changed and I thought that would be the end of the revelries on that Midsummer's Eve.

Then I saw a crowd gathering round a boy who held something in his hands. It was wriggling and mewing piteously. A cat! I thought, and instinct told me to whom that cat belonged. It was Mother Ginny's. I knew the boy slightly. I had seen him on the quay looking for a chance to earn a few pence doing odd jobs for the fishermen.

He shouted: "Here's a way to fight against them witches. They ain't going to get the better of the likes of we."

He held up the cat by the scruff of its neck.

"Mother Ginny's Devil's mate. Satan's gift to the wicked old witch."

The cat moved and must have scratched him for with a yell of pain he threw the animal straight into the flames.

I felt sick. I knew that Jacco was equally affected. We loved our animals, both of us; our dogs were our friends and the kitchen cat, which Mrs. Penlock declared was the best mouser in Cornwall, was a special favourite.

Jacco had his hand on my rein, for I had started forward.

"No," he hissed. "You can't."

Then I heard the scream of an animal in pain and there was silence.

The boy was crying out, excusing himself: "Look what 'un done to me." He held up his bleeding hand. "'Tis the only way to save ourselves. It 'as to be done . . . a living thing they allus say. Well, that's it . . . the witch's cat. That'll be one of 'em out of the way."

The moment of horror had passed. Everyone seemed to be talking at once. They were forming a group round one figure. I saw the grey robe in the midst of them. He was talking to them but I could not hear what he was saying.

Suddenly they all started to move. Some of them had carts, others horses. Jacco said to me: "Come on. We're going. We're going now . . . this minute."

[41]

As I followed him I kept hearing the cry of the cat and I just wanted to go back to the safety of my room. I could not stop thinking about Rolf there with them, Rolf . . . our friend . . . the one of whom I had made a hero . . . and he was there in the midst of them—a sort of leader.

Jacco was not making for home.

"Jacco," I said. "What. . . ? Where. . . ?"

"We're going to the woods. That's where they're going."

"Why?"

"That's what we've got to find out. At least I've got to. You can go home."

"I'm coming too."

As we came into the woods I could hear voices in the distance. I wanted to go back, to creep into bed. I had a horrible fear that tonight was going to be like no other night I had ever known. I kept saying to myself: If my father were here this would never happen.

But it was happening. And I had to see it.

"Be careful," said Jacco. "They mustn't know we're here. They'd send us home if they did."

We knew the woods well and we went a roundabout way, for both Jacco and I knew their destination. They were already at the clearing in the woods and their torches gave an unearthly light to the scene.

The first thing I noticed was the grey robe. He was there. He was leading them . . . inciting them. I could not believe that this was the Rolf I had always known. He had always been so kind, so understanding about everything. He could not be so cruel. I knew that he loved the old customs. He liked to experiment. I could imagine that he would wonder how easily people would revert to less civilized days.

I saw the cottage through a gleam of light. They were close now, waving their torches. They were all shouting and I could not hear what was said except that it was something about the witch.

Then someone called: "Come out, witch. Show yourself. Don't 'ee be afraid. We won't 'urt 'ee . . . leastways no more than 'ee have hurt us."

I gasped. She had come out of the cottage. She must have been in bed for she was in a nightgown, her grey hair streaming about her shoulders. Their torches lit up her face and I saw the fear there.

I felt physically sick and would have turned away but Jacco was close to me and I could not move. His horrified eyes were fixed on the scene.

"What do you want with me?" she screamed.

"You'm going to see, missus. What'll us do with her?"

Someone spoke. They were all listening. Could it be Rolf telling them what to do? I wondered.

"That'll do . . ." shouted someone. "What they've allus done. Duck her in the water. If she drowns she's innocent. If she floats it's with the help of the Devil and proves she's one of his."

"Where did the Devil kiss 'ee, Mother Ginny?"

There was a burst of coarse laughter.

"Oh no," I murmured. "She's only an old woman."

Jacco nodded, his eyes staring at that terrifying scene.

They had attached a rope about her waist. She was screaming and fighting them. One of the men gave her a blow which knocked her to the ground.

"Jacco," I cried, "they'll kill her. We've got to stop them. Papa would."

Jacco rode forward. "Stop it," he cried. "Stop it."

No one took any notice of him. They were all intent on getting Mother Ginny to the river. She called curses on them as they dragged her along the ground.

I was sobbing. "We must *do* something. What would our father do?"

But we lacked his strength and authority. We were only children and whatever we did would be of no avail. There was murder in the air. I had seen something in those people that night which I never would have believed could be there. For the first time I had witnessed the fury of a mob. These people who went about their ordinary daily rounds had undergone a remarkable change. There was a side to their nature which I had never known existed. They were cruel. They delighted in inflicting pain. They wanted revenge, an eye for an eye. Tregorran's mare; the Cherry baby; the rain; the heat; the Poldeans' boat. They wanted revenge and they were going to have it. And Rolf was there . . . leading them on . . . making them aware of how witches were treated long ago. Rolf . . . whom I had so much admired; who had been a hero to me, whom I had loved. That was the most startling and disturbing revelation of all. They were uneducated people . . . ready to be led . . . but he . . . I felt I knew what was in his mind. He was obsessed by the old ways, old customs. He wanted to see if people would react today as they had long ago. But this was a human life . . . I felt I could never trust anyone again.

I wanted to go to him, to tell him I was here, to beg him to stop this. But he was their leader. I could never forget that. Jacco and I were, after all, only two children. We could not stop them even though Jacco was my father's son.

I wanted to shut it all out of my mind, forget what I had seen, go right away. I did not want to know what was happening by the river. I feared something even more terrible was going to happen. But even if I did run home, I should never forget.

I could hear the shouts by the river.

"She won't sink," said Jacco.

"No, the river's not deep enough."

"Not by the banks. If they throw her into the middle . . . They say witches don't sink. The Devil saves them."

"But either way . . ."

"She'll be saved," insisted Jacco.

Then the boy came out of the cottage. He sped across the clearing. He was very close to us. I held my breath. I thought: What will they do to him?

I was aware of him; he was crouching among the trees quite near us.

The shouts sounded farther away; then they were near again. They were coming back. They were dragging Mother Ginny along. Her clothes were sodden and mud-stained; her hair hung grey and slimy about her face, which was deathly pale. I thought she was already dead.

I heard myself praying to God to do something . . . to send these people away . . . to let Mother Ginny go back to her truckle bed.

The people were shouting like a drunken mob. They were drunk in a way—not with strong drink but with mob frenzy.

She lay on the grass and they were all round her. I could not see her now.

Then someone cried: "The Devil saves his own."

"Not for long," said someone else.

Then suddenly, with a shout, someone threw a torch at the thatched roof. It ignited immediately. The thatch was alight. Someone threw another torch and the cottage was a blazing mass.

The mob stood back to admire its handiwork. I could see Mother Ginny now. She had risen to her feet and stood staring at the cottage. There was silence as she tottered towards it. She went along the path to the door and walked into the flames.

There was a silence which seemed to go on for a long time. I think they were all waiting for her to come out. But she did not.

Someone shouted: "That's her and her cat gone. What of the boy . . . the Witch's Varmint?"

There was silence again. My heart was beating rapidly. I heard a sound very close to us. Jacco moved his horse slightly. I heard him whisper: "Jump up behind me."

Then I saw Digory and I felt a wave of relief sweep over me.

"Come on," said Jacco. "Quick."

We moved silently through the woods.

"Where?" I asked.

"I'm thinking," said Jacco.

I glanced at Digory, who was clinging to Jacco; his face was white and all the bravado had gone out of him. I felt very tender towards him at that moment.

We were free of the woods and Jacco began to canter.

"Do you think they will follow us?" I called.

"Might do. If they knew where we were."

I could see the grey towers of Cador. We went up the incline and Jacco stopped suddenly.

"I know," he said. "The Dogs' Home."

"Oh yes," I cried. "That'll do."

The Dogs' Home was an old shed a little way from the stables. Jacco used it for anything he needed for his pets. Our father had said that if he had them he must be able to look after them; they were his responsibility. He had a key and no one else had one.

"It's the safest place," he said.

We went on to the shed. Then Jacco dismounted, pulling Digory with him. The boy seemed in a state of shock and hardly to be aware of either of us.

Jacco always carried the key of the shed with him. Now he opened it and we went inside. There were dogs' baskets and sacks of pease with which Jacco fed his peacocks. It smelt like a granary.

"You'll be all right here," he said. "No one would dare come here. We'll get you blankets and food, so you needn't worry."

Digory still did not speak.

"Now," said Jacco, "we're going to see you're all right. Annora, you get some blankets for him. You'll have to be quiet. First let's stable the horses."

We left Digory in the shed, locking him in. He was still stunned. I wondered how much he had seen of the terrible thing which had happened to his grandmother.

As we left the stables, Jacco said: "We'll keep him there until our father comes home. He'll know what to do."

I felt an immense relief. Yes, our father would know what to do.

"None of this would have happened if he had been here," I said. "Mother Ginny is dead. She couldn't have survived in that fire. She walked right into it."

"She killed herself."

"No," I said, "They killed her." And to myself I murmured: And Rolf was one of those who killed her. How could he? And yet I had seen him. Rolf. *My* Rolf. I would never have believed it possible if I had not witnessed it with my own eyes.

I was glad of something to do. It stopped my thinking of that terrible scene. But I knew I should go on thinking of it . . . always.

The task before me was not easy. I had to tread very carefully for fear of arousing attention. I did not know who was in the house. How many of them, I wondered, were still in the woods? But they would soon be coming back. They had done their wicked deed. Surely they would want to get as far away from it as possible.

I went into the linen room and took some blankets and a pillow. I went to the Dogs' Home where Jacco was impatiently waiting for me. He seized them and made a bed of some straw. Digory stood there—his thoughts, I knew, far away at that terrible scene—and when we told him to lie down, he obeyed us as though in a trance.

Jacco knelt beside him. He was gentle. This was a new side to my brother and I loved him the more for it.

"You'll be all right now," he said. "They won't come here. We'll keep you here till our father comes home. He'll know what to do."

Jacco stood up and looked at me. "First thing in the morning we'll bring him some food. Have to be careful with old Penlock."

I nodded.

"Here's the key," went on Jacco, turning to Digory and putting it into his hand. "Lock yourself in when we've gone. Don't open the door to anyone except us. Understand?"

Digory moved his head slightly.

I wanted to weep seeing him thus, denuded of that reckless bravado which had been such a part of him. I was discovering something about Digory, about Jacco, and so much more about the baser instincts of people whom I had always before thought commonplace. But what I had learned tonight of that other one whom I had idolized—that was what hurt and bewildered me most.

We went into the house cautiously. I crept up to my room, undressed and got into bed.

I lay looking through the window at that slim slice of moon and I could not shut out of my mind the sound of voices, the weird light of torches, and all that had happened on that terrible night.

I had roughly been jerked out of my childhood and I should never be the same again.

I did fall into an uneasy doze just as it was getting light, but my sleep was haunted by nightmares. I woke up sweating with horror. Will it always be like this? I wondered. I can never forget. I should be haunted forever by the memory of Mother Ginny walking into the flames. But most of all by a figure in a greyish robe leading the mob.

As soon as I awoke I remembered the boy. The terrible adventure was not over. I tried to imagine what his feelings would be on this morning. His whole life had changed. He had lost his home and his grandmother, who was the only family he had. What else had he? Only us. How I wished my father were home. I kept telling myself that if he had been, this would never have happened. He would have stopped it before it went so far. He alone could have put an end to those proceedings.

As soon as I went downstairs I found Jacco waiting impatiently.

"We've got to get some food for him," he said.

"I don't suppose he feels much like eating. I don't."

"He'll have to eat. See what you can get. You go to the kitchens more than I do, so it will be best for you to get it. You'll have to be careful."

"I know, "I said. "Leave it to me."

There was a subdued atmosphere throughout the house. How

many servants had been in the woods last night? I wondered. Some of them might well have remained on the moor or perhaps they did not get farther than the quay.

We had to make a pretence of eating breakfast although it was an effort to do so for both of us.

Afterwards I made my way to the kitchen. I was aware of an unusual silence.

Mrs. Penlock was seated at the big kitchen table with Isaacs and some of the others.

This was clearly not the moment to go to the pantry. I should have to bide my time.

"Good morning," I said, trying to appear as usual.

"Morning, Miss Annora."

"Is—is anything wrong?"

There was a brief silence, then Mrs. Penlock said: "There was a fire last night, Mother Ginny's house was burned to a cinder . . . and her in it."

I looked steadily at them. "How . . . how did it happen?"

After some hesitation Isaacs said: "Who's to know how fires start? They do and that's about it."

They looked down at their plates. I thought: I am sure some of them must have been there. Murderers! I wanted to shout at them. That was who killed Mother Ginny.

But I must be careful. I had to think of Digory.

I must get away or I should betray something; and yet on the other hand I had to show curiosity. Hadn't I been told a hundred times that I had my nose into everything? "Curiosity killed the cat," Mrs. Penlock had told me on more than one occasion.

"There . . . must have been a cause."

"It's easy done," said Mrs. Penlock. "Her always had a fire going. Sparks fall out and a place like that—it gone in next to no time."

"Is she dead? Are you sure?"

"Reckon," said Mrs. Penlock.

"And," I went on, "the boy . . ."

"There ain't no sign of him. He must have gone too."

"That's terrible."

"Well, her being a witch, you'd have thought the Devil would have come to her aid."

"And he didn't?"

[48]

"Seems not."

I hated them all in that moment. How dared they sit there lying to me. They knew, all of them, how she had died.

I wanted to shout at them, telling them that I knew, that I had been there and seen it all. Then I remembered the frenzy of the mob last night and I thought of the boy who had been saved. If they turned on him they might devise some terrible end for him as they had for his grandmother.

I said: "It is . . . terrible." And I ran out of the kitchen.

Jacco was waiting for me.

"Well?"

"They are all there. I couldn't get anything. They are pretending it was an accident. They said sparks must have fallen on the roof and set it on fire."

"Well, what do you expect?"

"It's lies . . . all lies. They did it. They killed her."

"We've got to save the boy. So what about the food?"

"I'll have to seize the opportunity."

He nodded.

"Let's go to the Dogs' Home to see how he is," he said.

I was glad that it was sheltered from the house, for the shrubs round it were considerably overgrown.

Jacco rapped on the door. "Let us in," he called.

We heard the key in the lock and there stood Digory. He still had the dazed look on his face.

As we went in Jacco said: "We're going to bring you food. All you have to do is stay here. You'll be all right. In a few days my father will be home."

Digory said: "There's nothing . . . nowhere. It's all burned down . . . and me granny . . ."

I went to him and put my arms round him.

"We're going to look after you," I assured him. "My father will know what to do."

He just stood there like a statue that has no life.

"Come on," said Jacco. "You'll want to eat something. You'll feel better then."

Later that morning I was able to get into the pantry. I took milk, bread and a piece of cold boiled bacon.

Jacco said: "That'll do for a start."

And we took it to the Dogs' Home.

Digory was still in a daze but we made him eat a little.

Jacco and I went into the woods on the afternoon of Midsummer's Day. The smell of burned wood and thatch hung about the place. It was a pitiful sight to see that burned-out shell of what had once been a home. The grass was scorched and there was something eerie about the scene. I felt that forever after it would be a haunted spot . . . haunted not by the so-called witch but by the evil of those who had killed her.

There was a subdued air in the town. The hot sun beat down on the fourteenth-century bridge which crossed the river near the quay and where the boats were moored. There had never been another Midsummer's Day like this.

One of the fishermen sat on an upturned boat mending his nets.

"Good day," we said.

"Good day, Mr. Jacco, Miss Annora."

He was intent on his nets. Everyone seemed less loquacious than usual.

Jacco said: "So there was a fire last night?"

"Oh, aye. So 'tis said."

I thought: Where were you last night, Tom Fellows? Were you one of those who tormented that old woman? You were there perhaps, waving your torch, setting that home on fire. It may not have been your torch which lit the fire, but you are all guilty, all the same . . . every one of you who let it happen.

"Mother Ginny's cottage was burned down," said Jacco.

"Oh, aye, so 'tis said."

"And she was in it."

"So they'm telling me."

"It's a terrible thing," I said.

"'Tis so, Miss Annora."

"And," demanded Jacco, "what of the boy Digory?"

"Don't 'ee ask me, Mr. Jacco. I know naught."

I thought: That is what they will all say. They know naught. They are all ashamed. They are all going to pretend they were not there.

We moved on. We spoke to some of the others and it was the same with them all. They had all heard of it and it was a terrible thing to have happened—even to a witch, some added.

[50]

I said angrily to Jacco: "They are all going to plead innocence."

"The guilty always do."

"There were a lot of them in the woods last night."

"They will all say they were on the moor or the quay or in their beds."

To all of them we mentioned Digory. Nobody called him the Varmint now. They believed he had been in the cottage and died with his grandmother. That certain respect which was due to the dead was accorded him.

"He'll be safe in the Dogs' Home," I said. "They think he's dead."

"We'll keep him there."

"Till our father comes home," I added.

I waited two days before I tried to see Rolf. I could not imagine what I should say to him if we came face to face. I had always felt there was a special understanding between us—but that was over now. I blamed him more than I did people like Mrs. Penlock. They were ignorant. He was not. He was clever; he had incited the people to behave as they did. Why? Perhaps he wanted to experiment. He wanted to see how close people of today were to their ancestors. He wanted to discover how far a modern mob would go in its savagery. I had always understood his desire for learning; but this was sheer callousness.

I could never forget it and whenever I saw him I would remember him in the midst of that crowd . . . urging them on.

But I had to talk to him. I rode without Jacco to Dorey Manor.

How grand it was becoming! It lacked the antiquity of Cador but it had stood there for three hundred years—just a Manor House, but the woods were now extensive and my father had said they must have almost as many pheasants as we had at Cador.

But I was not interested in these matters at the moment.

I rode into the stables and left my horse with the groom as I always did. Then I went to the house. I pulled the bell at the side of the iron-studded door and a maid appeared.

"Oh good afternoon, Miss Annora. I'll tell the master you are here."

I went into the hall with its linen-fold panelling so beautifully restored. Shortly afterwards I was mounting the wooden staircase decorated with Tudor roses of which Rolf was so proud. I was ushered into the drawing room and Mr. Hanson came forward to greet me.

"My dear Annora, this is a pleasure. Have you come to have a cup of tea with me?"

"That would be nice, thank you."

He turned to the maid who had brought me up. "We'll have some tea please, Annie," he said. Then: "There, my dear. Sit down. When are your parents coming home?"

"Very soon now."

"It was very sad about your grandpapa. But it was expected. I daresay you're missing them. I shall want to be asked over to hear how things are in that corner of England—and I don't doubt your parents stayed in London for a while, so they should be well informed of the latest news."

"Yes, they would of course have a little time there."

"You're wondering where Rolf is. I guessed you came to see him, eh?"

"Oh, Mr. Hanson . . ."

"Don't apologise. I understand. I know you like to talk to Rolf . . . and so does your brother. He's well, I hope."

I said Jacco was very well.

"A sad thing about that old woman."

"Oh yes . . . on Midsummer's Eve. Is . . . Rolf out?"

"That is what I'm getting to. He's away, my dear. He'll be away at least another week."

"He went away then?"

"Yes. Staying with a friend who's going to the University with him. They're going to study something . . . ancient documents or something. You know the sort of thing."

"Oh . . . I see."

I felt bewildered and while Mr. Hanson went on talking about something—I forget what, for I was not paying much attention—the tea came in.

I had to spend nearly an hour with him, and all the time I was thinking of Rolf. He must be ashamed of the part he had played on that terrible night and like everyone else connected with it was trying to pretend it had never happened.

[52]

* * *

We gave ourselves wholeheartedly to the task of keeping Digory hidden. Jacco did not mention the figure in the robe whom we had seen that night. Some of them did wear fancy dress on the night of the bonfire, bringing out old smocks and hats which their grandfathers had worn. I remembered that the robe had been mentioned in his presence, but Jacco was the type to forget things like that, particularly if he was interested in something else at the time. I was glad he did not refer to it and I was certainly not going to bring the matter up.

Then my parents came home.

I had never seen my mother so sad. She had loved her father dearly.

We had to choose the right moment to speak to our parents and the opportunity did not come until after dinner.

I thought the meal would never end. There was a great deal of talk about Eversleigh and the family there. They had wanted to bring my grandmother back with them but she had said that she felt too distraught for travel just yet. We must all be together soon.

"So we shall be going to Eversleigh," I said.

"It's such a long journey for her to come here," my mother pointed out. "Perhaps we could meet in London. It would do your grandmother good to get away for a while, I am sure."

We kept talking about Grandfather Dickon and what a wonderful man he had been and how strange it would be without him.

My father said: "That was a terrible thing about the fire."

"That poor woman," said my mother.

"And the boy too," added my father.

There was silence. Jacco looked at me warningly. There were servants about, he implied. As if I would have forgotten the need for secrecy even now.

As we rose from the table, I said: "We want to speak to you . . . Jacco and I."

"Somewhere quiet," said Jacco.

"Am I included?" asked our mother.

"Of course," replied Jacco.

"Something troubling you?" My father spoke anxiously. "Come into my study at once."

[53]

So we told them how we had gone out, how the cat had been thrown into the fire and how the mob had gone into the woods. I did not mention Rolf.

"Oh, my God," said my mother. "They are savages."

"Go on," said my father.

"When they threw her into the river," said Jacco, "the boy ran out."

"No one saw him but us," I added.

"He was hiding close to us," went on Jacco. "They threw the torches at the roof and she . . . walked into the fire. I took him up on my horse and I brought him away. We escaped."

"Good boy. You did well. What happened to him?"

"We kept him in the Dogs' Home. He's been there all this time."

"I took him food from the pantry," I added.

My father put an arm round us both and there were tears in my mother's eyes as she looked at us.

"I'm proud of you," said my father. "Proud of you both. We'll bring the boy out now."

I looked at him fearfully. "You've no idea what the people can be like. Nobody could know who hadn't seen them. They're not like the people we know generally . . . They were mad . . . wicked . . . cruel. They might harm Digory."

"They will not," said my father. "They will know they have to answer to me."

"What will happen to Digory?" I asked.

"He'll work for us. he will be under our roof . . . under my care."

An immense relief swept over me.

I knew that my father would know what to do.

We went at once to the Dogs' Home. When Digory saw my father he made as though to run but Jacco caught him and said: "It's all right. He's one of us."

I saw my father's lips turn up at the corners at that and he said in a wonderfully gentle voice: "He's right, my boy. Everything will be all right now. You're going to live here . . . work for me, and I look after people who do that."

Digory was silent. He had changed a little from that boy whom we had at first brought here, but the hunted look remained in his eyes. He was suspicious of everyone except Jacco and me. I knew that he

[54]

had gone into the woods at night and seen that burned-out cottage. I could well imagine his emotions at the sight. If I had grown up in that terrible night, so had he.

He had lost that impish bravado, that desire to show he was as good as—no, better than—the rest of us. There was in a way a sort of resignation, an acceptance of the tragedy of life; but I knew, too, that there was a burning resentment.

My father said: "First we'll find a bed for you."

"They'll take me . . . like they did me granny. They threw her in the river. They tried to drown her. Then they burned her all up."

"They will not dare," said my father. "I shall make them understand that. Come to the house with me now."

He was still reluctant, but Jacco took him by the arm and he trusted Jacco. I felt my spirits lift because of the trust he had in us.

We walked to the house and my father told Jacco to take Digory into the small room which led from the hall and to come out when he called to them.

Then he rang one of the bells and in a short time Isaacs appeared.

"Isaacs," he said, "I want all the servants assembled in the hall."

"Now, Sir Jake?"

"Immediately."

"Very good, sir."

I could almost feel the tremor which passed through the house. I was aware of running footsteps, whispering voices. In a very short time they were all present, forming two lines with Mrs. Penlock at the head of one and Isaacs at the other.

My father addressed them very seriously: "A wicked and most shameful event took place during my absence. Senseless savages murdered a defenseless old woman. Oh, I know that you are telling yourselves that the fire in the woods was an accident, but in your hearts you know it was not so. It is hard to believe that anyone today, people we meet in our everyday life, who before this had seemed ordinary decent folk, could be guilty of such a crime. I am not asking you to come forward and confess your guilt—if any of you are guilty you will know that and have to live with your consciences—but let me tell you this: there will be no more savagery on these lands, for the simple reason that anyone who is caught performing these evil deeds will no longer be on this land. On Midsummer's Eve an old woman was sent to her death. She had a grandson living with her.

Providentially that boy was saved from a mob of hooligans. He has been deprived of his home and his guardian and he is now under my care. He will work here; he will live among us. He has suffered a great deal and we shall remember that. If I hear of any persecution of this boy, it will be worse for those who are guilty of it. Jacco, come out now."

Jacco came out, Digory with him.

There was a gasp through the hall, and I had never heard such silence.

My father laid a hand on Digory's shoulder.

He went on. "This boy, Digory, is now a member of my household. I hope that is clear to you all." He turned to John Ferry, the head groom. "Ferry," he said. "You've got a spare room over the stables. The boy can use that until we decide what he is going to do here."

"Yes, sir," said Ferry.

"Take him now. He'll no doubt need to learn a lot if he is going to work with the horses."

"Yes, sir."

Jacco said: "You can go with Ferry. He'll do as my father says."

Digory still did not speak. How different he was from that truculent boy I had met in the woods.

John Ferry said: "Come on, me lad."

He grasped Digory by the shoulder and they went to the door, Digory still walking as though in a trance.

My father said: "Oh . . . Ferry?"

Ferry paused and turned. "Yes, sir?"

"Remember what I said."

"Yes, sir. I will, sir."

At a sign from my father the servants were dismissed.

"You two come into the drawing room and talk to your mother and me," he said to us. "There's a great deal I want to ask."

So we went and we sat up late telling them all that had happened on that terrible night.

I felt happier than I had since it happened. It was wonderful to know that my father was there to take care of everything.

In the days that followed I thought that was the perfect solution in view of everything that had happened. Digory had a home; he was assured of good meals every day, and he had my father's protection.

[56]

But, of course, there are no perfect solutions. Digory had lost his grandmother and he had taken a great pride in her and the fact that she was not only the seventh daughter of a seventh daughter, but she was also a footling—she had been born feet first and that meant she had special powers. Moreover she claimed to be of a Pellar family— one of those whose ancestor had helped a stranded mermaid back to the sea and for such services had been blessed with special powers. A fearful disillusion had come to Digory and added to his misery, for her powers had proved useless against the mob, and she had been unable to take her revenge on them. His pride was shattered and his freedom lost.

He loved horses and would rather work with them than with anything else; but he was no longer free. He was at the beck and call of John Ferry, and although there was no persecution—for that had been most forcefully forbidden by my father—at the same time there was no friendliness either.

He was a wild spirit and if his granny was a Pellar, so was he.

He was morose and said little to the other stable boys; he did what he had to do grudgingly and his love was for the horses and never spilled over to his fellow human beings. Perhaps for Jacco and me he had a certain feeling. He did not forget that we had probably saved his life on that memorable night. Apart from us he appeared to have no friendly feeling for any others.

He was different; he was apart.

Moreover his presence was resented, although none dared show it. But resentment was there all the same. Nobody could really forget that he was the Witch's Varmint.

Jacco and I had made him our protégé. We were fond of him because we believed we had saved his life, and every time I saw him I experienced a glow of satisfaction and pride because of this. And I was sure that Jacco felt the same. There is nothing which endears such a person to one so much as the knowledge that one has done that person a great service—and what greater service could there be than to save a life?

He never sought company. I fancied he lived in a little world of his own where he, the Pellar boy, was all-powerful. He had a deep-rooted pride in himself; he did not need other people—unlike the rest of us, who seemed to depend so much on one another.

He liked the Dogs' Home. There was a little window in it. He broke it and climbed through. He made it his little sanctum, the place where he could be quite alone. When Jacco discovered the broken window he had it repaired and gave the key of the place to Digory. I think that key became his dearest possession.

He might have felt some gratitude towards Jacco and me but he had been too deeply wounded to trust anyone completely; he avoided us, and I believed that was because he hated to feel indebted to anyone; for just as we had that glow of satisfaction for having saved his life, his pride was hurt because he had been so dependent upon us.

Every day I waited for the return of Rolf. I longed for it and dreaded it. I wondered what I would say to him. I would demand to know how he could have behaved in such a way. Already I had begun to think that all that had happened on that memorable night was because of him. He was a natural leader and he had taken charge. He had goaded them on because he wanted to see if people of our century reacted in the same way as they had in an earlier one. At times I could not believe it of him and then I reminded myself that I had seen it happen.

He did not come back. Mr. Hanson came to dinner. He said Rolf was going straight to the University without coming home first. He doubted he would see him for some time.

Rolf had always had his absences. Mr. Hanson talked of his son as though he were a law unto himself. He spoke with such pride and affection. I wondered what he would think if he knew.

I was glad in a way that I did not have to see him. While I did not, I could pretend to myself that there was some explanation.

It was a sad summer. My mother tried hard to hide her unhappiness and she did to a certain extent outwardly; but I could sense how deeply she mourned her father.

The memory of what had happened on Midsummer's Eve hung over us all. I did encounter some of the people who, I was sure, had been present in the woods and I could not believe that they were the same who had taken part in that fearful atrocity. They had become as strangers to me . . . just as, I told myself, Rolf had.

Change had come from all sides and my life would never be the same again.

My father's presence helped a lot. I went riding with him and he talked about what was going on in London.

"One day you'll have to go up to London and have a season, Annora," he said.

"Must I?"

"I suppose so. You have to see something of the world. You'll have to find a husband. You're not likely to have much choice here."

"That's a long time away."

"Yes. But time passes quickly. Your Aunt Amaryllis will soon be busy with Helena."

"Oh, Helena is a lot older than I."

"Is it six years? It seems a good deal now but when you get older it will seem nearer."

"I'd rather stay here."

"See how you feel later on. Life here might seem a little restricting to a lively girl."

"You like it here."

"Don't forget I've settled down. It's a good place to settle down in. When you are young you want to go out into the world. It makes you appreciate this more."

"What a life you've had."

"Not many men in my position can boast of having been a prisoner of Mother England." I saw the faraway look in his eyes which came when he referred to those years in Australia. "I'll tell you what," he went on. "One day you, your mother, Jacco and I will pay a visit to Australia. I have some land out there. Would you like to see where your father toiled in the years of his captivity?"

"We'd all go! Oh, that would be fun."

"One day we will."

We were riding when this conversation took place and then suddenly we turned a bend and Cador came into view. It always amazed me when seen from a distance for it was then that one appreciated its grandeur.

"It is magnificent," I said.

"I'm glad you like it."

"It looks so grand . . . so bold. As though it's saying, 'Come and take me if you can.'"

"That was what it was meant to say in the days of the marauding barons."

"Nobody ever succeeded in taking it."

"No. There were skirmishes. Gallons of boiling oil must have been poured from those battlements. You can see the marks of the battering rams on the gate. But you're right. No one succeeded. It would take more than brute force to get a footing in Cador."

"Then it is safe."

"Yes. Only cunning could find a way in."

"You're proud of it, Papa."

"Aren't you?"

"Of course."

As we rode home he went on talking about the house, how one of the towers had been damaged during the Civil War when the King had sheltered there, for no Cadorson could ever be anything but a staunch royalist. Cadorsons had stood firmly beside Edward IV during the Wars of the Roses and had played a big part in that conflict.

"Much of the history of England is written on this house, Annora. It's something to be proud of."

Mr. Hanson came to dine with us frequently. Rolf did not return. There was always a great deal of talk over the dinner table and at this time there was trouble in various places. We were a backwater and sometimes seemed apart from the rest of the country, but as my father said, what happened in London would affect us all eventually.

Jacco and I had taken the meal with our parents ever since we were out of the nursery. My mother said she had dined with her parents at an early age and she thought it was good for us to listen to adult conversation. We were delighted with the arrangement and I was sure she was right and we did profit from these occasions.

Having stayed in the Capital, my father had returned with a greater awareness of what was going on. A year or so ago the old King had died. He had been ailing for a long time and was almost senile. He had been dominated by his brother, the Duke of Cumberland, who was rather a sinister character and had been suspected of trying to murder the little Princess Victoria who was living with her forceful mother at Kensington Palace.

All these scandals and intrigues fascinated me. I daresay a great deal of it was exaggerated but it did give me an interest in what was going on in the country.

As soon as the old King died, Cumberland was dismissed by the new monarch, William IV, who had married the Princess Adelaide and they were shortly to be crowned.

"Perhaps we will go to London for the coronation," said my father.

"There's a lot of trouble up there, I believe," said Lawyer Hanson.

"Oh yes," replied my father. "It's due to this Reform Bill. And not only that. There is unrest everywhere among the working classes. They are determined to revolt and form unions against the employers. My wife's relation, Peter Lansdon, is right at the centre of it."

"Oh, that Peter Lansdon," said the lawyer. "If he goes on as he is now he could be Prime Minister in due course."

"Peter is a very ambitious man and seems to succeed in everything he touches."

There had always been a lot of talk about Peter Lansdon. The family connection was rather complicated, which was mainly due to the fact that Grandfather Dickon had married Grandmother Lottie late in life when he already had two sons by a previous marriage. My mother's half-brother, David, was the father of Amaryllis, so my mother was almost the same age as she was and they had been brought up together more like sisters than niece and aunt. It was always difficult to explain these relationships to people.

It was Amaryllis who had married Peter Lansdon, and their children were Peterkin and Helena, who were sort of second cousins to me.

However, Peter Lansdon was a very colourful character. He was an enormously successful businessman. He exported rum and bananas, I think from Jamaica, where he had spent his childhood. Having succeeded magnificently in business, he had turned his attention to politics and, as was to be expected, he rapidly began to make himself heard.

My mother had a great aversion to him. She never spoke of this but I could see how she felt whenever his name was mentioned; then a certain stony expression would creep across her face and she would become very silent.

The rest of the family admired him; and Jacco and I thought it exciting to have a relation whose name appeared in the papers now and then and of whom it was said that he might one day hold the highest post in the Government.

"Peter thinks there will have to be reform," my father was saying. "Not only with franchise but with the workers. He thinks it would be better to placate them now than to have them forming societies which will attempt to force employers to do what they want."

The lawyer nodded gravely. "All very well," he said, "but the more these people get, the more they will want."

"They haven't very much at the moment," my father reminded him.

My mother said: "I don't think workers on the land realize how lucky they are when they have a benign squire who is prepared to look after them."

Mr. Hanson agreed. "They have that and at first they are grateful. But people grow accustomed to what they have and start to want more. It's a difficult situation. If they are given more, mark my words . . . once they get it they will want more and more."

"What is generally known as the vicious circle," I put in.

Everyone looked at me and my father smiled. "You have hit the nail on the head, Annora," he said.

Rolf came back in August. I was riding with my father when we met him. He looked no different and smiled at me in that warmly affectionate way as though everything was as it had always been.

He told us that he was interested in a house his friend's family were buying. They were restoring it and he had been helping them to make decisions. It had meant exploring old records, for the place was very run-down and much of the original character was in danger of being lost.

It was hard to believe that he was the same person who had leaped over the bonfire and led the mob to destroy an old woman.

He came to dine with us and the talk was all about the Reform Bill and the unrest among the workers. Then it turned back to property and Mr. Hanson's desire to buy more land. He talked with pride about the pheasants they were breeding in their woods. "We'll have a good shoot this autumn," said Mr. Hanson proudly.

"Luke is determined on that," said Rolf.

"Still giving satisfaction, that fellow of yours?" asked my father.

"Couldn't be better," Mr. Hanson told him.

"I can see Lawyer Hanson will soon be becoming Squire Hanson," said my father.

"Our place will never be a Cador," said Rolf regretfully.

"But yours is a wonderful old house," my mother consoled him, "and you're making an excellent job of the reconstruction. That staircase of yours is magnificent."

"Put in for Queen Elizabeth," said Mr. Hanson. "Rolf tells me those carvings of the Tudor roses and the fleur-de-lys are the best of their kind."

"But you are the lucky ones," said Rolf, "to live in a place like this and know your ancestors have been there through the ages. That makes a difference."

Rolf was not the only one who was interested in Cador. I discovered someone else who was and I must say that was a surprise.

October had come. All through September there had been talk of the Fair. On the first and second of October St. Matthew's Fair was held in the marketplace in East Dorey. Jacco and I had been taken often when we were young, usually by one of the grooms. We had bought comfits and gingerbread; we had seen the fat woman and the bearded lady; we had had our fortunes told by Rosa the Gypsy; we had done it all.

Now that I was nearly twelve and Jacco was fourteen we felt ourselves to be too sophisticated for these simple pleasures and, rather condescendingly, said we did not want to go.

The servants, of course, would all go. They had been talking about "Matthey's Fair" for weeks. Even Mrs. Penlock liked to have her fortune told.

My parents were out visiting and would not be home until late; Miss Caster was taking tea at the vicarage. I think the general idea was that I was going somewhere with Jacco; he, however, had other plans.

Thus it was that on that October day the house was deserted, and I realized that it was very rarely that I found myself alone there. In a house like Cador—even though it has always been one's home—one is very much aware of the antiquity, of the intruding presence of another age when there is no one around to remind one that it is the present day.

I had been reading in my bedroom and decided that I would go for a ride. I would go and look at the Hansons' wood, of which they were so proud. It was about half the size of ours, a fact which I knew Rolf deplored. He had said: "One day our woods will rival yours." I wanted to see him, to force myself to talk with him about that night. But somehow I had always held back. I think in my heart I was trying to pretend he had not been there and sometimes I almost succeeded in convincing myself that this was so. Suppose I talked to him. Suppose he admitted what I suspected, that it had been one of his experiments. I did not want my feelings for Rolf to change. But I feared they would. I feared they had. I was rather bewildered and I seemed to be more so every day. If only it had been someone else, someone I did not care about. I found it very hard to stop caring about Rolf.

I was trying to shake off these thoughts as I came through the solarium, and as I did so I had the eerie feeling that I was not after all alone in the house. How is it that one is aware of a presence? An unexpected movement? A footstep? The creaking of a door? Was it being stealthily opened?

These thoughts crowded into my mind as I went to the peep in the alcove and looked down on the hall.

It looked the same as usual. There was the long table at which Oliver Cromwell's soldiers had sat when they came searching for the King; the weapons on the wall which had been used by Cadorsons long since dead; the family tree spreading out on the wall . . . everything that I had seen many times and grown up with.

And yet there was that uncanny feeling that someone was there.

Then I saw him. From beyond the screens he came stealthily, looking about him with a kind of wonder: Digory.

What was he doing in the house?

I watched him for some time. He examined the family tree; then he came to the wall and very reverently touched the weapons; he turned to the table and picking up one of the pewter goblets, examined it closely, put it down and stood for a moment staring rapturously at the vaulted roof. Then he began to tiptoe cautiously up the stairs.

I was at the top of the staircase when he reached it.

"Hello, Digory," I said.

He stared at me silently, a look of blank dismay on his face. Then he spluttered indignantly, "Why don't 'ee be at the Fair?"

"Because," I said, "I remained at home. I had no idea, of course, that you intended to pay a visit."

He turned and was about to dash down the stairs but I caught his arm.

"It doesn't matter," I said. "You looked as though you liked the place."

"I weren't doing no wrong."

"I didn't say you were. Why aren't *you* at the Fair?"

He looked contemptuous.

"You preferred to come to Cador," I said. "You do like it, don't you?"

[64]

"It ain't bad at all."

"I remember in the woods you used to ask me about it. You wanted to know all the details."

I saw the shadow cross his face and I reproached myself. He would probably be remembering that in those days he had a granny and a home.

I said gently: "I'm glad you like this house, Digory. I'm glad you came in. I'm going to take you round and show you everything."

He looked at me suspiciously.

"It's all right," I assured him. "You know I'm your friend . . . Jacco too."

He relaxed a little.

I said: "Do you like working in the stables?"

He shrugged his shoulders.

I remembered a bird I had once seen. Jacco had found it when it fell from its nest. We fed it. I kept it in a cage. It seemed content for a while; then it started to flap its wings against the bars. I opened the door and set it free. Digory was like a caged bird. He was well fed, he was safe, but he was not free.

"I'm going to show you the house," I said.

He tried not to look excited but he could not hide his feelings from me.

"Come on," I said. "We'll begin at the bottom and go right to the top."

"All right," he said.

"There's a dungeon down there. Would you like to see it?"

We came through the kitchens and descended a short spiral staircase.

"It's very cold down here. Mrs. Penlock uses it as a place to store things. That's very different from the old days."

We made our way past shelves upon which stood jars and bottles, and we came through a narrow passage to the dungeon with its iron gate.

"You can look in," I said.

"There's nobody in there," said Digory as though disappointed.

"Of course not. People don't put their enemies in dungeons nowadays."

"Some might," he retorted grimly; and again I saw the memory of that night in his eyes.

"Not now," I insisted firmly and I thought: I was wrong to bring him down here.

"Let's go up," I said. "It's cold down here."

So we went through the kitchens, past the ovens which had done service for hundreds of years, past the roasting spits and the great coppers, through the buttery to the laundry rooms. Then up to the great hall.

I talked to him about the wars which had beset the country and told him what part my family had played in them. I took him to the dining room and explained what the tapestries on the walls were depicting. He listened in rapt attention, which surprised me. I talked of the Wars of the Roses and the Great Rebellion, that conflict between Cavalier and Roundhead which had rent the country. I felt like Miss Caster giving a history lesson, but he was interested; he wanted to know.

I showed him the solarium and peeps, which fascinated him; he stood, for a long time, looking down into the hall and then the chapel. I took him to the turrets and we went out and walked along the battlements. I would not have believed that a house could have made such an impression on him. But then it was a wonderful house; it had been kept in good order over the centuries; it had been loved and cherished; and although it had been restored from time to time, there had been great care not to destroy the antiquity. That now seemed all around us. Perhaps it was due to the fact that we were alone in it, but as I talked to him I had the feeling that we were two young people walking back through the centuries.

He had had no schooling; I suppose he had never heard of the events to which I referred before, but he was fascinated by them; and now and then would ask a pertinent question.

We stood for a while looking out to sea.

"Just imagine, Digory," I said, "from out there Cador would have looked just the same five hundred years ago. Isn't that wonderful?"

"How do you know?" he demanded. "You wasn't here."

"No. But it hasn't changed so it must have been the same."

He looked steadily at me and said: "You've got the Devil's kiss on your forrid."

I put up my hand. His was there before mine. He touched the side of my temple just beside my left eye. I knew what he meant; it was a little mole. My father called it my beauty spot.

I had never thought very much about it.

"What do you mean—the Devil's kiss?" I asked.

"They do say that's how it be when the Devil kisses 'ee."

"What nonsense. I have never even met the gentleman—let alone been kissed by him."

"He do come in the night when you be sleeping."

"What a horrible thought! It's a mole. My father likes it. He says it's attractive. Who says it is anything to do with the Devil?"

"Them," he said; and again there was that look of hideous memory in his eyes. "Them says as how it's the Devil as does it."

"I'm not afraid of them."

Again I had spoken rashly. *He* had been afraid of them; and so should I have been in his place on that terrible night.

I felt very sorry for him. I put a hand on his shoulder. "Listen, Digory," I said. "We've got to forget all about that. It's over. It was cruel. It was horrible. But it's done and nothing can be done to change it."

He was silent, staring ahead, seeing it all, I knew; and I was seeing it with him. I could almost smell the burning thatch.

"We've got to go on from there, Digory," I said. "You've got to get used to the stables. You're fond of the horses and it's good to work with what you love. Ferry is kind to you, isn't he? My father insists that he should be. It's a better way of life . . . to be part of a household like this . . . better than running round stealing fish. You could get caught."

He shook his head.

"Yes, you might, Digory. If there's anything that bothers you, you only have to tell us . . . tell me or Jacco. We'll always help if we can."

He looked blankly at me and there was still in him that which reminded me of the caged bird.

He said: "Tell you what. I'll get rid of your Devil's kiss."

I put my hand to my temple.

"Oh, it's all right, Digory. It doesn't bother me. My father says that when I grow older I'll call attention to it. Blacken it to make it stand out and make people notice my eyes."

"There's them," he said.

And he meant that frenzied mob.

I could see that he wanted to attempt to charm away my mole and that this was his way of showing appreciation for what I had done for him. "Never brush aside people's attempts to repay you," my mother had said. "You may not want repayment but their pride demands that they should give it. Do take it graciously."

I saw what she meant now.

"All right, Digory," I said. "You shall charm away my mole."

We came into the turret and went down through the house. Every now and then he would pause and gaze wonderingly about him. I was pleased and felt I had seen a new side to his nature; he might be uneducated but he had an eye for beauty. He seemed to find it difficult to tear himself away from the tapestries and I had to tell him again about the wars which had inspired them.

I did not know how long this tour of the house had taken but I did realize that time was passing. Isaacs might return; and Mrs. Penlock was only interested in having her fortune told and would not stay after that had been done.

I said: "They'll be back soon."

A look of fear came into his face. He was then all eagerness to get away. I was leading him to the front door but he was anxious to leave by the way he had come, which was through an open window in one of the kitchens.

I felt then that I was a little nearer to understanding him and as soon as Jacco came in I would tell him what had happened and suggest that we try to see him now and then and make him realize how secure he was and that while he was under my father's protection, he was safe from the savagery of a superstitious mob.

I was unprepared for the sequel. It happened two days after our tour of the house.

Jacco and I had been out with our father. Jacco had to learn a good deal about estate management and he was often with my father on his round. I was free to accompany them whenever I wished and that was often because I was very interested in the people who were Cador tenants.

As we came into the stables John Ferry came hurrying out.

"Oh, Sir Jake," he said, "there be trouble. 'Tis about that boy . . ."

There was a faint tightening of the lips which betrayed the unspoken comment: "I could have told you so." This indicated that Digory was in some sort of trouble.

"What's happened?" asked my father.

"Slattery have caught him red-handed, Sir Jake," Ferry explained. "A tidy-sized piece of beefsteak he had . . . was stowing it away in a bag when he was caught. No doubt about it, sir. There was the steak in his bag."

"What was the point of stealing steak?" demanded my father. "He's well fed here, isn't he?"

"There's them that's thieves by nature, sir. They do it natural. It's a habit of a lifetime."

"Where's the boy now?"

"Down at Slattery's. Slattery's going to charge him. But he said he'd tell me first and I could tell you like . . . seeing as how you've taken the boy in."

Jacco and I were looking at our father anxiously. He said: "Come on. We'll go to Slattery's and sort this out."

Tom Slattery, the butcher, was a fat red-faced man with a slight resemblance to the pigs which hung up in his shop, except that they had oranges in their mouths and he had broken teeth. He always wore a blue-and-white striped apron, faintly bloodstained, over his grey trousers and my memory of him is standing over a slightly concave board with a chopper in his hands.

We left our horses tethered to the rail and a few steps from the shop and went in.

In the parlour behind the shop cowered Digory, trying hard to hide his terror. We were surprised to see Luke Tregern, the Hansons' gamekeeper, with Slattery.

"Good day, Slattery . . . Tregern . . ." said my father. "What's all this about a pound of beefsteak and the boy?"

"Well, Sir Jake," said Slattery, "he be nothing but a thief. Not that we ain't known that. 'Tis no surprise, as you might say. I had me back turned for a minute and I hears a shout. 'Twas a mercy Mr. Tregern here just come into the shop. See him take it up, he did, and when I spins round there he is stuffing it into his bag all ready to dart out of my shop."

"That's the case, Sir Jake," said Luke Tregern. "I caught the boy in the act."

[69]

He looked rather pleased with himself.

"He's been thieving all his life," said Slattery. "Slippery as an eel, that one is. I'd never have known he'd been in and out of my shop if it hadn't been for Mr. Tregern here."

"I'm glad I came in when I did," said Luke Tregern.

Digory turned defiant eyes up to my father.

"Is this true?" asked my father. "Did you steal the steak?"

Digory didn't answer.

I could not restrain myself. I said: "Why did you do it, you foolish boy? You get enough to eat, don't you?"

Still he did not answer.

"There must be a reason," said Jacco.

"Tell us why you stole the steak," said my father. "Were you hungry? If you don't tell us, how shall we know what to do about you? If there is a reason, you must tell us."

There was another silence. Then he lifted a finger and pointed at me.

"My daughter!" said my father. "What has she to do with it?"

"'Twas for her," said Digory.

"I don't understand."

"Had to be secret meat. No one to know where it come from . . . or it don't work."

"What is he talking about?" asked my father.

"Devil's kiss," said Digory.

Then I understood. I touched my temple. "Was it this?" I asked.

"You know," he said. "You wanted it done."

I said: "I think I understand. Digory wanted to do something for me. He noticed this." I pointed to my mole. "He was going to get rid of it for me. Was that what the beefsteak was for, Digory?"

He nodded. "It has to go on. Then I put on the brew. After that . . . 'tis gone in two days."

"But why did you steal it? I could have got some steak in the kitchen for you."

"'Tas to be secret. *You* can't know where it do come from."

I said: "It is all clear to me. Digory was trying to do me a good turn. He was going to remove this mole because he thought it was not good for me to have it." I looked appealingly at my father. "You can understand it after . . . after . . .

My father nodded.

"He wanted to repay us . . . Jacco and me."

Jacco said: "It's quite simple. He was going to take away Annora's mole and she wasn't to know where the steak came from or it wouldn't work."

"I have never heard such nonsense," said my father. "You see, Slattery, this is a children's game. Leave the boy to me. I'll deal with him." He put a sovereign on the table. "That'll take care of the steak and you can keep it as well as the money. I don't suppose it came to much harm in the boy's bag. Now I'll leave you to your business. Thank you for sending to Ferry. Shouldn't attach too much importance to childish games. I'll give the boy a talking-to . . . and my daughter, too."

We came out of the shop, Digory with us. I noticed that Luke Tregern was looking after us with a rather quizzical expression, and I had the feeling that he was disappointed in the way in which the situation had turned out. I supposed he thought he had been rather clever in spotting Digory's action and should have been commended for it.

My father said sternly to Digory: "Never take anything that doesn't belong to you, boy, or you'll be in trouble. Now go back to your work."

Digory ran off at great speed and my father turned to me: "As for you," he said, "I don't know how you could be so stupid. He might have disfigured you with his witches' potions."

"I only thought that he wanted to do something to repay us, and Mama says we should remember people's pride and respect it."

"I suppose she is right. But that young idiot will have to take care. There's enough feeling against him already. There's a great sense of guilt throughout this place for what happened that night. Nobody wants to take responsibility. I daresay your mother will tell you that people hate to feel guilt and try to justify themselves. If they could prove Mother Ginny's grandson to be a thief, they'd feel a little justification. So if you have any influence with that boy, tell him to take care."

"We will, won't we, Annora?" said Jacco.

I nodded in agreement.

When one is young and innocent of nature, one believes in easy solutions. The fairy tales always told us that they lived "happy ever

[71]

after." I accepted that. It was comforting and pleasant. I had thought that when Digory had a good bed to sleep in and was assured of three meals a day, and worked with horses which he loved and had my father's protection, he would live "happy ever after."

Comfort could not change Digory. He was wild; his freedom was what he most desired. In the days before the fire he might have lived frugally; he might have gone hungry now and then; he had lived dangerously, outside the community; and people were suspicious of him because his grandmother was a witch. But he had been proud, subservient to nobody—and he had been happy.

What happened I supposed was inevitable. He might have avoided it for a time, if he had had better luck; but the outcome would have been the same.

And this time there was no way of saving him.

He had made the Dogs' Home his. He slept there, though it must have been less comfortable than the room over the stables which had been allotted to him. There was a clearing behind the Dogs' Home and here he made fires and cooked for himself.

He did not like the company of the other stable lads; Ferry tolerated him but I guessed he was hoping he would be caught in some misdemeanor so that he could have the pleasure of seeing him removed and proving my father in the wrong. He did not understand that my father would not feel that at all. But Ferry was hoping for the boy's downfall—as I guessed most of the servants were. Mrs. Penlock never said a word against Digory but she had a very significant sniff when his name was mentioned.

It was about two weeks after the beefsteak incident.

Ferry came to the house, triumphant. He wished to speak to Sir Jake. I had seen him coming and, guessing from his attitude that this meant trouble for Digory, I contrived to be there.

Ferry stood, cap in hand, turning it round and round as he spoke.

"'Tis that boy again, Sir Jake."

"What's wrong?"

"He be in jail, Sir Jake."

"What?"

"Caught. In the Hanson woods, sir. Pheasant in his bag. No mistake about what he was up to this time."

My father looked at him blankly. "The idiot," he said. "What was he doing stealing a pheasant? He's fed . . ."

"There's some as is natural thieves, sir, and that boy's one of them. When you think where he comes from . . . It was Mr. Hanson's gamekeeper who caught him. Mr. Tregern, sir. He got him charged right away. Serious offence, this, sir."

"Very serious," agreed my father. "All right, Ferry."

Ferry touched his forehead and retired.

I stared in dismay at my father.

"It appears," he said, looking at me ruefully, "that this time the young fool has got himself into serious trouble."

How right he was!

Jacco and I were very distressed, looking upon Digory as our protégé as we did. How could he have been so foolish! With our father's help we had been able to extricate him from the beefsteak incident but this was another matter.

"Can you get him freed?" asked Jacco of my father.

"He's already in the hands of the law. Hanson's gamekeeper took quick action. I've no doubt they'll get Slattery to speak against him."

"Couldn't you forbid him to?"

"No, my son. I can't interfere with the course of justice. It's true what Slattery says. The boy's a natural thief. If he escaped the consequences of this there would be another incident before long. We've seen that of the beefsteak. You would have thought that would have been warning enough."

"It's just bravado," I said.

"It is a luxury which, in his position, he cannot afford."

It soon became clear that there was nothing to be done. My father asked Mr. Hanson if he would talk to his gamekeeper and this he did. He came back and told us that Luke Tregern was adamant. There was not doubt of the boy's guilt and he could not have people walking off with the pheasants. If this sort of thing was allowed to go on he could not be responsible. It would be an impossible situation for him. The last thing Mr. Hanson wanted was to lose such an excellent man. Moreover, as he hinted to my father, they both knew enough about the law to understand that it could not be trifled with to gain special favours for certain people.

My father said to us: "Of course I see his point. It is a pity about that beefsteak—and Tregern was the one who caught him at that. I warned the young fool and he has flouted me. No, there is nothing to be done. The boy has got to learn his lesson—a hard one it will no doubt be, but it is his own fault and perhaps the only way to instill some sense into him."

I wanted to go and see him, to talk to him; but that was not possible.

Jacco and I rode out to the moors and lay on the grass making wild plans to save him. But there was nothing that could be done. Even we had to realize that.

"How could he have been such a fool?" I kept demanding.

"He just liked taking risks. It made him feel good. It reminded him of the old days when he lived with his grandmother. Our father is right. If he had not been caught over this he would have been over something else."

Jacco shook his head. I think he was coming to the conclusion that there was nothing to be done to help Digory. He had a grudge against the world. I could understand that. He had seen what they had done to his granny on that night and he hated everybody. He did not completely trust even us.

He was tried and there was no question of his guilt. As my father had said, Slattery and Tregern were only too ready to give evidence against him. The beefsteak episode was recalled and there was no mention of the reason he had attempted to steal it. In any case it was not a question of why he had stolen it but that he had. As Digory worked for my father and his only relative had died recently leaving him homeless, he had been treated leniently on that occasion; but the boy had not learned his lesson; he was a born thief and could never be anything else.

We wanted no such people in this country. He was sentenced to seven years' transportation.

We were all greatly shocked by the sentence. It seemed unduly harsh. His background went against him; and the evidence as given by Slattery and Luke Tregern was the final blow.

My father and I went for a ride together and talked about Digory.

My father said: "It takes me back years. You've heard the story. I killed a man who was attempting to assault a gypsy girl. I was sentenced to seven years' transportation . . . just as this boy has been. His seems a trivial offence compared with mine. A man's life against that of a pheasant."

"What you did was right. What Digory did was wrong."

"Yet I killed. But I had people to speak for me. Your grandfather was a man of great influence and your mother forced him to save me from the gallows . . . which might so easily have been my fate."

"Don't speak of it. I can't bear it."

"Well, my darling. If that had been the end of me there would never have been Annora. That would have been a real tragedy."

"Don't joke. And what about Digory?"

"He'll serve his term. He'll come through . . . as I did. Perhaps it's not such a bad thing. Out of these misfortunes good can come. I grew up in Australia. When I look back I see myself as a feckless fellow with romantic notions. Going off as a gypsy! Imagine that! What folly! I was pulled up sharply and I realized the seriousness of life and when I had served my term I emerged as a reasonable man, ready to take on my responsibilities."

"I can't stop thinking of Digory being sent away like that. He'll be so frightened."

"Yes. It's a frightening ordeal. But he'll come through. After all, it's not as though he was happy here. What happened that night has scarred him deeply. Perhaps the best thing is a complete change, an entirely new life. If he can come through it, it might not be all bad."
He was silent for a while. Then he said: "This brings it all back to me, Annora. I can see myself on that ship, arriving in a new country . . . But after a while I grew accustomed to it. That's one lesson of life. To accept . . . and to remember all the time that whatever tragic times one has to live through, they can't last forever. There has to be change. So there will be for Digory."

"I wonder if we shall ever know. I wonder if we shall see him again."

"For that, my dear girl, we must wait and see."

We rode back to the house in a solemn and melancholy mood.

Scandal
in High Places

———— 🍎 ————

For a long time I could not stop thinking of Digory. Every now and then his image would crop up in my mind and I would see him as clearly as though he stood beside me, stuffing fish into the bag he carried, throwing stones into the river, standing accused in Slattery's shop. What was it like being sent away for seven years?

I talked about it a great deal with my father, who was by no means reticent about his own experiences. I had always found it easy to put myself in the place of others and I could imagine the arrival in that strange land, coming up from the dark interior of the ship to the blazing sunshine, the humiliation of being branded a felon. It had happened to my father and now it was happening to Digory. Perhaps being marched up in a gang to do hard labour or being selected by someone to whom one became a slave . . . My father had been considerably older than Digory when he had undergone that ordeal; and he had had so many qualities which Digory lacked. My father had come through. But how would Digory fare?

After he had departed I had long talks about him with Jacco. At first my brother was very interested but it was not long before other matters claimed his attention and his interest waned.

It was inevitable, and in time I should be the same, I supposed.

Then Jacco was going away to school and that seemed a great tragedy. I was wretchedly lonely for a while and I used to long for holidays. Then he would sometimes not come home but spend them with a friend. In their turn his friends came to us. Sometimes I was allowed to join them and we would ride, swim, fish and skate or go sailing with the fishermen. But there were times when I was clearly shown that my presence was not desired.

So with all this I, too, forgot Digory; and it was only when I went to the burned-out cottage that I remembered and felt a pang of remorse because I had forgotten.

There had been, in any case, a conspiracy to forget that Midsummer's Eve. I remember the following one. We went to the moors in the carriage, my father driving, and it had all been—in comparison with the previous one—very sedate. The bonfire was lighted; the songs were sung and no one attempted to leap over the flames.

It was a fact that people did not like to go to the clearing in the woods near the remains of the cottage. Even in daylight they would take a detour rather than the shortcut which passed it. Some of them must have remembered and felt a deep shame. But Mother Ginny was dead and her grandson far away. That night and its aftermath were best forgotten, they would tell themselves.

I saw much less of Rolf than formerly. He had so many friends at the University and was often going away on archaeological digs and all sorts of investigations into the past. His father came often and talked of his activities with the utmost pride.

When I did see him he seemed just the same as he used to. It was I who had changed. I no longer idolized him. Perhaps he noticed this and was less interested in me because of it. Once or twice I was on the point of referring to that night but my courage failed me right at the last moment and nothing was said. I was beginning to convince myself that I had not seen that grey-robed figure in the heart of the mob and thought how silly I should seem if I talked of it.

The years slipped by at a great rate. I had a new governess. We went to London now and then, and when we did we always made the journey to Eversleigh.

My grandmother had died a year after my grandfather. My mother was heartbroken at the loss of both her parents for there had been a very special relationship between them; but as she said, we must not grieve for my grandmother for she did not want to live without my grandfather.

Eversleigh was different after that. David and Claudine were getting old and Jonathan had already taken over, although I supposed he would not inherit while David was alive.

I liked Jonathan, and Tamarisk, his wife, was interesting. She was very beautiful and I had a special interest in her for I discovered that she was in fact my half-sister. Sometimes I found it difficult to keep up with all the intricate relationships in our family but I suppose it is the same in most.

My father said to me one day: "I don't believe in subterfuge and nor does your mother, so you might as well know. I was something of a rebel in my youth. You know I went off with the gypsies."

"Of course. I think it was a most exciting thing to do."

"It was a foolish thing to do but as I have often told you, one can never be entirely sure what are the good things and what the bad; it is what grows out of them which affects our lives so deeply. If I had not been a gypsy I should never have met your mother and that would have been the worst possible thing which could have befallen me. But when I first knew her she was only a little girl . . . about your age. I met Tamarisk's mother. She was a sad girl and very lonely . . . and we danced one night round the bonfire . . ."

"Midsummer's Eve," I cried.

"No. We were celebrating the victory of Trafalgar. We were all very merry and rather careless. . . . As a result of that night, Tamarisk was born. I am Tamarisk's father."

I said: "Strange things happen on nights like that. People become . . . not themselves. Perhaps it has something to do with bonfires."

Then I was thinking of that fearful night again . . . even more than I did of my father and the girl who was Tamarisk's mother.

She had died, I learned, having Tamarisk, and that was why Tamarisk had been brought up by my family and so she had known Jonathan all her life.

They loved each other very much, those two. I could sense it—although Tamarisk could be very angry with Jonathan, but it was a strong, fierce love which made her angry, and she was ready to attack anyone who criticized him. She was the same with her children; she had two boys, Richard and John; they were wild and rebellious but very lovable.

I always enjoyed the Eversleigh visits. I loved the country and the nearby sea and those two old houses not very far from Eversleigh—Grasslands and Enderby—which seemed part of the family estate. My mother had lived in Grasslands with her first husband, for she had been married before; and Enderby belonged to Peter and

Amaryllis Lansdon. It had been left to Tamarisk but Peter had bought it a long time ago and it was used really as a country home, for the Lansdons were mainly in London.

My father had sold our house in London some years before. We did not need it. There was the family house in Albemarle Street which was not often occupied nowadays and we could use that on our visits to London. The Lansdons had a big house in Westminster. That always seemed to me a most exciting house. It was tall and imposing and from some rooms there was a view of the river.

Peter Lansdon was a Member of Parliament—a very important one. When his party was in power he had had a high post in the Government and led a most exciting life for he was a man with many business interests in the City. He exuded power. Amaryllis was so proud of him. His daughter Helena and his son Peterkin—the name had been given to him when he was a baby to distinguish him from his father and it had remained—were very much in awe of him.

I was very fond of Helena and Peterkin. Helena was about six years older than I; Peterkin four. Helena had been presented at Court—an ordeal which Mother had said I should have to undergo. Helena had hated it, she told me. Everything depended upon a girl's being a success. If she was she was envied; if not she was despised. Helena had been despised, except by her mother of course. Amaryllis was one of those innocent, sweet and gentle women overflowing with sympathy and good will. But Helena told me that her father was disappointed. He had wanted her to make a good match.

I could understand that. Uncle Peter had made a great success of everything he had undertaken and he expected his children to do the same.

I said to my mother once: "I don't think two people could be less alike than Uncle Peter and Aunt Amaryllis."

I remembered how her face hardened as it often did when Uncle Peter was mentioned. She said: "You are right. There could not be two people less like each other."

"Then I wonder why they married," I said.

My mother remained silent with that rare hard look about her mouth. There was no doubt that she disliked Uncle Peter.

I could not do anything but admire him. He must have been very good-looking when he was young and now that he was no longer so he looked distinguished, with a touch of silver at his temples and those rather lazy eyes of his which always seemed to express amusement at the world and a confidence that he could easily conquer it. He enjoyed living. The trouble was that such a father must be very hard to live up to; and both Helena and Peterkin felt inadequate— Helena because she had failed to pass the coming-out test and had turned into her twenties without having been asked in marriage and Peterkin because he was as yet undecided as to what he intended to do with his life; and of course, his father would have been showing signs of success when he was at his age.

I felt some trepidation at the prospect of a season, though, of course, if I failed to pass the test I knew my parents would not want me to care very much. They wouldn't look upon it as failure. But then I was lucky to have unusual and very understanding parents.

I was almost eighteen when a trip to London and Eversleigh was proposed. That was in the year 1838.

It was the end of May and my birthday was at the beginning of September, a few months away.

My mother had said: "Now that the old King is dead and we have a young Queen on the throne we shall have to think about your coming out."

"That is going to entail a lot of preparations, I'll swear," said my father.

"Amaryllis did it for Helena, so I suppose I can manage."

"It will mean a stay in London," said my father. "By the way, I want to go up shortly. Did I tell you I had had another letter from Gregory Donnelly?"

"Oh, what's going on out there?"

Gregory Donnelly was the man who was looking after my father's property in Australia. I had heard his name mentioned from time to time.

"He wants to buy the property," said my father. "It might be a good idea to sell. It really seems quite absurd to keep it. It's just a sentimental notion. I want to say, I went out as a slave and now I'm the owner of property there."

"Why not let him have it if he wants to buy?"

"I'm thinking of it seriously. But I think I ought to go out just to have a look at it."

My mother looked alarmed.

"You'd come, of course."

"Of course," she repeated.

"I should come too," I added.

"Certainly you shall come. Jacco too. We'll all go."

"I wonder," I said impulsively, "if we shall find Digory."

There was silence, almost as though they were trying to remember who Digory was.

Then my father said: "My dear girl, it would be like looking for the needle in the haystack. People come in from miles away looking for convict labour. He could be on the other side of Australia . . . Victoria, Western Australia, even Queensland. It's a big place, you know."

"Poor boy," said my mother. "I am afraid he would have had a hard time of it."

"No doubt he has settled in by now," added my father. "One does after a time. We'll think about this trip really seriously, shall we?"

"You have talked about going so often," I reminded him, and I really did not think anything would come of it.

When the Hansons came we discussed the proposed trip with them. They were very interested.

"If the land is profitable," said Rolf, "it seems a shame to sell it."

"It is too far away to handle," replied my father. "This estate is enough for me."

The Hansons talked a great deal about their own estate, which had been growing larger over the years. They were constantly buying land. My relationship with Rolf had changed once more. When he came to Cador I guessed it was to see me. He explained his interest in Dorey Manor far more to me than he did to anyone else. He had given up all thought of the law. He wanted to be a landowner on a large estate as my father was. That was what appealed to him and he grew lyrical talking of the land.

As for myself I thought about him a good deal. He still had a very special effect on me. I was, in a way, in love with him as I had been when I was a child. He was very interested in me, too, and my parents watched us with a certain smug expression which I believed meant that they thought we would marry one day.

Should we? I felt very uncertain about my feelings for him. Physically the prospect filled me with delight while in my mind memories of that night would intrude and torment me. I was certainly excited by him; I loved to be near him; I fought against those memories and tried hard to assure myself that there had been some mistake; but always there would be that shadowy third, that figure in the grey robe who could not be made to disappear.

Once when I was riding with him I led the way into the woods past the burnt-out cottage. I longed for him to talk of that night and the part he had played in it. But I could not bring myself to mention it. I had a fear that he would say, "Yes, I was there. I was the one who led the mob to what they did. I wanted to know how they would react in such a situation and whether they would be as their ancestors had been before them." And I felt that once he had admitted that, all would be over between us. And, illogically, although I longed to hear, that was the last thing I wanted to know. I obviously preferred to go on in uncertainty rather than be faced with the truth, which would finish my relationship with him forever.

I was very young and inexperienced of life. Days were so dull when he did not come. I wished I was older, more capable of knowing myself, more able to understand my feelings. I should be able to face this, to ask him what really happened and to accept the truth—whatever it might be. But I was not.

"When does the proposed visit to Australia take place?" he asked my father.

"Oh, it needs a certain amount of planning. Besides, I'm not sure about it. I want to turn a few things over in my mind first."

I said to my mother afterwards: "I believe this is going to be like all those other trips we were to make. Papa is too fond of Cador to want to leave it for long."

She was inclined to agree. "I shall try to persuade him to sell that property to Gregory Donnelly and cut off all ties with Australia," she said.

"I somehow don't think he wants to do that. It must have been a very significant part of his life and he wants to keep a stake in it."

"I'm not sure that all this hoarding of memories is good. Anyway we shall be going to London and Eversleigh soon. I want to see Amaryllis and you'll enjoy being with Helena. She will give you all the dos and don'ts about coming out."

"Shall I have to do all that?"

"It seems necessary for a young lady to be launched. You'll have a season of course . . . parties and balls and that sort of thing."

[82]

I grimaced.

"Oh come, Annora, you'll enjoy it. You've got to see the world. You can't be shut away in Cornwall forever. One day you'll marry. It's a good idea to meet people first."

"It seems a bit crude. Helena thought so . . . being paraded to show your charms like cattle at a show . . . and if you don't come up to standard it must be awful."

"Poor Helena," said my mother. "She's a nice girl. I sometimes think men are quite stupid. They pass over the girls who would make the best wives."

"I'm glad Uncle Peter isn't my father. He's too ambitious . . . for himself and for his children."

My mother's mouth hardened in the accustomed way when he was mentioned and I wished I had not brought him into the conversation.

"Yes," she said. "You're lucky. I always thought my father was the best in the world, but you are as lucky in that respect as I was."

I flung my arms around her. "I know. That's why I'm so sorry for Helena . . . though I don't think he has actually *said* anything. It is just that he is there and everything he does goes right. Papa is wonderful and everything *he* does is right, but he doesn't make you feel . . . degraded . . . if you are not so good yourself."

"He wants you to be happy . . . above everything . . . and so do I."

"I know."

"Do you like Rolf?" she went on.

"Why do you ask?"

"I just wondered. I don't think he's indifferent to you."

I felt flustered. I stammered. "Yes . . . I like him all right."

"Just that?"

"Oh . . . I like him . . . very much, I suppose."

She smiled. "Your father and I like him very much."

I did not answer and she changed the subject.

At the beginning of June we left Cador. Jacco was to join us later, so my father, my mother and I travelled alone. We were to spend a few days in London before going to Eversleigh. We went to the family house in Albemarle Street and the very next day Amaryllis and Helena came to see us.

They invited us to dine that evening—an invitation which we were delighted to accept.

I thought Helena looked happier than I had seen her for a long time, and I wondered what had happened.

While her mother was talking to my parents she and I slipped up to my room and she was all eagerness to tell me.

"What's happened?" I demanded as soon as we were alone.

"I . . . I've met someone."

"Oh?"

"He's so charming, Annora. I have never met anyone who is so nice and so kind. That's what I like about him. He's not like any other young man. He's gentle . . . and I think he doesn't like the social round any more than I do."

"Who is he?"

"Well, the funny thing about it is that he is really quite important . . . or at least his family is. He is young . . . younger than I am actually, two years younger, Annora . . . but he is so *nice* . . ."

"I know. You said that before. Do tell me more about this *nice* young man."

"He's John Milward. Lord John Milward. You've heard of the Milwards?"

"I confess to ignorance."

"A very important family . . . Dukes of Cardingham. Only John is a younger son, thank goodness. That he should notice me is quite amazing. We met at a dance. I was hiding behind some of the plants trying to pretend I wasn't there . . . and he came upon me and we talked a bit and discovered that we were both doing the same thing . . . trying to look as though we were not there. It was the first time I'd ever enjoyed one of those occasions. It was funny because he said it was the same with him."

"And you've seen him again?"

"Oh yes. I've seen him at other places and when we're somewhere together, we always find each other."

"That's wonderful. And what does your father say?"

"He doesn't know. Nobody knows yet."

"I expect they've noticed you. From what I've heard those mamas with marriageable daughters have eyes like hawks."

"I do hope they haven't because I don't suppose anything will become of it."

"Why shouldn't it?"

"He's very young."

[84]

"Your father wouldn't object."

"Oh no. He'd be delighted. The Milwards are one of the oldest families in the country."

"You think *they* would?"

"I don't know."

"Well, our family is not to be sneezed at."

"Father is a merchant. Of course the Milwards are notoriously impoverished and I believe my father is very rich."

"Let not Society to the marriage of wealth and breeding admit impediment."

"Oh, Annora, it has made such a difference."

"I can see it has. I do hope all goes well. Won't it be wonderful? I shall look forward to visiting the country seat. You'll be Lady John Milward. Fancy that!"

"I'm so glad he is only a younger son."

"I think it is wonderful, Helena."

We joined the others.

I did not mention, even to my mother, what Helena had told me for she had been insistent that it should remain a secret. I just hoped fervently that all would go well with her. She seemed like a different person when she did not seem to be apologising all the time for her inadequacies.

It was rather a splendid dinner party that evening, though it was only a family affair. A great deal of entertaining was done in the house in the square and it seemed impossible for a dinner party to take place in that splendid dining room without a certain amount of ceremony. Aunt Amaryllis said we were lucky because Peter was able to join us; and it was probably his presence which added dignity to the occasion.

"Very often his work takes him away," Aunt Amaryllis explained. "There is always some important committee, particularly now he is concerned with parliamentary affairs."

She spoke of him in almost reverent tones. I thought it must be rather uncomfortable to live with such a man. I knew it was for Helena and Peterkin but Aunt Amaryllis was like an acolyte serving in the master's temple.

Uncle Peter told us how glad he was to see us in town.

"We're spying out the land," my father told him. "We shall have to be thinking about Annora's coming out."

"It is a little late, I suppose," said my mother. "She'll be past eighteen."

"There have been delays all round because of what has been happening," replied Aunt Amaryllis. "The Court has been in disarray. The King's been ill for so long and poor Queen Adelaide too. Now we have a new young queen on the throne, things will change, I have no doubt."

"Have you seen her?" I asked eagerly.

"We were at the Guildhall dinner in November," said Uncle Peter.

"What is she like?"

"Delightful," said Aunt Amaryllis. She turned to Helena and Peterkin. "You've seen her, haven't you, riding in her carriage?"

"She looks very young and very sure of herself," said Helena.

"I suppose she would have to be sure of herself," added Peterkin.

"She certainly seems full of confidence," said Uncle Peter. "I believe it is a good thing for a country to have a young queen for whom the people can show affection. They are tired of doddering old gentlemen."

"Peter!" said Aunt Amaryllis in a kind of shocked delight.

"It's true, my dear. George was almost senile at the end, and William was adept at making a fool of himself." He lifted his glass: "Long live Victoria. God save the Queen."

We all drank to that.

"You'll be here for the coronation?" said Aunt Amaryllis.

"Well . . ." began my father.

"Oh come," said Uncle Peter. "It's an historic occasion."

"We have to see how things are at Eversleigh."

"Jonathan's taking care of that."

"There was a time," said my mother, looking at Uncle Peter, "when you were of the opinion that he would not be able to run Eversleigh successfully."

He gave her a strange look, almost as though there was some understanding between them and he found it hard to suppress his amusement. "It was one of my mistakes," he retorted. "Rare, you will agree, but nevertheless a mistake."

"The coronation festivities will be exciting," said Aunt Amaryllis.

"Several state balls, levees, a Drawing Room and a State concert," added Uncle Peter.

Aunt Amaryllis looked at her husband with pride and then at her children. She said to them: "Your father will of course be able to go to any that he wishes to."

Uncle Peter gave her a fond look and I thought: She is the perfect wife, which is one who thinks her husband is always right, laughs at his jokes and loves him without question. There must be very few perfect wives. It was typical of Uncle Peter that he should have acquired this rarity. My parents loved each other dearly, but there were often disagreements between them. It had been the same with my grandparents; Tamarisk and Jonathan lived a tempestuous existence; yet they were all love matches. Only Aunt Amaryllis, from a husband's point of view, must be the perfect wife.

"My dear," he said fondly, for who would not be fond at such blatant admiration, "I shall have to wait and see whether my presence is commanded. I daresay we shall attend one of the balls." He looked at me. "I'm afraid, my dear Annora, that we shall be unable to take you with us as you are not yet out."

"I didn't expect to go," I told him. "And shall we be in London?"

My father hesitated. He said: "I don't really want to extend my stay. I am thinking of going to Australia and there will be a great many things I have to do at home before I can leave."

"To Australia," said Uncle Peter. "How interesting." He added with a smile: "The scene of your youth, eh?"

"Exactly. I have property there."

"It will be very interesting."

"Peter has a wonderful project in view, haven't you, Peter?" said Aunt Amaryllis.

He looked at her with a kind of tender exasperation, but I knew that behind it he was pleased, because we were now going to hear of another of his triumphs.

"My dear," he said reproachfully, "they will not be interested . . ."

"But of course we are," insisted my father. "What is this new achievement? I know they are commonplace with you, Peter, but we country folk like to hear of the great exploits of government. Is there an election coming up?"

"Not in the immediate future. The Whigs are not very secure, as you know. Melbourne, of course, gets on very well with the Queen."

"Yes," said my mother. "Even in the country we hear what a good relationship there is between them."

"It means," went on Uncle Peter, "that the Whigs, through one man, have the Queen in leading reins. That sort of thing won't be tolerated long."

"You mean by the Tories?"

"Exactly."

"So what diabolical schemes have you hatched for unseating your enemies?" asked my father.

"Nothing unconstitutional. It will happen naturally."

"And when Sir Robert Peel's government is in power . . ." said Aunt Amaryllis, looking proudly at her husband.

"A post in the government?" asked my father. "Well, we expect that of you, Peter. But we have digressed. What about this triumph of yours? You were just about to tell us."

"We are all eagerness to hear," said my mother, looking rather coldly at Uncle Peter.

"Well," began Uncle Peter with a show of reluctance. "Nothing is settled yet. A commission is being set up. There is a great deal of vice in the Capital. Drugs . . ." He glanced at me and hesitated. I guessed he was thinking of my youth and the inadvisability of discussing unpleasant realities in my presence. "Disreputable conduct," he went on. "The chairing of this commission will go to a politician."

"You?" said my mother in a rather blank voice.

He smiled at her and I saw that understanding flash between them. He seemed to find it very amusing. "I'm not sure," he said. "It's really a matter of party politics. Actually I believe it is a toss-up between myself and Joseph Cresswell."

"Peter says that if he could get it and it was a success . . . the road would open," said Aunt Amaryllis. "What do you think, Peter? The Home Office?"

"When Melbourne's Whigs are defeated and Peel's Tories are supreme," said my father.

"Yes, that will have to come about first," agreed Peter. "But it has to be . . . sooner or later."

"So really," added my father, "it is a question of either you or Joseph Cresswell."

"I think one could say that with some certainty."

"Surely they would not be so foolish as to give the post to Joseph Cresswell," said Aunt Amaryllis rather heatedly.

"They do not all possess your discernment, my dear," said Uncle Peter, giving her another of those fond glances.

My father said: "Cresswell is, of course, a well-known man. He's had a great success with the Commission for Canals. He is very able. I daresay in the next Melbourne ministry he'll qualify for a very high post."

"Certainly he will. That's if he gets this and makes a success of it."

"That's not going to happen, is it?" asked my father. "It's going to you, isn't it?"

Uncle Peter lifted his shoulders. "Melbourne will be behind Cresswell and his power is increasing every week. He certainly knows how to handle the Queen, and that makes him important to his party."

"But as you say, he is on shaky ground."

"I think this matter will be resolved before we get rid of this government."

"That looks like good luck for the enemy."

"Don't call Cresswell that. We're good friends out of the House. I respect and admire Cresswell. He's a good politician . . . although on the wrong side, of course." Uncle Peter laughed. "But none the less an admirable man. He's a good family man . . . and Melbourne, with his record, needs such around him. We visit now and then. They are a very pleasant family, aren't they, my dear?"

"Oh, they are charming," said Aunt Amaryllis. "I like them all very much. Young Joe is very nice . . . and that girl Frances."

"Oh, full of good works," said Uncle Peter. "As you see, I have a formidable rival."

"I don't doubt you have more irons in the fire."

"It's always wise to," said Uncle Peter.

Soon after that we left the men at their port and went with Aunt Amaryllis to the drawing room.

"I do wish you were staying longer in London," said Aunt Amaryllis.

"It would be nice," agreed my mother, "but we have to go to Eversleigh."

"It must be very sad there for you now that your parents have gone, Jessica."

My mother nodded. "It can never be the same, but I do think Claudine likes to see us and there are Jonathan and Tamarisk."

"Those two are all right. My mother comes up now and again but my father does not like to leave the place."

"Oh, Amaryllis, how things have changed!"

"Life does, but we have been so fortunate, Jessica, you and I in our marriages. You and Jake, Peter and I. I do hope Helena and Peterkin and Annora will be as lucky. Jacco, too. I wish Peterkin would decide what he wants to do. Helena, why don't you try to persuade Annora to stay with us while her parents are in Eversleigh?"

Helena's face lighted up. "Oh, that would be lovely."

She looked appealingly at my mother and then turned to me: "Would you like to, Annora?"

"Yes," I said, "I should. I'd love to see all the festivities for the coronation. I'd like to be with you, Helena."

"I don't see why you shouldn't stay up here," said my mother. "Ater all, you'd really enjoy that more."

"We'd look after her," said Aunt Amaryllis. "Wouldn't we, Helena?"

"It would be lovely," said Helena.

The next day it was decided that when my parents left for Eversleigh, I should stay in the house in the square until my parents returned.

I first met John Milward in the Park. My parents had gone to Eversleigh and I was very much enjoying being with my cousins. When he was away from the house Peterkin seemed to change his personality; he became much more relaxed. I thought that was another example of how trying it must be to live in the shadow of such a successful father.

I shared a bedroom with Helena which was a pleasure to us both because before going to sleep we would share confidences. I learned quite a lot about her and how she had always felt herself to be dull and stupid because she found lessons difficult. Coming out and discovering that she was not attractive to the opposite sex had been the *coup de grâce*.

But now that was changed. John Milward had come into her life.

Sometimes Peterkin would join Helena and me and we would go out together. Our favourite jaunt was to the Park which seemed a source of never-ending delight to me. We enjoyed walking and would stroll through St. James's Park and Green Park to Hyde Park and Kensington Gardens. There we would walk by the Serpentine and stand at the edge of the Round Pond looking beyond to Kensington Palace where the Queen had spent her childhood. She was at

Buckingham Palace now and I always hoped that we should catch a glimpse of her riding in her carriage. Everyone seemed delighted that we now had a young girl for a queen.

We had just entered Hyde Park and Peterkin pointed out to me Apsley House, the home of the Duke of Wellington.

"And," he was saying, "in case you should fail to see it and pay due homage, here is the great Achilles Statue set up in honour of the Duke."

It was a massive figure, meant I supposed to display the might and grandeur of the masculine figure—a symbol of the power of the great Duke.

I read the inscription which stated that it was dedicated to Arthur Wellesley, Duke of Wellington, and his brave companions in arms; it had been cast from cannon taken at the Duke's victorious battles including that of Waterloo. It had been erected through subscriptions of the women of England to do honour to military glory.

"There has been a lot of controversy about it," said Peterkin. "Some think it vulgar. Others that it is a work of genius."

"Isn't that always what happens to works of art?" I asked. "Most things are criticized before people know what they ought to think, and when they are proclaimed works of genius everyone agrees, and it is as though there had never been any other opinion. Lots of people have to be told what they should think."

"When I look at that," said Peterkin, "I think of joining the army."

Helena said: "You were thinking of going into Parliament a little while ago."

Peterkin grimaced. "Fancy following our father! Everyone would say, He's not what his father was!"

"Perhaps you would be better," I suggested.

"That would be impossible."

It was just at this moment that two young men came strolling towards us and before I was told I knew, from Helena's expression, that one of them was John Milward.

"Well," he said, "fancy meeting you." And I could see, from the manner in which he looked at Helena, that their arrival was no surprise and I remembered that she had been rather insistent that I see the Achilles Statue, and it was she who had kept us lingering there.

"Annora," she said, "this is Lord John Milward."

He bowed over my hand. Yes, there was something very pleasant about him. What struck me most was his youth. He looked younger than Peterkin, and Peterkin was two years younger than Helena. He seemed a little weak to me; he had large brown eyes and a gentle expression. Perhaps I had looked too long at Achilles.

He was smiling at Helena and I thought with pleasure: He is surely in love with her.

I was being introduced to the other young man and as soon as I heard his name I remembered. He was Joe Cresswell and that meant he was the son of the man whom my father had laughingly called "the enemy."

We stood for a while talking. Peterkin explained that we were taking a walk through the Park to show Cousin Annora some of the sights. Joe Cresswell was interested and I told him I came from Cornwall; and we talked for a while about that county of which he knew a little.

I walked ahead with Peterkin and Joe Cresswell; and Helena and John Milward fell in behind. We strolled along near the Row and Peterkin explained to me that this was once called the Ring and was a sort of parade for fashionable people to show off their fine clothes.

Joe Cresswell said: "I've something to tell you, Peterkin. I think I may be standing at the next election. I'm one of the candidates up for selection anyway, and my father says he thinks I have a good chance."

"That's excellent news," said Peterkin.

"If I get it. The general opinion is that the party will be out at the next election."

"Yes," said Peterkin, "everyone seems to think that is very likely."

Joe Cresswell turned to me. "I'm sorry, Miss Cadorson. This must all be rather boring for you."

"No. Not in the least. I am very interested to hear about it. Being in London is like breathing different air. It is all so exciting. I'm afraid we are a little dull in the country."

"Some prefer it," said Peterkin. "It depends so much on one's personality."

"I think," said Joe Cresswell, "that I should always want to be where things are happening."

We came to the Serpentine and walked along its banks. Joe Cresswell asked me how long I was staying. I told him I was not quite sure. My parents were visiting relatives in Kent. When they returned to London we should all go home together.

"Annora will be coming out next year," said Peterkin. "But she is going with her family to Australia before that, I believe."

"Those are the plans at the moment," I explained. "But it is all a little uncertain."

We sat down on a seat and watched two children with their nurses throwing breadcrumbs to the ducks.

Helena came up with John Milward. "We're going to walk on a little way," said John. "We'll see you later."

Peterkin and Joe Cresswell exchanged smiles.

I liked Joe Cresswell; he was very relaxed. He talked about his home and mostly of his father, to whom, it was obvious, he was very attached.

"I hope he gets this job," he said. "He's set his heart on it. Sorry, Peterkin. If my Pater's in, yours will be out."

"He can win some other time. You think this is more or less settled, do you?"

"Between ourselves, Miss Cadorson, I am sure I can trust you . . . but Lord Melbourne has hinted . . ."

"I suppose he would have a lot of say."

"Of course he'd rather it went to one of our party."

"It seems a very important matter," I said.

"These things are important in politics, Miss Cadorson. One thing leads to another. That is why it is such an exciting game."

"When will your by-election come up?"

"In a few months."

"You've got a good chance if you're nominated," said Peterkin. "It's a safe Whig seat and your father is a name."

Joe Cresswell smiled. "I don't really want to get through on my father's name."

"You can't help it," retorted Peterkin. "It's even the same Christian name. Just Joe . . . instead of Joseph. You could hardly be nearer than that."

"Yes, I suppose so. And if *you* went in you'd have your father's name."

"I should live in the shadow of it. That's one of the reasons against politics. I wouldn't mind going into his business but he doesn't want that. He says I'm not cut out to be a businessman."

"What then?"

"I don't know. But I do rather fancy politics."

There was a silence for a while. Then Joe Cresswell turned to me. "I shall look forward to your season," he said. "Next year is a long time to wait. I hope you are not going back to Cornwall just yet."

"I daresay I shall be here a few weeks longer."

He gave me a very pleasant smile.

"Then I hope I shall see you again . . . soon."

Helena and John Milward came back and we decided it was time we returned.

That had been a delightful morning. Helena was in the realms of bliss and I had to admit that I had enjoyed my encounter with Joe Cresswell, son of that other candidate for high office.

That evening was one of the rare occasions when Uncle Peter dined with us, and during the course of the meal the meeting in the Park was mentioned.

Uncle Peter beamed on us.

"Didn't you think Joe a very pleasant young man, Annora?" he asked.

"Yes, Uncle. I did. I thought he was very interesting."

He turned to Aunt Amaryllis. "We should ask the Cresswells to dine," he said.

"Before . . . the decision?"

"I think very soon, my dear. I don't want people to think there is any ill-feeling between us . . . just because he has the better chance. We're the best of friends really. That's how it is in politics. You're the bitterest enemies across the floor of the House, but outside all that enmity evaporates. Yes, let us have them to dine soon . . . Cresswell and his wife." He glanced at me. "And you might ask young Joe, too."

Within three days they came. It was a very enjoyable evening. I very much liked Mr. and Mrs. Cresswell. He was rather serious— and very precise, I imagined; she was jolly, rather scatter-brained, just the opposite of her husband—but very domesticated, kindly, motherly, not in the least clever. Yet they seemed ideally suited. I was pleased to meet Joe again and he was put next to me at dinner so that we had a good deal of conversation together, and I learned more about his hopes of following in his father's footsteps.

"Like the Pitts," I said.

"You're flattering us . . . at least myself."

"You never know. People have to wait for chances. Then greatness emerges. We have to wait and see."

Uncle Peter looked on us benignly as though he was rather pleased that we were getting on so well together.

We had a little music afterwards. Helena sang and I played a few pieces on the piano with Joe turning over the music for me.

I thought how creditable it was of both Uncle Peter and Mr. Cresswell, with this important post coming up which was going to mean so much to the one who held it—to be so friendly with no sign of bitterness between them.

There was some talk about the Cresswells' country home in Surrey. Mrs. Cresswell said it was always full of young people at the week-end. The Cresswells had a large family—three girls and three boys. Joe was one of the younger ones.

Mrs. Cresswell must have noticed how well I was getting along with Joe for she said: "You must visit us one week-end, Miss Cadorson. Do . . . before you go back to Cornwall."

"It would have to be soon," said Aunt Amaryllis. "Sir Jake is a man who makes quick decisions. He could well arrive next week and declare they must all go back to Cornwall to prepare to go to Australia."

"Australia," said Joe. "That's interesting."

"My father has some property there. He was there once . . . a long time ago."

Aunt Amaryllis looked faintly uneasy and Uncle Peter amused.

"It will be tremendously exciting," said Joe.

"Well, we must fix this visit soon," said Mrs. Cresswell. "What about next week-end?"

I looked at Aunt Amaryllis. "Why not?" she said. "If you would like that, Annora."

"I should very much," I said.

"Of course," went on Mrs. Cresswell, "Helena and Peterkin must come with you."

So it was arranged.

I saw Joe quite frequently, even before the week-end. There was another meeting in the Park when he appeared with John Milward. Helena was delighted. She felt she was a connoisseur of romance and she scented one between Joe and me.

I did not want to go as far as that. I liked Joe. But I could not think of him without seeing Rolf. I compared them and, charming as Joe was, he did not stand up well to the comparison. I suppose it was because when I was young I had set Rolf up as an ideal. He had seemed incomparable; and in spite of everything he remained so. There was a certain power about him which, I supposed, was the essence of masculinity. My father had it; so had my grandfather to a great degree even in his old age. Joe lacked it. Joe seemed vulnerable as none of those others did. One felt about them that no matter what happened they would rise above it. The fact was Joe seemed boyish almost when I thought of him beside Rolf. There was no doubt in my mind that, but for the fears which had grown out of that terrible night, I would have been deeply in love with Rolf. Perhaps I still was. That was why I clung to my original image of him, deceiving myself, telling myself that there was some mistake. Yet I had never been able to bring myself to ask him outright; and the reason was that I feared the answer.

Was I always going to think of Rolf? Would he always come between me and anyone else of whom I might grow fond?

Joe was interested in me. At least that was what Helena thought; and, I believed, so did Uncle Peter and Aunt Amaryllis. Aunt Amaryllis liked young people to be happy together and therefore she thought it was pleasant for them to fall in love, particularly if they were suitable in their parents' eyes. I think Uncle Peter was pleased because he was anxious to show that in spite of the rivalry between himself and Joseph Cresswell, there was no rancour.

So we came to that week-end which turned out to be one of the most pleasant I had enjoyed for a long time.

The Cresswell home was in Surrey in the midst of the lusciously green Home Counties which are so different from Cornwall where the landscape is wild and a little fey. Here fields looked as though they might have been mowed and the trees as though they were pruned; they did not get battered by spring gales as ours did now and then. There was an atmosphere of prosperity which one even sensed in the lanes. Buttercups and daisies abounded in the fields and on the journey down we passed through several little villages with their greens, ancient churches and almshouses all so neat and orderly and very attractive. Our Cornish villages lacked the opulence and the well-planned architecture even of the small cottages.

Rolf had once said that it was the difference between Anglo Saxon discipline and Celtic *laisser faire*.

The Cresswell house was large and the rooms cosy. As soon as one entered it one had the impression that it was not meant as a show piece but to be lived in. In the big drawing room with its French windows opening on to a lawn, there were books everywhere; some on the floor; there was a great fireplace with a long stool in front of it. It was a room in which one immediately felt at ease for one knew there would be a complete lack of ceremony.

Mrs. Cresswell was waiting to greet us. She embraced us warmly and said how glad she was that we had come.

Did I mind sharing with Helena? She had a larger houseful than she had anticipated. Frances had come.

"Dear Frances," she said. "She is usually so busy. It's lovely to have her here."

I was introduced to those members of the family who were present. Two of the girls were married—one living in Sussex, the other in the North. Flora, the daughter from the North, was staying in the house with her two children.

"The house is bursting at the seams," said Mrs. Cresswell, "but I admit to being not in the least displeased by that."

Flora was a charming young woman and her two children were delightful. Joe's brother Edgar was a doctor with a practice not far off, and he just called in for dinner with his wife. I was most interested to meet Frances Cresswell.

She was very serious and it was obvious to me, even on our first meeting, that she had a purpose in life. She was rather like Joe with a look of her father.

"This is my sister Frances," Joe told me and there was pride in his eyes.

"I'm very glad to meet you," I said.

"And I you," she replied. "Joe has told me a great deal about you."

Peterkin joined us.

"Frances is doing very good work," he said. "Frances, you are a wonder."

"You wouldn't say that if you saw me sometimes," she replied. "I can really be a shrew."

"I expect you have a lot to put up with. Frances runs a Mission in the East End of London, Annora."

"A Mission?" I asked.

"That's what they call it. We try to do what we can for people who

[97]

are unable to help themselves. There's a terrible amount of poverty in London, you know. The contrasts in big cities have to be seen to be believed."

"What sort of things do you do?"

"We try to help people in trouble. We have kitchens where we dispense soup and bread to those who haven't enough to eat. We have beds for those who are homeless. We try to sort out their difficulties and do what we can. Alas, there is little we can do . . . but we try."

"I've been to help," said Joe. "It is very revealing. It can be upsetting but gratifying in a way just because one is doing something, however small."

I was ashamed of my ignorance. London had always seemed to me especially grand and opulent even. I had seen poverty in the two Doreys. I knew of bad harvests and bad weather which prevented people's going fishing; I knew there were accidents in the mines which robbed a family of its breadwinner. But then there were squires like my father who would alleviate suffering. But in the vast city it would be different. There, there were no squires, no benevolent landowner who looked on his tenants as his responsibility. There had to be people like Frances.

I wanted to hear more.

"I'll tell you what," said Joe. "If you are interested you could come down one day and see for yourself."

"I should like that," I said.

"I've been," Peterkin told me. "It's depressing but it is something which people ought to know about. Don't you agree, Frances?"

"I certainly think people should know what is going on about them," said Frances.

"I'll come with you when you go," said Peterkin.

Just before we were going in to dinner, John Milward arrived. It was moving to watch the joy in Helena's face when she realized he was to stay for the week-end.

It was a very merry meal—quite different from those in the house in the square. Everyone seemed to be talking at once; they were a vociferous family, these Cresswells, and they all seemed to have different points of view on every subject and were determined to make themselves heard.

There was a great deal of argument and laughter.

Mrs. Cresswell lifted her eyes and smiled at me. "I'm afraid this is how it always is when the family gets together," she said.

Afterwards we played guessing games and charades. Then we all trooped back to a large room which was called "the play room."

"This is where they played when they were children," said Mrs. Cresswell. "They still play here, if you ask me."

There was a piano at one end of the room but no carpet on the floor, which was polished. Joe sat down and played the piano and we all danced. Mr. Cresswell was my partner for a time. Although he was considerably quieter than his sons and daughter he seemed to enjoy everything.

"I hope you don't find us too exuberant, Miss Cadorson," he said.

"I'm enjoying it so much. They all seem to have a capacity for getting a lot of fun out of life."

"They are a wonderful family in spite of their old sobersides of a father. Of course, it's my wife they take after more than they do me, which is a good thing."

"I don't think that is entirely true," I told him. "They are all tremendously proud of you."

"And I of them. I expect I sound like a doting old man to you."

"No. I think all this is just what a home should be—and you are part of it."

"What's that Joe is playing now? Sir Roger? You'll need a younger partner. Oh look. Edgar is taking over from Joe. He doesn't play so well, but he'll be adequate. Joe will want to be your partner."

Mr. and Mrs. Cresswell sat out for Sir Roger de Caverley. I often remembered afterwards how they looked sitting there smiling, she tapping her foot to the music, looking on at their friends and family with perfect contentment.

When we retired to bed Helena and I lay awake for a long time talking about the evening.

"Wasn't it fun?" said Helena.

"It was," I agreed. "Especially for you when your devoted admirer arrived."

"That was just like Mrs. Cresswell. She would do that. She invited him especially for me."

"She's a lovely woman," I said.

"Mr. Cresswell is so different, but very nice."

"I think he is a very good man, and he deserves his family. After all, we make our own happiness, don't we?"

"Sometimes others unmake it."

"It's up to us," I said.

Was it? I thought of Helena before John Milward had come along. It was pure chance with her. If he had not appeared on the scene she would have been the same old Helena . . . shy, diffident, feeling herself to be unattractive so that she convinced others that she was.

I was too tired to ponder the matter and slipped gently into sleep.

On the Sunday morning we made up a party and went to church. We sat in the Cresswell pew, filling it. It was a thirteenth-century church and the memorials on the walls told me that the Cresswells had worshipped here for generations.

After the service we stood outside the church for a while and I was introduced to certain people of the village. I said I wanted to look round the graveyard. Graveyards always interested me. I liked to read the inscriptions on the tombstones and imagine what the people lying under the ground had been like when they were alive. Old people . . . young cut off in their youth . . . and babies. I liked to be alone on these occasions so that I could absorb the silence of the graveyard, the stillness of the air. It seemed to bring back the past and I could feel I was back hundreds of years.

I had wandered a little away from the others who were standing outside the church and as I strolled round to the back of the building I found myself face to face with the vicar, who had just come out of a side door. He was still wearing his surplice.

He smiled at me and said: "You are with the Cresswell party, I believe."

"Yes," I replied. "I was looking at the churchyard. The inscriptions on the gravestones inspire my imagination."

He nodded.

"You are here for the week-end, I suppose."

"Yes."

"People come down often to stay with the family. It is a great pleasure to see them all in church. We owe a lot to the Cresswells in this village."

"They must have been here for generations."

"There have always been Cresswells here . . . for four hundred years, I reckon. They were always good to the people, but the pres-

[100]

ent Mr. Cresswell surpasses them all to my mind. We're very proud of him in the village. He's a rising politician. They'll tell you here that he ought to be Prime Minister. There are many who think he would make a better job of it than Lord Melbourne."

"I can see he has many local supporters."

"It'll come. He'll get the honours he deserves. There is a chairmanship coming up."

"Yes. I have heard of that."

"When he gets that it will be a big stepping-stone. It is important that we get the right men governing us. We want our rulers to be clever and shrewd but at the same time with a sense of morality. Unfortunately most of them seem to be lacking in the latter."

"I am sure you are right."

"Here I am running on. My wife says that given half a chance I'll start to preach a sermon. It has been pleasant talking to you. I hope you enjoy the rest of your stay with us."

"Thank you," I said.

I heard Joe calling and I went round to the front of the church to meet him. Then we all went back to the house.

At luncheon everyone talked a great deal. We sat long over the table unable to tear ourselves away. In the afternoon we went for a walk—Joe and I with Peterkin, Helena and John Milward. I was delighted to see Helena so happy; she sparkled and was quite talkative and even a little witty. How love could change a person!

The evening was very much like the previous one except that there was no dancing, this being Sunday. Joe and I played duets and the company sang hymns and ballads, both sentimental and humorous.

When we retired that night Helena was radiant.

She said nothing until we were in our beds. Then she whispered: "Annora?"

"Yes?"

"Are you awake?"

"No," I said. "Asleep."

She laughed as though that was hilariously funny.

"Come on," I said. "Tell me all about it."

"You guessed."

"I guessed something had happened. You look as though you have just kissed the frog who has turned into a prince."

"He's asked me, Annora."

"You're engaged."

"That's right."

I leaped out of bed and jumped on to hers, hugging her.

"Oh, Helena, I'm so pleased."

"It was while we were out walking this afternoon. He asked me to marry him . . . just like that."

"Oh, Helena, I'm so pleased."

"I can't believe it."

"Everyone else will. They only have to see you two together to guess what is in the wind."

"Was it so obvious?"

"As clear as daylight." I kissed her and went back to my bed.

"Does his family know?"

"Well, not yet. And we're going to wait until they do before we announce anything."

"Is he afraid they won't approve?"

"John doesn't think there'll be any trouble. But they are such a proud family . . . one of the oldest dukedoms. You know what people are like. Of course, they are not very well off. . . ."

"Your father will be pleased."

"I think so. There'll be no difficulty there. He's been hoping for something like this ever since I was 'out.' He spent a lot on my presentation and it seemed as though it was all wasted. Now I'm exonerated."

"You make it sound like a business transaction."

"Coming out is . . . in a way. But when people fall in love . . ."

"Ah, that is different. They're outside the transaction but it still exists for the fond parents. Did your father say he was disappointed in your performance?"

"Not in words. But I guessed. I felt he despised me."

"Well, he will have to change his mind now. The great Milwards, eh?"

"A younger son," she said with a giggle and added fervently: "Thank goodness."

"I'll be all right. I daresay it would have been different with the heir, but a younger son has more freedom to fall in love."

"Oh, Annora, isn't it wonderful! But not a word yet. You won't tell, will you?"

"You can rely on me. But it will come out soon. I have a very reliable set of bones and I can feel it in them."

"Oh, Annora, I'm so glad you stayed with us. I hope you won't go yet."

"So do I," I assured her.

We lay awake for some time talking.

That was a wonderful week-end. I was sorry that we had to leave next morning.

Nothing was said about Helena's engagement. John Milward was evidently waiting for the right moment to approach his father. I had always felt he was a rather nervous young man.

I wondered if Aunt Amaryllis guessed.

Perhaps not, for there was a great deal of excitement everywhere about the Queen's coronation. It was exhilarating to be in London at this time.

The streets were full of people from all over the country. A few days before the event was due to take place they were making beds on the pavements and camping out all night, so determined were they to get a good view of the procession.

Uncle Peter was very busy. He was on several committees and we hardly saw him during those days. He would be very occupied on the great day.

The Cresswells had a town house in St. James's Street through which the procession would be passing and I, with Helena and Peterkin, were invited to join a party which would be watching from the windows.

What an impressive sight! The bells were ringing all over London. I was deeply moved as I watched the procession. So many foreign dignitaries had come to take part in it and prominent among them were the Queen's German relations. Oddly enough, Marshal Soult, our enemy of not long ago, represented France. I was amazed at what a tumultuous welcome the people gave him. But most moving of all was the sight of the little Queen looking so young—almost a child— in her robes of crimson velvet and gold lace, with a diamond circlet on her head.

I did not see her return from the Abbey but I could picture her riding back through the streets to Buckingham Palace in the robes of state, carrying the orb and sceptre.

After the ceremony we went back to the house in the square accompanied by Joe. There was a cold supper and after that several of us went to watch the fireworks in the Park.

It was a day of great rejoicing.

I was so glad that I had remained in London for such an occasion and was sorry that my parents had missed it. When they came it would mean that we should be leaving soon for Cornwall; and that was something I was not really looking forward to for I had become so caught up in Helena's affairs. I wanted to see her officially engaged; moreover I was interested in the Cresswell family—especially Joe. My friendship for him was growing fast.

Helena was very excited because she was going to one of the State balls which were being given in honour of the coronation.

"I'm sorry you can't come, Annora," she said.

I smiled. Not long ago she would have been congratulating me because I did not have to go.

She had a new rose pink dress and she looked prettier than I had ever seen her look before. It was not so much rose pink which suited her as happiness.

I watched her set off with her parents and Peterkin. I knew that John Milward would be at the ball. I hoped he would soon speak to his father. The long wait seemed to me to be a little ominous. I supposed it all depended on how much they needed money and whether Helena's father was rich enough to supply a settlement which would be satisfactory to them. Yes, indeed, it was quite a sordid transaction or would have been except for the love of the two central characters.

Joe called with his sister Frances. I was delighted to see them.

"I thought you would have gone to the ball," I said to Joe.

"My parents are there. They'll represent the family. It wasn't exactly a royal command tonight."

Frances said she had no time for such occasions. She was in London to see if she could get a firm of tailors to pay their buttonhole-makers more money.

"I thought with all this euphoria about the new reign and coronation they might be in a generous mood."

"And are they?" asked Joe.

"Not a bit of it. I'll probably have to resort to threats. Expose them in the press or something like that."

"You will see that my sister is a very militant lady," said Joe to me.

"You are coming to see us one day, aren't you?" she asked.

"I am planning to bring her along next week," Joe told her.

"Oh good. Bring Peterkin. He shows real interest. This is a lovely house, isn't it? Such large rooms. Just what I need."

Joe said to me: "Frances is looking for new premises."

"We're very cramped. If I had another house . . ."

"What about the money?" asked Joe.

"Father is very generous. I could get him to make a subscription and lobby some of the M.P.s. Many of them declare their concern for the poor. But their sympathy does not always go deep enough to reach their pockets."

"I expect your father has been very helpful," I said.

"We couldn't have got very far without him. How many rooms are there in this house?"

"You couldn't afford anything like this," cried Joe.

"Not in this neighbourhood—but it wouldn't be much use here anyway. I'm interested in all houses at the moment."

"Would you like to see over this one?"

"I'd love that," said Frances.

So I showed them the house. She said: "What I could do with this!"

We had come to the very top. There was one room which was reached by a short staircase.

"What's up there?" asked Frances.

"That's my uncle's study. It's out of bounds. No one is allowed up there. Only my Aunt Amaryllis goes in to clean it."

"*She* cleans it!"

"Yes. He won't allow anyone else to go in. He says servants disturb things. Only Aunt Amaryllis is allowed in. She goes twice a week to clean it."

"How very odd! There must be something very important up there."

"Oh, it is only his files and papers and things. It's always kept locked. Along here are the attics . . . the servants' quarters."

We went downstairs and were soon talking of the coronation and what difference a new queen would make to the country.

I was awake when Helena came in from the ball.

I sat up in bed and looked at her. She was positively radiant.

"Well," I said.

"Everything was wonderful. The Duke and Duchess were there.

They received me most graciously. Papa and Mama were with them. They are all delighted. It's all right, Annora. It's settled. I'm officially engaged to John. It will be announced in the papers in a day or so. I think there'll be an early wedding. It was hinted that there would be . . . as soon as all the settlements and things have been arranged. Annora, you must stay for my wedding.''

"How exciting! It is like a fairy story."

"The ugly duckling who turned into a swan."

"No, the princess who didn't know how beautiful she was until her lover came and told her so."

"Oh. Annora, you say the nicest things. I'm glad you're here. You've brought me luck."

"What rubbish! You brought it all on yourself . . . you and your John. Now there is only one thing for you to do."

"What's that?"

"Live happy ever after."

"I shall never get to sleep tonight. I don't want to. I just want to lie here thinking about it."

There was not much sleep for me either. I lay there listening to her telling it again . . . the arrival, the gracious reception from the Duke and Duchess, and everyone showing approval of the most wonderful match that ever was.

I did not get to see Frances Cresswell's Mission then because the blow fell before that could be arranged.

It was two days after the coronation ball. When I went down to breakfast Amaryllis was there with Peterkin. They were absorbed in the morning papers.

"I wonder who it can possibly be," Aunt Amaryllis was saying.

"It says a prominent and highly respected politician."

"I daresay his name will soon be revealed."

"They'll withhold it for a while to make it more tantalising. I wonder if Papa has any idea."

"He wouldn't know anything about a man like that."

"What is it all about?" I asked.

Peterkin, who was helping himself from the sideboard at that moment, said: "A real scandal. Someone is in deep trouble. What are you having, Annora? This ham is good."

"Thanks," I said.

He set a plate before me.

"The papers are full of it. It happened last night. This fellow has been caught with a woman of a very dubious reputation. There was a brawl in her room and another fellow . . . he said he was her husband . . . attacked him. The police were called and they were all arrested."

"Who could it be?"

"We shall know in time."

"I hate this sort of thing," said Aunt Amaryllis. "It's so bad for everyone."

"I daresay the man in the case hates it more than you do, Mama," said Peterkin.

"It will distress your father. It must be someone he knows of . . . for it says a well-known politician."

"The seamy side of life shows itself sometime," said Peterkin. "By the way, Annora, what about Wednesday for our trip to Frances's Mission?"

"That will suit me very well."

It was later in the day when the papers revealed the name of the man about whom, by this time, everyone was talking.

I heard the paper boys calling out in the streets and ran downstairs to hear what they were saying. One of the servants was already there. He was carrying a paper and his eyes looked as though they were ready to pop out of his head.

"What is it?" I cried.

"They've named him, miss. Would you believe it . . ."

"Who? Who?" I demanded.

"It's Mr. Joseph Cresswell."

I could not believe it. It could not possibly be true. There must be a mistake.

Aunt Amaryllis was very upset. She kept saying: "It's a misprint. They have the wrong name. Not that nice, kind, clever Mr. Cresswell. It must be another Cresswell."

We were all sure there must have been some mistake, and were waiting for Uncle Peter to come in and hear what his reactions were. When he arrived we all clustered round him.

He looked shaken. He reiterated what we had all said. It must be a mistake. It could not be true.

[107]

"How could they have got hold of his name?" asked Peterkin.

"The only thing I can think of is that the real culprit gave a false name. The first one he thought of was Joseph Cresswell. After all his name is well known to the public."

Aunt Amaryllis breathed a sigh of relief. "Of course that's the answer. Trust you to put your finger right on it, Peter."

"I *hope* that's the case," said Uncle Peter. "But it has already done him a lot of harm."

"But if it is proved that his name has been falsely given people will regard him more highly because he has been wronged," I suggested.

"My dear," said Uncle Peter, "it is only conjecture on my part."

But it did not turn out like that. The man who had taken part in what the papers called "The Brothel Brawl" was indeed Joseph Cresswell. His story was that his carriage had knocked down a young woman in Panton Street. He had alighted to make sure she was all right and as she had appeared to be shaken he had taken her to her home. It was true that he went into her room but was not there for more than a few minutes when a man burst in and accused them of immoral conduct.

I believed the story. It seemed perfectly plausible to me. If the vehicle in which he was riding had knocked her down he would consider it only courteous to take her home. I could well imagine how it happened. Of course he took her in to make sure she was suffering from no ill effects.

What a terrible situation for him!

Chloe Kitt was the young woman; she was known to be a prostitute; she had an apartment next door to a men's club of a not very savoury reputation; and the rooms were let out by the club usually to women of easy virtue.

The man who had burst in on them was not Chloe's husband, only, as she said, an intimate friend.

It seemed likely that blackmail might have been the original object. It was not, after all, such an extraordinary situation. What made it so unusual, of such immense interest, was the fact that a well-known politician was involved.

The charge was breaking the peace and was to come before the magistrate's court.

"He was a fool," said Uncle Peter, "to go home with a girl like that."

"He wouldn't have seen any harm in it," replied Aunt Amaryllis.

"He was concerned because it was the carriage he was riding in which knocked her down. That was obviously why he went home with her."

"It's unfortunate. No matter what the outcome of all this there are going to be many who think the worst and it *is* worse because Joseph Cresswell has set himself up as a defender of virtue. The chairmanship of this committee . . . well, it is about the abolition of vice."

"It certainly won't go to him now," said Peterkin.

"Hardly likely to, I should think," agreed Uncle Peter.

"Then you . . ." began Aunt Amaryllis.

"Oh, my dear, don't let's talk about that now. This is a tragedy for Cresswell. I'd have given a lot for it not to have happened. I wouldn't want to walk over him in such circumstances."

"Of course you wouldn't," said Aunt Amaryllis. "I'm sorry I mentioned it. But the thought came to me. I do understand. It is just how you would feel."

He took her hand and patted it. "I know, my dear. But this is just not the time."

"It'll make all the difference to Joe, I expect," said Peterkin. "I doubt whether he'll be selected as a candidate for that by-election which is coming up. It'll be a tragedy for the whole family unless it can be proved to be a fabrication by this Chloe. Why should she. . . ?"

"Probably meant blackmail," said Uncle Peter. "And they played it wrongly. They didn't think the police would come."

"Oh dear!" sighed Aunt Amaryllis. "How wicked some people can be! I am so sad for that nice Mrs. Cresswell . . . and all the family."

I kept thinking of them as I had seen them during that happy week-end, and I too felt very sad. I wondered what effect it would have on Joe.

Peterkin said to me: "Let's go and see Joe. I want them to know that I, for one, believe Mr. Cresswell is telling the truth."

I was glad, for I wanted to do just that.

We walked to the house in St. James's Street and on the way we passed several newsvendors.

"All about it," shouted one. "Read about Chloe's lovers," called another.

I said: "They go on and on about it."

"That's how they are. If it had not been a well-known person we should have heard nothing about it."

The blinds were drawn at the windows of the house. We went through the gate and mounted the steps past the two stone lions who stood like sentinels on either side of the door.

Several people stopped to look at us, wondering, I supposed, who we were to call at this house of shame.

The door was eventually opened by a maid who first of all peered at us through the door's glass panel.

Peterkin said: "Good morning. Is Mr. Joe Cresswell at home?"

"No sir. None of the family's here."

"We want to get in touch. Is Mr. Joe in Surrey?"

"I ain't to say, sir," said the maid. "They've all gone away and that's all I can tell you."

While we were talking I heard a crack and the sound of breaking glass.

"That's the third stone we've had at the windows. I think it would be better if you was to go. They might think you family."

She shut the door.

Peterkin and I looked at each other in dismay. He was very angry.

We walked away from the house while several people who were passing watched us with curiosity.

"I wish," I said, "that we could see Joe. I'd like him to know we don't believe all this."

"Perhaps we could write to Surrey. I think he must be there."

"Yes, just to let him know that we are thinking of him."

I wrote to him that day telling him how sorry I was and how we all believed in his father. "This will all blow over," I wrote. "Everyone who knows your family realizes it can't be true."

I received a short note from Joe thanking me for my sympathy. He told me nothing of his plans and did not suggest a meeting.

In due course the case came before the magistrates. They were all fined for breaking the peace—including Mr. Cresswell, which was an intimation that the story he had told was untrue.

It was a trivial case—there were hundreds like it every day; but it was the end of Joseph Cresswell's career.

I wondered what was going on in his family. I was sure kind, motherly Mrs. Cresswell would believe her husband; and so would every member of the family. But would there be a niggling doubt?

Who would have believed that so much happiness and contentment could be destroyed by such an event?

If only the papers would allow the matter to rest it would have been easier; but they went on. "Our reporter talks to Chloe"; "Chloe's lovers"; "Chloe Kitt's early life, telling us all how she had been left an orphan and had had to fend for herself and had been helped along the road to perdition by men like Joseph Cresswell."

Peterkin and I went down to Frances's Mission.

It was a big house situated on a main road from which narrow streets branched off. As we passed I caught a glimpse of the traders in those streets. Stalls had been set up and various goods were displayed—old clothes, fruit, vegetables, hot pies, lemonade and ballads. There was a great babble as the salesmen shouted the qualities of their wares.

On one corner of the street was what appeared to be a lodging house and on the other a gin shop from which two women came lurching in the company of a man.

We hurried past.

We mounted the steps to the front door. It was open and we went in. There was a sparsely furnished hall and as we were wondering how to make our presence known a young man appeared. He was of medium height, brown-haired and grey-eyed; and I was immediately struck by his earnest manner.

"Can I help you?" he asked.

Peterkin said: "We want to see Miss Cresswell."

"She's not in at the moment. But she should be very soon. She was called out suddenly. Do come in and sit down."

We followed him into a room. It contained two chairs and a table and little else. He offered us the chairs and seated himself on the table.

He said: "Is there anything I can do? I'm one of Miss Cresswell's helpers."

"We only came to see her."

"Wonderful, isn't she?" he said. "Here we all admire her very much." He frowned. I guessed he was trying to tell us that here they were all behind the Cresswell family.

He chatted for a while and told us that he had been with the Mission for two months and was finding it very rewarding; and while we were talking Frances came in.

"Thanks, Matthew," she said. "I see you've been entertaining my visitors."

"Good day," said Matthew. "It was nice meeting you."

When we were alone, Frances took Matthew's place on the table.

"It was good of you to come," she said. "This is a terrible business."

"It's so ridiculous," said Peterkin.

"I know. But it's deadly damaging nonetheless."

"What is going to happen?" I asked.

She lifted her shoulders. "My father will have to disappear from public life. After all he has built up! And he had such plans. It was almost a certainty that he would have been on this vice committee. He would have been so effective."

"How is the family taking it?"

"Stoically. They are all standing by him. Joe, of course, is the one who will be most affected."

"Do you think it will ruin his career?" I asked.

"Well, for the time being . . . yes. He is the son of his father . . . same name and everything. Oh, it was a bitter blow to us all. For myself it does not matter. It's just that I can't bear for my father to be put through all this. It's so malicious."

"I wrote to Joe," I told her. "I had a short note back."

"I think they all just want to be left alone."

"I'm sure that's how I should feel," said Peterkin.

"Joe thinks that our father was trapped into the situation."

"Trapped?"

"It's a wild idea, of course, but Joe is in no state to reason."

"Frances," said Peterkin, "if there is anything we can do . . ."

"There isn't really. The best thing is to leave them all alone for a while. Something will work itself out."

"You're just carrying on here as usual."

"It makes no difference here. The people who work with me are marvellous. Matthew Hume whom you just met is typical. They just want to help people, to make society a little more tolerable for the unfortunate. As for the people who are living in this neighbourhood, they are not censorious. Moreover they can't read . . . most of them. They understand how easy it is for these girls to fall into prostitution. They would say, Oh they have to live—and that's one way of doing it. They wouldn't condemn my father—even if the accusations were true—as much as those who pay them so little for their work or wouldn't give them a few pence for a decent meal. It's a different set of morals. I suppose morals are tuned to the sort of society in which we live and the middle and upper classes take a highly moral tone on these matters. You must be without reproach and if you do stray, make sure you are not found out. A sin is a sin only when it is public knowledge. Hypocrisy is the order of the day."

She spoke without bitterness and I liked her more than ever.

This was not the sort of visit we had planned though we did look over the house. She had rows of beds in the upper rooms where she housed the homeless; then she took us and showed us the kitchen where a cauldron of soup was simmering on the fire.

"It's all so inadequate," she said. "I want bigger premises. I want more and more houses like this so that I can do some real work."

When we left Peterkin said what a fine job she was doing, and I wholeheartedly agreed.

In the papers that day there was a notice which caught my eyes. William Gardiner had been chosen as the prospective candidate for Bletchfield. That was the one for which Joe had been hoping.

Whatever had happened on that fateful night in the prostitute's bedroom had had a far-reaching effect.

My parents were in London. I left Uncle Peter's house and went back to the one in Albermarle Street with them.

They told us the news at Eversleigh, and of course they had heard of the Cresswell scandal. I guessed from their comments that they believed the story, which was an indication that most people would by the manner in which he had been presented in the press, and who did not know the family.

I told them that I refused to believe the accusations against Joseph Cresswell and then they were all sympathy.

"This sort of thing can happen," said my father. "A false step taken innocently enough . . . and it can influence one's life."

My mother said thoughtfully: "This will mean that Joseph Cresswell is out of the running for that chairmanship."

"Yes, of course," I replied. "And poor Joe has lost his chance to stand as candidate for Bletchfield."

"What a tragedy," said my father.

"They are very brave," I told them. "They are the most wonderful family. It has made us all very sad, and I was having such a marvellous time before it happened."

"It's good news about Helena," said my mother.

"Yes, isn't it?"

"They are very thrilled at Eversleigh."

"The wedding is going to be in August. It's quite soon but there doesn't seem to be any reason for delay. The two families are well satisfied."

"I daresay Peter is," said my mother shortly. "He'll revel in connections with an ancient dukedom."

"But what is so nice, Mama, is that Helena is so much in love and so is John Milward."

"I suppose Peter will be able to supply the necessary settlement," she said.

"Apparently. There doesn't seem to be any hitch about that."

"The Milward estate is ready to collapse, I believe," said my father. "The heir made a good marriage and saved it in the nick of time, otherwise it would have been a ruin by now. But still more is needed."

"Your father has something to tell you, Annora," said my mother.

"Yes. I have come to a decision, Annora. We are definitely going to Australia."

"When?"

"The beginning of September."

"So soon? Helena is being married in August and I promised to be at her wedding."

"We're not going till September, so why not? We'll have to get back soon. There'll be certain things to see to. We must be back by next summer. Then we'll start planning that season for you. I want to talk to Amaryllis about it. She'll help a lot. She'll have everything ready when we embark on the project."

"I don't look forward to it."

"A necessary evil. But this wedding of Helena's . . ."

"I must stay for it, Mama. She expects it."

"You and she have become greater friends even than you were before. I'm glad. I always felt Helena needed a good friend beside her."

"She has her John now. She dotes on him. She is quite different."

"Yes, I have noticed. But this wedding in August . . . As we're going away for a long time it might be a little difficult."

"Mama, it is not only that. It's this Cresswell matter. I have become quite friendly with them and I feel I know them very well. I stayed with them for a week-end . . . Helena, Peterkin and I. I felt so happy with them. There's a son . . . Joe. It's awful for him. He was going into Parliament and now he has lost his chance. They are shutting themselves away in Surrey and when they come back to Town I did want them to know that I don't believe all this rubbish . . ." I trailed off. "Well, there's that . . . and Helena's wedding."

"I see," said my father, "that you want to stay in London."

He looked at my mother. She was thoughtful for a while. Then she said: "Why not? You could stay with the Lansdons and help Helena with her preparations." She glanced at my father. "We could go back and do everything that has to be done and on our way to Tilbury come and collect Annora and then we could all go off together. How's that?'

"It needs a bit of consideration," said my father. "Is that what you'd like to do, Annora?"

"Well, I do miss Cador and Jacco and you two, but . . ."

"It's only a little while longer," my mother put in. "If you come back with us you'll be wondering what's happening here. You stay, Annora. I'm sure it can all be worked out satisfactorily."

So it was decided that I was to stay in London. My parents would go back to Cador and make their preparations for departure to Australia. Then they, with Jacco, would pick me up in London and I would leave with my family for the trip.

Helena was delighted; and I had to admit that this was what I wanted. I had a strong feeling that I must be on the spot for whatever happened next.

Something did happen soon. I was walking in the Park with Peterkin. The Cresswell affair had drawn us closer together and I had discovered a depth in Peterkin's character which I had not know was there before. He cared deeply about the Cresswells and often we talked about the tragedy which had befallen the family.

He saw a great deal of Frances.

He said: "She is the one who is able to cope with it more than the others because she is more of a realist. Her life in the East End has made her so. She can stand aloof from it and look in as an outsider—while one part of her is deeply concerned for those she loves. She says it has ruined her father's career in one direction. He will have to leave politics, but that is not the end. In Surrey they refuse to believe the story. Everyone in that village is rallying round him. I think that must be a great consolation."

We were talking thus as we walked along, passing the Achilles Statue and going across to Kensington Gardens, and as we were approaching the Round Pond we saw a young man coming towards us.

My heart leaped for it was Joe Cresswell.

"Joe," I cried and ran towards him holding out my hands.

He took them, held them firmly and smiled at me.

Peter was beside us. "Joe! How good to meet you! So you are back in London."

Joe said he was here only for a short while.

"You're staying in St. James's Street?"

"Yes. I steal in and out like a thief," he said. "Though there aren't now so many people hanging about looking at the house as though they are expecting some monster to emerge."

"Where are you going now?" asked Peterkin.

"Aimlessly wandering . . . just thinking."

"Oh, Joe," I cried. "I'm glad we've seen you. We've thought so much about you."

"Thanks for your letter."

"Let's sit down here," said Peterkin, indicating a bench under an oak tree. "It's easier to talk sitting."

So we sat.

"Joe, have you any plans?" asked Peterkin.

He shook his head. "There doesn't seem to be anything. Parliament is off as far as I'm concerned."

"It wasn't all that much of a safe seat," consoled Peterkin.

"I was going to make it safe."

"And now?"

"My father is on the board of several companies. There will be opportunities . . . when I am ready."

"Oh Joe," I said and touched his hands. He took mine and gripped it hard.

"You know," he said, "this was a put-up job."

"What do you mean?" asked Peterkin.

"That business with my father—it was all staged."

"By whom?"

"That's what I have to find out. Someone arranged the accident and that there should be a brawl and the police called in."

"Why?"

"A man in my father's position will always have enemies. If one of them feels strongly and has the means . . ."

Peterkin said: "Yes, yes," in a soothing sort of way, and I could see that he thought he was talking wildly—as I did. Poor Joe! Both Peterkin and I had the utmost sympathy for him.

"You see, it was simply not possible for my father to have gone there for any other reason than to help that girl he believed his carriage had knocked down."

"It wasn't your own coachman who did it?"

"No. It would never have happened if he had been driving. It was a hired vehicle. It wasn't always convenient to take the carriage. That's what makes me think. I reckon it was done on purpose to trap him, and he just walked into it."

It seemed a little far-fetched. The driver would have had to be in the conspiracy as well as the girl and the man who had made the brawl and those who sent for the police. No. I believed that Mr. Cresswell had gone into the girl's apartment because he felt responsible, as the vehicle in which he was riding had knocked her down. What had happened was a run of bad luck.

But both Peterkin and I listened sympathetically. We knew how badly Joe must be feeling—so we let him run on.

After a while Joe said he must go. He was grateful for our sympathy, he told us, and it had done him a lot of good to talk to us.

He took my hand as we were parting, and Peterkin, perhaps feeling that there was a special understanding between us, walked on and left us together for a few seconds.

Joe said: "Annora, I want to see you alone."

"Yes?"

"Can I come to the house? Is there a time when you would be alone there?"

I thought rapidly.

"On Wednesday," I said. "Helena and her mother are going to the dressmaker's. They'll be away all the morning. I think Peterkin is going to see Frances. And Uncle Peter is never there. Come on Wednesday at ten o'clock."

"I don't want to see anyone else. Not the servants . . . no one. You understand?

"They're usually in the kitchen at that time. If you come at ten I'll watch for you and let you in. No one need know. Or would you rather I met you somewhere?"

"No. I'd rather it was in the house . . . if we can be quite alone."

"Wednesday then," I said. "I'll look out for you at ten o'clock."

I was disturbed. I kept asking myself why Joe should want to see me alone, and the idea occurred to me that he might be going to ask me to marry him.

We had seen a great deal of each other and there had undoubtedly been a rather special rapport between us. At a time of acute distress, he might well turn to me for comfort.

And there was Rolf. I could not stop myself thinking of him. I had tried to dismiss him from my thoughts because before that memorable night I had been convinced that one day I would marry Rolf. It was a childish fantasy, of course. Hadn't I once thought of marrying my father? But Rolf had been so much a part of my innocent childhood—though I had ceased to be innocent after that fearful night. I must stop thinking of Rolf for I could never be completely happy thinking of him because from that night had sprung all my fears and doubts. It was not only that I was disillusioned with Rolf—but with life.

I wanted to escape from those memories. It might well be that the best way to do so would be through marriage with someone else.

I had to give this serious contemplation. If Joe were to ask me and I said No, that would make him more unhappy than he already was. It seemed to my inexperienced and romantic mind that if he asked me I must therefore say Yes. I could not bear to cause him further pain; and if I became engaged to him I should be able to comfort him. It would be a way of saying, I believe in your father. I want him for my father-in-law. I was sure that it would comfort the entire family. But I wished I could stop thinking of Rolf.

I was very uneasy on that Wednesday morning. I was afraid that at the last minute Aunt Amaryllis and Helena would cancel their visit to

[118]

the dressmaker's. It was hardly likely that Uncle Peter would be in. If Peterkin decided not to go out, that would not be too bad. I could explain to him more easily.

But all went according to plan.

At ten o'clock I was at the window which looked out on to the street. Joe was waiting. I listened. The house was quiet. The servants were all in the kitchen having the snack which they had about this time. I hurried down to the door and let Joe in.

I took him to a small room which was rarely used. He looked very distraught and was pale, I noticed. He took my hand and pressed it warmly.

I said: "We are free from interruptions here. The servants won't emerge from the kitchen for half an hour at least, and everyone else is out."

"Thank you. Oh, thank you." He looked around the room. "Oh, Annora. I could do with a drink."

"Oh, yes. I'll go and get something. It isn't kept in this room. I won't be long. You'll be all right here. No one will come."

He nodded.

I sped down to the cellar. I had to be careful because I did not want the servants to hear. They would think it so odd that I had not asked them to bring the wine. I had rarely been down here. It was dark. It was some little time before I could find what I wanted. Then I must find glasses. I must have been away for more than five minutes.

All the time I was pondering on his strange behaviour. I could not understand why he had asked so soon for wine.

There was a surprise for me when I reached the room. He was not there. Of course, he had been very nervous. Had he thought that someone was coming and made his escape?

It was all very strange.

I set down the wine and looked out on the street. There was no sign of him. It was very mysterious.

I went upstairs. No one was about. I stood listening. I thought I heard a sound from above.

Cautiously I went up the next flight of stairs. I was standing at the bottom of those steps which led to Uncle Peter's sanctum. I looked up and to my astonishment saw that the door was open.

Uncle Peter must be home.

"Uncle Peter," I called.

There was no answer. I went up and looked in. Joe turned to face me. He looked pale and shaken.

I cried: "What are you doing here? This room is always locked. How did you . . ."

"Hush," he said.

I advanced into the room. I had never been there before. It was as I had expected it would be—an office. There was a big desk and several iron filing cabinets.

"It's Uncle Peter's private office," I said.

Joe was putting some papers into his breast pocket.

"I'm ready to go now," he said.

"You must come down at once. This door is supposed to be locked. How did you get in?"

He did not answer that. He just said: "Let's get down."

I said: "I don't understand. Someone must have left the door open."

We came silently down the stairs to the hall.

"I must go now," he said.

"No, no, Joe," I cried. "I want to know what you were doing in Uncle Peter's room."

I drew him into the little room into which I had first brought him.

I said: "You have taken something. Joe, what are you doing?"

"There was something I wanted. Understand, Annora, I have to do this. You'll understand in time and you'll see why."

"But I don't understand. How did you know the door was open?"

"It wasn't. I opened it."

"You . . . you haven't a key. No one has a key except Uncle Peter and Aunt Amaryllis."

"I learned how to open locked doors. It's an art. Someone at Frances's place taught me how to do it. When you know how, it's not difficult."

"Frances's place!"

"Yes. Someone whose profession it is to unlock doors."

"You mean a thief . . . a criminal!"

"Look," he said, "I don't want to involve you in this, Annora."

"But you unlocked the door. They'll know you've been there."

"I can't relock it. They'll just think they forgot to lock it."

"But what did you take?"

"I can't tell you now, Annora. I must go. I have to go now . . . at once."

"So you came here . . . just to do that?"

"I knew you'd help me. We've always been good friends. I knew you'd be on my side. I must go now . . . quickly. Goodbye, Annora."

My first thought was that no one must know he had called. I took back the wine and the glasses. Then I went to my room.

I had thought he was going to ask me to marry him and he had come to steal something from my uncle's study. I felt stupidly bewildered and very, very uncertain. Should I tell them? I felt a certain loyalty to Joe. And yet what of Uncle Peter?

I tried to shut out of my mind the memory of Joe standing in Uncle Peter's room putting papers into his breast pocket. I could not stop thinking of him any more than I could of Rolf leaping over a bonfire.

I was in a terrible state of uncertainty. I simply did not know what I should do.

Helena returned full of excitement about her trousseau. I pretended to listen to her prattle and did not hear a word of it.

I expect Aunt Amaryllis thought she had failed to lock the door. She would be very upset and perhaps hastily lock it and say nothing about it. She would hate Uncle Peter to think she had been careless where his instructions were concerned.

I was quite bemused. I could not understand it. I did not want to discuss it even with Peterkin.

And then suddenly I learned what it was all about.

Following on the Cresswell case it was like another chapter in the same story.

"Corruption in High Places. Well-Known Politician in dubious Clubs Scandal": "Exclusive story in the *Gazette*": "Read all about it."

"I should have thought," said Aunt Amaryllis, "that everyone is tired of reading about these political scandals. I believe a lot of them are made up just to make sensational headlines and sell the papers. I shall not read it."

But of course she did.

The Cresswell case was nothing to this.

"Mr. Peter Lansdon, the well-known politician, and the expected choice for the new Vice Enquiry, is revealed as the man behind many of the leading clubs which are the haunts of prostitutes and gamblers. This multi-millionaire, whose daughter is about to marry into one of our oldest families, has made his fortune out of vice. Documents have been brought to us to prove this. There is no doubt of their authenticity."

It seemed that the house in the square was to be dealt a similar blow to that which had befallen the Cresswells.

There were crowds round the house and we could not go out. Aunt Amaryllis was stunned. She declared that it was all lies. Peterkin was bewildered. He told me that he had never really understood what his father's business was. There were warehouses dealing with imports from Jamaica he had known, but it seemed these were a cover for other, more lucrative interests; and he had always wondered why his father did not wish him to go into his business.

"This will ruin Uncle Peter," I said, "as the Cresswells have been ruined."

"It will be the end of his parliamentary career," said Peterkin. "He'll still have his businesses. Knowing him I daresay he acts within the law. It has always been known what those clubs were and they have not been abolished. I think too many people in high places are interested in them. They want them to remain. It's the old hypocrisy. Let them remain but don't let us know about them. I wonder why it has come out just now."

I did not wonder. I knew. This was Joe's revenge. He suspected Uncle Peter and he had determined to avenge his father. I could imagine his feelings seeing his career destroyed and his father branded as a lascivious hypocrite; he had looked about for one who had brought this disaster on his family and had suspected Uncle Peter. What had he known about Uncle Peter? And had my uncle set a trap for Joseph Cresswell? There was no doubt that he had wanted this chairmanship. Could it really have been as Joe had suspected?

Uncle Peter was the one who amazed me. He almost shrugged it aside. He faced us all at dinner with what I can only call equilibrium.

"Well," he said. "It's out at last. Yes, this is how I have made my fortune. You have all benefitted from it and so there is no need for you, at least, to take up a sanctimonious role. All the charities which I have upheld have profited from it. When they asked me for money they did not want to know how it had been earned. I have been at great pains to keep the nature of my business from you all, not because I am ashamed of it, but because I thought it might distress you. And there is no doubt that it would have had a restricting effect on my activities. Now it is out. There have been other occasions when I thought it might have been discovered. I shall follow Joseph Cresswell's example and resign my seat and slip out of politics for a while. It is a pity. I could have done so much and my ill-gotten wealth would have been of great service in many causes. However, as far as I am concerned, there are other roads which will be interesting to follow."

He went on calmly eating his dinner.

I talked to Aunt Amaryllis afterwards. She said: "I am so sad, Annora. This is all my fault. Somebody stole papers from your uncle's study, and he got in because I had left the door open."

I said: "Aunt Amaryllis, there are ways of getting in even when doors are locked. It is quite easy with people who do that sort of thing for a living."

"You mean thieves? Do you think we had a thief in the house?"

"We must have done," I said grimly.

Helena was worried.

"I don't know what effect this will have on the Duke," she said.

"It will depend on how much he wants your father's money," I replied bitterly.

"That it should have happened now! I thought it was too good to be true."

I comforted her. "It'll be all right," I said. "John loves you. What your father does is nothing to do with you."

There was silence from the ducal family for some days. Then Uncle Peter received a letter. The Duke felt that in view of recent revelations it would be understood by a man of the world that an alliance of the two families was now not desirable.

Poor Helena was heartbroken.

I felt guilty. If I had not let Joe in that day . . . But I was sure he would have found some other means. He was so intent on revenge.

I thought Helena was going to be ill; she lost interest in everything. It was a sad, quiet household. I heard some of the servants whispering to each other. They were going to give notice. They could not be expected to work in such a household. But none of them did. Whatever Uncle Peter's profession, he kept a good staff and paid them better than most; and weighing the matter up they must have decided that it was better to forget about a little vice for the sake of comforts and good posts.

I had to admire Uncle Peter. He went on as though nothing had happened. It was true that he followed Joseph Cresswell's example and resigned his seat. He just washed his hands of politics.

He was so rich that he could snap his fingers at respectability. I thought how different he was from Joseph Cresswell.

There were a few enquiries about the clubs, but their activities were well covered up. They were run as clubs, and gambling was not against the law. As for prostitution, occasionally there were attempts but nothing could be done to stop it entirely. We were a country in which the freedom of the individual was considered to be of the utmost importance. Any attempt to curb it would result in an outcry. Uncle Peter had been careful not to break any laws. He had protected his interests well and it was almost as though he had prepared himself for the kind of accusations which were being brought against him; and being the man he was, even the press grew tired of vilifying him and his activities.

He was not such an obvious victim as Joseph Cresswell. The one who really suffered was Helena.

I did see Joe again. He was in the Park and I think he wanted to see me for he felt he owed me some explanation.

I was with Peterkin when we met him.

We faced each other, tongue-tied. Neither of us could think of anything to say. On one hand I understood his need to avenge his father; and on the other I saw him as the destroyer of Helena's happiness.

At last Joe said: "I've been hanging about here for several days hoping to see you." He looked at me anxiously. "I didn't know whether you would want to see me again."

I was silent and Peterkin said: "Why?"

Joe looked at me. "You knew, didn't you?"

I said: "I think I had better explain to Peterkin. One day when you were all out, Joe came to see me. When I went out of the room to get some wine he went up to your father's room, forced the lock in some way and got into your father's papers. I suppose they gave details of his business."

"Listen," cut in Joe. "I knew my father had been trapped. He would never have gone home with that girl except to help her. And I guessed that the whole thing had been planned in order to blacken my father's reputation. Wouldn't you. . . ?"

"In your case perhaps," said Peterkin.

"I wasn't going to let it rest. I got hold of that girl . . . Chloe. I threatened her, I bribed her, and at last I got the story. She had been commanded to do what she did. She wasn't knocked over. The driver was in it and so was the man who broke in. It was a well-organized plot. And who was able to set that in motion? Your father. He hadn't seen the girl himself. His minions told her what she must do. But she had caught glimpses of him once or twice going into the private offices where the books and records were kept. She had found out who he was when she had seen pictures in the papers. My father had said long ago that this woman who called herself Madame Delarge was not really the owner. There was someone behind her. I thought I knew, in fact I was almost certain. You see, there was the motive."

"You mean this chairmanship?" said Peterkin.

Joe nodded. "My father was his rival in more ways than that. It was a despicable thing to do. I had to have my revenge. Wouldn't you?"

"For my own father . . . perhaps not," said Peterkin. "For yours . . . yes, I understand, Joe."

He looked at me. "So you don't blame me?"

I could not answer him. I could only see Helena's wretched face. *I* had let him into the house. I was responsible for Helena's misery. I knew I could never love Joe. There was a barrier between us as Midsummer's Eve was between Rolf and me.

"Annora," he went on, and laid his hand on my arm.

I said: "You didn't tell me why you wanted to come to my uncle's house."

"How could I?"

"You sent me from the room on a pretext so that you could go upstairs and break into my uncle's study."

"It was the only way. You wouldn't have helped me do that. And how could I have asked you to?"

"No, you certainly could not."

"I had to do it, Annora."

"Yes," said Peterkin. "I see how you felt."

[125]

"It has done no good," I cried. "It has not helped your father and it has ruined Helena's happiness."

"If John Milward can't stand out against his family, he wouldn't have been much of a husband."

"Helena doesn't think that and I . . . I don't know what to think."

We sat wretchedly looking at Achilles, so strong, so formidable, and it made me think of the weaknesses of mankind.

After a while we got up to go.

Joe took my hands and looked at me earnestly. "Annora," he said. "Do try to understand."

"I do understand. It was revenge you wanted. Two scandals instead of one."

"I'm going to clear my father's name," said Joe.

"How?" asked Peterkin.

"I'm going to make Chloe's confession public."

"My father will treat it all as if it were of little significance," said Peterkin.

"His parliamentary career will be ruined as my father's has been."

"He has already finished with politics. He says the whole world is his field. You'll do no good. You will just bring it all up again and it will be more distressing to your family than ours."

"I suppose," said Joe sadly, "this means that communication between us is impossible."

We said goodbye. Peterkin shook hands with Joe, and Joe held mine for some time looking at me appealingly; but I was too bewildered to give him the encouragement he obviously sought. I could not get Helena's sad face out of my mind.

"He's right," said Peterkin as we walked away. "It does make friendship between our families out of the question."

I think Joe did try to get Chloe's account of what happened into the press, but he failed to do so. I imagine this was due to Peter's influence because, as had been said of him before, he had his fingers into many pies. He could do a great deal of manipulation in many directions and I was sure that if he had not been taken by surprise and the story of his business had not been given to a particularly scurrilous newspaper in the first place he would have been able to prevent the facts being published. But of course, once the story was out all the papers had to make what sensation they could from it.

Joe must have been frustrated in his schemes but at least he had driven Uncle Peter from Parliament.

Moreover there was a great deal about the coronation festivities in the papers and people were more interested in that then anything else at the moment.

A Coronation Fair had been opened in Hyde Park and the Queen herself had been there to see it. Accounts of it filled the papers and the people were so busy reading about that, that the impact of Chloe's story would be lost upon them. They had finished with Joseph Cresswell and Peter Lansdon. They had both supplied scandalous titbits which had been gratefully received, but the element of surprise had gone; they had both been knocked off their high perches and there was nothing else which could be done to them. The coronation festivities, the Queen with her little figure and regal manner—that was what they wanted to read about. She reviewed five thousand troops in Hyde Park and the people cheered her wildly. Everything was going to be different now we had a young girl on the throne to take the place of those doddery rather boring old gentlemen.

One morning John Milward called at the house. He looked very young and rather frightened, but he had come to see Helena and I was pleased about that. He had not left it just to his father to break off the marriage.

When I saw Helena she had regained her radiance.

"I wanted you to be the first to know," she said. "It's going to be all right."

"You mean. . . ?"

She nodded. "We're going to be married. Oh, it won't be an expensive wedding. Who wants that, anyway?"

"Not you," I cried, hugging her.

"We shall be poor."

"You'll have your allowance."

"John will have to do some work or other." My heart sank a little. I could not imagine John's doing some work or other.

"But we don't care. He's going to defy his family. He doesn't care about being cut off. He only cares about me."

"Oh, Helena, I'm so glad. I misjudged him. I thought he was weak."

"We're going to be very strong."

"It's wonderful."

"Do you think Papa. . . ?"

I thought about that enigmatical man and it occurred to me that, wicked as he must be, he would not be one to stand in the way of his daughter's happiness. In fact I could imagine his delight in snubbing the Duke.

At least Helena's happiness was saved.

For a whole week Helena continued in a state of bliss. She saw John every day. She had been so unhappy that no restrictions were put on her by Aunt Amaryllis, who was delighted at the return of John for Helena's sake. John came to the house and was alone with Helena for long periods of time. They walked in the Park together.

He had left the ducal roof and was sharing rooms with a bachelor friend of his. I said to Peterkin: "He's got more spirit than I thought. I wouldn't have believed he could have stood out against his family."

Peterkin agreed with me.

How wrong we were to think all was well! His family must have brought great pressure to bear on him and John, after all, was not the man to withstand it.

He did not even come to tell Helena himself; he explained by letter. She showed it to me.

My dearest Helena,

I am so sorry but I cannot go on with this. You have no idea what I have had to put up with from my family. It's not just being cut off. Where would we live? My father says I shall have nothing . . . nothing at all. They are all against me, Helena. I can't stand it. I know I should never be any good at earning a living. What could I do?

I love you. I shall always love you. But it has to be goodbye.

John

I have never seen such misery as I saw in Helena's face. I cursed him. He should never have come back. It would have been better if she had just had the one blow.

I tried to comfort her. I said that perhaps if he was so weak it was better for them to part. She would not have it. Her heart was broken. Life had become intolerable to her.

Those were wretched days.

I wanted to leave London. I wanted to put all that had happened behind me. But I did know that I was the only one to whom Helena could talk and I felt I could not leave her.

My parents wrote to say that in view of our departure in September, and the scandal about Uncle Peter and because there was to be no wedding, I should return home. I would have to make certain preparations and although they had been going to pick me up on the way to Tilbury, it would now be more convenient for me to return home so that we could all set out together.

When I mentioned the matter to Helena she looked stricken although she said nothing.

Then I had an idea. "Helena," I said, "why don't you come with me? You'll get right away and there is nothing like leaving something behind to get it out of your mind."

She replied that nothing could get this out of her mind; but I could see that she was so eager not to lose me that she wanted to come.

So very soon after that Helena and I left for Cornwall.

I was glad to be home. It was good to see Jacco again. He was always particularly affectionate after long absences.

My parents were very kind and gentle to Helena and I fancied she seemed a little better away from the place where so much that was tragic had happened to her.

Rolf was away. His father had died suddenly of a heart attack. "Poor Rolf," said my mother. "He is very sad. He is away now, staying with friends in the Midlands. It was such a blow. We were all so fond of Mr. Hanson."

Later I had several talks with my mother, who was of the opinion that Helena was better off without John Milward since he lacked the courage to stand out against his parents. After all, he was of age.

My mother and I used to go for long walks together along the cliffs during the mornings. Helena usually stayed in her room until luncheon. That seemed to be what she wanted and we thought we should indulge her all we could.

It gave me a chance to be with my mother. I was realizing how much I had missed her while I had been away.

One day as we lay on the grass of the cliffs looking out to sea watching the seagulls flying high and then swooping down to capture some item of food, she said to me: "Tell me, what did Peter Lansdon do when the news about his connection with these clubs came out?"

"Do? Oh nothing much. He was quite nonchalant about it. Yes, it was true, he said. And then he reminded his family how they had benefitted from his money."

"Poor Amaryllis."

"Don't worry about her. She thinks Uncle Peter is always right. It's Helena I'm sorry for."

"I've got something to tell you, Annora, about your Uncle Peter. I've told your father. It was a secret even from him but now I can tell you. I said I thought you should know and he agreed with me. I know you liked Joe Cresswell. But what about Rolf?"

"What about him?"

"Your father and I used to think that you and Rolf would make a match of it one day. I know he is a little older than you but now you're growing up that's not so much. What we want is your happiness of course. We've always had such a soft spot for Rolf . . . living so close . . . being like one of the family really. At one time you admired him so much. We used to laugh about it. So did Mr. Hanson. It was almost an understood thing between us. Then you seemed to change."

"I was growing up."

"But you *do* like him, don't you?"

"Yes, of course I do."

"Your father would be very pleased. He says we know Rolf and that's what we like about it."

"You never really know people," I said quickly. "Not *all* about them."

"Well, we all have our secrets . . ."

I knew that she was uneasy, that she was thinking about what she had said she would tell me, that she was reluctant to do so and that was why she had gone on talking of other things, as though postponing the moment.

"Remember, my darling," she said now, "what we want more than anything is your happiness. Of course we'll like you to be somewhere near us. Parents are like that, but we have to remind ourselves that it is not for us to choose. I hope you'll talk to us. Sometimes talking can help."

"I know it can and if there was something I wanted to talk about I'd talk to you . . . first."

She kissed me. There was a brief silence and still she was hesitating. I imagined she was steeling herself. She said quickly: "Has this Joe Cresswell disappointed you in some way? You shouldn't blame him for his father's affairs, you know."

"I don't. In any case I believe his father was innocent of what they blamed him for. I suppose you read about the case?"

She nodded.

"Isn't it time you told me what you were going to?"

She hesitated and then said quickly: "I . . . I knew about Peter Lansdon's affairs. I discovered long ago, before I married your father."

"You didn't say," I said.

"I couldn't. He blackmailed me. It was a case of double blackmail."

"You!"

"Yes. You see, my dearest child, out of necessity, people sometimes do things you would least suspect them of. You've lived all your life sheltered and not really coming face to face with emotions and temptations which beset most of us at some time. You know your father was my second husband."

"Yes, of course."

"My first husband was a good, kind, gentle man. I married him without really being in love with him. It was always your father . . . but you know about him and his term in Australia. There's no secret about that. My first husband was hurt in an accident. He was crippled before our marriage. I tried to be a good wife to him . . . and then your father came back. You don't understand yet what love can be like. It was necessary to us both. I was your father's mistress before my first husband was dead. Peter Lansdon found this out."

"Oh, Mama . . ."

"It was a desperate situation."

"He blackmailed you."

"In a way. He's a strange man. He is bent on one thing—getting on in the world, making everyone dance to his tune. He is the most ambitious man I ever knew. I found out something about him . . . I found out that which has now become public knowledge."

[131]

"About the clubs?" I said.

"Yes . . . the sort they were. He was up to his tricks even then. Juggling with events so that he could be in the right place at the right moment."

"Do you think he arranged what happened to Joseph Cresswell?"

"I am sure he did. It was his way of working. I found out this and we made a pact. He would keep quiet about your father and me if I would about him. I agreed. He was not the sort of man to break his word . . . unless it was necessary for him to do so. He doesn't want revenge on people for the purpose of harming them. He acts only to bring benefit to himself. I feel I know him so well. It was your Joe Cresswell who exposed him, wasn't it? And you thought that was wrong . . ."

I said: "He told me he wanted to see me. He came to the house and when I went out of the room to get some wine for which he asked, he went upstairs and broke into Uncle Peter's room. You see, but for my carelessness he wouldn't have got into that room, he wouldn't have had his proof. Helena would still be engaged . . . almost married by now to John Milward."

"And you're blaming Joe?"

"What he did was wrong. Nothing has been put right. He wanted to prove that his father had been trapped . . . and no one wants to know about that now. He can in any case only rely on Chloe's evidence and nobody trusts her. She's a well-known adventuress. It all seems so unnecessary. Why couldn't he let it rest? It's done no good to his father and it's ruined Helena's life."

"You're right," she said. "But you must understand Joe's feelings."

"I do. But I can't forget the sight of him when I came into that room which he had forced open and saw him putting those papers into his breast pocket."

"I just wanted you to know, Annora, that we are none of us perfect. Your father and I . . . well, we were very much in love . . . and there was my husband, a helpless invalid. You see, we are all weak. Do realize that, Annora. Don't judge people too harshly."

I lay there staring out to sea, rather bewildered by what she had told me. I could picture Peter Lansdon laying down his rules. She must not tell and he would not tell. And my mother had entered into the bargain with him to save her first husband from the knowledge that she had a lover; and because her love for my father was so strong she could not resist it even though she was committing adultery.

I must try to understand Joe.

But I should always remember his standing there with the papers in his hands as I should remember Rolf that Midsummer's Eve.

After that talk with my mother, I tried to reason with myself. I expected too much from people. I must try to understand Joe's motives. I must try to convince myself that Rolf's feelings had got the better of him. He had thrown himself wholeheartedly into the past; he had imagined that he was living centuries ago when people tortured witches; for a night he had shed his shell of civilization and become one of those people whose customs interested him so much.

I must be understanding. I must realize that I was, as my mother said, young and I had seen little of the world.

But I could not forget.

Preparations for our departure were going on apace.

"I wish you weren't going," sighed Helena.

"You'll feel better when you're back in London. It won't be as bad as it was. They are right when they say time heals."

"I can't go back, Annora. I don't want to. I wish I could stay here."

Then the idea came to me. "Helena, why shouldn't you come with us to Australia?"

I saw the wonder dawning on her face.

There was a great deal of discussion about it. My mother wrote to Aunt Amaryllis. She had always had great influence with her. "I was like the dictatorial elder sister," she used to say.

The result was that both Uncle Peter and Aunt Amaryllis thought it might be a good idea for Helena to accompany us.

Helena brightened considerably at the prospect and I even saw her smile once or twice.

About a week before we were due to leave Rolf returned.

He came over to see us at once. He looked melancholy and I had never seen him like that before.

He visited us frequently and talked a great deal with my father about the estate, which was solely his now. He had been looking after it for years because he, not his father, had been the one who had built it up. "But there is a difference," my father said, "when something is entirely your own."

Rolf contrived to be alone with me when we went riding together.

He said: "I wish you weren't going away, Annora. You're going right to the other side of the world and you'll be away for a long time."

"It wouldn't be worthwhile going just for a few weeks."

"Then there is the journey there and another back. I missed you while you were in London. Did you think of Cador?"

"Often."

"When you come back, I want to have a long talk with you."

"What about?"

"Us."

"What do you mean . . . you and me?"

He nodded.

We were walking our horses and he turned to me and said: "You seem to take such a long time to grow up."

"The usual time I suppose."

"Will you think of me while you are away?"

"Quite a lot, I expect."

"When you come back we'll make plans . . ."

I felt a sudden happiness. He could mean only one thing. I smiled at him. He looked different with that air of melancholy about him.

I thought of what my mother had said. "One must try to understand people." She and my father had broken laws. People did at times. One must not judge them too harshly. One must grow up. One must understand something about life.

In that moment I wondered why I had ever thought there was a possibility of my marrying Joe. I knew I loved Rolf. But I wished I could forget that terrible night.

When we returned to the stables he helped me to dismount and kissed me.

I felt rather glad that we were going away. During the trip I would sort out my thoughts. I would come to terms with myself. I would make sure that, whatever had happened on that night, I was going to marry Rolf.

On the High Seas

—— 🍏 ——

It was the beginning of September when we set sail. We stayed a few nights in the house in Albemarle Street before going on to Tilbury to join the cargo ship in which we would be sailing. I was sure the excitement of the coming journey was good for Helena. She was still very sad and at times lapsed into deep melancholy, but I did feel that she had come a little way from the terrible lassitude which implied that she simply did not care what became of her.

Amaryllis was sorry that she was going but at the same time she felt that it was the best thing for her. As for Peter Lansdon, his resilience continued to amaze me. He behaved as though there was nothing extraordinary about a man who had aspired to become a leading politician being at the same time, to put it crudely, a brothel owner. He simply shrugged off politics and I had no doubt that he would soon be applying his immense energies to something else.

We went to the house in the square for dinner and it was almost as it had been in the past. He was insouciant, talkative and informative about what was going on. I did notice once the sardonic smile he sent in my mother's direction and I guessed he was reminding her of that long-ago pact, and telling her that exposure did not worry him all that much. Yet he had gone to great lengths to keep the nature of his business secret. He was, no doubt, making the best of an ugly situation, and in spite of everything I knew about him, I could not help feeling a grudging admiration for him.

He did talk a great deal about the Queen and Lord Melbourne and the growing certainty that there would soon be an election which would put Melbourne out.

"And what Her Majesty will do when she loses her beloved minister, I cannot imagine. Stamp her little foot, no doubt. But it won't do any good. And they say she has an aversion to Peel. Well, one has to admit he is too serious a politician to appeal to a young girl . . . and of course his lordship has all the charm in the world, to which is added a somewhat scandalous past." He smiled at us in a kind of wry triumph. "It seems odd that the naughty prosper in this world and the good are considered somewhat dull." I could see that he was certainly not going to let adversity deter him.

I think my father was inclined to admire him, too. He had always been one to look lightly on the sins of others. My mother naturally felt a great antipathy towards him and I could well understand that, after what she told me of the anxiety he must have caused her all those years ago.

I had several talks with Peterkin. He told me he had seen Joe at Frances's Mission and Joe had given up all thought of politics. It was the only thing he could do. He would not have a chance this time, but it might be that in a few years the name would be forgotten and he would pursue his ambition. For the time being he had gone up North and was working with a company in which his father had interests.

As for Peterkin himself, he was seeing Frances frequently and becoming more and more interested in the work she was doing.

He said: "My father is not averse to this. He thinks it is good publicity to have a son who is interested in social welfare; and it makes a nice touch that I am working with the daughter of Joseph Cresswell, because as you know there have been rumours that my father trapped Joseph Cresswell into that situation. So for once I have his approval of what I am doing." He smiled at me. "It suits me. For the first time I feel I am doing something I really want to do. My father has given money to the Mission . . . a sizeable sum, so that Frances is going to get that house she wants. Of course, Papa likes the press to know where the money comes from."

"I suppose he feels it's a sort of expiation."

"Not him. He just feels it's a neat touch for people to ask if the money goes to do such good service does it matter how it was come by?"

[136]

"He's very cynical."

"He's just about the shrewdest and most cunning person I know."

"And you and Frances—you don't mind using his money?"

Peterkin looked at me quizzically. "No. I suppose we ought to. Frances and I have talked about it. Not that she thought of refusing it for a moment. Frances would take money from any source if it helped with her work. She needs that money. If you could see some of those people, you'd understand. Frances is a very wise young woman. 'If good cometh out of evil,' she says, 'let's make the most of the good.'"

I thought a good deal about them all and it was brought home to me that life is not neatly divided between good and evil; and after that I began to make less critical judgements.

After that brief visit we went down to Tilbury to join our ship which was taking ready-made garments, corn, oats, sugar, tea and coffee as well as some livestock out to Australia. There were only a few passengers so I supposed we should get to know our fellow travellers well during the voyage.

Helena and I shared a small cabin with two bunks, one above the other, a little cupboard for our clothes and a small table on which was fixed a mirror. It was fortunate that most of our baggage had been put into the hold until our arrival. My parents had a similar cabin next to ours and Jacco was sharing with another young man.

It was an exciting moment when we slipped away from the dock.

The Captain invited us to his cabin. He was a pleasant man with a dark curly beard, the same dark curly hair and heavy-lidded brown eyes.

"Welcome," he said. "I hope you are going to have a pleasant voyage with us. Have you travelled on a cargo ship before?"

We said we hadn't and my father added that he had been out to Australia, but had travelled on a different kind of ship and that was more than twenty years ago.

"Things have changed," said the Captain. "In fact they are changing all the time. There are three other passengers besides yourselves. A young man who is going out to study something and a couple who want to settle. We should all get along fairly well. It just needs a little give and take if you know what I mean."

"I understand," said my father. "To be in such close proximity for so long could in some cases be rather trying."

"We shall try to make the voyage as pleasant as possible. There are card games, and there is a piano in one of the rooms. We have a good pianist among us. We'll make it tolerable but the main purpose of our voyage is to carry goods. That is why we are never quite sure how long we stay at certain ports, or even which ports we shall be calling at."

"We understand all that," said my father. "What we want is to be taken to Australia as quickly as possible."

"Then we shall be able to satisfy you. I have invited the other passengers here so that we can all get acquainted. Ah, here are Mr. and Mrs. Prevost. This is Sir Jake and Lady Cador and their son and daughter . . ." He looked at Helena and added, ". . . and their niece."

We shook hands. The Prevosts were a pleasant-looking couple in their early thirties, I imagined, and while we were exchanging a few pleasantries with them the other passenger arrived. He was the one who was sharing a cabin with Jacco and as soon as he came in I thought there was something familiar about him.

"This is Mr. Matthew Hume," said the captain, introducing us.

The young man smiled as we shook hands. He looked steadily at me and said: "We have met before."

"I thought so," I replied. "I was wondering . . ."

"Frances Cresswell's Mission."

"Of course. You let us in when we called."

"We only met briefly but I remembered."

"That's a strange coincidence," said my father. "There are only three passengers apart from my family and one of these knows one of us."

"It was just a case of hail and farewell," said the young man. "I was working at the Mission."

"I know something of it," said my mother. "I believe it does very good work."

His face lit up. "Wonderful work," he said. "Frances Cresswell is a remarkable woman."

"Well," put in the Captain, "it is a pleasant surprise to find that you are not absolute strangers. We dine in half an hour and by that time I hope you will have decided that you are going to get along very well together during the coming weeks."

"I'm so excited to be going," Matthew Hume told us. "I've been trying to get a passage for some time. I am longing to see Australia."

"We can't wait," said Mrs. Prevost. "Can we, Jim? It's going to mean so much to us."

By the time we went in to dinner we felt we knew each other quite well.

We sat at table with the Captain and his Chief Officer and I found myself in earnest conversation with Matthew Hume. He seemed to want to talk to me. I supposed because I was not exactly a stranger. The Mission kept coming into the conversation. He said that he had at one time thought of going into the Church and then he had visited Frances's Mission and had been amazed by what he saw there.

"Dear Frances," he said, "she looks to people like me to help all the time. She said she wants people with a social conscience, people who were born into the world of wealth—or comparative wealth—to give something of themselves to those who were born in less fortunate circumstances. Frances knows exactly where she is going, and as soon as I went to the Mission I began to feel I did."

I nodded and thought of Peterkin. "My cousin feels like that, I believe," I said.

"I have seen some terrible sights," he went on. "Heartrending. And I've been to some of the prisons. That's why I am going out here . . . to study the conditions of those who have been transported. I am going to write a book about it. I want to call attention to it. I think it is wrong. I think it is evil. We've got to stop it."

He was fervent and he seemed to me very young. I wondered how old he was. Twenty-three? Hardly that.

"I have had the honour of meeting Mrs. Elizabeth Fry," he told me. "She has talked to me about prisons and she has done a great deal . . ."

We were interrupted by someone's asking the Captain about the ports we should call at and wondering how long we should stay at them.

The Captain said it would depend on what had to be set ashore and what taken on board. We would be informed of when we must return to the ship.

"But we should like you to obey orders in that respect," he said. "The tides have to be considered before the wishes of the passengers, especially in ships of this kind."

The Prevosts were talking about what they wanted to do.

"We're going to acquire a little land," said Jim Prevost. "It's going very cheaply. Life was getting difficult at home. Trouble over the

Reform Bill, the Corn Laws and the bad harvests. They say the climate out there is just wonderful."

My father pointed out that in no part of the world could the climate be relied on and there were such things as droughts and plagues in Australia. He knew because he had lived there for nine years. True, that was more than twenty years ago, but the weather patterns had not changed.

The Prevosts looked abashed and he went on quickly: "I am sure the advantages will make up for the disadvantages. And I have heard that in some parts of Australia no price at all is asked for the land."

The Prevosts brightened and my father began to talk about his experiences of farming in Australia.

So the evening passed.

Helena had hardly spoken, but she did display a little curiosity in her surroundings and I was sure the voyage was going to be of great interest.

I could not be anything but exhilarated to be at sea. The crew was friendly and ready to explain anything we asked and the weather was benign even in the notoriously hazardous Bay of Biscay.

Helena wanted to stay in the cabin a good deal. She was quite ill which seemed a bad omen when we were not experiencing any really bad weather. She said it was the movement of the ship. Jacco and I revelled in the life. We would race each other along the open decks which were rather restricted, but we enjoyed it; then we would lean over the rail and look right down into the swirling sea-green water.

There was so much to learn about the ship and we awakened each day to a feeling of excitement.

My father and mother used to walk along the deck arm in arm with a smile of contentment on their faces while he talked about his experiences as a convict for he said the journey and the prospect of being in Australia again brought it all back to him most vividly.

There were our fellow travellers, too. The Prevosts were so enthusiastic about their project and they were constantly trying to corner my father to make him tell them all he knew. One evening, when he was in a particularly mellow mood, he told them that he had been sent out as a convict, recounting the story with a certain amount of wit, making light of his sufferings so that it was quite entertaining.

When Matthew Hume discovered that my father had actually experienced life as a convict he was beside himself with joy.

"First-hand knowledge!" he cried. "That is what I am after."

"I daresay it has changed a lot since my day," my father reminded him. "Life is changing all the time."

"But what an opportunity!"

He would sit beside my father, notebook in hand.

"Such a piece of luck," he said.

"It wasn't for my father," I reminded him.

He was serious. "But look. Here he is now, a man of standing, and he has gone through all that."

"He did have an estate to go to and a title waiting for him."

"I want the whole story," said Matthew.

He was very earnest, a little lacking in humour, but he was a young man with a purpose and I liked him for that.

I said to my mother: "There is an innate goodness about him."

She replied: "He certainly has reformation at heart, but it is often like that with the young. They have dreams of making this and that right and often they are not very practical. Their world is made of dreams rather than reality."

"Don't tell him that. He is intoxicated with his dream."

Our first port of call was Madeira where we were putting off goods and taking on wine. It gave us an opportunity to go ashore and my father arranged for us to go round the island in a carriage. My parents and the Prevosts were in one, Helena, Matthew Hume, Jacco and myself in another.

It was a beautiful sight with its mountains and magnificently colourful flowers and it was wonderful to be ashore after being so long at sea. We were all rather merry—with the exception of Helena, but we did not expect her to be otherwise as she never was. We had a meal in a tavern in Funchal close to the red stone Cathedral and the flower market. Then we went back to the ship and very soon were at sea again.

We were a day out from Madeira. At dinner we had been more vociferous than usual, talking of our experiences in Madeira and telling each other that we must make the most of the next port of call.

We were all given a taste of the Madeira wine which had been taken on board and we were very convivial. Glancing at Helena I saw the sheen of tears in her eyes. I thought, She is not getting any better. Is she going on grieving for the rest of her life? After all, as my mother had said, if John Milward had been man enough he would have defied his parents. I wanted to say to her: "Think of the Prevosts going out not knowing what they are going to find. Think of that nice earnest Matthew Hume with his mission in life. Helena, you will have to make the best of it."

When we retired that night I wondered if I could talk to her. But it seemed there was little one could say to someone who was so wrapped up in her grief.

I did try.

We were in our bunks—she was in the one above—and the ship was rocking slightly as it often did.

I said: "This is like being rocked to sleep."

"Yes," she answered.

"Are you sleepy?"

"No."

"There is something I wanted to say. Couldn't you try to be interested? Everything is so new to us. Madeira was lovely but you might have been anywhere. I don't think you noticed anything."

She was silent.

"You've got to try to forget. Don't you see, you'll never get over it until you do."

"I'll never get over it, Annora. There'll be something to remind me always. You don't understand what happened."

"Well, tell me then."

"I don't think I can. Though I suppose you'll have to know. Annora, I think I'm going to have a baby."

"Helena!" I whispered.

"Yes. In fact . . . I'm almost sure."

"It can't be."

"It is. You see, when John came back . . . and he was going to defy his family . . . it happened. Nobody had ever really cared for me before. It seemed wonderful. And now it's all finished and I'm going to have this little baby."

I felt so shaken I did not know what to say.

I wanted to get up and go straight to my parents and ask them what was to be done.

I could only say: "Oh, Helena, what are you going to do?"

"I don't know. I'm terrified."

"I daresay my mother will know what to do."

"A baby, Annora. Think what that means. I'll never be able to go home. What would my father say?"

"He can hardly set himself up as a pillar of respectability," I reminded her.

"I know. That makes it worse."

"I'm glad you told me, Helena."

"I've wanted to . . . ever since I knew."

"When. . . ?"

"I think about April."

"That gives us time to work something out."

"What can we work out?"

"What can be done. My mother will know what is best . . . and so will my father. It's a good thing you're here with us."

"I know."

"A baby," I said softly. "A dear little baby. In a way it's wonderful."

"It would be," said Helena, "if . . ."

"But still there'll be the baby."

I couldn't stop thinking of the baby. I saw it . . . fair-haired, rather like Aunt Amaryllis, with a sweet flower-like face. For a few moments I forgot Helena's dilemma contemplating it.

"I haven't known what to do. Sometimes I've thought it would all be settled if I jumped over the side of the ship."

"What an awful thing to say! Put that right out of your mind. This is going to give us problems but we're all here to help—my parents, Jacco, me—all of us. It'll all come right. It really will and there'll be the dear little baby."

"I can't think of it like that. There's too much to be faced. I never thought this would happen. I thought we were going to be happy together."

"You should perhaps let John know."

"I couldn't do that."

"Then you could be married."

"No, no." She sounded hysterical so I said quietly: "No, I suppose not. Do you mind if I tell my mother?"

"I don't want anyone to know."

"But they will know in time and they'll help. I know they will."

"I feel so much better now you know."

"Poor Helena. What you must have gone through . . . and all because of what happened . . ."

I thought, If it hadn't been for that chairmanship they would have gone on as planned and nobody would have known.

"Helena," I said, "you have been very sick. Ever since you came on board."

"Yes, I think that's what it was. I feel awful sometimes in the mornings."

"You should have told me right away."

"I couldn't. But you know now."

"Helena, I want to tell my mother in the morning. She will know what is best to be done. Do let me tell her."

After some hesitation she said: "All right. And you'll help me, won't you, Annora?"

"We all will. I'll do anything in the world, I promise."

"I'm so glad to be with you."

"I'm glad we're here. It will be all right, Helena, I know it will."

"I feel it might be, now that you know," she said. "It's like a great weight being lifted from my mind."

I felt immensely gratified, and a great tenderness swept over me and with it a desire to protect Helena.

I took the first opportunity of talking to my mother. I told her that I had something very important to say and that I wanted to talk to her alone.

We found a spot on deck. The sea had turned choppy and we were alone there. We sat down on a bench and I burst out: "Helena is going to have a baby."

I had rarely seen her so startled.

"A baby!" she echoed.

"Yes. She thought she and John were going to be married, you see."

"Oh yes. I see."

"What shall we do?"

My mother was silent for a while. Then she said: "Poor girl. No wonder she's been looking as though she would like to jump overboard."

"She did actually mention that."

"For Heaven's sake, watch her. She could be hysterical. Then goodness knows what would happen."

"I want to reassure her. I've told her we'll look after her."

My mother nodded. "It's a good thing we are going to Australia. That'll help a lot. No one will know her there and we'll manage it. When?"

"She thinks April."

"I see. Well, that gives us time."

"But what are we going to do?"

"There is nothing we can do here . . . only reassure her. We've got to make her see that it is not such an unusual situation and she is by no means the first girl to whom it has happened. . . . Then we'll decide what we're going to do when we get to Sydney. She should take care of herself now. I'm glad she is in with you. Just reassure her. Don't let her get overwhelmed by a sense of guilt. I'll speak to your father. He'll know what to do when we get there. We'll arrange it all. As I say, it is a good thing we are not at home. That could have been decidedly more difficult. I daresay they have midwives and doctors in Sydney. Lots of children must be getting born out there. We'll see to it all. Don't let her worry. That's the great thing."

"I think she is glad not to be at home."

"Amaryllis would have helped all she could."

"She wouldn't want her father to know."

"He's in no position to condemn anyone," said my mother shortly.

"I shall tell her you know and that you have said you will help. What will happen when we take the baby home with us?"

"We'll deal with that when the time comes. Let's get her out of that suicidal mood and make her see that what has happened to her is not all that unusual and above all that she is with her family and we are going to help."

"Oh thank you. I knew you'd make it seem better."

She smiled at me and pressed my hand; and we went on talking about it for a long time. My father came and found us.

"I wondered where you were," he said. "What is this? The women getting together for a little peace and quiet?"

My mother looked at me and said: "I've just heard a startling piece of news."

"Oh?" He looked from her to me and she went on:

"Helena is going to have a baby."

"Good God!" he cried. Then: "John Milward?"

I nodded.

"He'll have to marry her."

"She won't hear of his being told."

"Though," went on my father, "how we'd get him out here I can't imagine."

"This must be treated with the utmost tact, Jake."

"Is that an indication that I should keep out of it?"

"No, no!" I cried. "We very much want you in it. Mama thinks it will be fairly easy until we get the baby. What then . . . when we have to take it home to England?"

"We could invent a marriage which was fruitful in a short time, and a husband who came to an untimely end."

"You're going too fast, Jake," said my mother. "Let's get Helena in the right frame of mind. Let's not think so far ahead as that. Annora is being so helpful with her."

"I am going to tell her that you know and understand," I said, "and that you don't think she is wicked or anything like that. I'll tell her that Papa says it often happens and there is nothing for her to be ashamed of because she loved John and he loved her; and it was only due to his proud family that it turned out like this."

"You're putting words into my mouth."

"But you do feel that. You're not condemning Helena."

"Heaven forbid."

"I'll tell her that. I'm going to see her now. She'll be lying on her bunk as she almost always is. I am glad we all know. Now we can do something about it."

I went back to the cabin. As I thought, she was there lying on her bunk.

I said: "Come down, Helena, where I can see you. I've told my parents. My father says it happens to lots of people and it isn't going to be so very difficult. They know exactly what we shall have to do."

She had climbed down and stood facing me.

I went to her and put my arms round her. She clung to me and again that desire to protect her swept over me.

Now that we knew, Helena was a little brighter. She had lost that desperately frightened look. She was often sick and felt ill but some of the despair had gone. I think that from then on she started to think about the baby and, in spite of everything, that could not fail to bring her some joy.

She was probably meant to be a mother; and I think that if she could have married John and settled down to bringing up a big family she would have found perfect happiness.

She did spend quite a lot of time lying on her bunk. Pregnancy was not easy with her but I think the mental anguish had been greater than physical discomfort.

I spent a good deal of time with Matthew Hume; we were becoming good friends. Jacco got on very well with Jim Prevost. Jacco would, in due course, join my father in the management of Cador and he was already learning something about the estate and that meant he had a knowledge of what was going on in some of the farms.

Jim Prevost would talk of little but the land he was going to acquire and therefore he and Jacco had a good deal in common.

Matthew Hume interested me because of that earnestness of his. He was a man with a purpose, and very unusual, for although he was ambitious to a great degree to succeed in what he was doing, it was rare to find such an ambition which was not self-centered.

He had brought one or two books with him and the subject of all of them was prisons. He could hold forth eloquently. He had seen the inside of Newgate once when he had gone there with Frances to visit one of the people she had been looking after and who, she believed, had been wrongfully accused.

"Frances is wonderful," he said. "So strong. She could force her way in anywhere. She has a way with her. Oh what a place, Annora. Dark high stone walls without windows. It's opposite the Old Bailey at the west end of Newgate Street. I shudder every time I see it. Do you know there was a prison there in the thirteenth century? Imagine all the people who must have been locked up there. The suffering, the misery that has gone on in that spot! It's not the original building standing there of course. It was burned down during the great fire of London. This one was built over a hundred years after that in 1780. You've heard about the Gordon Riots? Well, it was almost destroyed then by fire and lots of the prisoners were let out. People don't care about prisoners. They put them away to be rid of them. They are a nuisance. A child steals a loaf of bread because he is hungry and he goes to the same place as a murderer. It's all wrong. People don't care enough. That great lady, Mrs. Elizabeth Fry, worked hard for them. I am privileged to have met her."

[147]

"Did she come to Frances's Mission?"

"No. I wrote to her. I told her of my interest in prisons and prisoners and she invited me to call on her. I went to see her in her house at Plashet. It was a great experience. I talked to her of Frances and the work she is doing. She was so interested. She is no longer young, alas, but she has devoted her life to reform. She spoke heart-rendingly of a visit she had paid to Newgate more than twenty years ago. She said she would never forget the sight. There were women there . . . three hundred of them with their children . . . some who had never been brought before a court of justice. They had no bedding. They slept on the floor. Their rags scarcely covered them. She could do little then but take them clothes, and this she did. She called on her friends to help. She worked for these people. She has given her life to this cause. She formed a society for the improvement of female prisoners. Goodness flowed from her. She has had a school and a manufactory set up in Newgate. Not only did she confine her efforts to Newgate but she has visited prisons all over the country and even in the Continent. Annora, I want to do something like that with my life."

"Frances feels that too."

"Frances is different from Mrs. Fry. Mrs. Fry is gentle. Frances is without sentiment, almost cynical. Frances is angry with society."

"She gets things done. That is what matters."

"Oh yes, I greatly admire Frances."

"I think my cousin Peterkin Lansdon is impressed by Frances's work, too."

"You feel like that when you go to her Mission. You feel there is something there worthwhile. It's a good thing to devote your life to such a cause . . . like Mrs. Fry. I think of her often. And there is so much more which needs to be done. Transportation, for instance. I think that is a very cruel way of treating men and women."

I told him the story of Digory.

"Seven years for stealing a pheasant! Torn from his home, from his family, for such an offence . . . and a boy, a young boy!"

"He had no home and family. He was by no means innocent. He was a thief and I believe always had been. I often wonder whether he would have changed if he had had the chance."

"Perhaps you will see him when you get to Australia."

"My father thinks that very unlikely. He says he could have been sent anywhere in Australia."

"I shall be travelling all over Australia. I want to get first-hand accounts from prisoners. Why they were accused. What the journey out was like. What happened to them when they arrived."

"My father, of course, told you something of his experiences. He was fortunate. He was allotted to a man who was just, even though he demanded a great deal from his workers. My father became a friend of his. And my father has some land over there which he has kept for years."

"I know. His is a most interesting story. His was, of course, a rather special case."

"Yes. He always says it would have been the gallows for him had it not been for my mother, who forced my grandfather to save him from that fate."

"Well, before I die I want to see transportation abolished. I want to see our prisons changed. When I have my information and my book is finished and published I want it to be widely read. I want it to awaken people's consciences. I want a bill brought in to change the law."

"You are very determined, Matthew."

"The way to get something done is to make up your mind you are going to do it."

"You are so . . . selfless."

"It is easy for me to be. Quite a number of people have to work to keep themselves and that has to be their first consideration. I am fortunate in having inherited an income which keeps me adequately if not in comfort. I can devote all my time to what I really want to do and don't have to be bothered with that tiresome business of earning a living."

"It's a great help."

"I thank God for it."

"I am so glad you are here," I said.

As we approached the Cape we encountered storms. Our ship seemed to have become frail—vulnerable to rough winds and high seas. There were times when it was impossible to stand upright. Helena wanted nothing but to lie in her bunk but Jacco and I went on

[149]

deck for we found the fresh air good for the queasiness which I think we all felt to some extent.

We clung to the rail and watched the angry water pounding against the ship's side. I think we were both wondering whether our flimsy craft could continue to take such a battering.

The crew were all at their posts and had little time for us. Jacco and I cautiously made our way to one of the benches which was slightly sheltered from the shrieking wind.

"I wonder what it's like to be thrown into the sea," said Jacco.

"We'd not have a chance."

"They say your whole life flashes before your eyes."

"I should have imagined one would have been thinking about the present rather than the past," I commented wryly. "Trying to keep afloat would take up all your energies, mental and physical."

"The Chief Engineer said this morning that he had seen worse storms. But perhaps we haven't seen the end of this."

"How cheerful you are!"

"Mrs. Prevost is laid low and I don't think her husband feels very well either. Where is Helena?"

"In her bunk. I wonder if she is very frightened. Perhaps I ought to go down and see."

"Mind how you go."

"I shall take the utmost care."

I went to the cabin. "Helena," I called. "I think the storm is abating. How do you feel?"

There was no answer.

"Helena," I said again.

I looked up. She was not there.

I was amazed. She must have gone up on deck and she had said she felt very unwell that morning and the movement of the ship greatly upset her.

I looked into the cupboard where our clothes hung very closely together as the space was so limited.

Her raincoat and boots were missing.

So she must have gone on deck.

I felt a thrill of fear run through me. She would have to walk so carefully up there. And what was her intention?

I went on deck. There was no sign of her. Jacco was not there either.

"Helena!" I cried. My voice was lost in the howling of the wind. "Helena, where are you?"

I clung to the rail and looked down with horror at the swirling waters.

Yesterday when the sea had been rough I had said, "I hope the ship can stand up to the weather. It seems a little frail." And she had replied: "If it didn't that would be an answer to everything for me, wouldn't it?"

Even that she could have had such a thought disturbed me.

Now that conversation came back to me and with it a fearful apprehension.

I felt numb suddenly. I remembered the hopeless look in her eyes. True, I had felt she was better since we all knew. She had my support and that of my parents and Jacco. None of us had allowed a shadow of reproach to come into our attitude; it had been as though we believed there was nothing reprehensible about an unmarried girl's bringing a baby into the world—and that was, without doubt, contrary to general convention.

We had all declared we would be with her. She was not alone.

And yet . . . I could not get those words out of my mind.

I hurried along the deck. Perhaps she was still there contemplating this terrible thing. Quite a lot of people thought of it when they were in a situation which seemed too tragic to face, but carrying it out to the conclusion was another matter.

I had to find her.

I went on calling her name. If I had stayed with her instead of going on deck . . . I ought never to have left her. I should have seen the mood she was in, read the despair in her eyes. How many girls over the centuries had found themselves in such a position after recklessly submitting to the demands of a lover? And how many had taken this way out?

I thought of Aunt Amaryllis who loved her daughter so dearly. I thought of Uncle Peter. What would he think when he heard his daughter had been unable to face the consequences for which he in a way was responsible? John Milward was responsible. Joe was, too, because he had exposed her father and his action had cost Helena her future happiness. I was responsible for not taking care of her, for not seeing the danger signals. It seemed to me like a chain of guilt and I was a link in that chain.

"Helena!" I cried desperately. "Where are you?"

No answer . . . just the mocking shriek of the wind and the sound of the sea battering the side of the ship.

I staggered along the deck. I must find my father and mother. I must give the alarm. But what could be done? The ship could not turn round and go back. How would they ever find her in such a sea?

I went along the deck as quickly as I could. The wind tore at my cloak; my hair was streaming about my face. I was wet with the spray for the seawater was spilling over the decks.

I clung to the rail and made my progress as quickly as I could. At the end of the deck was a small alcove overhung by a life boat. It was a little sheltered from the wind.

As I approached I saw someone huddled there.

"Helena!" I cried in joy.

Yes, it was indeed Helena and she was not alone. Matthew Hume was sitting close to her.

I hurried into the comparative shelter of the alcove.

"Helena," I gasped. "I wondered where you were. You gave me a fright."

She did not speak. She lifted her eyes to my face and they seemed full of tragedy.

Matthew said: "She's all right now. She's going to be all right. You've nothing to worry about now."

"Annora has been very good to me," said Helena. "She is the best friend I ever had."

"I know," he said.

She looked at me. "Annora, I was going to do it. It would have been so easy. I thought that in this weather they could have thought—or pretended to think—I had fallen over."

"What are you saying, Helena?"

"I came up to do it. I thought it the best way. I was thinking I couldn't go on. It was best for me and the little baby. You see, my child won't have a name . . ."

"It will have a name," I said sternly, "Your name."

"But that's not good for a baby. It's a stigma. It's not good to come into the world at a disadvantage. It's bad enough without."

She was talking as though she were in a trance. I had almost forgotten Matthew Hume.

[152]

Then he said: "Come and sit with us, Annora. It's a little sheltered here."

I sat down beside Helena.

"I was so worried," I said.

"I'm sorry, Annora."

"If you had . . . do you realize how unhappy we all should have been?"

"Just for a while. It would have been forgotten soon. This time next year you would hardly think of me at all."

"What nonsense! I should always think of you." I suddenly realized that Matthew Hume knew our secret.

I said to him: "I'm sorry you've been brought into all this."

"I thank God I was. It was fortuitous. Here I was just at the right moment. There is a purpose in it. I was sent on this ship for just this."

He was, of course, an idealist and I thought at the moment I needed someone who was practical, like either of my parents.

"Yes," said Helena, "I was going to do it. I wanted it to seem like an accident. It could have. It could seem as though I had come up here for some fresh air and fallen overboard."

"Helena, how could you think of doing such a thing? How could you hurt us so!"

"I didn't think. I just believed that it would be better for us all."

I put my arm round her and held her against me.

I said: "I am going to take you back to the cabin. You're going to lie down."

"No," she said. "I want to stay here. I feel comforted by you . . . both of you. Matthew knows about everything. I've told him."

"I knew there was some trouble," he said. "I did not know of what kind. I have just been praying that I could help, and this was God's answer. I was here at the right moment."

"You saved me from that," said Helena.

"Thank you, Matthew," I said.

"Now we have to convince her that she must never try to do this again. It's wicked. It's criminal. It's taking life . . . your own and your child's."

"Yes," said Helena, "I know. But I felt so lost and frightened. I really don't know how I can go on. I know that Annora and her parents will look after me until the baby is born, but what then? I've got to go on for the rest of my life with everyone knowing that I have a child and no husband. How can I do that?"

"You can," I said. "We're going to help you."

Silence fell on us and we sat there for a long time listening to the sea thrashing the sides of the ship.

There seemed to grow up between Helena and Matthew a special relationship. He had saved her and I was sure he could not help feeling a glow of satisfaction because of that. Anyone would be gratified to save someone's life—but with Matthew it went deeper than that. He had made it his mission in life to succour his fellow human beings and Helena had given him the most obvious chance he had ever had.

He talked to her a great deal about his object in life. I would come upon them sitting in the alcove; he would be talking and she would be staring out to sea; whether she was listening or not I was not sure, but she sat on silently while he talked.

We went ashore at Capetown—a party of us, as we had done in Madeira. It was wonderful, after so much rough weather at sea, to be on dry land and in warm sunshine. Moreover Capetown will always be for me one of the most beautiful places in the world. I think it was because I felt happy on that day.

I was so relieved that Helena was still with us. I could not have borne it if she had succeeded. In my heart I should have blamed Joe and I could never forget the sight of him, standing there putting the incriminating papers into his pocket. Between them he and Uncle Peter had ruined Helena's life; and I had played my little part in the drama by making Joe's task easy.

But she had been saved in time by Matthew and from now on I was going to be extra watchful. I looked at the blue calm waters, the great Table Mountain and the beautiful Bay and I felt more at peace than I had for a long time.

The day passed all too quickly and we were at sea again. Now we were in the calm and peaceful waters of the Indian Ocean and delightful weather seemed to have its effect on us all.

Helena said to me: "I wish I could go on sailing like this forever. I never want this to stop. But it will have to soon and then . . ."

I said: "Remember we are here with you, and when the baby is born we are going to love it so much that everything will have been worthwhile."

"Promise you won't leave me," she said. "Promise you'll stay with me forever."

"I will be with you as long as you need me."

She smiled and seemed almost happy.

We were astounded when the news broke.

Matthew announced it after we left the dinner table. There were my parents, Jacco and I, and of course Matthew and Helena and the Prevosts.

Matthew said: "Helena and I are going to be married."

We all stared at them. We had seen no real sign that there was any special attraction between them. Of course they had talked now and then, but Matthew was so enthusiastic about his mission in life that he talked earnestly about it to anyone who would listen.

For a few seconds no one spoke. Jacco recovered himself first.

"Well, congratulations. They say this sort of thing does happen on ships."

"Helena and I have made up our minds," said Matthew. "We shall be married as soon as we reach Sydney."

My mother kissed Helena and I said: "I hope you will be very happy, dear Helena."

"This calls for a celebration," said my father. "I wonder what they can offer us."

Helena was blushing and the unusual colour in her face made her look quite pretty. Matthew seemed delighted. His face was shining with virtue; and the thought came into my mind that the proposal was another of his good works. He looked very young and I thought: Is he being very noble? And does he understand what this means?

Helena stood there holding Matthew's hand. There was a look in her eyes which I had noticed in the alcove during the storm. She was like a drowning person clinging to a raft. I felt very uneasy.

My father was saying, "I am going to organize something. We must drink to this engagement. I'll see what I can get. We'll ask the Captain to join us in half an hour in our cabin."

We left Helena and Matthew walking the deck and went down to my parents' cabin.

"Well, this is a surprise," said my mother.

[155]

"It's Matthew performing another of his good deeds, I believe," put in Jacco.

"I feared that," added my mother.

"He is so earnestly good," I said. "He really does want to spend his life helping others."

"Supplying their needs," mused my father. "What does Helena need most now? A husband. So Matthew offers himself."

"And Helena . . . what does *she* think, I wonder," said my mother.

"Helena is so lost and bewildered," I told them, "so frightened that she will cling to anyone who offers help."

"This is a very special sort of help," said my mother. "Oh dear, I hope it works out well for them."

"He has the rest of the voyage to think about it," my father reminded us. "Perhaps it was all suggested on the spur of the moment. It may be that by the time they get to Sydney . . ."

"Who knows?" I said.

"They'll be able to marry easily in Sydney if they are still in the mind to," my father explained. "There won't be a lot of ceremony. They are so used to girls coming out to be married and so they get through the performance with the utmost speed."

"She was so worried about the baby," I said. "That's what she is doing it for."

"I understand that is her reason," put in my mother. "As for him . . . I imagine he has rather a simplified picture of life."

"Most good people have," I replied.

My father looked at me and smiled. "There speaks our wise girl. Now listen to me. This is their affair. What we think of this hasty marriage is of no account. They have to work it out for themselves. They have to live it. It's up to them."

"It may well be that it will work out all right," said Jacco. "I should imagine Matthew is just about as easy-going as anyone could be."

"As long as he can pursue his own virtuous road," said my father. "And Helena knows him up to a point. I know their acquaintance has been brief, but they have met every day, so compared with friendships at home when a friend or lover is seen perhaps once a week, their meetings on this ship are tantamount to months of acquaintanceship on shore. Let us wish them good luck and hope that all will be well."

"There is nothing else we can do," my mother pointed out. "They have made up their minds."

Helena, I thought, because she needs marriage for her baby and he because he needs to make sacrifices and do good works.

I wondered if they were really the right reasons for a marriage.

The Captain arrived with two bottles of what he said he kept for special occasions. Mrs. Prevost was tittering with excitement and even Mr. Prevost seemed to have forgotten his absorption with the land for a while. The Captain made a little speech in which he said that it was not the first time romance had come to his ship. There was nothing like ships for romance.

Helena and Matthew stood there accepting the congratulations— Helena still flushed and looking almost happy, or perhaps that was relief; and Matthew had a look about him of such shining pleasure which could only come from the awareness of his virtue.

He was a very good young man and I felt that I loved him for saving Helena from the rough stormy sea and then giving her a chance to escape from a situation which she found so intolerable that she was ready to die to be rid of it.

The days began to speed by. The atmosphere of the ship was changing. We were about to leave that closed world in which we had lived for so many weeks. It had been rather an unreal world, I thought, looking back. Now we were coming into reality.

People changed subtly. The Prevosts were abstracted and in Jim Prevost's eyes there was a look of faint anxiety. He had been so sure on the way out that he was going to find what he wanted. Now he was not so sure. As for his wife, I thought she seemed a little nostalgic, as though she was suddenly realizing all she was losing. After all, it must be a great wrench to go to a new country, a new life. I could understand their feelings.

And Matthew? He was becoming very excited at the prospect of finding the material he needed for his book. I could see the dreams in his eyes. He was going to marry Helena; she was to be his disciple who would share in his work. He had a simple uncomplicated way of ordering his life. Helena had changed too. It may have been that the baby was having an effect on her. Perhaps it seemed to her now like a living person—her very own child. I wondered how often she thought of John and whether she was peacefully contemplating a life ahead with Matthew. I think she was still in a bemused state, but I believed she felt herself fortunate to have found a man who would act as father to her child.

As for myself and my family—it was different with us. This was merely a visit and when it was over we should all go back to life as it had been before.

My father was perhaps a little quieter than usual. I daresay he remembered a great deal of that part of his life when he had come to her in chains—figuratively—a prisoner of Mother England, to submit to the humiliating ordeal of being chosen as someone's slave during seven years of bondage. And my mother would share his mood for their lives were so closely interwoven, and even, at periods, when she was a child, she had known him and thought of him in that land overseas.

Jacco was exuberant. He was longing to explore. He had found the entire voyage exciting and interesting, as it had been for me but for Helena's problems.

And so we came to Sydney.

I stood on deck as we approached what has been called the finest harbour in the world. And what a sight is was! It was early morning; the sun was just coming up and the sea was pale aquamarine, calm and beautiful. My father, standing beside me, slipped his arm through mine. I turned to look at him and I saw the faraway look in his eyes. I knew he was thinking of arriving here all those years ago. I turned from him to look at the magnificent harbour with its cove-like indentations fringed with foliage and numerous sandy beaches.

My mother came and joined us and we stood silently together.

It was some time before we could go ashore. We had said our goodbyes to the Captain and those members of the crew with whom we had become friendly. The Prevosts were with us when we went off. They said we must keep in touch and my father explained that we should be staying at the Grand Hotel in Sydney for a little while and then we should be going to a property he owned some hundred or so miles north of Sydney. It was known simply as Cadorsons and was near a place called Sealands Creek. Knowing a little of the land, he would be happy to advise them at any time they cared to call upon him. That seemed to give them a certain comfort and it was clearer than ever that now their dreams were about to be realized they were growing very apprehensive.

Helena and Matthew were to stay with us for the time being. I knew that Helena wanted to stay with me, but Matthew wanted to go off in search of material as soon as possible. But for the time being we should all stay at the hotel until my father had discovered what accommodation there would be for us at the property at Sealands Creek.

We went from the dock to the Grand Hotel in our buggy and as we rode along my father expressed his amazement at the change in Sydney since he had last seen it.

"It is quite different," he said. "When I was last here the narrow streets were quite dangerous because of the pigs, dogs and goats which would be getting under your feet. The buildings were shacks. Now the streets have been made wider and the buildings . . ."

"Well, it was rather a long time ago," said my mother.

"Yes. I heard that Macquarie had worked wonders."

I said: "It must be an extraordinary experience . . . coming back after all these years."

He nodded. "It brings it all back. I can see myself standing on deck with the rest of us, half blinded by the brilliant light after weeks shut up in the hold, waiting to be selected by those who would be our masters for the next seven years. But that is all in the past. Here I am with my family, and soon I shall be seeing the property I managed to acquire in spite of my degrading arrival."

"You should be proud," said my mother. "How many could do what you did?"

"Quite a number, I assure you. Just look at this city. It might be an English provincial town. It shows what can be done with energy, determination and convict labour. Look at those warehouses. Some of them are quite imposing. I would never have believed it."

We had arrived at the Grand Hotel which though it did not quite live up to its name was comfortable. There were red felt curtains everywhere held back by brass chains. They added a cheerful colour to the surroundings.

We were regarded with some curiosity by the people in the foyer of the hotel, but I expect they were accustomed to arrivals from England for I learned later how many people, like the Prevosts, were coming out attracted by the cheapness of the land and the labour of convicts which meant that they could start to build a fortune without a big initial outlay.

My father had arranged for the bulk of our baggage to remain at the docks until it could be sent straight to the property.

And so we had arrived in Australia.

Outback

The days which followed were full of new experiences.

Helena and Matthew went through a marriage ceremony in accordance with the custom here; and my parents with Jacco went to the property which was some two hundred miles north of Sydney. I wanted to go with them but Helena was so frightened at being left without me that I said I would stay behind. My father's idea was that he and my mother should "spy out the land" and find out what living conditions at the property would be like. He knew there was a dwelling house and that in the interests of the property it had been added to over the years; but he did want to make sure that conditions would not be too primitive, and before we moved out he wished to investigate.

The manager of the property had come to Sydney to welcome us. He was a man of about thirty with strong features and dark curly hair. His skin was very bronzed and his hearty manner seemed to us a little brash, but I think that was more or less natural to people here for although they had originally come from England, life here had changed them. I had the idea that some of them despised us for our courteous manners and more refined way of speaking. Gregory Donnelly was a man of the country. Strong, uncompromising, independent, contemptuous of those unlike himself, a man who would be ready to face any difficulty and, I imagined, make a good job of extricating himself. He was what Mrs. Penlock would have called "a real man." I felt a faint revulsion towards him on the first day we met.

"Hi . . . ya," he said. "So here you are, *Sir* Jake. I've been expecting you for years. We've got a lot to show you."

"This is my wife," said my father.

"Lady Cadorson," replied Gregory Donnelly, bowing his head with a gesture of respect which he managed to convey that he did not feel.

"My son . . . my daughter . . ."

Did I imagine it or did his eyes linger on me with a hint of speculation? I felt myself growing hot under his scrutiny. I felt he was trying to see too much of me, to sum me up in a somewhat crude manner.

"So what's your plan, Sir Jake?"

"I'm coming out to take a look at things. We all want to come out. We have two more with us . . . a relative of my wife and the man she will be married to very soon. We didn't expect they would be with us, and I am wondering what accommodation there is out there. That's what I want to make sure of."

"Well, there ought to be room. There's a shack adjoining the place which I could move into. Casual labour use it, but there's no one there now."

"We'll come and take a look," said my mother.

"That's best, Lady Cadorson. I don't promise the ladies there'll be what they're used to."

"We shall probably be able to get a few things in Sydney," suggested my mother.

"Reckon there'll be no trouble at all. It's a fine town, Sydney. Every time you come in there's something new. Buildings seem to spring up overnight. There's plenty of labour about. Should be another cargo coming in soon."

My mother looked horrified to hear human beings referred to as cargo—criminals though they might be.

Gregory Donnelly had a meal with us and there was a great deal of discussion about what would be needed. Helena and Matthew had been introduced to him. I saw his quick appraisal and dismissal of Helena which angered me. There was an arrogance about him which I found distinctly irritating. He was a disturbing man; his essential masculinity made one think of relationships between men and women and I would rather not be disturbed by such thoughts.

Matthew was very interested to meet him and I could see that he was preparing to ask him many questions.

There was no lack of conversation. Gregory Donnelly made sure of that.

Jacco asked how long the journey out to the property would take.

"Depends," said Gregory Donnelly. "Good horses might do the journey in a couple of days. You can take a buggy. There are two inns where you can spend a night. I usually camp down somewhere. I know the place. Been coming in and out of Sydney for years."

"You make it sound simple, Mr. Donnelly," said Jacco.

"I'm Greg," he said. "We don't stand on ceremony out here. I don't know myself as Mr. Donnelly. That all right with you, Jacco?"

"That's all right," said Jacco, and Gregory Donnelly turned his eyes on me.

"That goes for all round," he went on. He looked rather apologetically at my father. "Better to fall in with the ways of the natives. Makes for the easy way."

"I'm quickly realizing that," said my father.

And from then on he was Greg.

The nicest thing about him was his pride in his country. He talked of it with glowing enthusiasm. "There's something about a town that grows under your eyes. There have been men here whose names will always live in Sydney, though they've gone now. Their names are on our streets. When you think a short time ago there was nothing here . . . Settlers are coming in now. Oh no, Miss, er . . . Annora, we're not all convicts now."

"We know that," I retorted. "There were two people on board with us. They've come out to get land."

"Going cheaply, ha. Well, why not? Get the place going. We've got a lot to be thankful for. MacArthur brought the sheep here. We call him the father of the sheep industry, and that is quite something now. We've got wool and we've got meat. Why, they call some wool Botany Bay. That was where they first came out to with their load of prisoners and when they saw this harbour they came here and they called the place after some important gent in England."

"Viscount Sydney," said my mother.

[163]

"That's the fellow, but Macquarie is the man who made the place what it is. He said this was going to be a capital city of the world and believe me it's fast becoming one. He's built roads, houses, bridges, factories . . . We've even got our own newspaper. Yes, the Sydney *Gazette*. You can read all about it in there."

Matthew said: "I'm interested in the convicts. I'm writing a book about them and I've come to collect information."

"Well, take my advice, Matt." He had already taken upon himself to give what he considered an appropriate version of Matthew's name. "Don't let them know what they're saying is going into a book or they'll shut up like clams. You've got to get them to talk naturally. Let it come out in conversation. I'll show you a few of them on the property. They'll be ready to talk."

"That will be wonderful," cried Matthew.

"I see you're looking at me hopefully. Well, sorry to disappoint you. I'm not one of them. Came from Yorkshire. My father was a settler and it was Sir Jake here who put him in charge of the property. He died five years ago and I took over. I wasn't born here, but then, who was? But I've adopted it. It's my country and I'm proud of the way it's going."

He talked a great deal about the city and the property, the price of wool, of droughts, plagues of insects and of forest fires, which were a continual source of anxiety during the summer months.

I found myself listening with interest and wondered what my father thought of him.

I discovered later that evening.

"He's certainly got a good opinion of himself," said Jacco.

"I think we might well find a great number of his sort here," my father pointed out.

"Surely there could only be one Greg," said my mother. "Really he is most forceful . . . democratic, I suppose he would call it . . . insisting on Christian names so soon."

"I thought your manager might be a little more subservient," I said.

"We mustn't expect that here. I imagine they are no respecters of position. It's the way of the country."

"He's brash," I said.

"I thought you took quite a dislike to him," Jacco told me. "I thought he should have shown more respect to Papa."

[164]

"Oh, he wasn't disrespectful," my father defended him. "That's what you call masculine dignity."

"I thought it was arrogance," I insisted.

"I believe he's a good man from what I gather," said my father firmly. "Well, we shall find out."

"I don't see why we should delay looking at the property," said Jacco.

"No reason at all. We'll go as soon as Greg can arrange the transport." He looked at my mother.

"I'll be all right on horseback," she said. "I've been riding all my life, haven't I? A few miles of this bush or whatever they call it isn't going to worry me."

"It'll be a bit rough going. We shall stay the nights at those inns."

"Well, I must say I don't fancy bivouacking—even under the expert guidance of our Greg."

"No. I shall insist on the inns."

"Helena can't come," I said.

"Oh dear," said my mother.

"Matthew can take care of her," put in Jacco. "After all, that's his job now."

"She's nervous still. She clings in spite of everything."

My mother said: "I think Annora had better stay here while we investigate. She's right about Helena. The poor girl is in a nervous state. She went through a lot with poor little John Milward. To my mind he ought to know what's happened. Anyway, you stay here, Annora. We'll report. Trust me to see that when you come to the property you have as much comfort as I can get for you."

"I'm longing to see it all."

"So are we all," said Jacco. "I don't see why Matthew Hume can't look after Helena."

However it was finally decided that I should stay and a few days later my father and mother and Jacco set out, under the guidance of Greg, to see the property. They had acquired good horses and all that they would need for the journey. It had all been arranged with efficiency, said my father, by Greg.

Helena and I were together all the time. Matthew was out all day and would come back full of excitement. He talked to people and when he returned he kept to his room writing copious notes.

The relationship between him and Helena was a very unusual one.

[165]

I was sure he thought that he had done his good deed by marrying her and there his responsibility ended. Helena said: "It was wonderful of him, but it is not like a marriage, Annora. It couldn't be . . . after John. There couldn't be anyone else for me."

"Not after he deserted you!"

"He didn't know about the baby."

"He ought to," I said.

"Oh, I couldn't bear that. I wouldn't want him to come back to me because he thought he ought to. I think that would be something between us all our lives, and it would have its effect on the child. He might resent it because it was due to the child that he had come back. After all," she added with unexpected rationality, "if he had wanted to marry me, he would, no matter what anyone said. I mean if it had been the most important thing in the world . . ."

We took one of the buggies and went to the shops. There we bought clothes for the baby. I think Helena enjoyed that. We rode through the town and when we saw Hyde Park, we felt quite near home.

"These are our people, Helena," I said. "We shouldn't feel that we are strangers in a strange land."

"I'm glad to be here with you, Annora. What should I have done if I had had to face all this at home?"

"There would have been a way. There always is."

"But this was like a miracle. Your planning to come out here . . . and then my coming, too. Suppose I had been at home!"

"Your mother would have helped you."

"I know. But I think I should have died of shame."

"People don't die of shame."

"I should have done what I nearly did."

"No more talk of that," I said briskly. "I think this gown is absolutely lovely. Oh, Helena, I can't wait for the baby. I'm already thinking of it as ours."

It was quite a pleasant morning really. When we were back in the hotel we examined the clothes, put them away carefully and talked of the baby. I was thinking of my parents and wondering what they were doing. I imagined them, riding out in this strange land, and beside them, leading them, would be the boastful Greg.

Those days seemed long. I was waiting impatiently for the return

[166]

of my family. I longed to hear what they had found at Sealands Creek.

Matthew was exuberant. He was succeeding beyond his expectations. He was taking Greg's advice and not telling those he spoke to that he was recording their words. That way they spoke frankly.

When we dined in the evening he talked continuously of what he had discovered that day. He did not ask what we had been doing or how Helena was feeling. I have noticed since how so many of those who devote themselves to doing good for the masses have little time for the individual. True, Matthew had married Helena as an act of uncalculated goodness; but that was a spectacular event. It was the small things he had not time for.

I started to tell him about our shopping expedition but changed my mind.

"I met this fellow," he was saying. "He's been on the hulks before he came out. What luck for me! I have very little on the hulks. He told me they lived on board and left the hulk each day to do ten hours' hard labour. His hulk was in the river . . . some of them were in the docks. He described it to me so that I could almost see it. I'm getting it on paper tonight so that I don't forget a detail. There is a lower deck with a passage down the middle . . . and on each side of the passage the space is divided into wards. They have about twenty of them all jammed together for there is little space. There are no beds. They sleep in the darkness on the floor. It's a terrible life. Many of them are glad when they leave the hulks for the journey across the sea. What these people suffer! It's uncivilized. It's got to be abolished sooner or later. I'm going to see this comes about. I'm not going to rest until I do."

"I suppose," I commented, "this is how things get done in the world. People like you protest forcibly through the right channels."

"That's so. Many of the men riot. They ill-treat . . . or attempt to ill-treat . . . their guards. That's not the way. It has to be done peaceably . . . with words . . . words. That is where the strength lies."

"And it is people like you, Matthew, who do it. I wish you all success."

"I can't do much until I get into Parliament and when I do that, all

[167]

that I learn here will be of the utmost use to me."

How could one talk to such a man about baby clothes!

My parents came back without Jacco.

They said: "He's staying. He's quite fascinated by the place and he's all right with Greg and the people there."

"It's better than I thought it would be," my mother explained. "It's a long rambling sort of house, all on one floor. There are several rooms though, and we can all sleep there in moderate comfort. Greg, who was living there, says he'll move out while we're in residence. There's a sort of cottage close by to which he can go. They call it a shack. The temporary hands sleep there when they come to help with shearing and that sort of thing. There are other shacks too where the workmen sleep. It's quite a little village in a way. Apparently there are acres of land so your father is quite a landowner here. He says Greg's been adding to it when the opportunity has arisen and he's made quite a place of it."

"I'm impressed," said my father. "He's certainly done a good job."

"You're not going to get so pleased with it that you want to stay?" I asked anxiously.

My father laid his hand on my shoulder. "Don't be afraid of that."

"But we shall have to stay until Helena's baby is born," my mother pointed out.

"Yes, I know."

"After that we'll go. I think that will be quite long enough . . . even for Jacco."

"And we'll make ourselves as comfortable as possible while we're here," said my mother. "We're going shopping tomorrow. I want some beds and linen chiefly. And we shall take some food with us. There is a township nearer than Sydney but that is a bit primitive. I think about a week will be enough to do all we need."

There followed a week of activity. My mother and I shopped. Sometimes Helena came with us. She was moving into a stage of greater discomfort now and became very tired by the middle of the day. I insisted that she rest, which she did without much persuasion.

She was to come with us and so would Matthew at first, but naturally he would want to move about, otherwise how could he find the material he sought. He would be out looking for it, of course, and

[168]

while he did Helena would be staying with us.

We were now in the height of summer and the heat was trying. My father said it would be more tolerable in the country. Unfamiliar insects plagued us considerably and seemed to take a special fancy to our English skins. The flies were a pest. I had never seen so many.

At home it would be winter and from afar that seemed preferable to this overpowering heat. Each morning we were awakened by the sun streaming into our rooms; and there it stayed all day and no blinds could keep it out.

The day before we were ready to leave Greg arrived. I heard his voice before I saw him. He was talking to my father in the foyer of the hotel.

"I thought you might need a guide. It's easy to get lost in the bush. So I've come to offer myself. Some of the stuff's arrived. I've set it up where I thought you'd want it. If it's wrong, no need to fret. Some of the boys will soon shift it round to please you."

My father said: "That is good of you. I thought I knew my way. Remember, it's not my first visit; we did find our way back. But it will be a help to have someone who is familiar with the country."

"Good-o," said Greg. "We'll start at dawn tomorrow. Then we can get a good way in the morning. We can pull up for rest somewhere out of the sun if that's possible. Think it might be. Then start off again in the late afternoon. That way we avoid the worst of the heat."

I could see that he was going to put himself in charge; but I did realize that as he was on familiar terrain it was better so.

Helena could not ride and there was a buggy which Greg would drive. My mother and I would ride in it with Helena. My father and Matthew would go on horseback.

It was rather pleasant in the early morning. We set off with Greg in the driving seat, taking charge of the two grey horses. With the sun not yet up in its full fury the air was comparatively cool. We left the town behind and came into the open country. Gregory talked over his shoulder to us as he drove along pointing out the great eucalyptus trees which were such a feature of the landscape.

"We call them gums," he said. "All over Australia you'll find gums."

The yellow bushes enchanted me. They seemed to be as ubiquitous as the gum trees.

"Wattle," he said. "That's another of our plants. When you see wattle like that you know you're in Australia."

"We call it mimosa at home," I said.

"That's wattle," he said firmly.

Now we had come to what he called "the scrub," which consisted of stunted shrubs. "You have to be careful not to wander out here. You can get lost. People have been known to walk for days looking for the way and then find themselves back where they started because they've been walking in circles."

There were some beautiful birds. I recognized the parrots and cockatoos and he pointed out others—lyre birds, regent birds and fly catchers.

"*They*," I said, "must be very useful here."

"You're referring to our fly population. You have to admit there are a few in the world who love us."

The morning was wearing on and the sun climbing high.

"Soon," shouted Greg to the riders, "we'll call a halt."

He found a patch of trees—tall eucalyptus. There was not a great deal of shade. The country was rocky here and he led us to a mass of projecting stones beneath which it was almost like a cave.

"There's a little creek here," he said. "It should give the horses some refreshment. And the boulder will give us a little shade. This is where we stay."

It was pleasant lying under the boulder while my mother handed round cold meat and bread which we had brought with us. There was ale to drink.

Greg had stretched himself out close to me. He said: "Now we'll stay here. No hurry. No use going off till it's a bit cooler. We'll do better that way and we'll just about get to a little place I know where we can stay the night. They are few and far between . . . these accommodation places. Not enough to keep 'em going. This one's run by a couple whose main business is farming. Taking the odd guests is a bonus. It helps to make ends meet."

"You know your way around and we're lucky to have you, Greg," said my father.

"Should do," replied Greg, conceding the point. "I've been hereabouts quite a bit."

I asked Helena if she were comfortable and she said she was.

"I should try to sleep," I said.

[170]

"We should all try to sleep," added Greg.

So having eaten we lay there through that hot afternoon. I half dozed and found myself thinking of all that had happened in London and how far away all that seemed from this land of hot sun, bright birds, tall eucalyptus and the seemingly endless scrub. I thought of poor tormented Joe and wondered what he was doing now; I thought of Rolf who had a habit of forcing his way into my thoughts. Would he be riding round his estate making plans to enlarge it?

I had fallen asleep.

I was awakened by movement all around me.

I heard Greg cry: "Come on now. Time to get moving."

And soon we were riding through that sun-baked land. We went at a good pace. Greg said: "Want to make sure of our beds for tonight."

It was just getting dark when we arrived. It was a small house of one storey. A woman came to the door as we approached. She must have heard the clatter of horses' hoofs and the wheels of the buggy. It had not been the most comfortable of rides, particularly the last part when we had travelled at some speed.

I looked anxiously at Helena. She was pale but that was not unusual.

"Was it very uncomfortable?" I whispered to her.

"Well . . . a little."

"We do go at a spanking pace."

"But you feel safe with Greg," she said; and I had to agree with that.

We were taken in to a room which was already laid for a meal. Steaks were cooking on a big stove in a kitchen where the heat must have been intolerable.

"I've made some dampers," said our hostess. "They should go down a treat."

And we sat down and ate as we were, although Mother, Helena and I would have preferred to wash first. But we were hungry and the food tasted good.

The woman and her husband—Gladys and Tom Pickory— hovered about us while we ate. They kept refilling the tankards from which we drank beer. We were far more tired than we had realized and I could scarcely keep my eyes open.

There were only two rooms available. My mother, Helena and I were put in one, my father, Matthew and Greg in the other. We were given some water in which to wash but there was not much of it. However we lay in the one big bed and were soon fast asleep.

We were to leave at dawn, the procedure being as before so that we could get as far as possible before the intense heat of the day.

I had a few words with Mrs. Pickory before we left. She said Mr. Donnelly had told her he would endeavour to bring her a party. He had called in on his way to Sydney. "Sometimes he calls in and stays a night on his journeys back and forth. He tells other people about us. We're working this up into a real little business, thanks to Mr. Donnelly."

I noticed how her eyes shone when she spoke of him as though there was something godlike about him. I supposed it was that innate masculinity, that sense of power which appealed to some people. Even Helena had said she felt safe with him.

Then we were off again. The scenery all around was the same as we had seen before. I could understand how people got lost in what Greg called the outback.

With customary efficiency he found us a spot to rest and eat just as he had on the previous day and in due course we were on our way to the next house of accommodation; and after that it would be Sealands Creek and Cadorsons.

We were going along at a fair pace when something happened. My father called: "Look out. The wheel's coming off."

Greg brought the buggy to an abrupt halt. He leaped down and stood for a few seconds looking at the wheel. My father had dismounted.

"I can see what it is," said Gregory. "I've got tools in the buggy. Wouldn't travel without them. It'll take a little time, though."

He was looking round him. "There's a bit of shade over there. Not much. But it will have to do. All right. Ladies out. We'll get to work."

I sat down with Helena and my mother close to a wattle bush. The heat was intense and the flies swarmed round us. As we fought them off I watched the men at work.

Gregory was giving orders. Of course he would, I thought. But in these circumstances he would know what to do. My father worked with him. Matthew stood by trying to help but I doubted he was much use.

[172]

It was almost two hours before we were able to resume our journey.

Darkness was descending on us. "We can't get to that house tonight," said Gregory.

"What do you propose?" asked my father. "Go on through the night?"

"The horses need a rest. There is only one thing for it. We'll camp. Leave it to me. We'll look for a spot. I do this journey fairly often to and from Sydney. I think I know where we might stop for a rest . . . and we'll be off early in the morning."

So that was what we did.

There were sleeping bags in the buggy—one for each of us women; and there were a few rugs which would serve for the men.

Gregory said: "We'll light a fire. That'll scare off any dingo who might feel like investigating. Come on, everybody."

We gathered branches of what he called boree—a kind of wattle which he told us made good firewood, and he produced a tin with a lid and a wire handle.

"It's a billycan," he said, "something a man can't do without in the outback. It'll brew us some hot tea in no time. You'll see."

My mother said: "You seem to have taken precautions against any eventuality."

"That's what you learn in the bush, my lady."

"We're certainly grateful for your experience," added my father.

We watched him make tea; from the buggy he produced cups for us to drink out of. They were tin but in spite of that the tea tasted good. We were very thirsty.

With an air of efficiency Gregory washed the cups and the tin can in the creek and put them back in the buggy.

"Now a good night's sleep," he said, "and we'll be off at the streak of dawn. We might make Cadorsons by sundown."

I lay in my sleeping bag looking up at the foreign sky with its unfamiliar stars. I found the Southern Cross which indicated clearly that I was on the other side of the world and made home seem very far away. I could not help thinking of what I called the cosy years; riding round with my father or Jacco, waiting for Jacco to come home for holidays, wondering what companions he would bring with him. But it had not been all cosy. There had been that Midsummer's Eve which was something as fearful and horrifying as anything that had ever happened. Rolf . . . leaping over the fire, Rolf whom before then I had believed to be like one of the knights of the Round Table. Perhaps all men had their weaknesses . . . Joe with his ambitions and theft of Uncle Peter's papers; John Milward who hadn't the courage to face his family; Uncle Peter with his dubious clubs. It was a harsh world.

Thinking of that Midsummer's Eve brought Digory back to my mind. Where was Digory? Somewhere under these stars? I wondered if he was finding life tolerable. He might be only a few miles away. While we were here I could try to find him. It might be difficult but not insuperable. Perhaps the omniscient Greg could be of use.

I should be wary of asking favours of him. I felt that might be rather unwise.

I dozed and woke suddenly to find someone standing over me. I started up. It was Gregory.

He put his fingers to his lips. "Don't want to wake the company," he whispered.

Floods of relief swept over me. I remembered that my father and mother with Matthew and Helena were within a few yards of me. I felt safe. For a moment, coming out of my sleep, I had thought I was alone with this man . . . alone out here in this wild country, and the thought terrified me.

"What's the matter?" I asked.

He knelt down beside me. I could see his eyes gleaming in the starlight.

"All's well," he said. "I just came to see how you were."

"Why?"

"I wanted to make sure you were comfortable."

"I'm as comfortable as can be expected."

"Not like a nice feather bed, eh?"

"Indeed no."

"Be better when we get to the house. We'll make you comfortable there. That's what I aim to do, Annie."

"My name is Annora," I said.

"Very classy. I like Annie. It's more friendly."

"I do not like it."

"Never mind, Annie. You'll get used to it."

[174]

I heard my father's voice. "Anything wrong?"

"No, no." Gregory was getting to his feet. "Thought I heard something prowling. Dingo, I reckon. They get a bit bold at night."

"It'll soon be time for getting up," said my mother.

"A couple of hours yet," replied Gregory.

I watched him move away and I lay there, my body trembling. There was something about his manner which filled me with apprehension.

We were ready to continue the journey at dawn. The day seemed very like the previous one, the country more or less the same, too. The land was dry and when we came to a creek Gregory looked at it anxiously to see how much water there was.

He said: "The greatest curse of this land is drought. Give us rain . . . just a little of what you get in the Old Country and I can tell you this would then be God's Own Country."

He was quite informative as we rode along, telling us how he had come out as a boy and fallen in love with the place right away.

"It grows on you, takes a grip of you. It may be that some of you will be affected in this same way," he warned.

Just as the sun was beginning to fall before the horizon we arrived at our destination. It was bigger than I had imagined—a rather long low house of one storey. There were several buildings round it which looked like outhouses. We had ridden a long way without seeing any sign of habitation, so I imagined we were fairly isolated.

Jacco came running out of the house.

"I was afraid you wouldn't make it before sundown," he said.

He looked different. He wore no coat and his shirt was open at the neck; his face was bronzed; the country was already changing him.

"It's lovely to see you, Jacco," cried my mother. "How are you?"

"Fine, fine. I've had a great time. Come on in. Hello, Greg. Good to see you."

Gregory leaped down. "Where's everyone? They ought to be here. The ladies are exhausted. Maud got anything good brewing?"

"She has," said Jacco.

Several people were coming towards us . . . men in buckskin trousers and open-necked shirts.

Jacco said authoritatively; "Wally, see to the horses."

A woman came to the door of the house. She stood under the

porch watching us. She was tall and rather plump, Junoesque in fact. She had abundant dark hair which, piled up on her head, made her look even taller than she actually was.

A young girl whom I judged to be about fifteen came out and stood beside her.

"This is Maud," said Jacco to me. "She's a wonderful cook. And Rosa . . . that's her little girl."

Gregory said: "Let's get in. Introductions can be made in the morning. What we want now is food and a bed."

There was a big room which was a kind of living room and another of the same size which was a kitchen. The rest were bedrooms—five of them, apart from one room which was an office. Several oil lamps were burning in the living room and places were laid at a long wooden table.

There were steaks and hot bread called dampers, with tankards of ale; and Maud and the young girl waited on us.

I was too tired that night to take in my new surroundings. All I wanted was to sleep.

My dreams were jumbled. I was at the Midsummer bonfire and Rolf was there. He stepped out of his robe and he had horns on his head and cloven feet. Then he changed into Gregory and Joe was there saying, "I had to do it, I had to do it." Then I was alone right out in the scrub and Rolf was coming towards me. Then it was not Rolf but Gregory.

It was a nightmare and I was glad to wake from it.

I was soon asleep again and when I awoke it was to find the sun streaming into my bedroom and what had awakened me was a jeering laugh which was immediately followed by another.

I sat up in bed. Then I remembered. This was the kookaburra, the laughing jackass, of which Gregory had told us. It was the first of many times I was to hear it. But it seemed appropriate that it should awaken me on my first morning here.

The days were full of new experiences. I seemed to learn such a lot in a short time. Jacco was a mine of information. He had the advantage of having been in the outback much longer and he had eagerly absorbed everything with a fervent admiration.

He accompanied us round the property—Gregory was with us of course. We met the men who were working there. The place was apparently so large that it took several days to ride round it so of course we could only see a fraction of it. We were, as they said, "in sheep and cattle" and some of these grazed some miles away. There was one man, a jackeroo, who spent his time riding round the property, just to make sure animals were getting the attention they needed and that fences were kept in good repair.

The men lived in the rather roughly constructed shacks dotted about the place. Some had wives and children, all of whom worked in some capacity on the property. Their attitude amused me. They were in some awe of my father as the owner of the land but at the same time they regarded him with a certain contempt because of his manners and his cultured form of speech. He was an English gentleman—a breed which was not greatly admired in this part of the world. I heard one of them tell Jacco that in time he would grow into a fair dinkum Aussie, which I supposed was just about the highest compliment they could pay an Englishman. It was clear to me that Matthew was utterly despised. He was not practical; he was a dreamer, an idealist—something which there was no call for in this part of the world. As for my mother, Helena and myself, we were women, and by nature of our sex, second-class beings, suitable for one purpose only—to serve their needs in all directions.

I was most interested in Maud who, in spite of the fact that she was a woman, could keep them in order. I think they applied a special judgement to Maud. She cooked in the great kitchen where, regardless of the heat, there always seemed to be a fire going with pots on it, simmering away.

She was the widow of one of the men—a man for whom they had had the greatest respect—who had come out originally to have his own farm, and this he had done; but it had been destroyed by a forest fire and he had been left with nothing, and a wife and small daughter to keep. He had found work at Cadorsons and had proved, as Gregory said, a good right-hand man. Unfortunately he had suffered from a chest complaint which was the reason why he had come to Australia in the first place. But the climate could not save him and he had died. Maud was left with ten-year-old Rosa. That was five years ago. I thought she was a fine woman. She hated the coarseness of the men and often chided them for their habits. She guarded Rosa like a dragon and I soon began to understand why; Rosa was young and pretty and there was a scarcity of women on the property; men regarded Rosa with lustful longing.

Maud had taught Rosa to read fluently and write well. She wanted the best for Rosa.

My mother was very sympathetic and when we were all together she talked about the possibility of sending Rosa to school. My father said we should wait awhile before suggesting anything impulsively. What we needed first of all was a good midwife for Helena. That should be our primary consideration.

"There is another matter," he said. "I think Greg is after buying the property. He's the sort of man who wants to be in complete control."

"He is that already it seems to me," said my mother.

"He wants to be known as the master. It's understandable."

"What do you think? Will you sell?"

"I don't know. It's one of the things I want to decide while we are here."

"Jacco is very interested in it."

"My dear, Jacco's future is with Cador. Can you see him staying out here forever? Bringing up our grandchildren in this wilderness?"

"Heaven forbid that he should stay out here," cried my mother.

"Of course he wouldn't want that. He'll be longing to get home after a while. It's the novelty with him. He's seen little of the world. I think I shall probably sell to Greg, although I've always liked the idea of having a foot in the country. To see how it has come along since I was last here . . . well, it is just a miracle. I think there's a future here. People work. They have to. There aren't the distractions we get at home. Perhaps that is why they have made such rapid progress.

"We've got plenty of time to decide."

"Yes, Helena's affair will keep us here for a bit."

"I'll ask Maud about a midwife," said my mother. "I'd like her to be here well before the baby's due. I wonder if there is a doctor."

"I shouldn't think so . . . not nearer than Sydney."

"That's rather alarming."

"We'll be prepared by the time the baby is due."

"It's something of a responsibility. Poor girl, she seems so listless. What she would have done without Annora, I can't imagine."

"I think she's looking forward to having the baby now," I said, "and when it comes that will make all the difference."

"I'm sure you're right," agreed my mother.

The days slipped by quickly. I scarcely saw anything of Jacco. He was out all day. Matthew was planning to go on a trip farther north. He had spent his days talking to the men and making notes. Several of them were convict labour and he wanted their stories. I often wondered whether the tales the men told him were true because I had seen them with an amused look on their faces when he made notes in his book. They were the sort who would think it a great joke to, as they would say, "Lead him up the garden path."

He was a man obsessed with one idea. I imagined he did not concern himself very much with Helena nowadays. At first it had pleased him to have done his knightly deed. Now his thoughts were of a greater achievement.

He talked continually during meals when we were all gathered round the table.

"Imagine living on those ships going out!" he cried, hitting the table with his fist. He could be really vehement on this subject which was strange because on all other matters he was such a mild man. "Murderers, footpads put together with those who had stolen a handkerchief or a loaf of bread. Do you know they were kept below for a week after sailing out . . . shut down below, of course. They had to remove the hatches from time to time or they would have been suffocated. The women made the most of their sex . . . selling themselves to the marines for a tot of gin. We've got to stop this. I'm going to do it. My book is going to be a revelation."

I said: "I wonder what happened to Digory and if he survived."

Then we talked of Digory and the terrible thing that had happened to his grandmother and how he had been left alone.

Matthew listened intently. He said: "I'll find him. His story would be worth recording—particularly as I know something of his origins."

"How I should love to know what became of him," I went on. "I should be relieved if I could hear that he had settled down . . . perhaps acquired a bit of land."

"Let's hope that he came through," said my father. "He was a boy who wanted to be alone. He did not seem to care much for the companionship of others."

"It was because of his circumstances," I said hotly. "Who was there?"

"You and Jacco did a good deal for him."

"And so did you."

"I don't recall that he was particularly grateful."

"He didn't know how to show it."

"He showed it by stealing . . . unnecessarily. I could have understood it if he had been hungry. I'm afraid what happened to Digory was inevitable."

"I shall see if I can find him and get his story," said Matthew.

He was leaving the next morning for Sydney.

"I shall make the Grand Hotel my headquarters while I'm there," he told us. "So that is where you can find me if I am wanted. From there I hope to be going to various parts of Australia . . . at least where I am likely to find the information I need."

"Have you any idea how long you'll be away?" asked my mother.

"So much depends on my success. When I have collected enough material I shall want to set about the writing."

"And Helena . . . her time is not so far off."

He smiled at me. "I know she will be safe with you."

Words trembled on my mother's lips. I knew she wanted to say that at such a time a woman wanted her husband with her. But of course this was no ordinary marriage and I supposed we should all be grateful to Matthew. We must remind ourselves that he was an earnest philanthropist and there was not time in his busy life to be delayed in his work by anyone—even though it be his wife.

The next morning we said goodbye to Matthew. I think Helena was relieved to see him go. It must be trying to be continually reminded that you owed so much to one person. Not that he reminded her; but Helena could not forget.

My father was out a great deal with Gregory and Jacco was invariably with them. They would sometimes leave before we rose in the morning and come back before dark. Often we would sit out of doors in the evenings. The men made fires and cooked in the open air and it was quite pleasant when it was cooler after sundown. The men would sing songs which they had brought from home. "Coming Through the Rye," "Sally in Our Alley" and "In Good King Charles's Golden Days." One of the men had a musical instrument which he called a Didgeridoo. It was a long wooden tube which boomed when blown; another had a banjo. They would grow very merry.

Gregory was always there. I would hear his voice above the rest. He had said that the convivial evenings were part of his duties.

"You've got a group of men about working hard all day . . . they've got to have something to look forward to in the evenings. A little get-together with a bit of singing gets us all friendly," he had explained. "It keeps their minds off the women and there are not enough of them to go round. It's a consideration."

Our arrival had added considerably to the female population. I had seen some of the men and girls together and I guessed that they were more than normally friendly. I noticed the way in which the men looked at the women . . . even us. I felt that there was a certain amount of tension in such a situation.

That Maud felt it I knew, because of her careful watch on her daughter. If any man talked to Rosa her mother's eyes would be immediately upon them. It must be worrying to have a pretty young daughter in such a community.

Gregory determined to show us the country. We saw a great deal of him for although he had given up the house when we came and had gone to one of the shacks, he dined with us every day.

One day he told us about the boat.

"You see we are not very far from the sea. An hour or so on horseback gets us there. I often take a trip. I like to get some good sea breezes. We are less than two hours from Smoky Cape. You can bathe there if you've a fancy to. We must go there one day. I've got a little boat house there and my boat, well . . . she's a humdinger, I can tell you."

I went with my father, Gregory and Jacco. Helena was unable to ride and my mother stayed behind with her. We had a picnic and then Gregory took us sailing. He managed the boat with skill and it was a wonderful feeling to be sailing along on the open sea.

We kept close to the coast.

"Storms can blow up pretty fast," Gregory told us, "and we've got precious cargo aboard." This with a wink at me.

He still disturbed me. I would find his eyes watching me, calculating almost.

I thought of what he had said about the men and women and I felt he was summing me up, waiting. That made me very uneasy and when I was in my room alone at night I was thankful that my father and brother were close by.

That was a very enjoyable day in spite of the few uncomfortable moments Gregory gave me. I thought that perhaps I was imagining something which was not there. Sometimes I would think of myself

[181]

alone in the house with him and that filled me with something like terror . . . a certain sort of horror, like that which I had felt as a child when I had conjured up images of giants and hobgoblins and trembled at the thought of them . . . and in a way longed to see them in reality.

"We must use the boat more often, Greg," said my father.

"It is at your disposal, Sir Jake. Please use it when you feel the desire to do so."

After that my father often went out in the boat, sometimes with Gregory, sometimes without him. My mother and I sometimes accompanied him. Jacco, of course, was very keen on sailing. Helena did not go at all. Her time was getting very near.

Maud told us that she herself had helped to deliver babies on the property. "They arrive now and then as you'd expect and sometimes the midwife doesn't get here in time, so I've had to learn something about it."

"My mother says that we must have the midwife in residence several weeks before the baby is due."

She agreed with this and it was arranged that one of the men should go over to a township some fifty miles away and bring back Polly Winters with him.

This was done. She was small and plump with merry dark eyes, high-pitched laughter and a continual flow of chatter. She was in her mid-thirties, a widow. Men died often in this country.

"Don't be put off by her frivolous manner," said Maud. "She is a good midwife. She likes what she calls a good time but when she is doing her job she really is very good indeed."

Polly Winters examined Helena and declared herself satisfied: then she set about entertaining us with tales about the many children she had brought into the world.

She slept in the empty room which was conveniently next to Helena's; she went through the layette and said what else was needed. When she talked of the coming baby she was intensely serious; and then as soon as she stopped she would be giggling and one would have thought she was incapable of her delicate task.

I saw her often from my window. She was always talking to one of the men; and the nature of her conversation was obvious. She would roll her eyes and assume an archness which seemed very girlish and did not fit one of her age; she would almost caress them as she talked; and they responded readily.

My mother said she did wonder whether we had chosen wisely.

I reminded her that there was no choice. Polly Winters was the only midwife around and she had had to be fetched from fifty miles away.

But we could not help liking Polly. She was so good-natured, ready to help in anything that came along, full of laughter and seeming to find life very enjoyable. It was only when a man appeared that she became giggly and rather stupid.

We did not expect the birth for another three weeks but as my mother said—and Maud agreed with her—in view of the fact that Helena seemed a little delicate and it was so difficult to get help quickly, it was right to keep Polly with us.

I did enjoy riding and often went out with my father or my brother. We never strayed far from the house. My father was always careful to make sure of the landmarks. He said Gregory was right to warn us for it was the easiest thing in the world to get lost in such country.

There came a day when my father and Jacco had gone off to examine some aspect of the property with one of the men; Helena was resting. Polly liked her to and, as she said, put her own feet up in the afternoon. Whether she rested or not I could not be sure, but on one occasion I heard whispering coming from behind her door and now and then a suppressed giggle. I guessed that Polly was giving expression to her appreciation of one of the men about the property. It was not what one would have expected of a midwife with this very important task looming close; but I had to remember that this was not home. Life was different here. No one could reproach Polly for her conduct; her services were too important to us. If Polly entertained men in her bedroom when she was "putting her feet up," it was not for us to complain.

The house was quiet. I felt restless. I had a longing then for home . . . not for London where so many dramatic and unpleasant incidents had recently taken place, but for Cador.

I pictured myself riding out of the stables and meeting Rolf. I had to remind myself that things were not always as they seemed and that people hid their true natures behind a veneer of good manners. Here at least people were more frank. Polly and her men . . . Maud and her desire for her daughter's welfare . . . even Gregory. At least he did not pretend to be a courteous knight.

I felt the need for fresh air. I would go for a ride. Not far, of course. It would be the first time I had gone out alone. But I had a desire to go by myself.

There was a faint breeze which was pleasant. I broke into a gallop and was soon in the heart of shrub land.

There was something grand about the landscape. Gregory had talked a great deal about it. He had told us about the natives—"abos" he called them. He had several of them working on the land. "Good workers when they work," he said. "But you don't know what to expect. They suddenly take it into their heads to get up and go . . . 'go walk-about,' they call it. Sometimes they come back, but like as not you'll never see them again."

I thought about them. Bewildered perhaps, trying to change their lives to fit in with these people who had come and taken possession of their land.

He had told us about the animals; the kangaroos with their young in their pouches. We had seen several; and the little ones they called wallabies.

There was so much to see that was new to us. We used to sit and talk over meals when my mother liked to keep everyone at the table for as long as possible.

Gregory always talked glowingly. It became more and more clear that he loved the land and had made it his own. Through him we heard of the plagues of locusts which destroyed the crops, the raging forest fires which could encircle a hamlet and destroy it and even threaten the towns, of the most frequent threat of all to the farms: the dreaded drought.

He talked of koalas and wombats and the beautifully plumaged birds seen in some parts. We did not see many of these at Sealands Creek, but occasionally he would point out a flying mouse or a lyre bird.

I enjoyed hearing Gregory talk about the country.

I rode on thinking of him. The property extended for miles and I felt that while I was on my father's land I was safe.

All the same there had been many warnings and I had to be careful.

I looked back. Far in the distance I could see the house. I dismounted, tied my horse to a dwarf shrub and sat down.

I thought about the strangeness of everything since I had come to London and once again I found myself going over it all.

Soon, I thought, we shall go home, and things will be normal again. And Helena . . . where would she go? Would she live with Matthew . . . help him with his book perhaps? She had shown no interest in it. But she would have the baby. I had a feeling that when that child came all her attention would be for it.

The heat was intense. I had been rather silly to come out at this time of day. I closed my eyes and dozed.

I awoke with a start and for the moment wondered where I was. Remembering, I rose to my feet. There was a mist in the air. I could not see the house now. I was not disturbed. I knew the direction. I would ride back at once.

Then I saw that my horse was not where I had left it and I began to feel afraid. I had not tethered him securely enough and he must have wandered off. The mist had obscured the sun and it was not so hot now. That was a blessing. But I wished I could see the house.

I started to walk. Soon the house must be in sight.

I went on. Time passed. The mist had not thickened but I could still not see the house. A group of eucalyptus loomed up beside me. Had I noticed them before? I was not sure. There was such a similarity about the landscape wherever one was.

A terrible fear came to me then that I might be lost. I remembered Gregory's warning. People walked for miles and then found they had been going round in circles.

I sank down beside a clump of shrubs.

Was I walking round in circles? Was I walking farther away from the house? I had no way of knowing.

The best thing was to wait until the mist cleared. That might be hours. Oh, how foolish I had been. I should have started back as soon as the mist began to rise; I should never have sat down and dozed. I should have taken the warnings more seriously. I should never have gone out alone.

Must I stay all night here? What of the dingoes? I should imagine they would be rather unfriendly. There were native cats . . . wild, I expected.

I was now very frightened. There is nothing worse than being undecided in such a situation. If only I knew what to do . . . to go on walking or to stay where I was.

And while I was trying to make up my mind I heard a sound which seemed to come from a long way off. It was the call I had heard one man give to another when they wanted their whereabouts known. "Cooee."

With all my strength I called back: "Cooee."

I waited tensely; and then the call came again. I answered it. It was coming nearer. I went on calling and the answer came back.

Then Gregory came riding through the mist.

He leaped from his horse and with his hands on his hips stood regarding me sardonically.

Then he said: "You little idiot. How many times have I told you. . . ?"

"I know. I know. But who would have thought it would suddenly be misty like this?"

"Anyone with any sense," he retorted.

He took me by the shoulders and shook me.

"You ought to be spanked," he said. He laughed familiarly. "And I'd like to be the one to do it."

I tried to wriggle free but he would not let me go. Then he bent his head and kissed me firmly on the lips.

I was furiously angry. I had been very frightened, almost on the verge of despair, and my relief had been intense when he had ridden out of the mist, and now here I was out here . . . in this mysterious land, and he had dared to do what I knew he had been threatening to ever since we met.

I freed myself and stood a few paces back from him.

"I'm glad you came, but . . ." I began.

"Well that's a nice start," he replied, mocking me I knew.

"How did you know I was lost?"

"The horse came back. He had more sense than some."

"He . . . came back?"

"Thank your stars he did. Otherwise you'd have been in for an uncomfortable time, young Annie."

"I have told you I don't answer to that name which is not mine."

"You're in no position to give orders now are you, Annie? You've got to knuckle under now and do what dear kind Greg tells you."

"Take me back to the house."

"Say please, Greg."

"Please."

"All right. That'll do. Come here."

"Please do not attempt to do that again."

"What if you were to ask me to?"

"That I can assure you will never happen."

"Don't be too sure of that."

"Do my parents know I'm lost?"

"No. No one knows. They would have been out of their minds to think their little daughter was lost in the outback. You're a precious little chick, you know."

"Perhaps you should remember that."

"Oh, I do. I do. Otherwise I wouldn't be handling you with the kid gloves. I'd be giving you something to remember me by."

"What would that be?"

"Would you like me to show you?"

"I really don't know what you are talking about."

"You will, Annie, One day you will."

"Are we going back?"

He nodded.

"You'll have to ride with me. I don't know if that will offend your ladyship's finer feelings . . . but there is only one horse."

"I realize that."

"Come on then." He leaped onto the horse, then leaned over to lift me up beside him. He kept his hands on me longer than necessary. "You'll have to hold me round the waist," he said. "Hang on . . . tightly."

"I know."

"All right. Let's go."

My relief was intense. Soon I would be home. The mist would not deter him.

He walked the horse through the scrub.

"You must have felt very pleased to see me," he said. "You were getting scared, weren't you? And you were right, too. It's no picnic spending a night in the outback, I can assure you, unless you are in the right company. That was a pleasant night we spent on the way out. Do you remember how I guarded you? Well, you wouldn't have had me there if I hadn't come out to look after you, would you?"

I was silent.

"Hold tighter," he said. "Don't want to fall off, do you? Do you know, I am really rather enjoying this. Riding to the homestead with my Annie's arms around me."

I took them away.

"Hey! Be careful," he said. "A sudden jolt and you'd be off."

I put my arms back. He patted one of my hands. "Do you know, Annie," he said. "I'm very fond of you."

I said: "How far are we from the house?"

"Far enough to give us time for a little chat."

"There is nothing to be said which cannot be said in the house. Let's go faster."

"Trust me to know how we go," he retorted. "I could see you becoming a fair dinkum Aussie . . . in time. This place will grow on you like it has on me. You're free out here. You've done with most of the rules and regulations . . . you go your own way . . . you're a real person."

"I feel I *am* a real person at home," I said.

"Oh, so polite . . . saying the right thing or what's expected of you. How do you know what people are really feeling?"

"Sometimes it's better not to know."

"That's something I don't agree with. Annie, let's get to know each other. You're so standoffish. Sometimes I think you don't like me very much. But that's not true, is it? That's just your English hypocrisy."

"In the language of the fair dinkums, it's true," I said.

He laughed.

"You and I would get along fine, Annie."

"Let us at this moment concentrate on getting back to the house."

"Tell me, do you have a lover in England?"

"You are being impertinent."

"I just wanted to know. It's important to me."

"As far as I'm concerned this conversation is over."

"As far as I'm concerned it's still on. I give the orders at the moment, Annie. Where would you be now without me?"

"I daresay I could find my way back."

"Shall I put you down so that you can do so?"

"Don't be absurd. Just go on . . . quickly."

"I must say you are the most ungracious maiden in distress I ever rescued."

"I suppose the others were eager to repay you for your services?"

"That's just about the case, Annie. Let's be serious. I like you. I like you very much."

I was silent. How much farther had we to go? I wondered. I was a little afraid of him and the alarming thought came to me that I was at his mercy.

"Just suppose that you and I got together . . ."

"Got together? What do you mean?"

"Suppose we married."

"Married! Are you sure you are feeling quite well?"

"Never better. It's been a dream of mine ever since I saw you to have your arms round me like this."

"Of necessity."

"Oh I'll settle for that . . . for the time being. It would be just right. You're the sort. Plenty of spirit. That's what I like. I reckon you and I were made for one another."

"And I reckon you have a touch of the sun. They say it brings on hallucinations."

"I'm just looking truth straight in the face. I want you, Annie. I think of you all the time. Now I've seen you, there's no one else who'll do for me. Think what we could make of this place. We'd expand. We'd have a house in Sydney. We'd have people . . . entertain . . . just so that you wouldn't miss the Old Country. You could play the gracious lady. It would be pretty good, I promise you. You don't say anything . . ."

"I'm just stunned," I said.

"You'd only have to tell me what you want and it would be yours."

"Very well. I want to go back to the house."

"You're a hard woman, Annie," he said, sighing deeply with mock resignation; and just at that moment the house loomed up out of the mist.

I was greatly relieved.

He leaped down and turned to lift me. He looked up into my face and we were very close to each other for a second or so. Clearly I saw his thick dark hair curling about his temples and the mockery in his eyes; and twinges of alarm came to me in spite of the comfort of seeing the house so close by and knowing my family was there.

He kept his hand on my shoulders and I said quickly: "Thank you for bringing me home."

"There's nothing I wouldn't do for you," he said. "Remember that."

I turned and ran into the house.

My mother came into my room followed by my father. Gregory had come into the house and told them how he had rescued me.

They were very disturbed.

"I cannot understand you, Annora," said my mother. "The times you've been told about going out alone!"

"I didn't go far. I should have been all right if it hadn't been for the mist."

"That's one of the hazards," said my father impatiently. "You should be ashamed of yourself."

"I am," I said. "Do stop scolding. I promise I won't do it again. I want to go home . . . soon."

"Well thank Heaven for Greg," said my mother. "And thank goodness your horse came back. It was wonderful of Greg to go and look for you."

"It was miraculous . . . the way he came across you," added my father.

"Well, he gave the bush call and I answered."

"There's not much he doesn't know about this country," said my father admiringly. "But we'll go home as soon as we can. I begin to feel a bit homesick, too. Don't you, Jessica?"

My mother admitted that she did.

"As soon as this business of Helena's is settled we'll go. And I think I shall sell to Greg. He's made a jolly good thing of this place and I fancy he'd do even better if it were his own."

"Promise me," said my mother to me, "that you will never do anything so silly again."

I promised.

She hugged me for a moment and I felt so glad to be back with them; but I heartily wished Gregory had not been my rescuer.

I found sleep difficult that night. I kept going over what he had said. There was such purpose in his eyes and I think it was that which frightened me.

Maud had said once on some very trivial matter: "Oh, Greg wants it and Greg always gets what he wants."

Ominous words. But I was my own mistress. No one was going to force me to do what I did not want to.

Sleep would not come.

It was midnight when I heard a movement near my window. There was someone out there . . . close to the door.

I stood at the window and looked down. It was Gregory. My heart was beating wildly. How dared he! Was he coming in? What did it mean? But the door was locked. It was always locked at night. He himself had said that we must lock up carefully because of prowlers who might be looking for something they could pick up. Bushrangers were hardly a danger. They would not attack a household where there were so many men about.

Did he think he was coming to me? For what purpose? The answer was obvious. Did he think he could overpower me with his magnetic charm—or whatever he thought it was? Did he think he was irresistible to me? To come to the house was a very bold thing to do. I only had to scream and I would wake my parents along the corridor. If my father caught him he would be dismissed. He would never have a chance of owning the place.

A movement along the corridor. Someone was there. I opened my door and peeped out. I saw Polly Winters in a low-cut nightdress exposing her considerable bosom as she went silently to the door.

I shut my door and listened. The front door was opened . . . just a whisper . . . almost imperceptible. They would both have had long practice of this sort of clandestine nocturnal event.

When I opened my door again, they had gone . . . into Polly's room.

I thought: This is intolerable. And under my father's roof when only today he had asked *me* to marry him.

The man is a monster, I told myself.

I went back to bed, but not to sleep. I lay there thinking about riding on the horse with him. I was more angry with him than I had believed I could ever be with anyone.

I had thought it would be a good idea to be ready for him when he left the house in the morning, to confront him and let him know I understood where he had spent the night.

I wanted to tell him how I despised him, and that I would let my parents know the sort of man he was. I would let him see that he was not the mighty conqueror he imagined himself to be.

I must have dozed for it was fairly late when I arose. I heard Maud in the kitchen. She always let herself in very early and two of the women came to help her get the breakfast.

So I was too late to catch him.

I did not tell my parents. I did not see how they could send him away. He was so necessary to the property. Why should I bother about his relationships with women? It was not as though Polly had not welcomed him. She must have arranged to let him in.

Helena was getting very near to her confinement. She was surprisingly calm. She said to me one day: "I feel so much better since Polly's been here. She's so comforting. She's always telling me about 'her little babies.' She does love them so much."

People had so many sides to their natures.

I tried Maud.

I said to her: "Don't you think Polly is too fond of the men?"

"Well, she's certainly fond of them," said Maud.

"And they of her, I imagine."

"Men are always fond of women who are fond of them. It flatters them and there's nothing they like better than a bit of flattery."

"Don't you think some of them like women who don't like them at all?"

"Oh, that's in a different way. That's the challenge. They like that, too."

"It seems to me they like all sorts."

"That's probably right."

"I er . . . believe Polly invites men to her room at night."

"That wouldn't surprise me."

"And you . . . think we should accept that?"

"There's not another midwife round here and once the baby starts to come she'll forget about the men. She's one of the best at her job. You have to put up with people's ways if they're good at what they've come to do."

"I see," I said. "That applies to the men here too."

She looked quickly at me. "That's always a problem. There aren't enough women in the country. They need them, you know. We have to shut our eyes to a lot of things out here which wouldn't be acceptable at home."

"I understand that."

"It makes morals not quite the same."

"Can't they marry?"

"Most of them do."

"You'd think Gregory . . ."

She smiled. "Oh he'll marry when the time is ripe. He's waiting."

[192]

"Waiting for what?"

"For the right moment."

"And in the meantime?"

"Well, he's a man like the rest of them . . . more so, perhaps."

I had an idea that she might know that Polly's nocturnal visitor was Gregory Donnelly.

She could shrug it aside. I could not. To me it seemed the height of depravity when, that very day, he had asked me to marry him.

All thought of the matter was driven from my mind because the next day Helena's pains started. It was amazing how Polly threw off her frivolity and put on the mantle of the midwife. The white coat she had brought with her was the outward symbol of her professionalism and that was certainly in no doubt when she took charge.

She gave her orders in a sharp crisp voice and we were all eager to accept her authority.

It was as though she had changed her personality entirely.

We had all been very anxious about Helena; her listlessness had disturbed us. Maud thought it was due to the fact that she had an indifferent husband. Both Maud and Polly had a poor opinion of Matthew; but there was, naturally, so much that they did not know.

Her labour went on for two days while the house was plunged into a state of fearful expectancy. Even Jacco was affected and talked in whispers.

We were all seated in the living room waiting. Polly had summoned Maud to help her, for Maud over the years had gathered certain experience and had on one occasion delivered a child when help was long in coming.

Our relief was intense when we heard the cry of a child.

Maud came down to tell us.

"It's a boy," she said.

I had not seen Helena so happy since the days of her engagement to John Milward. She sat up in bed holding the baby while we all stood round declaring our admiration for the infant.

Polly was beaming with satisfaction as though the baby was entirely her creation. All of us were deeply moved. As for myself I could not take my eyes from the baby. It seemed extraordinary that one could marvel at ten tiny fingers, ten toes and a blob of a nose but

I did—and so did my mother and Helena. The men were a little aloof though there was certainly general relief that Helena's baby had come safely into the world and that she, though exhausted now, survived her ordeal.

The days went quickly by; I was with Helena most of the time. I was allowed to hold the baby. Polly reigned supreme. She had promised to stay for two weeks after the birth for, she admitted now, she had been a little worried about Helena.

Polly bustled and twinkled and laughed; every time I saw her I thought of her lying with Gregory in her bed, making love. It was a repulsive thought—and yet there was Polly, so happy, so pleased with life, talking about little babies. "I reckon," she said, "they're the nicest things God ever thought of. Mind you," she added, "there's other nice things, too. But when I've just brought a little one into the world, I don't think there's anything as lovely as a little baby."

How strange people were! Polly, the baby lover and the wanton companion of men like Gregory Donnelly. If there had been love I could have understood it, but this was plain lust.

Rosa came in and held the baby. She was such a pretty girl and different from the young girls I had seen about the property. In a way she seemed younger. I expected this was because her mother sheltered her from the crudeness around her. Not an easy task, I imagined.

I thought again: I want to go home. And now that the baby is born we can start making our plans.

There was the baby's name to consider. Helena wanted to call him after John.

"After all," she said, "he is John's."

"Why not vary it a little? Jonathan is a name used in our family."

"Jon," she said. "John without the H. That will make his name a little different from his father's."

So the baby became Jon and we were soon calling him Jonnie.

Our time was taken up with the baby. I was learning a great deal from Polly; how to hold him; how he should be bathed; how to dress him; how to rock him.

"You'd be a good little mother," Polly told me. "Better see about getting one of your own."

She nudged me and went off into one of her fits of laughter. I flushed painfully thinking again of her and Gregory Donnelly together.

She was shedding her midwife's skin just like a snake does and becoming the flighty woman with promiscuous habits. There was nothing else snakelike about Polly Winters.

Soon she would be gone to some other homestead looking for a little baby to bring into the world and new men to comfort her at nights. And we should be gone, too. I had seen signs of restlessness in my mother.

I desperately wanted to go. I wanted to get away from Gregory Donnelly. He disturbed me. He aroused images in my mind which I wanted to banish. I supposed that was what people would call life. I wanted to remain apart from it for as long as I could.

There was one thing I would greatly regret on leaving Australia and that was that we had been unable to find Digory. I often talked about him to my father.

"I know how much you wanted to find him," he said. "You wanted to make sure that he was all right . . . making a life for himself. He seemed to me a survivor. But I agree with you that it would be good to know. Don't give up hope. We might find him even yet. Everywhere I go I make enquiries, but it is rather like looking for the needle in the haystack. But you never know what's going to turn up."

Rosa was often in the room we called the nursery. She adored the child. She confided in me that when she grew up and married she intended to have ten children.

"Do you want to be married?" I asked.

"Oh yes. But I've got to wait until I'm a little older."

"Have you decided on the bridegroom?"

"Oh yes," she said. "I've always known."

"Oh? Who is it?"

She opened her pretty blue eyes very wide as though astonished by my ignorance. "Mr. Donnelly, of course."

"Oh . . . Mr. Donnelly! Do you . . . like him?"

She nodded. "He's the finest man around here. My mother says he's the only one for me."

I was silent. I could understand Maud's reasoning. Rosa was not for one of the men from the shacks, not for one of the hired hands; she was for the master of them all; and that was Greg Donnelly. That he was a philanderer did not seem to affect Maud. Perhaps she believed that when he was married he would settle down.

She probably thought he would own the property one day. That was his ambition of course, and hadn't she said he was the sort of man who would get what he wanted?

Poor Rosa. I was beginning to understand a great deal. It was not that he wanted me. He wanted the property; and I was the key to the property. It belonged to my father and it was very possible that if Gregory Donnelly married his daughter, the property would be a wedding present.

It was all hideously clear.

I hated the man more than ever.

We were at dinner. In the room which had become the nursery now that Polly Winters had gone, the baby was sleeping. Gregory was dining with us as usual and I had become more aware of him. Every time I looked up his eyes would be on me and he would give me that meaningful smile which embarrassed and infuriated me. He was like a man who was biding his time. I began to dread these meals because of his presence.

My father was saying did we realize that we were already into May?

"It's eight months since we left home," he said.

"And time we were thinking of getting back," added my mother.

"It's been a great time here," said Jacco with a hint of regret.

"A wonderful experience," my father agreed. "But I often ask myself what has been happening at home during our absence."

"I suppose you have a good man there," said Gregory.

"Excellent. We couldn't have left otherwise. He's been in complete charge many times . . . but never quite so long."

"It will be summer there now," said my mother nostalgically.

My father smiled at her. "Oh, I know you can't wait to get back."

"What about you, Helena?" asked my mother.

"I . . . I don't know. I shall have to make plans."

"You won't want to wait here for Matthew. You'd better come back to Cador with us."

"Yes . . . I'd like that."

"Annora doesn't want to part with Jonnie, you know," said my mother smiling at me.

"I admit it," I said.

Helena smiled but I could see she was uneasy at the prospect of having to face life in England. Here she had been lulled into a certain peace. She had her baby and she was with us.

My father said: "I think we might make arrangements to leave at the end of June. That will give us time to see a little more. Greg, where is Stillman's Creek?"

"Stillman's Creek? Oh, that would be up north. Halfway to Brisbane, I think."

"Have you ever been there?"

"No. But I've heard of it. A fellow called Stillman came out here and got hold of the land for next to nothing. I don't know what happened to him. Droughts are a bigger problem up there than even down here. Are you interested in the place?"

"I just heard it mentioned and wondered if you knew it. I'd like to do a little more sailing before we go."

"Do it soon. We get some fierce winds next month."

"That would be fine," said Jacco.

"Could be too much of a good thing," Gregory commented.

The conversation turned to what was happening in the property and when we left the table Gregory followed my father to the stables. I saw that they were talking earnestly.

I guessed that our giving a definite time for our departure had made Gregory more determined to thrash out the matter of buying the property.

When they came back to the house I went to my parents' bedroom. It was the only place where we could talk in privacy; and both Jacco and I often went there to do this.

Jacco was already there and I expect he had the same idea as I had.

"Did you really mean we were going in June?" asked Jacco.

"Yes," replied my father. "Most definitely. We shouldn't have stayed so long but for Helena and her baby."

"What's going to happen to her when we get back?" asked my mother.

"We did say she could come with us," I reminded them.

"It'll work out," said Jacco.

"Yes," I agreed. "She'll come home with us and then we'll decide."

"Well, let's make the most of the time left to us," said my father.

[197]

"What about sailing tomorrow?" suggested Jacco.

"All right. Just the family, eh? Would you like that, Annora?"

"Just the family. Yes. Helena won't want to come."

"The four of us then," said my mother.

"Have you decided to sell the property to Gregory?" I asked my father.

"Yes, I think I have. It seems the reasonable thing to do. He's made an excellent job of it. All I had to begin with was a very small patch. His father was a great help to me. I was doing quite well before I left because I had some experience of the country during my servitude. I certainly chose the right man in his father; and his son is such another."

"He's a very masterful man," added my mother. "Just the sort who will get on and make something of his life."

"I'll have to put it into motion right away," said my father. "These things take a little time."

"Can he afford to buy?" asked Jacco.

"My dear chap, I shan't be hard on him."

"So you would sever all ties with Australia?" I asked.

"Well, my dear child, what do we want with it? Cador takes all my time. And it is going to take all Jacco's. We don't want property on the other side of the world. I don't know why I hung on to it for so long. This visit has been of the utmost interest, but would any one of us want to come again? Think of all the discomfort of the voyage . . . and we do miss certain amenities, don't we?"

"That is an indisputable fact," said my mother. "I think it is an excellent idea to hand it over to Gregory who is really superb in his way, and in his right element."

"He's a pioneer by nature. He'll get a good bargain and he deserves it. I told him I'd give him my decision within a few days. I think he knows what the answer will be. And then . . . it's home for us."

"And tomorrow we go sailing," I said.

"There are a few places I want to see," said my father. "But I can do that while we clinch the deal."

I went to bed that night with a feeling of relief. This strange experience was almost over. Soon we should be leaving the property to Gregory Donnelly—and that was what he wanted; we should be returning home to England which in spite of weak noblemen, aspiring politicians with grudges and prosperous brothel-keepers, was at least home!

I had no idea when I awoke that morning that this was to be one of the strangest and most tragic days of my life.

I was awakened by Helena who stood by my bed.

She said: "Jonnie is coughing and he's rather hot."

Immediately I got out of bed. I went to the nursery. I picked up Jonnie. He was a little feverish but he gave me that lop-sided toothless look which we interpreted as a smile.

I said: "I don't think there is much wrong with him, but I'll get Maud. She's had experience and will know."

I dressed and went to find her. She came at once.

"It's a slight chill," she said. "Nothing much, I'm sure. We'll just keep him warm and he'll be right as rain tomorrow."

Helena was a little panicky.

"Are you going to be out all day?" she asked.

I said that I was.

"I wish you weren't going," she said in a worried voice.

I hesitated. "All right . . . I'll stay. The others can go without me."

My mother was disappointed. "Really, Helena does make demands on you," she said.

"I don't mind. I can sail another day. I would be worried all the time about the baby if I came."

My mother kissed me and said, "Well, we're all very sorry you won't be with us, but I understand. You stay and look after Helena and the baby."

They went off early. During the morning the baby seemed normal.

"I told you so," said Maud.

"I get so frightened," Helena explained.

"I know. They call it first-baby nerves. You'll be better when you've had a few more."

Helena looked startled at the prospect and I thought: That will never be. Hers is the most extraordinary marriage. At first we had thought it was such a convenient way out. At least it had given Helena married status which was so necessary as she was to have a child; but I doubted whether much good would come out of it.

Matthew had not returned. We had heard from him and Helena had written to the hotel in Sydney where letters might eventually reach him. There was a small township near us where letters could be delivered and posted. One of the men went in three times a week to take and collect mail. In a letter Matthew had said that his research had taken him to Van Diemen's Land and he would send an address from there.

Helena had written telling him that the child was born but had had no reply to that so perhaps he had not received that letter. My parents had said that when we left we should have to let him know that we were leaving and that Helena was coming with us. But perhaps by then we should have had an address from Van Diemen's Land.

I had heard the term "husband in name only." Matthew was certainly that.

A wind sprang up during the morning. I heard Gregory Donnelly shouting to some of the men.

Maud was cooking in the kitchen and I went to her. "Is anything wrong?" I asked.

"Wrong?" she said.

"I thought I heard Greg shouting orders and there seemed to be a certain tension."

"It's the weather again. It's always something. They don't like this wind."

"It's unusual," I said.

"It comes now and then. They have to make preparations. It can do a lot of damage. I daresay Greg is making sure they take precautions."

I went to the baby. He appeared to be sleeping peacefully.

During the afternoon the wind grew fierce. I looked out of the window. The few trees were swaying; they looked as though they might be torn up. The wind battered them savagely; and I thought of my parents and Jacco.

They had been delighted at the prospect of wind—but not of this strength.

Gregory came into the house. I heard Maud talking to him.

"They wouldn't have taken the boat out in this weather," he said.

I ran out to him and he saw the anxiety in my face.

"What if they have taken the boat?" I asked.

"They wouldn't," he replied with conviction. "Nobody would on a day like this."

"But they left early. They might have been out at sea before it became so bad."

He looked away from me.

"I reckon they changed their minds," he murmured. "Your father was saying he wanted to do a bit more exploring."

I went back to Helena. She was still sitting with the baby who seemed to have recovered completely.

I wished that I had gone with them. Not knowing where they were was worrying.

In the evening the wind abated. But at sundown they had not come home.

I sat up all night waiting for them. Helena sat with me. We spoke little. We were afraid to put our thoughts into words. We just sat there, ears strained for the slightest sound of their return.

And so we waited.

But they never came back.

How I lived through those days which followed I do not know. I was completely numb. I could not believe that this terrible tragedy had overtaken me.

My father. My mother. My brother. The people I loved best in the world . . . all taken from me.

I could only console myself that I was dreaming. This could not have happened to such vital people. They had all been brimming over with life. I could not imagine a world without them. Always they had been there—the most important part of my life.

Helena tried to comfort me. She surprised me. She came right out of her lethargy to share my grief. Maud, Rosa, all of them—and particularly Gregory Donnelly—seemed to have undergone a change. He was quiet, gentle, and above all strong. But I wanted none of them. There was only one thing in the world I wanted and that was the return of my loved ones.

They had found the remains of the boat. It was washed up on the shore and Jacco's body with it. My father and mother they did not find.

I lived on in that strange half world from which I could not rouse myself; nor did I want to for to do so would have brought me face to face with the enormity of what had happened to me.

There was one terrible day when a man came to see me. He insisted on talking to me. He wanted to know about my father mainly. At first I talked and then suddenly I was so overcome that I begged him to go away.

He talked at length to Maud and Gregory and most of the people on the property. I learned afterwards that he was from the Sydney *Gazette*.

The story was headline news. My father with his wife and son were drowned. He had come out as a convict to serve a seven-year term at the end of which he had acquired land; then he went home to claim estates and title in the Old Country. However, Australia and his past had lured him back . . . to his death.

It was a story, of course, which appealed to the readers. It went on prominently in the papers for several days.

These papers were kept from me for a while, but in time I discovered them and I read them through my tears.

I was too numb to care what happened, what they said. I could make no plans. I just wanted to stay in my room and try not to think.

Sleep was my only relief and they made sure that I had it. They gave me something . . . and I was grateful for that.

And then I was ill.

That was perhaps a blessed relief. It was some sort of fever. They cropped my hair and for a long time I did not know what was happening to me, nor where I was.

Nothing could have been better for me really. What I craved was forgetfulness. I wanted to go into a long sleep and never come out of it.

It was August before I began to get well. The tragedy was a little farther away but I knew it would be with me all my life. I was like a different person with my short hair which was beginning to grow in a short bob which just covered my ears.

My only real interest was the baby. He was now nearly four months old, a beautiful child, a little like Helena. She used to come in in the mornings and put him into my bed. He would pull at my short hair and try to catch my nose in his chubby fingers. He helped to soothe me and to a certain extent he did charm away some of my sadness.

"He knows you," Helena told me.

How kind everyone was to me! Rosa used to come and sit with me and talk to me; she showed me her embroidery which her mother was teaching her. She was learning how to keep house. "I shall have to when I get married," she said. She was clearly looking forward to the day when she would be. She looked upon Gregory Donnelly as a god almost. I supposed that was how her mother had brought her up to regard him. That was wise, no doubt, for if the day ever came when she married him, he would be sure of her uncritical devotion.

I had hardly been aware of him during the weeks of my misery. I had indeed been aware of no one except the baby and Helena who had been with me most of the time and had taken on a new stature in caring for me, so that she no longer seemed the helpless creature she had been.

Maud made special dishes for me.

"Come on," she would say. "Just try a little to please me . . . to please us all."

I would eat just for that reason. I drifted along not caring about anything, trying not to remember. I wanted to forget everything of the past for there had been very little of my past in which they did not figure. They had always been there . . . my beloved ones . . . they had cared for me, guided me, watched over me, given me their very special love.

I used to make up fantasies. They had been picked up at sea; a ship had taken them somewhere far away. One day they would walk in. But Jacco was dead. They had found his body. But my father and my mother . . . where were they? I knew in my heart that I should never see them again.

I cursed the boat. I cursed the wind . . . everything which had taken them from me.

Then the letter came.

It was from the lawyers who had taken over from Rolf's father when he had died and Rolf had decided he did not wish to go into law.

They had heard the grievous news and they reminded me that on the death of my parents and my only brother, I had become the owner of the Cador estate. I was in possession of considerable property and wealth; and consequently there were many questions to be discussed. They thought it would be advisable for me to return to

England at my very earliest convenience. I would have to decide what was to be done about the Australian property. My father had written to them of his wish to sell and they understood there was a prospective buyer.

They were my obedient servants, Yorke, Tamblin and Company. I let the letter fall from my hands.

With it came certain reality. I had to come out of my fantasy world where I could delude myself into thinking this was a nightmare from which I should wake when my parents came into my room.

I had been ill; I had been in a fever; I had had hallucinations. No longer could I tell myself that.

I had to face the truth. They were gone forever. I was left desolate, alone, but a woman with responsibilities.

When Helena came in, I said to her: "We shall go home."

She nodded. "When you are stronger. You have been very ill. Just yet the journey would be too much for you."

"I've had a letter from the lawyers. I shall have to go back to Cador."

"When you go, I shall come with you. We shan't be parted, ever."

"No. We have suffered . . . both of us. But we have to go on. So you'll come to Cador with me?"

"I shall go where you go."

"I don't think I can face it yet, Helena. There are more memories there than here. It will seem that at home they are everywhere . . ."

"Perhaps you would rather not go to Cador?"

"Where else? London?"

She shivered.

"It would have to be Cador," I went on. "You see, Helena, Cador is now mine. I am sure they never thought of this. My father . . ." My voice broke and I forced myself to go on. "He was not old . . . and there was Jacco and there should have been Jacco's children . . . and to think of him . . . oh, Helena, I can't go on."

"Then let's stay awhile. You can stay here as long as you like. This is your place, isn't it, for all that it seems to belong to Greg Donnelly."

"I just want to drift. I can't go home yet. I'll have to write to these lawyers. I'll tell them I'll come when I'm ready."

She nodded. Then she said: "It suits us here . . . both of us . . . shut away from things that remind us and hurt us."

[204]

"Strange," I said, "I was so looking forward to going home."

I felt the tears falling down my cheeks. I realized with amazement that it was the first time I had wept since it happened.

The weather was less hot now. This was winter. It seemed rather like our spring. I hardly noticed the change. I did not notice anything. It was sunrise and then it was sundown . . . and I went on living in limbo. I did not want to emerge. I was afraid to, for then I had to face my loss.

"Time heals," Maud had said. I supposed the time-honoured cliché was true. It wouldn't have lasted so long if it hadn't been. Time did heal. It must. Did I feel any less bereaved, any less desolate than I had on the day they had brought me the news that that broken boat had been washed ashore?

I just wanted time to pass . . . to put as long as I could between myself and that tragedy. I only wished I could believe that in time it would be easier.

I was in my room a great deal. I had no desire to go out. I did not want to talk to anyone but Helena. I did not want to see anyone but her and the baby.

I would lie on my bed during the long afternoons, waiting for sundown and the night which followed, when I might sleep and escape into dreams where my parents would be with me. But then would come the awakening, that deadly realization that what I had thought I was experiencing was only a dream—and I was alone again.

That afternoon there was a knock on my door.

"Come in," I said thinking it was Helena.

But it was Gregory Donnelly.

I did not feel the apprehension or annoyance which I should have before. I was just indifferent.

"I have come to talk to you," he said. "May I come in?"

To ask permission was so different from the manner he had previously employed. But then everything had changed—even he.

I nodded wearily. He brought up a chair and sat down.

"You look better," he said.

I did not answer.

"We'll soon get you well. Maud says she thinks you're picking up."

[205]

Still I said nothing.

"I want you to know I'm going to look after you."

I said quietly: "Thanks, but I can look after myself."

"No," he said softly. "You need someone. I'll tell you what you need. You need a new life. You want to start afresh."

"Yes," I said. "I need a new life."

"I can give it to you. We'll do anything you want. We'll go away for a while."

"I shall go home," I said.

"Later . . . yes. I'll come with you. You'll need someone to help you."

"To help me?"

"A big burden has been thrust on you. You'll need someone beside you . . . someone who cares for you. You need a husband. Don't delay any longer, Annora."

For the first time since the tragedy I smiled. He was trying to please me. He even called me by my rightful name. He was not going to run the risk of irritating me with his Annie.

I thought, He is asking me to marry him. Why? He wants the property. But I have so much now. Perhaps his ambitions have grown.

Yes, I felt a little better. I allowed my dislike of him, my distrust of him full rein. It took my thoughts from my grief to a certain extent. I let him go on.

"You're young. You need someone . . . a man . . . to look after you. You need me."

I said then, taunting him a little: "I don't think you realize the extent of my responsibilities. I have estates in Cornwall . . ."

I saw the look in his face. He knew. Had he seen the lawyer's letter? Or had he guessed? He know that my father owned large properties in Cornwall and it was obvious that Jacco would be the heir. But they were gone, both of them . . . and I, the helpless daughter, was left.

I felt helplessness slipping away from me. I even experienced something I had never thought to feel again, pleasure in leading him on—this ambitious man who was destined for Rosa. But he would be ready to waive that proposition I was sure, this man who had proposed to me one day and that night had been most willingly enter-

[206]

tained in the midwife's bedroom! He was bemused by his ambitious dreams and they were robbing him of his natural shrewdness.

He went on eagerly: "We'll go to England. We'll live there. I can put a man in here . . . just as your father did. I'll find the right person. We'll go and live in England and you can leave all the difficult business to me. It'll be what *you* want. It's lucky that I am here."

"There was no luck at all about our coming here," I reminded him. "It was the most terribly unfortunate thing we ever did. If we hadn't come they would be here today."

"My poor little girl, I understand your grief. You have gone through so much. I know how it was with your parents and your brother. You were all so fond of each other. That was always clear and I understand. I want to make it easy for you. I've thought it all out. I've thought of nothing else since it happened. What can I do that is best for you . . . that's what I've been trying to figure out. I would have spoken before but I felt you wanted to be on your own . . . to grieve. But you can't go on grieving forever. You've got to begin to live again. Leave everything to me. I'll have it arranged. Just a quiet little ceremony. Everyone will understand . . . a girl on her own, miles from her home . . ."

I sat up suddenly. I felt my nerves tingling. I was alive again. My anger had done that for me.

I said: "I am sure you have made some excellent plans."

"You can trust me."

"Trust you, yes . . . to make plans. But in no other way would I trust you. You must understand that I am not so foolish as you appear to think. I know exactly how your mind works. You see me as the heiress. Land. That is your true love, I believe, that and nothing else. Through me you see the way to your darling. You've heard a great deal about Cador while we've been here. It makes this property very small, very insignificant, yet you've had your sights on this one for a long time. The greater glory now lies before you. All you have to do is to marry the helpless girl. You didn't think there would be any difficulty about that. All that charm . . . so you think . . . all that blatant masculinity . . . so irresistible to the poor stupid females. Please understand. Mr. Donnelly, I have no intention of marrying you. I know you asked me once before. I hoped I made myself clear then. I know that very same night you were creeping into the house to share the midwife's bed."

He looked at me in astonishment and then he smiled.

"You've no cause to be jealous," he said. "It was nothing. She was just there . . . a woman for the night. It makes no difference to us."

"You are right. It makes no difference because I am indifferent to what you do. If I had considered your proposal for a moment, let me tell you it would have made a great deal of difference. Please get this clear. I have never had any intention of marrying you, nor shall I ever have. Now will you please leave this room."

He stood up, smiling at me. Then he laughed.

"You've come alive," he said.

"Get out," I told him.

He bowed and went to the door.

There he stood looking at me.

"You have to admit that I have done something for you. I've put new life into you . . . even if you do hate me. Never mind. Hate turns to love . . . at least that sort of hate."

Then he was gone. I was trembling. I caught a glimpse of myself in the mirror. My cheeks had lost their pallor. My eyes were blazing.

He was right. I had at last come alive.

In a small house little escapes the attention of the observant and where Gregory Donnelly was concerned Maud was certainly that. She must have seen him come out of my room and a little later she herself came to see me.

She was faintly embarrassed and I could see she was wondering how to say what she wanted to.

She began by asking how I was feeling and I said that I seemed a little better. She was wondering about my plans.

"You wouldn't want to stay here, I know," she said. "You wouldn't want to make a home here."

"No, indeed not."

"I was, er . . . wondering about you . . . and Greg."

I felt again those waves of indignation which drew me out of my lethargy.

"What could you be wondering about Mr. Donnelly and myself?" I asked.

"Well, it was just that he gave me the impression that something

[208]

was fixed up between you." She looked round the room rather furtively as though expecting eavesdroppers. "If you don't mind my saying so, I don't think it would work out very satisfactorily."

I was on the point of saying that she should have no qualms about that for I had no intention of marrying Gregory Donnelly; but I was interested in her plans for Rosa and I thought she might be more communicative if she thought I was considering him as my husband. I wanted to hear about him; it was so long since I had been interested in anything at all—so I remained silent.

"It isn't the life for a lady who has been brought up as you have. Of course, he has a way with him."

Has he? I thought. He has a way of antagonizing me.

"He's a man who would always dominate a woman and I don't think you are the sort to stand for that."

"Yes," I said, "you wanted him for Rosa."

She flushed. "Who told you that?"

"Rosa. She seemed to think it was more or less settled."

She was clearly embarrassed.

I said: "Don't worry. It came out quite naturally. She seems to think he is wonderful. I am sure he would like that."

"He is very fond of Rosa," she said almost defiantly.

"I am sure he is. She is a charming girl."

"It was a sort of understood thing . . ."

"You mean an arranged betrothal?"

"We hadn't said much about it. It was understood. Rosa is a cut above the rest of the women here. You've seen her; you've seen them. I've given her a bit of education and she is very pretty. He wants a wife who's not just anybody . . ."

"Well," I said, "if Rosa admires him and he likes to bask in her admiration, I think it would work out very well."

"So did I . . . but now . . ."

"You mean when I came along?"

She was silent.

"I had more to offer, of course. I was my father's daughter . . ." My voice broke a little, but I went on: "I now own property in England. You see I am a very good catch for an ambitious man." She cast down her eyes and I went on: "Don't worry. He's Rosa's if she wants him. I have no intention of marrying him."

She looked up swiftly.

[209]

"He's determined," she said. "He's a man who gets his way."

"I daresay he has succeeded very well in that. But when he meets someone who is equally determined to have her own way there is nothing he can do."

She shook her head disbelievingly.

"It *is* so, Maud," I said. "What I don't understand is why you should want him for Rosa. She is a gentle, innocent girl. Could you let her go to a man like that?"

"He'd be good to her . . . if she were a good wife to him. And she would be. I'd see to that."

"You should know this man to whom you propose to marry your daughter. He has asked me to marry him. This was some time ago before . . ." I paused and could not go on for a few moments. Then: "He asked me and I refused. That night he spent with the midwife."

"He is a *man*," she said.

"You have a very poor opinion of his sex."

"If he had a wife he would be different."

"I doubt it. He is promiscuous naturally. That sort doesn't change."

"My Rosa is a lovely girl. I want the best for her. I don't want her to have just one of the cowboys, the sheepshearers, the hired hands. Greg is a big man out here. In a few years he'll be right at the top. That's what I want for Rosa."

"You are being very frank with me, Maud," I said. "I will be with you. Soon I shall be going home. I doubt I shall ever come here again. I have no intention of marrying Gregory Donnelly. In fact the idea is quite repulsive to me. Please set your mind at rest. If you are prepared to take such a man as your son-in-law, you are welcome as far as I am concerned. I understand that life might be hard for Rosa and that you want to make it as comfortable for her as you can, but I cannot imagine a woman having a comfortable life with that man."

"I know men," she said. "And I know Greg. He's ambitious. Perhaps that's first with him—but it is what I want. I want Rosa to have her own home and a carriage to ride in. I want her to be the lady of the property. I've suffered hardship with her father and I don't want any of that for Rosa."

"I understand, Maud. So put your mind at rest. Soon I shall be gone. Don't have any fear that I might spoil Rosa's chances."

"You are so vehement about him."

"I feel vehement. I don't happen to admire men who are so besotted by property that they would do anything to get it. I don't accept this promiscuity as you do."

"You haven't lived in a place like this where women are scarce. Men are men all the world over . . ."

"I shall keep to my view. I am going to start making plans now."

"He won't accept it."

"It is not for him to accept. It is my affair."

"He always gets his way."

"This is one instance when he won't."

"He'll find a way."

I shook my head.

"He was ready to wait for Rosa. . .until you came."

"He can go on waiting for Rosa. When did you propose the marriage should take place?"

"She is only fifteen. I have been thinking of when she is sixteen but that is a little young. Rosa is young for her age. I had been thinking of her seventeenth birthday but when you came I thought it was a long time to wait. Anything can happen in a few weeks."

"Don't worry, Maud. Oh dear, this *has* been a frank conversation."

"I didn't mean it to be. I just wanted to know . . ."

"Whether I was going to accept him. Have no fear. I assure you again and again the answer is most definitely No."

"But he won't take No for an answer. He never has done. He won't let anything stand in the way of what he wants."

"You'll see," I said.

She stood up. "Thank you for letting me talk to you and thank you for being so understanding."

"I'm glad I know exactly how you feel. Don't worry any more. In a short time I shall be gone."

"He'll never let you go."

"That, Maud, is a matter for me to decide."

She left me, still worrying, I was sure, unable to accept that this god-like creature could ever be thwarted.

Once again I had forgotten my grief for a brief spell. I was certainly stimulated by this battle with Gregory Donnelly; and I wondered how a loving mother could actually wish her daughter married to a man whom she knew as well as I did.

I received a letter from a lawyer in Sydney in which he informed me that my father had been considering selling the Australian property to the manager, Mr. Gregory Donnelly, and he thought I might think it a good idea to put the sale into negotiation. He had written to my father's solicitors in England who were in agreement with him, and in view of the tragedy, the sale seemed desirable. It was unwise to have property so far from home, the place had been excellently managed over the years and it seemed only right to sell it to the man who had done so much to make it prosperous.

I read the letter through several times. It was what Gregory wanted. Only he would prefer to marry me and not have to buy it. It seemed to me that I could make my feelings clear by agreeing to the sale and accepting the offer he had made.

That day, for the first time after my illness, I went out riding. I felt very feeble and could not stay long in the saddle. I thought of the long journey back to Sydney and then there would be the exhausting business of getting on the ship which would take me home. It seemed that they were right when they said I must get stronger. I had suffered from a virulent fever and goodness knows what else. Being in a debilitated state during those weeks I had been conscious of a death wish and had cursed the fates which had prevented my joining my parents and brother in their watery grave.

I wanted to go on mourning but I had to accept the fact that I had grown a little apart from the tragedy. I began to think with a faint pleasure of seeing Cador again. I knew memories would be very nearly unbearable, but I wanted to go home.

In a week or so I should feel less tired and then I would set about making arrangements to leave. I supposed we should need Gregory's help in getting to Sydney. I remembered that night when I had lain in my sleeping bag and had awakened to find him standing beside me. He had said something about defending me from prowling dingoes. I imagined myself on such a journey with him . . . with Helena and the baby. Jonnie was not really old enough for such travel.

There were so many problems to be considered.

I had not ridden far. I was too tired; moreover I had had my lesson about going too far from the house. When I came back to the stables Gregory was there.

He smiled at the sight of me and hastened to me.

"Ah, riding. That's a good sign . . . provided you keep close to the house. First time, isn't it?"

"Yes."

"Bit tiring, eh?" He attempted to lift me out of the saddle.

"Thank you. I can manage."

"You look like a medieval page with your hair like that. It's unusual. I like it."

I stood beside him. I said: "By the way. I have written to the solicitors in Sydney. I've told them to go ahead with the sale."

He raised his eyebrows but otherwise betrayed nothing.

"So," he said slowly, "the property is to be mine."

"When the sale is completed . . . yes."

"That's very gratifying."

"I'm glad you think so."

I turned away but he caught my arm. "Have you been thinking . . ."

"My mind is not usually a blank, so I suppose I have."

"I mean about us."

"Us?"

"Yes . . . you and me . . . us!"

"The sale of the property, you mean. Obviously . . ."

"No. My proposal."

"There was nothing to think about. I answered that on the spot. It doesn't require any meditation whatsoever."

"You are a stubborn woman."

"No. It is all very simple. I don't have to think about it. The answer from the first has been definitely No."

"Don't be too sure."

"I am absolutely sure."

"You'll change your mind."

"Good afternoon," I said. I knew that he was watching me as I went into the house.

He made me feel very uneasy. Perhaps it was due to Maud's assurances that he was certain to get his own way. He always had, she implied; and he always would.

That evening I was very tired. My illness had left me weaker than I had realized.

I said I would rest and not join them for the evening meal.

I had a good deal to think about. The sale of the property must not go through until I had left. I should hate to think that I was under *his* roof. I supposed that it could be arranged fairly quickly; but by agreeing that the sale should go ahead, I had made it necessary for us to make our plans about leaving.

Maud came in with a tray.

I said I was not hungry.

"I've brought you a little soup. It'll do you good. Try it. It just slips down. And there's some hot damper to go with it."

She sat beside the bed and I took the tray.

"It's made from the remains of the lamb . . . full of goodness. I always like to get the last bit of nourishment out of everything."

She watched me while I spooned the soup into my mouth.

She said: "I hope you don't think the worse of me after our little talk."

"No, Maud, I understand perfectly. I know how you must feel having a daughter like Rosa and wanting the best for her. It's natural."

"Well, there are few chances out here. I sometimes wonder if I ought to try to get back home. But what could we do there? I'd have to work and so would she. It wouldn't be much better than here."

"No. It seems that Gregory Donnelly is the big catch, especially when he owns this place."

"Is that going through then?"

"I think it very likely."

"You're wise. You wouldn't want to come out here again."

"There are too many bitter memories . . . but there will be at home, too. They are everywhere. There is no escaping them."

I had finished the soup. She took the tray and said: "Thank you for being so understanding."

That night I was very ill.

I knew it was the soup.

Oh, Maud, I thought, how little I knew you! Do you want to be rid of me so much?

I felt so ill at moments that I thought I was going to die.

It was about four in the morning before the griping pains and the sickness stopped and I began to feel a little better.

I sank back into my bed with relief. I was still alive.

Yet it had not been long ago when I was thinking longingly of death. I had wanted to be with them. I had felt it was unfair that they should go and I be left behind; but now I felt this overwhelming sense of relief. I was alive and I wanted to live.

Oddly enough it was anger which had begun to lift me out of my abject melancholy and now I had to be nearly poisoned to realize how much I wanted to live.

I lay there thinking of Maud, for it was Maud who had made the soup and brought it to me, who had been so eager for me to take it, and who had sat there watching me put every spoonful into my mouth.

She wanted me out of the way. She did not believe that I would not marry Gregory Donnelly; she could not conceive of any woman's not wanting him. And how desperately she wanted the right marriage for her daughter.

Who would have believed that she would go to such lengths?

I was in danger. I must get out of this place. Passions ran high in places like this. Life was not sacred here; there were too many hazards which made it cheap. People were fighting for their existences and if anyone stood in the way of what was the utmost importance to them they eliminated them.

But Maud! Calm and dignified Maud! Was it possible? Desperately she wanted that marriage for her daughter. She had betrayed herself to me when she talked of it. She wanted to see Rosa secure and in spite of all my protestations she did not believe I was not affected by his charms.

My body was limp and exhausted but my mind was active.

I went over that conversation we had had, trying to remember every word. I thought of her sitting by my bed, urging me to eat. Maud had done it. I would not have believed it possible but once again I was faced with the fact that one could never be sure what people would do in what to them was an emergency.

I felt too weak to get up the next morning. Nobody came, which was extraordinary. At length I got out of bed and went to Helena's room.

She was lying on her bed looking ill.

"Oh, Annora," she said. "I've had such a night. I have been so terribly ill. I am sure it was the soup."

"You, too. I thought it was just myself."

I went to the kitchen. No one was there. Were they all suffering from the poisonous soup?

A little later one of the women came over to the house.

[215]

She said: "Maud sent me. Everyone who took that soup last night is ill. I'm glad I didn't have any of it."

I felt a great sense of relief.

I was glad that I could go on thinking of Maud as I always had.

It took several days for everyone to recover.

Maud said: "It was all my fault. I thought the meat might be a bit off. But it didn't seem much. I might have poisoned the lot of us. I had two helpings. Serves me right. I wanted to finish it up. I hope you are feeling all right, Miss Cadorson?"

I said I was much better. Fortunately I had not taken a great deal.

There was no doubt that the soup had not been deliberately poisoned but the incident did have an effect on me; and the fact that I had felt so strongly that there might be a plan to get rid of me stayed with me.

I would look out of my window at the vast stretch of land and remember the day when I had been lost in the mist. I would awake in the night and listen for sounds. I kept thinking of the way in which Gregory had crept into the house to be with the midwife. There was a growing tension within me.

I was aware that Gregory watched me with a certain speculation.

I knew that Maud was watchful of us both.

There seemed to be a warning in the air. Get away. Get away while there is time.

We must get to Sydney. We must get a passage for England. There were a number of ships which sailed regularly.

Gregory was the one who could arrange it and yet I hesitated to speak to him. Somewhere at the back of my mind was the fear that if he knew I was really making plans to leave he might take some drastic action. I don't know whether it was due to the weakness of my condition or whether there was some uncanny force warning me; but I felt this strongly. I began to feel trapped. It was foolish. I only had to speak to Gregory, to tell him I had made up my mind to leave on such a date and that I wished him to make arrangements for our journey to Sydney. Once there I could book our passages myself.

Yet I did nothing.

Helena, too, was overcome by a kind of lethargy. She was uncertain what she felt about going home. There would be so many explanations. True, she was married, but her baby's age would indicate that he had been well on the way before the ceremony had taken place. And what a strange marriage. Where was her husband? Travelling round Australia looking for material, letting his wife and child go home without him.

I would have to discuss the matter with Gregory and I knew that when I did he would find some means of thwarting me.

It was a strange eerie feeling.

I had a restless night. I was beset by wild dreams; and I knew I had to act quickly.

I felt limp when I arose in the morning. I would speak to Helena and tell her we must make an effort without delay. This very day we must discuss it with Gregory. I would bring it up at dinner that night.

It was midafternoon when I heard the sound of horses' hoofs outside the house. A man had dismounted and was looking about him. I could scarcely believe my eyes. It was a dream. It must be. The fever had come back bringing strange images . . . some horrifying, some like this one . . . bringing a sudden incredible comfort, like the materialization of some longed-for dream.

"Rolf!" I cried.

I half-expected his image to dissolve before my eyes, but it did not. He came towards me, his arms outstretched.

I ran to him and flung myself at him.

"Rolf!" I cried. "Rolf, is it really you?"

He nodded, smiling. "Oh, Annora, dearest Annora . . . I have come to take you home."

It was truly Rolf. He was as calm and practical as ever. He told me that he had made preparations to leave as soon as he had heard the news because he knew how devastated I would be. I should need someone. I should need him.

All I could say was: "Oh, Rolf, Rolf, you really *are* here. Let me hold your hand. I'm afraid I'm dreaming. It's been like a nightmare . . . and I feel I'm still in it."

"You've come out of it now. We are going home just as soon as you are ready. I thought you would want to. It's best to get right away. I've found a man who can take us. He knows the country. He's got some conveyance he calls a buggy. There will be some baggage. Otherwise we could have gone on horseback. There are two inns we could stay at, and that's what we'll do. I've planned to leave here the day after tomorrow. He'll be with us then, buggy and all. We'll get to Sydney and I have tentative bookings if we can make it in time."

"You've arranged all that. Oh, Rolf, you're wonderful!"

He smiled. "Don't forget I was brought up to be a lawyer."

"And turned landowner instead. Oh, Rolf, it's so good you are here."

"Will you be ready?"

"Yes, yes. Oh . . . but there is Helena."

He looked puzzled.

"Helena and the baby. They'll have to come with us. You know my cousin Helena Lansdon . . . well, she's Helena Hume now. She's got a baby, the dearest little baby. They'll have to come, too."

"Oh," he said. "We'll have to do something about her passage."

"I couldn't go without her, Rolf."

Helena had come out carrying the baby.

"Helena," I cried, "this is Rolf Hanson. You remember him. You met him at Cador."

"Yes, of course I remember."

"He's come to take us home."

Rolf went to her and shook her hands. He looked at the baby.

"He's Jonnie," I said.

Rolf looked bewildered. I wondered if that was how people would look when they confronted Helena and her baby. One would see their minds calculating. How could she have a baby so soon?

"Helena's husband is away. He's collecting material for a book on convicts and transportation."

"Then he will not be coming home now?"

"No," said Helena. "He will be staying awhile. But I and Jonnie will go with Annora."

"Could you be ready to leave the day after tomorrow?"

"Yes, yes, I could," she answered.

Jonnie was holding out his hands to me. I took him from his mother and rocked him in my arms. He laughed and pulled at my short hair. I was aware of Rolf, gazing at us intently.

Maud came out to see what was happening.

"Oh, Maud," I cried, "this is a friend of mine who has come to take us back to England."

[218]

She came forward smiling, holding out her hand. I introduced them.

Rolf said: "I wasn't sure whether to write, but letters take so long. I thought the best thing was to come out as soon as possible. It takes a long time to come from the other side of the world. But at last I got here."

"You're very welcome," said Maud.

"Mr. Hanson will be here for two nights," I said.

I was thinking that there were two rooms which had been left just as they were—my parents' and Jacco's. I had asked that this should be so. I did not want anyone to touch any of their things and I did not feel capable of doing it myself just yet.

Maud seemed to follow my thoughts. She said: "The baby could go in with his mother and that would leave the nursery free."

"Yes, Maud. Thanks."

"I daresay you could do with something to drink," said Maud practically, "and to eat too, no doubt."

He agreed. "It's thirsty riding."

"Come along in, Rolf," I said. "How did you find your way?"

"I knew the address because my father had done considerable business with this place. I was given careful instructions in Sydney. I found the inns where I stayed the nights. Everyone was very helpful."

We went into the living room. "So this is where you have been staying." He turned to me with concern. "You've been ill, Annora."

"Yes, very ill. I had some sort of fever. That's why they cut my hair."

"It's becoming. It makes you look unusual."

"You'll get used to it. Oh, Rolf, I'm so glad you came. I'm longing to get home."

"I was afraid that I was going to miss you. I thought you might have started off already."

"No, because I was ill for so long. It has left me limp and easily tired. They didn't think I was fit to make the journey."

"It's hard travelling. You're thinner."

"Considerably."

"You'll be better when you get home."

"Nothing is going to be the same again."

[219]

"No. It's a fresh start though, Annora."

Maud was already setting out food. I sat with him while he ate. Maud came in and out with the food. She seemed as though she could not do enough to please him. I knew she was delighted with him because he had come to take me away. Moreover I think she was deciding he was the one for me.

I really felt I loved him then. He was like a saviour. He was different in every way from Gregory Donnelly; yet not less a man.

I said: "They are putting you in the nursery."

"I suppose there is not much room here."

"There are two rooms which I haven't let them touch yet. Their things are there—my parents' and Jacco's."

"I understand," he said. "They'll have to be cleared out before we go. Perhaps I can do it."

"No, I will. It is just that I couldn't bring myself to before."

"It's understandable. My poor, dearest Annora. How you must have suffered."

When he had eaten I took him to the room which would be his for the two nights he would be here. Maud had already taken out Jonnie's cot and put up the bed.

"It's only for two nights," I said.

"It will be absolute comfort after those inns."

"Rolf, it was so good of you to come."

"I had to, Annora. I thought of you all alone . . . without them. I'm so glad I found you. I pictured myself arriving to find you gone."

"I expect I should have gone but for my illness."

Maud came in with hot water for him to wash. He had brought a small bag with him and I left him to change.

It was later when he met Gregory Donnelly.

They stood face to face and I was aware of a certain bristling resentment in Gregory and a curiosity in Rolf.

Rolf carried off the situation with a good grace.

"Rolf Hanson has come to escort us home," I explained.

"You've come a long way," commented Gregory.

"I regret I did not get here earlier. One just can't step on to a ship without formalities. Arrangements have to be made. My great fear was that I should arrive to find Miss Cadorson had left."

"How did you get out to the property?"

"On horseback. I had instructions and stayed at the two inns on the way—the only two, I fancy."

"Oh, the accommodation houses. I know them well. You didn't lose your way?"

"I came near to it once or twice, but I had very good instructions and was given a rough map which was of inestimable worth."

Gregory was a little taken aback. Rolf had an easy manner. The difference in them, I decided, was that Gregory felt he had to be constantly reminding people of his superiority; Rolf didn't have to; it was obvious.

"When do you propose to go back?" asked Gregory.

"The day after tomorrow. I've arranged for a man to bring a buggy. We shall travel in that."

"The best way really. Mind you it takes longer. Who's your man?"

"A fellow called Jack Tomlin."

"Know him well. He's one of the best. He'll take care of everything."

"I can see I made a good choice."

I wondered what Gregory was feeling. He knew that I was definitely going now and that his grandiose schemes for marrying the little woman and acquiring her fortune were foundering.

"There will be a good deal to do," I said to Helena.

She agreed.

The evening passed. We sat for a long time over the table, talking. Rolf and Gregory had one passion in common: land. Gregory was greatly interested to hear that Rolf owned a large estate in Cornwall. They talked at great length about the differences in the land here and in England. I could see they were both very curious about each other—possibly regarding their relationships with me—but they talked amicably until it grew dark and Maud brought in the oil lamps.

When I retired I felt a lightness of spirit. I felt better than I had since the tragedy.

The tension had lifted, the eerie feeling had disappeared; I was being gently lifted out of a situation which had begun to alarm me. There was nothing to be afraid of now.

But that night I dreamed of Midsummer's Eve. Then we were

back in Australia and Rolf had just arrived. He was wearing a grey robe. They were cooking out of doors as they sometimes did and he leaped high over the fire and disappeared.

A strange dream. During the last weeks I had forgotten all about that Midsummer's Eve.

I was up early in the morning. Before me lay the task of going through their clothes . . . something I had shunned until now. But it had to be done. I had to sort out the little jewellery my mother had brought with her and her clothes. I would give the latter away. Many of the people on the property might be glad of them. And the same went for my father's and Jacco's.

I knew it was going to be harrowing and the sooner I did it the better.

Maud offered to help me. So did Helena; but I declined their assistance and set about the task on my own.

It was even worse than I imagined. I did Jacco's first. I tried not to let my emotions get the better of me, but each garment seemed to have some special significance. At one moment I just sat on the floor and gave way to my weeping.

It was no use. It had to be done. The clothes at least would give pleasure to some of the young men on the property. Or would they? Some of them might well despise the elegant cut and the good material. But what did that matter? They were only clothes.

I went to my parents' room and worked steadily.

In the pocket of one of my father's coats I found a little notebook. I remembered that I had given it to him. I sat down on the bed and looked at it. It was in red leather with his initials on it in gilt lettering. I thought about the Christmas Day two years ago. My gift to him . . .

I opened it. He had used it for addresses. There were several in London . . . often people I knew. And recently he had written in some in Australia. They were not in alphabetical order. In fact there was no index in the book; it was just a plain notebook with a little gold pencil fixed at the side.

I turned it over idly and came to the last address he had written.

"Stillman's Creek on the borders of Queensland and New South Wales? Some eighty miles from Brisbane."

That had been written in rather hastily and my mind went back to a scrap of conversation I had heard between my father and Gregory when my father had asked in what direction Stillman's Creek lay.

I wondered why he had been interested in that place.

I shut the book and put it into that pile which contained my mother's jewellery and those things I wanted to keep.

With an intense relief, I shut the door of that room and went out. The heartrending task had been completed.

The buggy was at the door. The baggage had been put into it. It only remained for us to say goodbye and we would be off.

They had assembled to see us go. Most of the people who worked on the property had come out. Standing a little apart from them was Gregory. Maud and Rosa were beside him.

I put my arms round Maud and kissed her.

I sensed her mingling emotions; sadness at parting and relief that I was going. She had believed until the last that Gregory would find some way of forcing me to marry him. Now the field was free for Rosa. I conveyed to her somehow that I understood.

"Good luck, Maud," I whispered. "I hope all goes well for you and Rosa."

Gregory was holding my hands and looking into my eyes with that familiar quizzical look. It was over. I had escaped him. He knew this and he accepted it as he accepted life generally, nonchalantly. He had what he had been waiting for so long . . . the property. He had lost the greater prize but he would take the cash in hand and waive the rest. That was his nature.

I could not help admiring him.

We set off. I gave one look back. Gregory was smiling that smile I knew so well; and Maud was standing there, her hand on Rosa's shoulder.

A Visitor
From Australia

And so we were sailing for England.

We should be well into the new year before we reached home, for there had been some delay in getting a passage for us all and we had had to stay in Sydney for several weeks.

Helena had written to Matthew and had left the letter at the Grand Hotel to be collected when he came there. In this she told him she was going home with me.

I knew that Rolf was puzzled by the marriage which in a short time had produced not only a baby but a husband who had gone off leaving his newly wedded wife who was not sure of his whereabouts.

But finally we were on board.

I realized that everything I did was going to bring back memories; and as soon as I stepped on to the ship I remembered the journey out and the fun Jacco and I had had, and how excited we had been at the prospect of seeing new places; but most of all I remembered that deep abiding security I had had—and which I had not realized until I had lost it—in the heart of a devoted and loving family.

But Rolf had come right to the other side of the world, leaving his beloved estates, to come to me because as much as anyone else I knew, he would understand my grief.

I must be thankful that I had such a friend.

At first I could not feel any interest in the ship. I did not care whether the sun shone or we were in stormy waters. I was hardly aware of the rough seas. Although I was glad to be on my way I dreaded getting home. I tried to imagine Cador without them.

Jonnie comforted me a great deal. I was with him as often as possible. I was sure he knew me; he was beginning to take an interest in the world about him now, and he grew more adorable every day. Helena understood and when she thought I was particularly depressed she would talk of him or bring him to me and put him into my arms.

Rolf noticed and remarked on my fondness for the child.

"He's always been with me," I said, "really as much as he is with Helena."

I realized my feelings towards Rolf were getting back to what they had been before that terrible Midsummer's Eve.

When I looked at him dispassionately it was brought home to me what a very attractive man he was. He was greatly respected throughout the ship. He was gracious; he had an easy manner; he did not thrust himself forward as Gregory Donnelly had done. In fact my acquaintance with Gregory Donnelly had made me realize how very much I admired Rolf.

I was taken back to those days of my childhood when I had set him up as a god, when my heart leaped with pleasure when I heard his arrival. How I used to fly down to meet him and he would lift me in his arms and give me a piggyback-ride when I wanted to show him something in the nursery.

Then had come that Midsummer's Eve when I believed that my god had feet of clay.

What had shocked me almost as much as the cruelty inflicted on Mother Ginny was Rolf's part in it. That had destroyed my feelings for him. I had continued to love him in a way, but my affection had been tainted by what I had seen and the awful realization that I did not really know him at all.

One grows very close to people during a sea voyage; one sees them every day at meals as well as about the ship. A few days of such intimacy is equivalent to months of an ordinary relationship.

Rolf was so tender, so tactful. Now and then he talked of home and when he saw that I was getting too emotional, he would steer the conversation away from that evocative subject.

It was such a comfort to know that he understood, even more than Helena did, what I was feeling.

[225]

And somehow I knew he was waiting. The fact that he had come out to Australia to bring me home, showed that he cared for me in a very special way. He had always been a good friend but this was more than friendship.

It was during these peaceful balmy nights when we were crossing the Indian Ocean that we sat on the deck together looking out on the darkening water, listening to the gentle swishing of the sea against the side of the ship as we talked.

He said: "I often think of you when you were a little girl. You used to rush to me when I arrived at Cador with my father. If you had something new, you always wanted to show it to me."

"Yes, I remember."

"You were very fond of me then."

"I thought you were the most wonderful person in the world. At least, you shared that honour with . . ."

The tell-tale break in my voice made him reach for my hand.

"I know," he said. "It was a gratifying feeling to be so regarded. When things weren't going well, I used to say to myself, 'I'll go to Cador and get a boost to my ego from Annora.' And then suddenly . . . it changed."

I was silent.

"Yes," he went on, "suddenly it changed. I thought sadly, She's growing up. She's not a child any more. She's more discerning. And I didn't like it at all. I did not come so much to Cador because I could not bear the change in your attitude towards me. I told myself that children were fickle and I was hurt."

"It was after that Midsummer's Eve," I said.

"That Midsummer's Eve," he repeated. "Ah, I remember. There was an awful tragedy. The house in the woods was burned down."

"Yes. With Mother Ginny in it. They were very cruel to her on that night. I was there . . . with Jacco. It was intolerable."

"You saw it! It must have been horrific."

"They set fire to her house. They dragged her to the river. I can never forget it. I didn't believe in anything after that. People I had known . . . doing that. I felt I could not trust people any more."

"I understand," he said slowly. "My father was greatly shocked. He told me about it when I came back."

"When you came back?"

"I had gone away on the afternoon of Midsummer's Eve. I went to a friend who was in my college. He lived near Bodmin. You remember how interested I used to be . . . well, I still am . . . in old customs and superstitions. He had found some old papers in his family's attics and he wanted me to look at them. I was going to miss the bonfires but old papers interested me more, so I went off. I was rather glad that I wasn't there in view of what happened."

"You weren't there?" I stammered.

I could see it all so clearly; the figure in the grey robe leaping over the bonfire; leading the mob on to harass the poor old woman.

Floods of relief were sweeping over me. It must have been someone else in the robe. Could the truth be that which I had always tried to convince myself was so?

Why had I not spoken before? How foolish I had been. I could have learned this long ago.

"Oh, Rolf," I cried. "I'm so glad you were not there. It was horrible . . ."

"You shouldn't have been there."

"My parents were away. Jacco and I went on our own."

"My dear child . . ."

"We thought it was adventurous . . . at first. But I am glad we were there. I think we saved Digory."

I told him then how we had gone out, witnessed the horror of that night and hidden Digory so that his fate should not be that of his grandmother.

"I learned something that night," I said. "I learned about people. I suppose those are the sorts of things one ought to know."

He put his arm round me and kissed me. Then he said: "I've always loved you, Annora."

I did not answer. I felt almost happy—as I had never thought to feel again, sitting there with his arm about me and the wonderful knowledge that he had not been there on that terrible night. It had been someone else in that robe. Why had I not thought that there could be more than one robe? I had come to a hasty conclusion which had embittered me for years and had changed my life in a way. Who would have believed that such a thing could have happened in one night? But I had already been made aware of how suddenly tragedy could strike and how quickly life could change.

He kissed me gently.

"I have been thinking a great deal about us, Annora. What is going to happen when you return?"

"I am dreading it. I can't imagine the place without them."

[227]

"It is something you will have to face. It will be hard at first."

"I know."

"I shall be near," he said. "I'll be there to help you. You'll need help in many ways. You have inherited Cador. Do you realize what that means?"

"I haven't thought much about that side of it."

"I guessed not. In a way it will help you. You'll have so much to think about. You've got to forget the past. You have to realize that everything is going to be different now. Your father cared a great deal about the estate once he came into it, and Jacco was being trained for when his time came. Now you have to take that responsibility."

"I was always interested in it . . . at one time more than Jacco was. I used to go round with my father . . "

"It will not be easy for you, but I am there . . . close. I want to be even nearer. Annora, we could be married."

I was silent. I was still thinking: he was not there. All these years I have misjudged him. I ought to have known he couldn't have been there. I wanted to make up to him for all the years of mistrust.

I thought of all the loneliness of returning to Cador without my family, and I saw at once that I had to stop brooding. I had to go on. And here was the way. I had lost my dear ones but I should not be alone.

I turned to Rolf and said: "Yes, we could be married."

Now that I had made the decision I felt better. I had a new life opening before me. Everything would be different but I should have someone to love me.

I used to say to myself, It was what *they* wanted. They had always been fond of Rolf. Rolf would know what should be done about the estate. His own lands bordered on Cador. We should join up. We should be as one.

Helena was delighted. She liked Rolf very much. I think she was perhaps a little envious comparing her own marriage with my prospects. But her great comfort was Jonnie. At least he had come out of all that had happened to her.

Slowly we made our way towards England.

We were docking at Southampton and were rather glad of this. It meant that we should go straight to Cador without calling in at London which would have been the natural thing to do if we had landed at Tilbury.

Helena was not really prepared to see her parents yet and I felt I did not want to talk of my loss to them. I knew how upset Amaryllis would be at my mother's death, for the ties between them which had been made in the days of their childhood had never been broken.

How moving it was to see Cador again and as I gazed at those ancient towers I had to suppress my unhappiness. I had to keep reminding myself that I had to make a new start. This great house and everything that went with it was mine. I had a great responsibility towards a good many people therefore. I had to stop mourning. There would be so much to learn but, I reminded myself, I should have Rolf to help me.

There was a warm but subdued welcome from the household. Mrs. Penlock burst into tears. I gripped her hands and told her we had to go on. Several of the others wiped their eyes and Isaacs said in a shaken voice: "We are glad you are home, Miss Cadorson."

I thanked them as best I could and I know my voice shook. I had schooled myself for this for I knew how emotional it would be.

I said: "I intend that everything shall go on as before." They cast down their heads and I went on: "I will talk to you all in the morning."

Jonnie was a great help. Faces brightened as they looked at him. He studied them all with curiosity and through her tears Mrs. Penlock exclaimed: "The little duck!"

So there I was back home, longing to be alone in my room and yet dreading it, for during that first night, memories would be as vividly with me as ever.

I have to put it all behind me, I kept telling myself. I have Rolf now. He will help me. Perhaps in time I can be happy again.

I rode round the estate the very next morning and called at several of the farms. Mrs. Cherry had nine children now; she was larger than ever and still laughed at every sentence she uttered. Even when she referred to my loss, her laughter was not far off. It was a habit. And the Tregorrans were as mournful as I remembered.

"These be bad days, Miss Cadorson," said Jim Tregorran. Miss Cadorson, I noticed, not Miss Annora.

They seemed bewildered. I supposed it was difficult for them to think of me as their landlord.

The first days were difficult. People were embarrassed. They wanted to tell me, I knew, that they mourned the loss of my parents and brother deeply, but they did not know how to do so.

Perhaps if I could have spoken of the tragedy it would have been easier. But I could not bring myself to do it at first. Perhaps later, I thought.

I went down to town. I rode along the quay. They touched their caps to me. Jack Gort was weighing fish from his tubs; he said, "Good day to 'ee, Miss Cadorson. Glad to see 'ee back." He did not mention my family, but I saw the sympathy in his eyes. Old Harry Gentle lifted his bleary eyes from the nets he was mending and said: "Welcome home, Miss Cadorson. Nice to see 'ee back."

Jim Poldean who was cleaning his boat sprang on to the quay to take my hand and shake it. He did not say anything but his expression told me how sorry he was.

They all felt they wanted to convey their sympathy; they had respected my father; they had been fond of my mother and Jacco. But they did not know how to express their feelings in words and I was afraid to talk in case I broke down. Being home seemed to bring them so much nearer, to make me so much more aware of all I had lost.

And as I rode back I thought: These were the people who drove Mother Ginny to her death.

Which one among them had been wearing a grey robe?

And there it was back again and with it a fearful apprehension. But he wasn't there, I kept telling myself. He was in Bodmin.

Soon he would be with me always. He would help me. I had been right about him when I was a little girl. I had thought he was wonderful then. Of course he *was* wonderful. He was good and kind, clever and resourceful, the sort of man who was born to be a leader.

When the news broke that I was to be married to Rolf there was general approval.

"This be very right and proper," said Mrs. Penlock. "'Tain't natural for a woman to be the squire. If God had intended it He would have made women men."

I thought that an odd sort of reasoning and I was glad that I could smile at it.

"Well then," said Isaacs, "I reckon Cador and Manor 'ull be one. That be spreading it a bit. Looks like nearly all the Duchy 'ull be Cador-Manor land."

That amused everyone very much.

I wished I could go quietly into the kitchen as I used to and listen to their talk when they forgot I was there.

I did hear one of the maids say: "If they wasn't to wait the year 'twouldn't do no harm. After all, this be special with her having known him so long and being all alone like."

"Mind you," said one of the others, "'twould have to be a quiet wedding."

They were all very interested, which was not surprising because their livelihoods were tied up in Cador land. That made me feel a great responsibility, which was good for me and brought me out of my brooding.

I went through the books with Bob Carter, our manager, who had looked after everything during my father's absence. I told him that everything appeared to be in excellent shape. He was gratified and said he hoped there would be no changes on the estate.

"I don't see any need to change anything, Bob," I said. "I have a lot to learn, but you can explain to me what I ought to know."

"That I will, Miss Cadorson."

And after the first shock of homecoming with its inevitable memories, I began to feel better.

Rolf took me round his estate. I was amazed at the size of it.

"It's flourishing," he said. "Luke Tregern looked after it well while I was away."

He told me that when the manager had retired Luke Tregern had taken over his post.

"Luke has done marvels," he went on. "I felt I could leave him in charge while I was away and I was not wrong."

I saw Luke in the office seated at a table working on some papers. He looked very smart in a velveteen jacket and gaiters, with a cream-coloured cravat. He stood up and bowed as I entered.

"Good morning, Luke," I said.

"Good morning, Miss Cadorson, and welcome home. My deepest sympathy for your loss."

"Thank you, Luke. Mr. Hanson tells me you are doing a very good job here."

"I trust so, Miss Cadorson. It is what I strive for."

He was handsome in a way and his clothes and manner rather indicated that he was aware of it. That was nothing to complain of, of course. In fact it was pleasant to meet someone who obviously cared about his appearance.

We chatted a little about the estate and then Rolf and I left.

"He's different," I said.

[231]

"Yes. I saw it at once when he came looking for a job. He's got drive, he's ambitious, Luke is. I think he'll get on."

"I should think so. He already has. From gamekeeper to manager is quite a step."

"You've got your good Bob Carter. Don't grudge me my Luke."

"I don't. I'm glad for you."

"It will be fine when we run the two together, Annora."

"Yes. I believe I am looking forward to that."

I was. It was gratifying that the people on the estate thought my coming marriage to Rolf was a good thing—which meant good for the estate as well as for Rolf and me. They believed and so did I that in the circumstances it was the best thing that could have happened.

When Aunt Amaryllis heard that we were home she wrote that she must come to see us; and in due course she arrived accompanied by her lady's maid.

My pleasure in seeing her was mixed with great sadness. She was very emotional; and I kept remembering stories my mother had told me of their childhood.

Her reunion with Helena was very moving. She had been so anxious about her daughter, I knew, and she told me how grateful she was to me for looking after her.

I replied that Helena had, at times, looked after me.

And we cried together.

But she was delighted with her grandchild. She could not keep away from him.

"You must come home," she said to Helena.

"I want to stay with Annora . . . just for a little while," Helena told her. "We have been through so much together. She has helped me through."

"I should have been with you, my dearest child. Bless you, Annora my dear. Such dreadful things to happen . . . and all at once."

How right she was! One thing had followed on another. It had been a disastrous chain of events.

"Your father would want you home," said Aunt Amaryllis.

"Would he?" cried Helena. "It's going to be difficult to explain."

"And your husband, Matthew. What of him?"

"He's in Australia. He will come home when he has collected the material he needs."

"Doesn't he want to see you . . . and the baby?"

"Mama," said Helena, "it is no use pretending. Matthew married me to help me. That was all. It is difficult to understand if you don't know him. He's that sort of person. He wants to do good for people. That's why he is going to write this book. He is a man who has to have a cause. I was in a difficult position and he saw a way of helping me out. He's a very rare person. But he is not Jonnie's father."

"Was it . . . John Milward?"

Helena nodded.

"Oh dear, what a terrible muddle. Your father could have sorted something out for you, you know."

"He wouldn't want me home. It would only add to the scandal about us."

"Oh, he'd deal with that. There are so many malicious people in the world. He's just been driven out of political life, that's all. It's a great loss to the country. He says it is very unprofitable in any case."

"But what about his business . . . all those clubs?"

"It's still as it always was."

"My mother told me that you were involved in Uncle Peter's business, Aunt Amaryllis," I said.

"Oh, just money and all that. He always insisted that I had my own income. He invested it for me. He says he has made me much richer than I was when I married him."

"But the money comes from . . ."

"He explained all that to me. His clubs are very necessary, you know."

"Necessary?"

"Well, it is not very nice to talk about, but there are aspects of human nature which young girls wouldn't know about. These baser sides to men's natures have to be satisfied or there could be real trouble. People get frustrated. In that way they do terrible things . . . run amok. There is rape and other things too terrible to talk about. Your uncle, Annora, is doing a real service."

I looked at her in amazement. My mother always said she was besotted about her husband and if he told her black was white she would believe him. She saw him as perfect and nothing could ever change that. How right my mother had been. I could imagine Uncle Peter's explanations to her, telling her of his nobility in running profitable clubs which kept just on the right side of the law and which were really a benefit to humanity—profligate humanity, it was

[233]

true—but they had to be considered for the good of the community at large.

"People just love something sensational," went on Aunt Amaryllis. "Even the Queen is not immune. There is all this terrible scandal about Lady Flora Hastings."

I said that being away we had heard nothing of this.

"Oh well, there is a feud going on between the Queen and her mother. They say the Duchess interferes too much and the Queen and she are not on the best of terms. Lady Flora is one of the Duchess's household and when her body became swollen the Queen's women put a rumour about that she was pregnant and it turned out that she wasn't. There was a great outcry about it. People are saying the Queen is responsible. Lady Flora's family are making a great fuss. I can tell you the story is all over London. So you see, even the Queen is not immune from what Peter calls the gutter press. She is not as popular as she was, but Peter says it will come back. It is just a temporary set-back . . . and that is how it usually is."

"We haven't had much chance to see the papers yet."

"Oh, they are full of these little scandals. Headline news today and forgotten tomorrow."

"And all that was said about Joseph Cresswell and Uncle Peter . . ."

"A nine days' wonder. Your Uncle Peter is doing so much good. He always did, but more so lately. And you haven't heard about Peterkin. He's engaged to Frances Cresswell. She is a little older than he is, but your uncle is pleased. He said it's a good thing. Peterkin is completely devoted to Frances and what a lot of good she is doing! Your father, Helena, has given them a great deal of money. It has been in the papers. They call him the Philanthropist of the Underworld. I would prefer just the Philanthropist, but he says it creates more interest to mention the Underworld. People notice and rather like it. Someone wrote an article saying that although he had made his fortune through the clubs of the Underworld he gave so much back to charity that he has to be admired. The clubs were for the amusement of people who were not of the highest moral standard, but if so much was done for a worthy cause, credit must be given where it was due."

So that was what Uncle Peter was doing now. He had been exposed so he turned about and became a philanthropist. He had given his wholehearted support to Peterkin. Frances must be very pleased. She would not care how the money had been come by, as long as it was there.

Should she have done? I was not sure. Immorality and morality had become oddly mixed.

Aunt Amaryllis was very pleased to have—as she thought—made us understand about Uncle Peter's business and to make us realize that, in spite of all the harsh things which had been written about him in the newspapers, he was really very noble.

She was very affectionate towards Rolf and delighted that I was engaged to marry him.

"Mama," said Helena, "I want to stay for a while. At least for Annora's wedding."

"Of course," she replied. "And you must come, Annora, with your husband to stay with us. Your Uncle Peter will be so pleased to see you."

Dear Aunt Amaryllis, she wanted the best for everyone and what was so comforting about her was that she believed so earnestly that it would come about that one began to share that belief.

Aunt Amaryllis returned to London having extracted a promise from Helena that she would go home after the wedding and that Rolf and I would visit them on the way to our honeymoon.

Rolf was making arrangements.

"We'll go abroad," he said. "I was impressed by Italy when I did the Grand Tour of Europe in my student days. I shall show you Florence. You will love it. And all the antiquities of Rome . . . and then Venice. What a country! Surely one of the most beautiful in the world."

I began to feel a little enthusiasm.

"You'll feel better when we are right away," he assured me, for he had always understood my moods. "Then we'll come back to our new life. We will be so busy there will be no time for brooding. We can go away when we feel like it. Between them Bob Carter and Luke Tregern can take care of things."

I was to be married in the chapel at Cador and it would be a white wedding as it was to take place in June.

Jennie Tregore, wife of one of the farmers, had been a dressmaker by profession before her marriage and she carried on with it when anyone wanted anything made. I decided I wanted something simple and that she should make it.

I often thought when Jennie was busy with the fittings, what an occasion my mother would have made of this. She would have wanted to go to London for my wedding dress. What excitement there would have been! How she would have loved it!

I must stop thinking along those lines. I told myself so a hundred times a day, but I still went on doing it.

I was thinking now about my honeymoon. I had always wanted to see Italy. My father had often talked about our going. Once more I was back in the past. I could see them all so clearly, sitting at the dinner table, Jacco arguing fiercely that it would be more fun to go to the mountains of Switzerland than the art galleries of Florence.

I must stop.

Yes, I thought. In London I will buy some clothes for my honeymoon. There! I was growing away from it if I could think about clothes.

I noticed that Helena was becoming more and more uneasy about returning to London. She was afraid she would have to face a barrage of questions.

"But your mother knows," I told her, "and she will explain everything to your father. As for him, he has a way of making things right even if they aren't. Peterkin and Frances will love to see you. They'll understand."

"I wasn't thinking so much about the family as people I shall have to meet—all those mothers who used to pity me because no one wanted to marry me, and when John did, looked on me with a sort of envy. They'll crow now. Besides, what are people really thinking about my father and his business?"

"They are thinking what he intends they should. He is a man of the world and now he is contributing in a very public way to charity. Your father is the sort of man who will be unperturbed by anything that happens to him. You must try to be like him, Helena."

"As if I ever could be! I'm not looking forward to it and you'll miss Jonnie."

"Very much . . . and you, too. But we have to go on, Helena. We can't just stand still. We have been through a lot and we have learned to grow away from it."

"You have that chance now . . . with Rolf."

"And so have you a chance . . . with Jonnie. Your mother will help. I think she is one of the kindest people I ever knew. You're lucky to have her."

"She's an angel but not a very practical one."

"You'll be all right. Helena, suppose Matthew comes back."

"I suppose he will in time."

"How do you feel abut him?"

"Very grateful. He's a good man, isn't he?"

"He is dedicated to his purpose."

"Yes. He's like Frances Cresswell in a way. Those sort of people want to do good. They are wonderful people . . . but they don't always care so much for just one person."

"Do you think . . . if he came back, you would be together . . . that you could love him?"

"I don't think I shall ever love anyone like that but John."

"He should have gone on with the marriage, defied his family."

"He just couldn't. He had to do what seemed right to him."

"If he had known about Jonnie . . ."

"I didn't want marriage on those terms . . . because he had to. I wanted him to marry me because he wanted to."

"He did want to . . ."

"But not enough. You're lucky, Annora. Rolf loves you . . . completely. There was a time when I thought you might marry Gregory Donnelly."

"Surely not. I loathed the man."

"He was so sure of himself. I thought he might find some way of forcing you to marry him."

"I can't see how he could have done that in any circumstances."

"Well, you're lucky. Rolf is our sort. You'll be very good together. You've got all this. Just fancy. It's yours. Oh, Annora, I hope you are going to be very happy."

"I'll try to be," I said. "And, Helena, you must, too. Don't forget. You have Jonnie."

"The dearest treasure in the world."

We laughed; and then she wanted to see how my wedding dress was progressing, so I took her to the room where Jennie was working and we had a discussion about pleats and tucks and Honiton lace versus that of Brussels.

Helena was getting ready to leave. The day after the wedding we should set out, Rolf and I, for our honeymoon, Helena and Jonnie for her father's London home. Rolf and I were to spend a few nights there before going to the coast.

Jonnie was almost walking now. He was just over a year old. He crawled along at great speed, then he would stand and after a few tottering steps sit down on the floor. There was no nanny. Helena had not wanted that. Most of the women in the house were only too glad to lend a hand looking after him if for any reason his mother or I could not.

I was going to miss Jonnie very much.

As my wedding day approached I began to grow apprehensive. It had seemed such a heaven-sent solution at first, for I knew that it would take me a long time to learn all that would be expected of the owner of Cador. Rolf was to teach me. He loved the place; he always had; and I needed someone to love me deeply. I wanted to be cherished. I had lost so much love. It was natural that I should turn to Rolf, the idol of my childhood who, knowing me so well, could understand the enormity of my loss. I often thought that if it had not been for that Midsummer's Eve Rolf and I might well have been married long ago. Perhaps before I had gone to Australia. But that night could not be forgotten; and it was brought back more vividly one day about a week before the day fixed for the wedding.

Rolf was still fascinated by the old customs of Cornwall. In his library at the Manor he had collections of books about them. He liked to take me there and he would get quite carried away talking of them. I was reminded of those times when he had visited us with his father and how he had held us all spellbound.

On this occasion he was talking about old cures which the Cornish had believed in years ago.

"There were white witches who did good with their cures," he was saying, "and there were the kind who practised the evil eye and put spells on people so that disaster followed. Just listen to some of the things they did." He opened a book. "Look at this. Whooping cough cured by filling a bag full of spiders and tying it round the neck of the poor child who had to wear it night and day. Here's another. For asthma. 'Collect webs, roll them into a ball and swallow.'"

"Spiders seemed to have had a beneficial effect."

"Styes on eyes treated by touching the eyes with a cat's tail."

"I believe they still do that."

"I've no doubt. Some old letters were found in the attics at Bray's

[238]

place. Tom Bray showed them to me. They are amazing. I must get him to show them to you."

We were standing at the bookshelves below which was a row of drawers. He pulled one out. "No," he said, "not here," Then he opened the next and I saw it. It was lying there and there was no mistaking it.

I stared at it.

"It's that old habit," he said. "I went to a ceremony once . . ."

"I remember hearing about it."

"This is what we wore."

"You showed it to me once before . . . long ago."

"Oh yes, I did." He had taken it out and slipped it on. I felt my heart racing. As he stood before me he slipped the hood over his head. His face was almost hidden.

"It's horrible," I cried.

He took it off and laughed at me.

"I must admit it is rather gruesome. I'll tell you why. It is very like the sort the executioners used to wear in the Inquisition. In this I looked as if I might have stepped out of an *auto-da-fé*."

"Yes," I said. "And you wore it . . ."

"At that ceremony. I thought it was going a bit far to dress up like that. I never went again."

He rolled up the habit and put it into a drawer.

"Why," he said, "I believe I frightened you. You look quite shaken."

He came to me and put his arms round me. "The time seems to drag," he went on. "It seems as though our wedding day will never come."

With his arm about me I felt better. It was true I had been shaken to see him in that robe. It had taken me right back to that fateful Midsummer's Eve.

After that it kept intruding into my thoughts.

The day before the wedding, I rode alone in the woods. On impulse I went to the clearing by the river. The remains of the burned-out house were still there. Nothing had ever been done about it.

It was on our land and I remembered my father had gone to look at it one day and he had come back and said that another cottage should be built there. He had set one of the builders to investigate.

But no one was anxious to work there. A rumour went round that to do so would bring bad luck to anyone who had anything to do with it. The place was bewitched.

I remembered my father's saying: "Better leave it till they've forgotten. They'll be working up all sorts of superstitions about the place. God knows who would want to live there. These things magnify and they thrive on them. No. No one would want the cottage. We'd better leave it alone."

A few years later he had made another attempt but he had met with all kinds of excuses.

After that nothing had happened.

I paused there, remembering. It all came back to me so clearly. The lighted thatch . . . the figure in the robe. Had he been the first one to throw the torch? I believed so. I remembered the cottage as it had been. Digory standing at the door with the cat; I could hear the final scream as the poor animal was consumed by the flames. I felt sick, physically and mentally. That people could do such things! They were savage, and yet by the next morning they had returned to their normal guises. One could never know the hidden depth of people's characters nor how they would act when confronted with certain situations.

I wanted so much to forget that night, but I could not. It had stamped itself indelibly on my mind.

The wind sighed mournfully through the trees; I felt cold though the sun was hot. Memories of those faces in the light of the torches kept coming back to me. The hooded figure which I had believed concealed someone I knew.

I rode home thoughtfully. I felt melancholy. Was it because I was going to be married in the morning? Surely a matter for rejoicing. It was a solemn occasion. Perhaps many girls felt as I did the day before they were taking the great step.

I thought: Maybe it is too soon. I should have waited. But on the moonlit night on the ship when Rolf had told me that he had not been in the woods on that Midsummer's Eve, it had seemed so right.

He had been to Bodmin. Of course he had. Why had he not said he was going? Why had he not mentioned it until now? How strange that we could go on under a misapprehension for so many years!

I wished I could disperse the memories of that night, but they kept coming back to me: the shouts of the people, Mother Ginny with her grey hair straggling about her ashen face. I could not forget it. Digory cowering in the grass, robbed of his bravado . . . just a terrified child.

Then I was thinking of Jacco, all the fun we had together, and how that night we had saved Digory. And my misery was back as heart-rending as it had ever been.

I wished I could have found Digory. Would that have helped? Digory would be all right, my father had said. He would land on his feet. Heaven knew he had had enough experience of fending for himself.

Why had I gone to the woods on the eve of my wedding? It was a foolish thing to have done.

I *must* forget that night. I must forget my doubts. They were natural enough. They came to all girls who were on the point of taking such a momentous step.

It was afternoon. I was in my room getting together a few things which I should take on my honeymoon. The house was quiet and I suspected Isaacs was taking a nap, which I believed he did at that hour. Mrs. Penlock too, I supposed.

Suddenly I heard her voice. She was talking to one of the maids. They must be coming in from the kitchen garden for I heard Mrs. Penlock say: "I think that will be enough. Miss Helena pecks like a bird. I don't think she wants to leave us."

One of the maids—I think her name was Fanny—said: "You'd have thought she'd have wanted to, wouldn't 'ee, Mrs. Penlock? It must be wonderful to go up to London."

Mrs. Penlock gave her familiar snort. "Full of thieves and vaga-bonds up there, if you was to ask me."

"'ee don't say, Mrs. Penlock!"

"I could tell 'ee a few things. Never mind now. We've got a wedding on our hands."

"Miss Annora don't look like a bride somehow."

"Be careful of that basket. She's all right. Best thing that could have happened. She needs someone to look after her. 'Tain't natural women being left with places like this. It needs a man."

"He's lovely, don't 'ee think so, Mrs. Penlock?"

"He's all right. Better than one of them smart lahdidahs from London what she might have got hold of."

I had to listen. I found their views amusing. I guessed they would soon pass out of earshot, but the basket must have been heavy and they were walking slowly: every now and then they paused.

"Soon be part of the Manor," said Fanny.

"Don't 'ee say such a thing. Manor'll be part of us, I reckon. Well, 'tas always been a dream of Mr. Hanson to get his hands on this place."

"But it'll be Cador still. 'Twon't be Hansons."

"'Course it'll be Cador, but she'll be his wife, won't she? And what's hers is his and I'm not so sure that what's his is hers. That's the way of the world. I reckon he be pleased with himself. I remember him coming here years ago . . . Heard him say to his father, 'I'd like to have this place.' I reckon he always meant to own it somehow."

"But he be sweet on Miss Annora."

"He is and all. Sweet on her and sweet on Cador, I reckon," affirmed Mrs. Penlock. "So it's sweet all round. Come on, Fan. Get a move on. We'll never get these done in time if you don't."

"Don't 'ee think this wedding's a good thing then, Mrs. Penlock?"

"I reckon it's about the best thing that could have happened to him. He'll have Cador, won't he, which is what he's always wanted."

Their voices were lost to me.

I sat very still. They were right. He had always cared deeply about Cador. He had been fascinated by it. It was the reason why he had restored the decrepit old Manor House. It was the reason why he had acquired land.

And in marrying me he would share it . . . perhaps own it.

I wished that I had not listened to that conversation.

Helena and I dined quietly that evening. I said I should like to retire early as there was so much to do tomorrow. So we said good night and went to our respective rooms.

My uneasiness was deepening, and try as I might I could not dispel it.

It was a long time before I slept; then I was haunted by dreams from which I kept waking, startled and alarmed. They were jumbled and seemed meaningless when I tried to recall them. My parents were in them with Jacco, Digory and Gregory Donnelly. It seemed to me that they were all warning me, that some great danger was threatening me.

Then I dreamed the most frightening dream of all.

[242]

I was in the woods and I saw torches through the trees. I went forward and there was the cottage with the roof aflame and holding the torch which had lighted it was a tall figure in a grey robe. The hood covered his face. I crept up to it. I could feel the heat from the torch and I put out my hand and touched the rough serge of the robe. The figure turned towards me and the hood fell back. Rolf was looking at me. He seized me. "Too late," he whispered. "Too late. I was there . . . I am here . . . now." He held the torch above my head and I screamed: "Let me go."

He answered: "No. It is too late."

"What do you want with me?" I cried.

"Cador," he said. "I want Cador."

I awoke. I think I must have cried out. I sat up in bed. I heard the creaking sound of a door opening. It was my cupboard. I caught my breath. It was Rolf, I thought, in the grey robe. He was there, menacing me, ready to step out and seize me as he had in the dream.

But I was not dreaming now.

I sat there, cowering back, my heart feeling as though it would burst out of my body.

"No," I whispered. "No, no. Go away."

Nothing happened. But it was there. The robe.

My eyes were growing accustomed to the darkness of the room. Now I could see clearly. I got out of bed. I was almost sobbing in terror. It was not the robe that I saw. The cupboard door had swung open and it was the dress which Jennie had made for me which was hanging there.

It was part of my nightmare but it seemed to have a frightening significance.

I shut the cupboard door firmly and set a chair against it. The catch was weak and a gust of wind would now and then blow it open, which was what had happened now.

That was all. It was just that coming after my dream it was like a symbol; and I thought suddenly: I cannot marry Rolf.

In my heart I did not believe him. He *had* been there that night. He was not the man I believed him to be. People are not always what one thinks them. I had thought Joe Cresswell was an honourable man and he had made me an accomplice in stealing documents to incriminate Uncle Peter. Uncle Peter had deceived people for years. I felt lost and alone. I had no experience of men. Gregory Donnelly had frightened me with his crude and meaningful glances, but at least I knew him for what he was.

And Rolf? He would not have lied. Or would he? He knew that I had changed after that Midsummer's Eve. He knew now why. He wanted Cador. He would have lied . . . for Cador.

And if he were indeed there that night, if it was he who had led on the mob to do that cruel thing, he was not the man I had loved so slavishly in my childhood. But he was kind and gentle, I knew. Part of him was; but people were made up of many parts.

He was obsessed by Cador. He loved the place. I saw the excitement in his eyes when he talked of it. Of course he wanted to marry me. I represented Cador in his eyes.

If I spoke to him, if I tried to explain, he would soothe me. I would believe him for a while . . . and then the doubts would come.

I could not marry him while I doubted him.

I had promised to marry him when I was not in a fit state to think clearly. I was stunned by the loss of the three people I loved unquestioningly. I had needed loving care and he had been there to offer it. He had given it ardently, it seemed; but was it for Cador?

The servants thought so. He had always wanted it. I remembered those eager conversations when my father was alive and Rolf and his father came to dine with us. He had wanted an estate of his own— and he had acquired one. But it was Cador that he really wanted.

I realized I had acted rashly. I needed time to think.

It was already morning and I could not marry Rolf this day.

It was no use trying to sleep. I got up and lighting four candles I sat down and wrote. I had torn up several sheets before I had completed the letter.

Dear Rolf,

This is a terrible thing I have to do, but I know now that I must. I cannot marry you yet. I hope you will not be too hurt. I think you will come to see that it is perhaps for the best. I have been foolish and rash, and the last thing I want to do is to hurt you, but marriage is such a big step and once the words have been said people are united forever.

I am behaving badly and you will despise me for this. I am

[244]

trying to find excuses for myself and I can only say that what happened so shattered me that I have felt lost and bewildered ever since. On the ship when we were together it seemed the right thing to do, a kind of way out for me. But marriage is more important than just that. Now that I am home, I am trying to think clearly, to be practical; and I am filled with misgiving.

I have been wondering for some weeks whether I have been rash. To me it seems such a short time since the tragedy.

Rolf, do please try to understand.

As you know I have always been very fond of you, but marriage is so binding, and I do not feel ready to take the step yet.

Forgive me, Rolf.

Annora

I sealed the letter. I must be sure that he received it at once. I did not want him to come to the chapel expecting the ceremony to go ahead.

As soon as it was light I dressed and went downstairs. I saddled my horse and rode over to the Manor.

As I arrived at the Manor stables I saw Luke Tregern on the point of going in. He looked amazed to see me, as well he might.

"Good morning, Miss Cadorson," he said, his eyebrows slightly raised, his teeth gleaming and his shrewd eyes alight with curiosity.

"Good morning, Luke. I have a letter here. Would you see that it gets to Mr. Hanson immediately?"

"I will indeed, Miss Cadorson. Are you well? Would you care to come into the house? I am sure Mr. Hanson will be up."

"No thanks. I just want him to get this note . . . as soon as possible."

"I will see to it."

I watched him as he hurried into the house; then I rode away.

I went back to my room. I sat there looking out of the window. My heart was still beating wildly and I was saying to myself: "What have you done?"

I went into Helena's room. She was surprised to see me.

"Good morning, Annora. Why, what's the matter?"

"There is to be no wedding, Helena."

She stared at me. "But . . "

"I can't explain. I just can't go through with it."

"But . . . Rolf . . ."

"I've told him. I wrote a note explaining. I've just taken it over myself. Luke Tregern is giving it to him."

"Annora!"

"I know it is a terrible thing I have done. But I had to. I *knew* I had to. Helena, I want you to explain to them all. Stop all the preparation . . ."

"Do you want to talk. . . ?"

I shook my head.

"Just do that for me. Will you, Helena?"

She nodded and went away.

There was a stunned silence throughout the house. It was like a place of mourning. The servants talked in whispers. I could imagine the conversation in the kitchen.

Rolf came over. Helena came to tell me that he was there.

I did not want to see him, but I could not refuse. I had already done him a great injury. I could not add to that.

He was waiting for me in the small room which led from the hall. He just stood there looking at me in silence.

I began to stammer: "Oh . . . Rolf . . . I'm so sorry. I just could not go through with it."

"Why, Annora? *Why?*"

"It's difficult to explain. I just know I can't. Oh, Rolf, what can I say?"

"To have come so near. . . !"

"I know. But I had to stop it . . . before it was too late. Please try to understand."

"I'm afraid I can't." His voice sounded cold, remote. I wanted to go to him, to fling my arms round him, to tell him that no matter what the consequences were I would marry him today in the chapel.

But he was looking at me with cold distrust. He had changed. I had never seen him look like that. He was controlling his emotions. The thought came to me, He is seeing Cador slipping out of his grasp.

I felt vindicated suddenly.

I had done the right thing.

I heard myself say almost coolly: "I'm sorry, Rolf, but I had to do it."

I thought he might plead with me and if he had done so, I might have given way. I loved Rolf. I had always loved him, but between us was that image of the man in the grey robe. I could not rid myself of the fear that he was the one who had worn it on that night; and I imagined that I would always go on believing it. It would be there always, a shadow between us.

"This is definite then," he said.

I did not answer. I wanted to say: "Wait. It might change." I might come to terms with this. I loved Rolf. I wanted to be with him. If only I could be sure that he had not been there that night. But he had already said that he was not there. The fact was that I did not believe him.

"There is no need for me to remain," said Rolf. "You have made it very clear to me. I can do nothing but accept your decision."

This cold, precise man was not like the Rolf I knew. He was deeply wounded I knew yet it hurt me that he could seem so aloof, almost indifferent. If he had raged at me I could have answered him, perhaps explained. Perhaps we could have made some plans. Perhaps we could wait awhile. Time . . . that was what I wanted.

But he had gone.

A terrible sense of loneliness swept over me. I knew then that I wanted him back. Even if he *had* been there on that night, I loved him enough to be able to understand that he was carried away by his desire to watch the behaviour of people and compare it with what had happened long ago.

But he had gone and I had wounded him so deeply that he would never forgive me for what I had done. It was the cruellest blow one partner of a prospective marriage could deal another. If I had broken it off even a week ago the blow would have been less acute. But to leave it until the very day of the wedding, that seemed heartless. I knew that was what he was thinking. He must despise me.

No wonder I was unhappy. I felt I was losing everything I cared for.

That day which was to have been my wedding day seemed as though it would never end. There was no one I could talk to, not even Helena. I could not tell her of my fears, that I did not trust Rolf. Why did I doubt him? He had said he was not there. Until recently I should have believed him—but what had happened in London had made me doubt human nature . . . and Rolf was human.

How bitter he must be feeling! I tried to tell myself that he would be in mourning for Cador, not for me, but I could not entirely believe that.

If only my parents had not died our marriage would have been a joyous occasion. I should have known that he was not marrying me for my possessions. But would memories of that Midsummer's Eve be as fresh in my mind even then?

I was afraid it was something I should never forget.

Helena had written to her mother to tell her that the wedding was not taking place for she would be expecting us to arrive in London.

"I haven't given her any reason," she said. "I have just written to say that the wedding is off and that we shall be here for a while."

She did not attempt to probe. Gentleness was one of her greatest qualities which went with a certain acceptance that things did not always go right. That was something she herself had learned through bitter experience.

The days dragged on. When I rode along the quay I was aware of furtive looks. They were all wondering why I had almost reached the altar before I decided to run back.

I did not see Rolf, but I heard he had left Luke Tregern in charge and gone away. No one was quite sure where.

That was a wise thing to do. Trust Rolf to be wise.

Helena said to me one day: "Annora, I think you ought to get away. Bob Carter can look after everything. He does now so what difference does it make? My mother is urging us to come to London."

I knew that she was right.

It was a relief to leave Cador.

Aunt Amaryllis was so kind and no one asked embarrassing questions. They just took it for granted that I had changed my mind.

Helena was welcomed back and Jonnie became everyone's favourite.

Peterkin said: "You've come just at the right time. You'll be able to come to our wedding."

Then he looked a little shamefaced as though it was tactless of him to refer to weddings. I hastily assured him that I should be delighted to come.

He had changed a good deal. He was wildly enthusiastic about his work and he and Frances were obviously very pleased with each other. Frances had been able to extend her activities considerably and it was all due to the support she had received from Uncle Peter. It was true that in the press there were constant references to the mission work which Miss Cresswell and Mr. Lansdon were doing. It was a piquant story for they were the daughter and son of those two men who not long ago had been in the news, suspected of questionable behaviour.

Uncle Peter amazed me. He was more ebullient than ever. He was full of energy, always engaged in some project, and I believed his business was flourishing. No one could shut down his clubs because he kept within the law. He maintained that worldly insouciance implying that they were a necessity in a less than perfect world and he almost succeeded in giving the impression that he was a benefactor to society.

In spite of my sorrow in my loss which still persisted and my guilt in having treated Rolf so badly, I began to feel a little better in London.

I remembered that there had been talk, when my parents were alive, of having a season. Had things gone differently this would have come about. But there was no question of it now.

Aunt Amaryllis could have launched me, I suppose, but the recent scandal might have made it a little awkward even if my parents' death had not made it quite undesirable.

Aunt Amaryllis had referred to it vaguely, but I had hastily brushed it aside.

"Perhaps later . . ." said Aunt Amaryllis.

But I did not feel like a young debutante. I certainly did not want to join that band of girls who were led forth to display their charms, both physical and financial, in the hope of acquiring a husband. I felt old by comparison; if not in years, in experience.

But there were moments in London when I could forget these matters which weighed so heavily on me. Aunt Amaryllis was determined to lighten my spirits. There were visits to the opera; there were rides in the Park and visits to the Mission in the East End. I was beginning to feel alive again.

I found the papers interesting. There was a great deal going on. The Flora Hastings affair was still being widely discussed and the Queen was decidedly out of favour on this account. Moreover there was another matter over which she was being severely criticized.

Her relationship with Lord Melbourne was the subject for sly jokes; his government had been defeated and she, being so devoted to him, had developed a great antipathy to Sir Robert Peel.

Uncle Peter discussed these matters at length when he dined with us. They were not frequent, those occasions, because he was usually busy somewhere else but, oddly enough, I found myself looking forward to them. I knew that he was amoral and my mother had hated him because he had blackmailed her—or rather they had blackmailed each other—before she married my father, and, of course, I knew the nature of his business; yet there he was, setting aside his misdemeanours, snapping his fingers at scandal and giving the impression that he had outwitted all his critics. I should not have admired him, but I could not help it; and his conversation was always lighthearted and amusing.

He told us wittily about the Queen versus Sir Robert Peel; how she called him the "music master," because of the nervous way he pranced on the carpet when he was talking to her, for she would not ask him to sit down and etiquette prevented his doing so without that invitation.

"Of course he is nervous in her presence. No cosy têtes-à-têtes as with dear Lord Melbourne. Odd, to think of a great statesman being nervous of a young girl . . . for that is all she is. But it is the crown, of course. Peel wants the Whig ladies dismissed from the Bedchamber and Tory ladies to replace them. The Queen says No; and Peel says, No Tory Bedchamber Ladies and no Peel for P.M. It is an impasse. And the result, the return of Melbourne to totter along in power for a few more months. An early election is inevitable and even Her Majesty cannot stop that. Then it will be the retirement of Lord M and the Whig Bedchamber Ladies, I fear."

"And what do you think will happen at the election, Uncle?" I asked.

"No doubt about it. A majority for Peel and the Tories."

I looked at him intently. It was the election he had been waiting for. But for the scandal he would have been standing and I had no doubt that he would have been elected. Then, of course, with his power and his money and his adroit cleverness it would have been a ministerial post for him. Being Uncle Peter he would most certainly have had his eyes on the Premiership. Yet there he was smiling nonchalantly, discussing it all amusingly with no sign of any deep regret. Yet he had wanted advancement in that direction so fervently that he had sought to disqualify Joseph Cresswell.

It was a wicked thing to have done. How could I admire him for anything after that? It seemed that I was becoming tainted with that worldliness myself, or was I beginning to understand that people are complicated with good and bad closely entwined?

The days slipped by. I was sleeping better and was a little more interested in food and what I should wear. Helena and I went shopping. We bought clothes for ourselves and Jonnie. The streets were full of activity and there was always something new to see. I was fascinated by the Flying Pieman, who did not sell pies but hot puddings, running through the streets with his tray on which his puddings steamed. He hardly stopped to serve his customers for he had deposited his wares early in the morning at various public houses where the food could be kept hot; then he sped through the streets from one to another so that the puddings could be served steaming hot. The ballad singers also interested me. They did a big trade if there was an execution. They would have accounts of the murder or verses reputed to have been written by the condemned on the eve of execution. It was all rather grim and for that reason attracted many buyers. There were ballad singers and groups singing madrigals. Those streets were so lively, and it was impossible not to get caught up in the excitement.

News came that Flora Hastings had died and that her death was due to a malignant growth. This had made her body so swollen that the false impression had been given that she was pregnant. The indignation of the people was great.

So easily swayed, they sanctified Flora Hastings and vilified the Queen—for they had to have a scapegoat. The papers were full of the affair. People walked about the streets displaying placards on which were written: "Murder at Buckingham Palace." The Queen was hissed when she rode out in her carriage.

"We shall see sparks flying at the funeral," said Uncle Peter. "The Queen and Melbourne must be uneasy. It's bad for them that she died at Buckingham Palace and the cortège will start from there. I'd be ready to swear that they will leave earlier than stated because they'll be hoping to get well away before the crowds become unmanageable. Anything could happen. It's to be hoped the Queen's advisers won't let her attend. I don't think it would be safe for her little Majesty."

She did not attend but she sent her carriage. A stone was thrown at it.

I said to Uncle Peter: "Why do they blame her? I suppose she only listened to her advisers."

"A monarch cannot afford to take the wrong side. No, Her Majesty is not to blame. She has the kindest of hearts and is most sentimental. This has been worked up between the Queen's household and that of her mother. Things are never quite as they seem, Annora my dear. There are intrigues and feuds where you would least expect them. Don't fret. Her Majesty is quite safe on the throne."

"But when she was crowned they cheered her so madly. They really loved her then."

"They'll love her again. The crowd's love is very fickle. It's like the weather. You can never rely on it. It is well to remember that it changes quickly. But everything blows over eventually."

It seemed to me that he was quite fond of me. He often talked to me which I thought was rather strange, as I must have seemed very young and inexperienced to such a worldly man.

One late afternoon when Helena and I returned from a visit to the shops, we were told by one of the maids that a gentleman was in the drawing room with Mrs. Lansdon and we were to go there as soon as we came in.

Giving our parcels to the maid to be taken to our rooms we went into the drawing room.

To our amazement Matthew was there.

Helena gave a little cry. He came to her, and putting his hands on her shoulders, kissed her.

Then he turned to me.

"I am so pleased to see you, Annora," he said, taking my hands. "I . . . heard. I was so sorry I was not there to help."

I shook my head and tried to fight back the emotion which reference to the tragedy always aroused. I said: "Matthew, how are you? How long have you been back?"

"Some little time," he said. "I went to Cornwall. Your letter said you would be there. They gave me hospitality for a night and then I started on the journey here."

Aunt Amaryllis said: "Isn't it wonderful? You must be very happy, Helena. You have been so long apart."

"How is Jonnie?" asked Matthew.

"He is well. You'll want to see him, of course."

I thought: Helena is keeping up the pretence that this is an ordinary marriage—and Matthew is helping her.

"He's in the nursery," went on Helena. "Come up."

They went. Aunt Amaryllis looked at me and said: "He seems a very pleasant young man. And so earnest. Before you came he was telling me about his research and his book. I do hope it is soon published. I think he is a very *good* young man."

I was amazed at the impact Matthew made on the family. He had always seemed to me rather insignificant apart from his ambition to do good. He had never shown great interest in anything but prison reform.

It was Uncle Peter, of course, who was behind it all.

When he had heard that Matthew had collected his material and had already written it in the form of a book he wanted to see the book and Matthew willingly showed him. Having read it Uncle Peter was enthusiastic.

"It must be published without delay," he said. "Leave it to me. It is a matter of making sure it receives notice. I know people, I know how these things are done. People should know of these evils."

He gave me a broad smile for he saw the amazement on my face; he knew that I was thinking of the work that he had kept secret for so long.

There was some motive behind Uncle Peter's interest. With Uncle Peter there would always be a motive.

Matthew was delighted. Before he had been in the house a few days he was Uncle Peter's devoted disciple. He listened to his views with reverence; he must have known the nature of Uncle Peter's business but like so many before him he was ready to forget that. It must have seemed to him that anyone who cared so much about prison reform was a good man.

Uncle Peter acted quickly. He found a firm which was eager to publish the book. A few adjustments would have to be made.

"Always the case," said Uncle Peter lightly, "with people who are not professional writers. The sooner we get the whole thing ready and out, the better."

Matthew had changed. I could see that he thought this marriage into which he had entered on impulse to help Helena was turning out very well for him. He had acquired the kindest of mothers-in-law who was ready to love everyone and a powerful father-in-law who was well disposed towards him and was welcoming him with open arms into his new family.

Uncle Peter set about getting people working on the book and I was sure a great deal of interest would be created.

I began to understand Uncle Peter's motive, for one evening when we were all at dinner he said: "You know, Matthew, it is not enough to write a book. A book is important. People read it and become indignant. This should not be, they say. And then something else catches their attention. The book could be a nine days' wonder. The battle will not be done by one single book."

Matthew looked crestfallen. "But, I thought, sir, to arouse people's consciences."

"And so you will. But consciences are fickle things and I repeat, it is not enough. You will have to plead your cause to the country . . . and there is only one way of doing that."

"I don't understand. Another book?"

Uncle Peter shook his head. "There is bound to be an election soon. Stand for Parliament, my dear fellow. Get in. Bring this matter up. That's the only way. It's Parliament that changes the law."

"It has always been a dream of mine to get into politics. I see that it is the real way to get these things done."

"Well, do you want my advice?"

"I'd be grateful for it. You have been so wonderfully good to me."

Uncle Peter smiled at him. "Start thinking about standing for Parliament *now*."

"Do you think I would be eligible?"

"We'll make you eligible. Now this book is going to make a stir."

"Are you sure of that?"

"We'll see that it does. That sort of thing is not left to chance. You'll have a certain amount of fame. Now, you'll have to have a place of your own . . . a little house in Westminster . . . not very far from here. You and Helena will entertain the right people. I know something about these things. Progress in all things is very much a matter of knowing the right people. That's not all, of course. But it plays a big part. You must have a house . . . a charming house . . . not too big. Just what is right for a rising young man whose main interest is doing the right thing for his country. You are shocked by some of our laws and you are going into Parliament to put that right. That is what politicians are supposed to be for. You have written your book. You have travelled to Australia to get first-hand knowledge. You have interviewed convicts. You'd get in easily in the right constituency. People are interested in reform. Think of the Reform Bill and the difference that has made. If you want to bring about Prison Reform there is only one way of doing it. In Parliament."

Matthew's eyes were glowing. He could see himself triumphantly reforming the laws of the country. Aunt Amaryllis was looking on with pride. She still grieved for my mother but she had a new son-in-law who had found great favour with Uncle Peter and was already a respected member of the family. Moreover there was Jonnie. Aunt Amaryllis was fast recovering her contentment.

Uncle Peter said: "We have never given Matthew and Helena a present, Amaryllis, have we? I have a suggestion to make. We're going to give them a house. I have seen a charming one, not a stone's throw from here. It's vacant. I passed it today. It's handy for the House of Commons and a small amount of entertaining. Small dinner parties . . . nothing very big . . . we'll get the right people there. And I am sure your book and your contacts will lessen the difficulties of being selected as a candidate."

There was a feeling of excitement round the table. I was thinking how clever Uncle Peter was. He was manipulating Matthew. He had already made him his slave. Matthew was a simple young man who really cared about the sufferings of others; he was fundamentally good. He was a perfect tool for Uncle Peter. No one could doubt Matthew's sincerity and that was going to be very useful to Uncle Peter.

I was wondering what his eventual motives were for there would be motives. He was doing something more than merely helping along the career of his son-in-law. I suspected he was going to use him as his mouthpiece. He himself was barred from Parliament; perhaps he intended Matthew to speak for him.

Uncle Peter was smiling at me. I had a notion that he guessed my thoughts and that they amused him.

About two days later I came face to face with Uncle Peter on the stairs.

He said: "My dear Annora, I want us to have a little talk soon."
I looked startled.
He went on: "I feel like a sort of guardian. I am your uncle and

[255]

you are a young woman of property and that means responsibilities
. . . heavy I fear for those young shoulders. It will be a private talk. I
tell you what we'll do. You and I will have luncheon together at my
club. Shall we say tomorrow?"

"Thank you, Uncle," I said. "I should like that."

It was true. I should. I found him very interesting. I wondered so
much about him and I was fascinated by the manner in which he was
directing Matthew. Perhaps I could ask him about it if we were
alone. I had a feeling that he might be very frank for he knew I
understood certain things about him.

At dinner that night he told Aunt Amaryllis he was going to take
me to luncheon at his club.

Aunt Amaryllis beamed. "That will be lovely for you, Annora,"
she said and she sent one of those adoring looks in her husband's
direction. I knew she was thinking what a wonderful man he was. He
was making Matthew and Helena so happy. He was such a good
father as well as a perfect husband.

His dignified carriage took us to the club. There he introduced me
to several members as his niece who was on a visit to London from
Cornwall.

A secluded table was found for us and he ordered what he thought
I should like.

He smiled at me across the table and said: "This is pleasant. I feel
there are certain things we have to say to each other. My dear child, I
know you are very sad at this moment. You have lost those who were
very dear to you and you thought you would rush into marriage . . .
and then you decided against it. You are rather bewildered, are you
not? You don't know quite what comes next. Moreover, you have
inherited a big estate which will have to be administered. You have a
good man there, I believe?"

I nodded.

"But, of course, you will have to return in due course. I was very
fond of your mother, very fond indeed. At one point, I might have
married her."

"She was always in love with my father."

"This was before your father's return. He was in Australia serving
his sentence. He had been sent away for seven years and your mother
was only a child when he went. Moreover she had married . . ."

"I know the story. Her first husband was an invalid and he died."

[256]

"And your father came back."

I looked at him steadily. "She did tell me about the blackmail."

"An interesting situation. There have been many cases of blackmail. I don't know how many there have been of double blackmail."

"Not so many, I suppose."

"And *I* suppose you think me something of a villain. That's what I want to talk to you about. I want to explain a good many things. You see, I admired your mother more than any woman I know. She was strong and passionate about life. She knew how to live." He must have guessed my thoughts again for he went on quickly: "Oh, don't think I am disparaging your Aunt Amaryllis in any way. I knew at once that she was the one for me. She has been the perfect wife. I love her dearly. Yes, Amaryllis was the one for me. I chose her because she was the sort of wife I needed. I saw that immediately."

"You seem to see everything. There was one thing though. You didn't see that Joe Cresswell would expose you."

"No. I did not see that."

"You should have . . . after what you had done to his father. People don't just allow others to treat them like that."

"I misjudged Joe. I thought he was spineless like his father. But he had something. Not enough though. Did you know they have moved to the North . . . the whole family? They have some business up there. Well, they chose the way they have gone . . . as we all do."

"They were ruined."

"They ruined themselves. It would have blown over. They lacked the good sense and courage to stay and fight it out."

"As you did."

"Yes, as I did. That is what I want to talk to you about, Annora. I want to help you get out of this slough of despondency into which you have fallen. You are so young, dear girl. Your whole life is before you. I do fully understand your feelings. To lose them all at one blow . . . It was shattering. And then all that it entailed. You found the estate was yours and you thought you would marry. He would have been a good husband, I think. What little I have seen of him would indicate that. But right at the eleventh hour you decided against it. Well, you know your own mind. But I think you hanker after him. Do you?"

"I don't know."

"I think, in your circumstances, a strong man to stand beside you would not come amiss. I think perhaps you will change your mind and marry Rolf Hanson after all."

I was silent.

"My dearest Annora, you cannot go on mourning forever. That is not the way to live. You must look for happiness. That is the real success in life . . . to be happy."

"It is strange to hear you say that. I should have thought for you it was money and power."

"You're right. But power and money . . . that *is* my happiness. Some people look in other directions. To get what you want. That is success, and you won't achieve it by giving way."

"I know you like to manipulate people. Are you thinking of doing that with me?"

He shook his head. "What I want to do for you is put you on the right road. I have seen you looking at me in a questioning manner. You are wondering about me, aren't you? You think I am a wicked man, worldly, cynical, power-seeking, ruthless. Perhaps you are right, but I do fancy that you have a sneaking liking for me which will not be suppressed."

I could not help smiling. He had described exactly what I felt.

"True?" he asked.

"Well . . . perhaps."

He nodded. "I knew. And you are nearly right. I don't like to see you drooping, fading away, suppressing your personality, drowning in your sorrows. Stand up and face them, Annora. You see how I've done it. I want you to take a lesson from me. You would have thought, wouldn't you, that when the news broke about my business, I should have been finished. A great many men would have been. Look at Joseph Cresswell slinking away with his tail between his legs. No. I saw I had to stand my ground and I did . . . and I got by."

"Circumstances worked in your favour. Peterkin and Frances with the Mission was one thing."

"Cresswell had the same advantage. After all, Frances is his daughter. I took advantage of what was offered."

"It must have been a god-send."

"It was good. I have made it beneficial."

"The money you gave to the Mission was accompanied by blazing publicity, I noticed."

[258]

"Exactly."

"And now Matthew?"

"Matthew is going into Parliament. I shall support him."

"Another gift from Heaven?"

"He is married to my daughter. It will be seen that I am a supporter of good causes."

"And when he is in Parliament?"

"I shall advise him, of course. He is a very amenable young man."

"He will be your slave."

"Oh come. Slavery is abolished now, you know. Let us say I may become his mentor. In five years' time . . . seven at most . . . I shall not be so very old. Perhaps then I can do what I've always wanted to. Be in Parliament myself. That is the ultimate power. To make the laws of the land, to build one's country into the greatest in the world."

"I see you are building the foundation of your future career which has been disturbed. You have had to start building again. But you are still determined to succeed."

"I am being very frank with you, Annora."

"I wonder why."

"Because you have been astute enough to see the way I am going. I am telling you this because I want you to see what can be done. I daresay you have had moments when you thought you would never be happy again. But you can and you will. But you won't do it if you sit nursing your sorrows. Get rid of them. Start again. Those who succeed in life are the ones who can pick themselves up and start again when they fall down. The longer you remain on the ground the harder it will be to get up. That's what I'm telling you, Annora."

"It is very kind of you to take so much trouble over me."

"I am expiating my sins towards your mother. She would agree that I owed it to her. She was a very courageous woman. Oh, I was very fond of Jessica. And here you are . . . her daughter. Remember what I have told you. Think of how far I have come since those days when the papers blared forth evidence of my villainies. I'm living it down, just as Lord Melbourne lived down his past. Did you know that man figured in two divorce cases? He had a mad wife who blatantly flaunted her relationship with the poet Lord Byron. Their story was one of the scandals of the age. Yet what happened to Lord Melbourne? He became Prime Minister and is now the Queen's most devoted and dearest friend. What Melbourne did, what I can do, *you* can do, Annora."

He stretched his hand across the table and took mine.

I said: "Thank you, Uncle Peter. You have helped me a lot. Should I go back to Cornwall?"

"I like your being here, of course, but you have to go back, don't you? You have to see that man again. I think you're hankering after him. I should find out. Then if he'll still have you, marry him. Do you still want him?"

"I think of him . . . often."

"You can't get him out of your thoughts. I've seen you look at Helena and Matthew . . . wistfully."

"It seems as if it might work out for them now."

"It does indeed. Helena is not of an adventurous nature. She takes after her mother. She wants a cosy life. She is ready to step in line. This rather stresses what I have been telling you. I know the story. I know that John Milward is the baby's father; but Matthew came along and he did his good deed. He married Helena to make life easier for her. He is a very agreeable young man. And now you see everything is going to turn out well for him . . . for them both. When he gets into Parliament, when he plays his part in bringing about Prison Reform he will have justified himself. His confidence will rise. I see a life of good works ahead of him for, mark my words, when he has done with Prison Reform, there will be something else. Helena will stand beside him, helped by her mother and me. She will provide the right setting for the rising politician. There will be little ones joining Jonnie in the nursery and Helena will realize that the best thing that happened to her was being jilted by John Milward and marrying Matthew purely for convenience in the first place."

I couldn't help laughing. "I don't think it is going to be quite as simple as that."

He looked at me earnestly. "But it will . . . if they make it so. You see what I'm getting at. Now this young man in Cornwall—you've known him all your life. I remember hearing that as a child you were his devoted slave. And then you grew up and were in love with him. Yes, you are. Don't think you can deceive me. And you turn him down on some whim . . . just because, my dear, you are immersed in your tragedy and not making the effort to grow away from it. You allow yourself to suspect he is marrying you for your possessions. He wants Cador. So? He would be a foolish young man if he did not. Of course, he wants Cador; and for that very reason he will make a good thing of it. If he didn't want Cador I should have a very poor opinion of him. How could he help you manage it satisfactorily if he didn't feel delighted in having a share in it?"

"You have a certain way of reasoning . . ."

"I have a realistic way of reasoning. You want to feel that he would marry you if you were a little match seller. But you are not a match seller and if you were it is hardly likely that you would have met this young man. No. He wants to marry you. He loves you but that need not stop his loving Cador as well. Get rid of those romantic notions. Look at life as it really is . . . as I always have. And you see me as I am. I have ridden the storms, haven't I? That is what you have to do in life, believe me."

If it were only Cador that stood between us he might be right. But my thoughts went back to that Midsummer's Eve.

I said: "When I was a child, I thought Rolf the most wonderful person on earth . . . at least one of them. He shared that honour with my father. Red-letter days were when he came to Cador which he did often with his father. Then something happened. It was Midsummer's Eve in Cornwall. They celebrate it there with old customs going back to pre-Christian days. There was a woman who lived in the woods. People said she was a witch. On Midsummer's Eve they burned down her house. There was one there . . . the leader in a kind of Druid's robe. I believe it was Rolf because I had seen that robe in his house. It changed everything between us. It occurred to me that I did not know him at all. I felt I could not trust anyone any more, not even Rolf. And early in the morning of the day which was to have been our wedding day, I realized that it was Cador he wanted . . . and I just could not marry him."

"Did you talk to him about it?"

"On the ship when we were coming home we had talked. He said he wasn't there. He was in Bodmin."

"Well?"

"I couldn't quite believe him. Oh, I did at the time . . . but later I had so many doubts. And then I thought that he was marrying me for Cador."

"And all because of that escapade."

"Escapade! It was such cruelty as I had never seen before. If my father had been there he would have put a stop to it."

"Let's suppose the worst: that he lied about this. He was young.

Young men have high spirits. Perhaps they drink a little too much. They do foolish things. They do things they regret afterwards. You must understand this. You have to forgive the sins of youth."

"This was no ordinary little peccadillo. You should have seen that woman's face . . . the terrible things they did to her."

"People get carried away. He is a man now . . . and you are in love with him. The best thing you can do is marry him. I am sure the man who is looking after the place is good. He must be for your father was prepared to leave him in charge while he was away. But I daresay he had means of knowing what was going on and he would have been advised from afar and gone home if it had been necessary. The best manager in the country needs a guiding hand. You have to give that. It's a great responsibility . . . all those tenants, people who depend on Cador. You've got to do your duty by the land; you have to make sure that all goes well with what your father and his forebears have built up. And Rolf is the man to help you. Go back and marry him if he'll have you after what you did to him. He will . . . for Cador's sake."

"Uncle Peter," I said, "you are the most amazing of men. I never thought I should be talking to *you* like this."

"Sinners are far more lenient than saints. That's another lesson you'll have to learn. I know all the temptations, good people don't. Therefore I understand how easy it is to fall into them. Take my advice. Go back. Talk to him. Tell him of your feelings . . . as you've talked to me. I'd like to see you settled. I tell you, I feel a responsibility towards you because I was fond of your mother. I'm fond of you, too."

He smiled and lifted his glass.

"To the success of Annora. May everything that is good come to her. And let me tell you that if she makes up her mind to get it, she will. That's a law of nature. Think about what we've said. And now I am going to take you back because I have a meeting to attend."

I said: "Thank you, Uncle Peter. You have helped me quite a lot."

He had. I felt my spirits rise. Had I attached too much importance to that Midsummer's Eve? I tried to shut out the memory of the stricken face of that old woman and the flames rioting among the thatch of her cottage.

A youthful escapade? No, I could not think of it as that. It had been a cruel and vicious act and only a man who had cruelty in him could have taken part in such a deed. But he had not been there. I must believe him.

And Cador? Uncle Peter was right. Of course he loved Cador. He always had.

I was in love with Rolf. I always had been. Hadn't I compared others with him? Joe. Gregory Donnelly. And always I had thought, But they are not Rolf. Yet I had turned my back on him. I thought of the last time I had seen him—cool, detached, almost as though he disliked me. It was natural that he should after what I had done.

Suppose I went back. Suppose I told him how I had felt. Suppose we talked—not just lightly but in detail about that Midsummer's Eve and his love for Cador—talked frankly as, surprisingly, I had been able to talk to Uncle Peter.

Helena was growing towards some sort of contentment. I had gone with her and Aunt Amaryllis to see the little house in Westminster. It was charming and I could see that Helena liked it. There were plans in her mind as she talked quite animatedly for her about the aspect of the dining room and the drawing room, and how her eyes shone as she planned what should be the nursery.

"Jonnie would love to play in that," said Aunt Amaryllis, beaming. It was all turning out as she would have wished, and her magnificent husband was going to buy this house for Helena and her husband. Moreover Uncle Peter was interested in Matthew's prospects and that meant he was going to make a great career for his son-in-law.

It was only when she turned to me that Aunt Amaryllis's eyes were clouded. She would be remembering my mother, my tragic loss, my desertion of my bridegroom almost at the altar.

And again I thought: Uncle Peter is right. I have allowed myself to brood, to become cynical, to look for a mercenary motive behind people's actions. I remembered my mother's saying that good things would always come to Amaryllis because she just simply failed to see what was not good.

I think there must have been some truth in that.

Now Aunt Amaryllis had both her children happily settled. The irritations which had beset them a short while ago when people who were jealous of Peter had tried to pull him down, were over. Nobody could ruin Peter however virulently they attacked him. Everyone must see what a magnificent man he was.

I thought of Peter choosing Amaryllis. He had said he might have married my mother. I doubted she would have had him, but if she had, Peter's marriage would have been stormy. He had chosen Amaryllis because she was just the wife he needed. What husband wouldn't want a wife who thought him perfect in every way? How rare such women would be. It was typical of Uncle Peter that he had one.

What he had said to me was true. Rolf and I belonged together. And Cador belonged to us.

While I was looking over the house with Helena and Aunt Amaryllis I said to myself: Go back. See Rolf. Ask his forgiveness for what I have done and talk . . . talk frankly. Tell him exactly what I feel.

The thought lifted my spirits considerably.

When I mentioned to Helena that I had decided to go back to Cornwall very soon, she was regretful, but she did not cling to me and beg me to stay as once she would have done. That was an indication of the change in her life. She was getting closer to Matthew. She was eager to get to the new house. She discussed how she would entertain there with her mother and was even drawing up lists of people who should be invited.

One morning, a few days after my luncheon with Uncle Peter I went downstairs and found two letters waiting for me. Both came from Cornwall. One was from Rolf; the other from Yorke, Tamblin and Company, the lawyers who had taken over the practice when Rolf's father had given up.

I hesitated over them and deliberately picked up the lawyers' letter first.

Dear Miss Cadorson,

A most extraordinary and alarming matter has arisen. It is difficult to explain by letter, but I think you should return to Cador immediately.

I assure you that it is of the utmost importance that you come without delay.

Your obedient servant,

James Tamblin

I was puzzled. To what could he be referring and why so mysterious?

I took up Rolf's letter.

"My dear Annora." I felt floods of relief sweep over me. At least he called me his dear Annora, so he could not hate and despise me as much as I had feared.

This is a most extraordinary matter. I really cannot believe it is true. James Tamblin, I know, is writing to you. I do think it is imperative that you should be here. It is a matter which will have to have thorough investigation, as you will agree . . .

How can I, I thought, when I don't know what it is?

I am afraid I was a little bewildered at our last meeting and you did not find me very sympathetic. Annora, we have to forget that. It's over. I still don't understand it, but I am trying to put it behind me.

I want you to know that if you need my help over this I am here to be of assistance. Remember, I did study law to a certain extent. So you must call on me at any time you think I might be of use.

Don't worry. We will go on as though nothing has happened. I am sure this ridiculous claim will be proved to be false.

I hope we can be, as we always were, good friends.

Yours,
Rolf

I read both letters again. They were maddeningly obscure. What could have happened? I must know. I would return to Cornwall without delay.

There was consternation throughout the household when I produced the solicitors' letter. Everyone was mystified.

"You see," I said, "that I must leave immediately."

They all realized that. Uncle Peter said I should not travel alone. He would have come with me but for important business which he could not possibly fail to attend to. He was going to send Mrs. Eggham to travel with Eggham and me. Eggham was one of the grooms.

"It's a pity they haven't done better with the railways," he said.

"It's about fifteen years since there was all that fuss about a train that went from Stockton to Darlington. Of course we were all sceptical then, and after that we began to expect wonders. And now if you go from London to Birmingham you have to break your journey and take the coach. The carriage will be comfortable and Mrs. Eggham is a pleasant woman. When do you propose to leave?"

"Tomorrow."

So I said goodbye to them and this time, although Helena expressed her sorrow at my departure she did not beg to come with me.

I set out with the Egghams who were to stay a night or two at Cador and then return to London.

The journey was uneventful and in due course I arrived at Cador. It was always an emotional moment to catch sight of those towers— and perhaps particularly so now that they belonged to me.

It was early evening when we arrived. They had all been expecting me. Isaacs was in the hall with Mrs. Penlock and a number of the servants. Bob Carter was there also.

I was conscious of the suppressed excitement and I knew the cause. They were all aware that something momentous was happening.

"Mr. Tamblin told us you'd be coming," said Mrs. Penlock. "We wasn't quite sure which day but your bed is aired and everything's ready."

"I had a rather disturbing letter from Mr. Tamblin," I said, looking from Isaacs to Mrs. Penlock. "Have you any idea what is wrong?"

They shook their heads. "We just know the lawyer wanted to see you, Miss Cadorson," said Isaacs.

"I thought something was wrong with the house. The roof . . . or something like that."

"The roof is in good order," said Bob Carter. "I'd have seen to that."

"So's everything else as far as we do know," added Mrs. Penlock.

"By the way, Mr. and Mrs. Eggham will want a room. They'll want to eat, too."

"We reckoned as you'd have someone with you, Miss Cadorson," said Isaacs.

"And we'm prepared," added Mrs. Penlock.

"They will probably stay for two nights."

"I'll have something on the table within the hour," said Mrs. Penlock.

I retired early. Travelling was so exhausting. I decided to go along to the lawyer first thing in the morning.

I rose early, breakfasted and prepared to leave the house. I rode down to the town. I knew the Yorke, Tamblin offices well for they had once been Rolf's father's.

Mr. Tamblin was obviously relieved to see me.

"Come into the office, Miss Cadorson," he said. "How glad I am that you are here. This is a most disturbing matter. Would you care for a glass of Madeira wine . . . or sherry?"

"No, thank you. I'd rather hear what is wrong."

"Mind you, nothing is certain, but this woman could prove that she is right and that could mean you would be dispossessed of everything . . . or almost everything."

"Please tell me the worst."

"A woman has arrived here. She is now staying at the Anglers' Inn. She is laying claim to Cador."

"Laying claim? What do you mean? How can she do that?"

"Her story is that your father married her mother in Australia in 1814, and that she is his legitimate daughter and therefore heiress to his estates."

"But that is ridiculous."

"So I thought. But your father was in Australia at that time and she says she has proof."

"Proof? What proof?"

"A certificate of marriage."

"It's nonsense. My father married my mother . . ."

"Her story is that he went through a form of marriage with your mother when he came back to England, but of course if as she says, he was already married to her mother, the ceremony he went through with your mother was no true marriage."

"That is quite impossible. All those years ago! Where has she been until now? Why didn't she come forward? Why does she wait until he is dead before she does so? What has she been doing all these years?"

"She said she did not know where he was. It was only when she read of him in the papers at the time of his death by drowning in Australia that she understood who he was. She knew nothing of his

[267]

wealth and title. She says that when he was drowned with the woman who thought she was his wife and his illegitimate son, and she read about it in the Sydney *Gazette*, there was no doubt in her mind. She knew she was reading about her father because it gave his history, how he went out there for seven years because he had killed a man for attempting to rape a gypsy girl, how when his term was served he had heard of vast estates and a title awaiting him in England. How he had left Australia and returned to England. She was only a child when he went away and never knew him very well, but her deserted mother used to tell her about him. She says that when he came into his fortune he wanted to forget his life in Australia, so he just walked out and went to England . . . and there he married. But she insists that marriage was no true one."

"She read of it in the papers. Do you think. . . ?"

"I understand what you mean, Miss Cadorson. She read of what had happened and thought she would perpetrate this fraud. Your father had been in Australia; he had returned to England. She knew that. She had the facts. That's what you mean. But her story is just possible."

"I don't believe a word of it."

"I do not want to. But she says there is a certificate of marriage, which states clearly that there was a marriage with Jake Cadorson. It is an unusual name and this allegedly took place while your father was there."

"Is this a real marriage certificate?"

"We shall have it examined of course. But I find this very disturbing."

"What sort of woman is she?"

"Young. A little older than yourself. That fits of course. Her story undoubtedly has a certain plausibility."

"And just suppose it is decided that she is telling the truth?"

"I am afraid she could claim the estate."

"You mean . . . Cador would be hers."

He looked grim. "There might be some arrangement."

"What sort of arrangement?"

"As you have lived at Cador as your father's legitimate daughter for the whole of your life to date, we might be able to preserve something. I cannot say. It will be a matter for the judiciary. I thought of calling in advice. You might decide to contest the case."

"I cannot believe that my father would marry a woman and then desert her just because he had inherited his family home."

"It is hard to believe. But people do the strangest things. He *was* out there. He had been a prisoner. He had lived a hard life. He may have, at some time, thought he would continue to live out there. He did acquire land and was working on it when the news came to him. It might have been that he did not think his wife—if that was what she was—would fit into the ancestral home or to life in England. It may be that he wanted to cut off all ties with the country of his captivity."

"He would not have left her. He would not have come back and married my mother."

Mr. Tamblin sighed. "What we shall have to consider is whether this certificate is true or false. I am of the opinion that a great deal will hang on that."

"Where is it?"

"She guards it carefully. She knows that her case rests on it. When the time comes she will let it go but not, I fear, to me, for she knows I act for you."

"What sort of woman is she?"

Mr. Tamblin paused. "She . . . er . . . is not the sort of person I should expect to be your father's daughter."

"What must we do?"

"I want to get a verdict on the marriage certificate."

"Does anyone know about this?"

"I confess to telling Mr. Hanson. He has some knowledge of the law. Occasionally we exchange views and have done ever since I took over the practice. Very often business concerns the people here, and he knows them quite well. It helps when dealing with people to know something about them personally."

"He did write to me."

"Yes, he said he would."

"But he did not give me any idea of the nature of the trouble."

"No. He would be discreet."

"So we must wait now for a verdict on the certificate?"

He nodded. "She is bringing it tomorrow. Her lawyer will be with her. Perhaps you would care to be here then. And would you object if I invited Mr. Hanson to come along, too?"

I said weakly: "No. I should not object."

"This has been a great shock to you, Miss Cadorson, and coming so soon after the tragedy . . . but what happened would never have arisen but for that. Oh dear, this is most distressing."

I said: "I will go now, Mr. Tamblin. I will see you in the morning."

I came out of the office and mounted my horse. I rode out of the town and up the hill to Cador.

Then I turned away. I could not bear to look at it just now. I had been so proud of it always. My home . . . and now my very own. But for how long?

Could the story possibly be true? No. My father would never have deserted that woman. He would never have married my mother under false pretences. It was not his way. She was lying. It was clear to me what had happened. There had been full coverage of the story in the Sydney *Gazette*. She would have read about his coming to Australia to serve his prison term, his acquiring a little land which he was working when news of his inheritance came to him. She would have read all that. It was a romantic story of the kind beloved by newsmen. And how simple for her to fabricate the story. The marriage, the flight of the man who vanished from Australia for years during which he lived his grand life in England where he had married, settled down and had a family. I could see how the idea would come to an unscrupulous schemer, and because of the great distance between Australia and England, it might be possible to make it work.

I wondered what was happening to my life. I had suffered the terrible shock of losing my family and that had been so sudden. They had left me in the best of health that morning and I had never seen them again. I had lost Rolf—due to my own uncertainty; and now, I was in danger of losing my home. It seemed as though fate was preparing to rob me of everything I held dear.

I could not believe that this was really happening. It could not be possible that my mother had not been married to my father all those years and that I was his illegitimate daughter, Jacco his illegitimate son. It was like a bad dream.

And yet Mr. Tamblin thought the story was not impossible.

I had ridden some miles without thinking where I was going. I had come to Croft Cottage, and it was almost as though I had been led there, for it was of sudden interest to me. It was a pleasant little house, just outside the estate, and my mother had bought it ten years ago. One of the maids was going to have a baby, I remembered, and the father was a farm labourer. A quick marriage was necessary and my mother had bought the cottage for them to live in. It was, therefore, my mother's property, and presumably did not belong to the estate. What a strange thought! If this woman's story was proved to be true this cottage could be the only home I had in Cornwall.

I rode round the cottage. It was empty because the family had gone up to the north of England just before we left for Australia. The husband's cousin had offered him a share in his farm as far as I remembered, and no one else had taken up residence in the cottage.

This was absurd. Of course the woman would be proved a fraud.

I slowly made my way back to Cador.

I summoned Isaacs and Mrs. Penlock to the drawing room. They came, their faces expectant. They knew something momentous had happened.

I came to the point at once.

I said: "A woman is now in the neighbourhood who says she is my father's daughter and that he married her mother before he married mine. She claims that Cador is hers."

Even Mrs. Penlock was struck dumb.

"She will have to prove her story, of course," I went on, "and if she succeeds there would be great differences here. The place would not belong to me but to her."

Isaacs had gone quite white. He looked very shocked.

Mrs. Penlock stammered: "Oh . . . the wicked woman to say such things. It be a pack of lies, that's what it be."

"That's what I think, Mrs. Penlock," I said. "It is what I hope. But of course such statements have to be examined, and Mr. Tamblin gives some credence to her story. She says she has proof. I think it could be well if you explained it to the servants. They know that something is happening, and I think it would be better for them to hear the truth rather than to listen to rumour. Particularly as this could affect their future very considerably."

Isaacs said: "I will make it known to them, Miss Cadorson."

Mrs. Penlock nodded. "Don't 'ee take no notice of this wicked woman, Miss Cadorson," she said.

"Unfortunately, Mrs. Penlock, I have to . . . until she is proved to be a fraud."

"She will be. Don't 'ee make no mistake about that."

I prayed fervently that she might be right.

I could settle to nothing. As I went about the house, I was thinking: It may be that I have no right here. It may be that I shall have to go.

The next day I went to the lawyers' office where Mr. Tamblin greeted me solemnly.

"Come in, Miss Cadorson." He whispered to me: "She is here . . . and so is Mr. Hanson. I will take you to her immediately."

Rolf took my hands and holding them firmly looked into my face.

"Good morning, Annora," he said; and I could see that he was telling me how disturbed and sorry he was.

I felt a little rush of relief because he was here. And then I saw her. Oh no, I thought. She is not my father's daughter.

She was tall and broad with large features, big china blue eyes and abundant hair with a reddish tinge. There was about her an air of aggression. No, no, no, I thought. He would never have had such a daughter.

"This is Miss . . . Maria Cadorson," said Mr. Tamblin. "And er . . . Miss Annora Cadorson."

She gave a little sharp laugh. "Well, I suppose we're sisters . . . or half-sisters, you might say."

I did not answer. I could not agree.

Mr. Tamblin went on: "I have already spoken to Miss Annora Cadorson of your claim. She finds it hard to believe, knowing her father so well."

"I never knew him," she said to me. "He was off when I was too little. He deserted my mother and left her to bring me up on her own."

I said: "My father was a man who always shouldered his responsibilities."

"Well, this was one he wanted to forget had ever been his."

Mr. Tamblin coughed and said: "Miss Maria Cadorson's lawyer will be here at any moment. He will bring with him the alleged marriage certificate. Until that has been seen, examined and verified as authentic, there is little to be said."

The woman looked at me; her expression softened. "Don't think I don't know how you're feeling. This must be terrible news for you. I know about the house and what sort of place it is. My mother used to

[272]

tell me about it. You see, my father couldn't stop talking of it, even though he thought it wouldn't be his then. He had run away from it to be a gypsy. His brother never liked him. They hadn't got on. Well, it made all the difference when it was his. He'd served his term and he was a free man. He could go back to England and claim his inheritance and he didn't want to take my mother and me with him . . . so he just walked out."

"There must be a mistake. My father would never have behaved like that."

"Oh, he did all right. There was my mother . . . left with a child to look after. She went back to her father. It was a blessing she had him to go to. But her place was here, in Cador, that place she'd heard so much about. She used to say to me that she felt she'd been there. He'd talked so much about it, you see. She was fascinated by it. Every day she used to talk about it to me. You'd think she'd been there. According to her my father was a great talker. He used to tell her about the dungeons where the food was stored because it was cool down there; and the kitchens with their roasting spits and the buttery and the laundry rooms. She loved to tell me about the dining room with its tapestries of the Wars of the Roses and the Great Rebellion . . . I wanted to know all about them after that."

I listened aghast. She was giving an exact description of Cador.

"What fascinated me most," she went on, "was what they called the peeps. I can't wait to see them. In that room called the solarium. I want to look through those peeps down into the chapel and the hall. I want to go out onto the battlements and look at the sea. But I think what's going to be my favourite are the peeps."

I thought: She knows the house. She knows it intimately. How could she unless. . . ?

She saw the effect her words were having on me and there was, I fancy, a malicious glint in her eyes.

She went on: "My mother tried to do some tatting. She said it was on the chairs in the dining room. 'Queen Anne's Tatting' she called it." She smiled. "My mother used to say that my father could make you see the things he was talking about."

Mr. Tamblin was looking uneasy, and I could see that Rolf was taken aback, for he, too, knew she was giving an exact description of Cador which could only have come from one who knew the house well.

I was relieved when her lawyer arrived.

She introduced him as Mr. Trilling. She had brought him with her from Sydney. He had read of the case in the papers of course. At the time, the whole of Sydney had been talking about it: the man who had been sent out on a seven years' term, had served it and come back to his death. It was something to catch everyone's imagination. Mr. Trilling said there was no doubt that Miss Maria Cadorson's story was true and the marriage certificate would prove that.

The dramatic moment came when he produced the certificate. Mr. Tamblin looked eagerly and he and Rolf studied it. I saw the blank dismay on their faces.

"It . . . would appear to be authentic," said Mr. Tamblin.

Rolf looked at me with a deep compassion which confirmed my worst fears.

"Of course," said Mr. Tamblin, "there will have to be a further inspection."

"May I see it?" I asked.

The document was put into my hands. I stared at the names: Jake Cadorson and Hilda Stillman.

Stillman . . . The name had a familiar ring.

"That was your mother," I heard myself say. "Hilda Stillman."

"That's right. My grandfather was Tom Stillman. He had quite a fair property. Stillman's Creek was the place . . . Named after him, you see. Because there was nothing there when he settled."

"Whereabouts is that?" asked Mr. Tamblin.

"South of Brisbane . . . Just about on the borders of New South Wales and Queensland."

The room seemed to be spinning round me. I was carried back to that day when I had been in my father's room sorting out his clothes.

I saw the little notebook which I had given my father. I remembered the words so clearly. "Stillman's Creek on the borders of New South Wales and Queensland."

He had the address. He had asked Gregory Donnelly where it was.

Hilda Stillman had gone back to her father when she was deserted. It was there that Maria had been brought up.

I could almost hear his voice . . . and Gregory Donnelly's answer. My father had known where she was and he was going there.

What did it mean?

Only one thing, it seemed. He knew of Stillman's Creek, the home of the girl who said she was his daughter.

What had he intended to do? To recompense her in some way? He would naturally want to see his own daughter. Was that the real reason why he had wanted to go to Australia?

She had talked of Cador as though she knew it. It was almost as though she had seen it. There could only be one answer. Her story was true. She was my father's legitimate daughter. I was a bastard. I had no claim to Cador. Not only had I lost my parents and my brother: I was going to lose my home as well.

Discoveries

I shall never forget those months. I think they were some of the worst I have ever passed through. My common sense told me that her story was true, but every emotion I possessed assured me that it could not be. My father would never have deserted her and her mother in that way. I could well understand that if he had in fact married that woman he would realize he had made a vital mistake and that the prospect of returning to England with her would fill him with dismay. She would certainly not fit in with the life at Cador. He might have wanted to desert her, but he would never have done so in the way it was suggested.

The matter was brought to court. Mr. Tamblin said it was imperative that this should be. I could not simply hand over the estates to a woman who had come along and asked for them. It was a court of law that would decide the merits of the case and legal documents would have to be drawn up.

Rolf was with me in those days. He was completely astounded by the turn of events. I should have liked to turn to him then, to tell him of my desolation and explain how I longed to be with him; and at this time I did not seem to care if he had been there on that Midsummer's Eve. But he was aloof. I suppose he could not forget the humiliation I had inflicted on him by waiting until the morning we were to be married to tell him that I could not go on with it.

There was a barrier between us. He was there helping me, advising me; he gave me his knowledge, his sympathy, his time—but the closeness which had once been between us was there no longer.

He agreed with Mr. Tamblin that the matter would have to go to court.

I dreaded it.

The woman told her story well. It seemed to fit in with everything. Her mother had met my father—so the story ran—in a hotel in Sydney where she worked as a barmaid. They had become friendly. He had finished his term of seven years and had bought a bit of property. It was called Cadorsons and was some miles north of Sydney. A daughter had been born to them—Maria herself. Then it appeared news of my father's inheritance had come to him. He had kept it from his wife. He had told her that he was selling the property to a man named Thomas Donnelly; and then went back to Sydney where she thought they were to remain until he bought a bigger property. But he had left her in Sydney and that was the last she saw of him. He had left her nothing and she was penniless. All she could do was go back to her father on his property at Stillman's Creek. There Maria was brought up. If anyone tried to pretend she was a bastard she had the means to prove that she was not.

When there was all the fuss in the newspapers about Sir Jake Cadorson with the story of his past, she realized that this was the father who had deserted her and her mother all those years ago. She learned about the property in Cornwall and had spoken to a few of her friends about it. They had told her that she ought to claim what was hers by right; and this was what she was doing.

The marriage certificate was scrutinized, and the verdict was given that it was authentic.

Her Counsel reminded the court that Sir Jake Cadorson was a man who was a little cavalier in his relationships with women. He had been known to have one illegitimate daughter who had been born in Kent the same year as he had been sent to Australia for seven years. That child had been looked after by others and he had not been in the least concerned about her welfare.

Our Counsel pointed out that he had been unaware of her existence until he returned to England and in any case was in no position to do anything about it as he was sent out of England for seven years.

It soon became clear to me in which way the case was going.

[277]

Everything seemed weighted heavily against my father. The marriage certificate was declared to be valid; Maria's story fitted exactly with what had been known to have happened. It was remembered that my father's crime had been to kill a man who, according to him, was assaulting a young gypsy girl, presumably, was the sly comment, a protégée of his during this madcap sojourn with the tribe.

They were vilifying him. That was what I could not bear. To prove the woman's case they had to make my father into a callous philanderer.

I could see from the first that we were going to lose. Her story fitted so neatly; I had to admit that if I had not known my father, if I had been looking in on the case from the outside, I should probably have believed her.

And the verdict. She was telling the truth. She had proved that she was my father's daughter, that his marriage to my mother was no true marriage, and that she was the rightful heiress to Cador.

After the verdict she came to me outside the court.

She said: "I don't want to hustle you. I know how it must be for you. You'll want to take some of your personal things. You're welcome to stay until you find somewhere else."

"I shall go to London for a while," I told her. "I want to get right away."

Everyone seemed to understand that.

A gloom hung over the house. The servants were very uneasy. They did not like the idea of a new mistress in the house. I had not realized before how fond they were of me.

Uncle Peter and Aunt Amaryllis arrived. They had come to take me to London and in a few days I left with them.

I did not know what I was going to do. At times I felt a burning anger; at others a listlessness.

I was angry at the reputation they had given my father. I knew that he had been wild in his youth. I knew that he was the father of Tamarisk and it was true that she was the result of a casual encounter, but he would never have deserted a wife and child. He would never have gone through a mockery of marriage with my mother. All the evidence might be against him but in my heart I just knew.

Aunt Amaryllis was very sad. For once she could not think that everything was going right.

Uncle Peter was thoughtful. I knew he was wondering what chance there might be of overthrowing the verdict. He would never accept defeat, of course. But I guessed from his demeanour that, like most, he believed my father guilty of all that had been said against him.

"God help me," I prayed. "If we had never gone to Australia, none of this would have happened."

Helena greeted me warmly and so did Peterkin and Frances. Since their marriage they were more absorbed in their work than ever. Helena had changed, too. She was a practiced hostess now and had lost a great deal of her reserve. She was pregnant once more and very happy about that. Matthew's book had been published and had attracted the notice that Uncle Peter decided it should. He was going to stand for the election which would shortly take place.

"It makes us all very busy," said Helena. "There is quite a big campaign. Father is putting up the money. He thinks it is certain that Matthew will win the seat. People know how good he is . . . after his book."

She was very sympathetic towards me.

"We followed the case every day," she said. "My mother wanted to bring you here but you had to be there, of course. Father thought it should have been tried in London instead of some little country court. He is wondering whether there could be another hearing."

She looked at me anxiously and I shook my head. "They've given their verdict. They wouldn't change it. I couldn't bear to go through all that again."

"But, Annora, do you believe it's *true?*"

"I would never believe that of my father," I said with conviction.

"No," she said soothingly, but I guessed she believed, as all the others did, that he had deserted his wife and child.

"What are you going to do?" asked Helena.

I said with truth: "I don't know."

"Something will work itself out. You'd always have a home here. I expect Tamarisk and Jonathan would like to see you at Eversleigh . . . my parents, too."

"I have to think, Helena. I don't know what I shall do yet."

Uncle Peter discussed my future with me. He was crisp and realistic as I expected him to be.

He thought it was a terrible calamity to lose Cador. That was what concerned him so deeply.

When I spoke about the damage they had done to my father's reputation he shrugged that aside.

"That won't hurt him now."

"But, Uncle Peter, you can't believe . . ."

He frowned. "I can believe he would have realized he had made a big mistake in marrying that woman and that he wanted to get away from her. But from what I know of him I am sure he would have made some provision for her. It was not his way to steal off and hope to lose himself. That he married the woman . . . yes, that's possible. He thought he was out there for the term of his natural life. He adjusted himself. He always liked women. I can see how it happened. But, my dear Annora, how can we be sure? We're wasting time in conjecture. Let's look at the practical side. We have to think about you. Have you any plans?"

I shook my head.

"Of course, *I* should like to probe into this more fully. I think they have skimmed the surface and come to an easy conclusion too quickly. I should like to get a man out to Australia to look into a few things."

"She had the certificate. The dates and everything fitted. That was what turned things in her favour."

"It's cleverly worked out . . . if worked out it is. But often there is a loophole." He looked at me through narrowed eyes. "The mistake was to have it tried down in Cornwall. It should have been in London with the very best people working for you. There was a great property at stake."

"Uncle Peter, I want to forget it."

"All right. Now what are you going to do? You're not without means. The family is comfortably off. You have some money from your mother. She can't touch that. It's Cador and your father's property that she is claiming; but I should have thought that a sophisticated lawyer would have brought forward more the fact that you had lived there all your life as his daughter with expectations. You should have been entitled to something. The whole thing was too blithely handed over to her . . . lock, stock and barrel."

"I have selected my very own possessions . . . a few pieces of furniture, ornaments, that sort of thing. Mr. Tamblin is arranging for them to be stored. Then there is Croft Cottage. That belonged to my mother. I suppose that will remain mine."

"A little property then."

"Yes, in need of repair."

"You should get Tamblin to arrange to have it put in order."

"I don't want to think . . ."

"I'll think for you. It may be small but it's a property. You might want to use it, or it could be let."

"You are so practical, Uncle Peter."

"It pays to be. I think you ought to do something, Annora. Have some purpose in life. You've seen the change in Helena."

"Yes. It's miraculous."

"And you know what you've got to do. You've got to pick yourself up. You've got to start all over again. Dear child, you have had a very bad time . . . blow after blow . . ."

"One leading to the other, of course."

"That is how life works. It's a pity you didn't marry that young man."

I was silent.

"If you had," he went on, "it would have cushioned the blow. I gather his Manor estate is growing and prospering. I remember your father's saying some time ago that it would rival Cador in a few years' time."

"You always think of the material side of everything, Uncle Peter."

"My dear, it is always a side to consider. All your creature comforts depend on it, and they are not called comforts for nothing. They soften the impact of the slings and arrows. If you had married him you would have a home." His eyes gleamed. "You could have found a soothing balm in rivalling your neighbour. What does this woman know about great estates?"

"She'll have Bob Carter to look after it for her."

"A lot depends on the one at the top. It would have been just what you need. It would have added a zest to life. Zest. That's what you want, Annora."

I said: "*You* would have enjoyed it. I know you would have found means of getting the better of her."

"And, you are thinking, in a none too scrupulous way."

"Perhaps."

"You don't trust me, do you? You have a long memory. You are thinking of what I did to Joseph Cresswell. It was fair enough to my mind. He wouldn't have been any good in that post. What did he know about the vice of underground London? I do know of it. I thought I was right in what I was doing. Oh, you are not going to agree with me, of course. It is amazing, Annora, how you have become involved in my affairs. Look at the good I am doing now. They are working wonders at the Mission—all due to my support. That can't be bad, can it? Does it matter how the money is come by if it does good in the end?"

"That is a question which has often been discussed."

"And have you found a satisfactory answer?"

I shook my head. "You have been good to me, Uncle Peter," I said.

"I've told you I always had a soft spot for your mother . . . and now for you. Listen to me. What you will do now is go with Helena and Matthew down to Mobury. There is a lot to do. We must get him in, you understand. You'll work for him. It's hard work. You'll persuade people why they've got to vote for Matthew Hume . . . the reformer. Read his book. It's illuminating. He's done a good job. He somehow gets right into the minds of those convicts and some of the stories are pretty grim. It'll carry you along for a while. Stop your brooding. I've told you before that you have to pick yourself up when life knocks you down. You've got to think about those poor devils who have been sent into bondage for some petty crime or perhaps for some political attitude. Then you'll realize how much you have to be thankful for."

"I'm thankful for you, Uncle Peter. You do me so much good. Talking to you, listening to you, has always helped me."

"Odd, isn't it, an old villain like myself?"

I said: "You are a very lovable villain and you almost make me feel your villainies are virtues."

"That, my dear Annora, is the very essence of villainy."

I supposed I felt happier in London than I could anywhere else. It was an interesting suggestion that I should travel down to Mobury with Helena and Matthew. My reunion with Jonnie had been rapturous. At first he had not known me but after a while he seemed to, and it soothed me considerably to play with him.

A great deal had been happening in the world. The Queen had married most happily.

"It's rather put Lord Melbourne's nose out of joint," said Uncle Peter. "But he doesn't seem to mind and I think all of us are glad to see the Queen happily settled."

She had regained the popularity she had lost over the Flora Hastings and Bedchamber affairs.

"There is nothing the people like better than a wedding," said Uncle Peter. "A royal wedding makes the people forget the intrigues of the boudoir."

There had been a hint of my having a season. I would have vehemently declined if the hint had been pursued. I think it was feared that the scandal which Uncle Peter had skilfully managed to divert might be resuscitated and it was well known that the Queen's husband was, as Uncle Peter said, most definitely prudish.

I was sure Prince Albert would not have agreed with Uncle Peter's views about directing dubiously acquired money into good causes.

I heard of the alarming incident when an attempt had been made to assassinate the Queen. True, it was only a brainless potboy and he had been declared insane, but it was sobering. The Queen behaved magnificently, of course, as most of her ancestors had in similar circumstances. But it was an indication that life could never be smooth for anyone.

In Mobury I got caught up in the excitement of electioneering, and it became to me a matter of the utmost importance that Matthew should win the seat.

I sat on platforms listening to his speeches. He was turning out to be quite an effective orator. He burned with zeal when he spoke of the necessity of prison reform. He harrowed his audience with stories of what he had seen first-hand. He wanted the laws drastically changed; he wanted better conditions for the poor. He had visited the Mission run by his brother-in-law and his wife, and he knew what he was talking about. People listened to him and were moved.

Helena would sit on the platform smiling and admiring. She reminded me of Aunt Amaryllis; and when I thought of how their marriage had come about I was truly amazed.

She had grown into marriage—and if ever there had been a marriage of convenience that had been one. But now she was contented, reminding me so much of her mother.

To see her thus set me longing for Rolf. What a fool I had been! I had allowed myself to turn away from happiness because of a dream . . . and something which had happened long ago. He had said he was not there and I had chosen not to believe him. Then I had convinced myself that he wanted to marry me to get Cador.

Perhaps I should go back to Cornwall. I could go to Croft Cottage. I should see Rolf often. Perhaps we could talk about Midsummer's Eve and perhaps I could explain how deeply it had affected me, how I had lost my illusions, for I had seen ordinary people turn into monsters of cruelty. It had had a great effect on me. It had changed me from a trusting girl into a doubting woman.

If I could see Rolf . . . if I could break through this barrier between us . . . if we could be together . . . if I could forget Midsummer's Eve . . . if I could believe him . . . if he again asked me to marry him now I no longer owned Cador . . . how happy I should be.

I would go back. But not yet.

Helena sat there, her hands on her lap, obviously pregnant. Uncle Peter had said: "That's a good thing. It shows a nice family life."

I thought of Joe Cresswell and wondered what he was doing now. This was where he would like to be. He had been very ambitious to follow in his father's footsteps and get into Parliament.

Uncle Peter had prevented that. I wondered afresh why I was so fond of Uncle Peter. He was such a ruthless, amoral man. Yet he always had answers to explain his wickedness, and he never failed to show me another side which differed from the obvious one.

Election day came. There was an air of excitement in the town. I drove round in a carriage with Helena waving banners. "Vote for Matthew Hume. Your Member who cares for the Unfortunate."

Uncle Peter came down in the afternoon. He expressed his pleasure with the manner in which the campaign had gone.

It was late that night when the results were declared. Matthew Hume was the elected Member of Parliament for Mobury.

What a celebration there was! Uncle Peter presided. We drank champagne to the success of the new Member, and he stood with Helena on one side and Uncle Peter on the other receiving congratulations. I felt quite carried away by the excitement, and for a while forgot my difficulties.

Back in London, the question arose: What was I going to do? It had to be answered.

I went down to Frances's Mission. I was surprised at the difference in her premises. She had a large house with many rooms in it. She told me that the old one was turned into a dormitory for the homeless.

Peterkin and she worked in harmony. They had the same ideals; they knew exactly what they wanted to do. Peterkin's gentle manner was a contrast to Frances's brisk one. Each seemed to supply what the other lacked.

"Ours," Peterkin told me, "is a marriage of two minds in complete harmony with each other."

I felt a touch of envy. Both Helena and Peterkin had found happiness. I was the only one to whom that desired state would not come.

When I suggested staying with them for a few weeks they welcomed the idea warmly.

Frances said: "We have people who come down now and then to help . . . society girls often who feel like a change and have the urge to do good. Some of them *are* good but they like to say they've been. My father has made the place fashionable."

I came in contact with poverty such as I had never dreamed existed. I went into attics where women sat sewing all day, often in poor light; some had children to feed. I noticed these women's eyes which looked as though they had sunk into their heads and I knew it was due to their working at their sewing half into the night—all for a pittance barely enough to keep them alive.

Frances said: "We're trying to get them to pay more for the work. I have some of them here sewing for us and I see that they get good food."

What I found most pathetic was the children. There was one little fellow—he couldn't have been more than five years old—who had been a chimney sweep since the age of three. He was terrified of the dark, sooty chimneys and had run away from his master. Peterkin had found him wandering in the streets. Frances dealt with him in her usual brisk, unsentimental way. When I was there he was doing little jobs in the kitchen. The little one was in the seventh heaven of bliss and his attitude towards Frances was one of idolatry.

"It makes you humble," said Peterkin.

There was the crossing sweeper who had been run over and crippled—a boy of some eight years. Frances took him in and found him some light job he could do about the house.

There were women whose husbands or paramours had ill-treated them. Their wounds horrified me. I learned a little first aid; I did some of the cooking; I turned my hands to several jobs; and like Peterkin, I felt humble, and so much better.

There was one young woman to whom I took quite a fancy. Her name was Kitty. She came to the house one day when both Frances and Peterkin were out and I was the first one who saw her.

She was in a pitiful state—unkempt and near starvation.

She stammered something about someone's telling her they'd help her if she came to this house.

I gave her some soup—there was always a cauldron of soup simmering in the kitchen. I spoke to her soothingly and told her we would look after her.

She looked lost and lonely and frightened. She was, I could see, really a pretty girl.

Frances came in and took charge and in a few days there was a great change in Kitty. She was bright and meant to enjoy life but she had had a bad time. She told us she had come up from the country to work in London. She had had a job as tweeny in a big house but the master had taken notice of her. The mistress found out and sent her packing with no money, no reference.

"It's an old story," said Frances.

I took a special interest in her; she seemed to like me too. She was very capable and almost took over the management of the kitchen.

The house was sparsely furnished.

"We don't waste money on fancy stuff," said Frances. "As much as my father-in-law has given us we still need more money."

There was a big room with a wooden table in it; this table was kept scrupulously clean and we used to eat there in the evenings. Dinner was usually between eight and nine o'clock and was generally a stew of some sort which was kept simmering on the fire so that it was ready at whatever time we sat down. After we had eaten we would sit there, with the candles guttering, tired after an exhausting day, and we would talk about the work we were doing and life in general.

The memories of those evenings would stay with me all my life. I can still recall Peterkin's hot anger about something particularly shocking he had seen that day, and Frances's almost clinical approach; and the views of the other young people who had come to help. We talked far into the night, sometimes absorbed by the conversations, at others too tired to move even when the clock struck midnight.

One day I had been out shopping and when I came in Frances was in the hall.

"Oh hello," she said. "Someone you know is coming to see me this evening."

"Someone I know?"

"Brother Joe."

"Joe? How is he?"

She lifted her shoulder. "He comes to London now and then and he always looks in on his little sister. Sometimes he stays for a few days and gives a hand."

"Is he here now?"

"No. He's been in and gone off somewhere on business. He'll be back this evening. I didn't tell him you were here. I wondered whether you wanted to see him."

"Why shouldn't I?"

"I didn't know." I realized that she, like some others, thought that at one time there had been a rather special friendship between Joe and me which had petered out when the scandal about Joe's father and Uncle Peter had been revealed.

I wondered what it would be like meeting Joe again.

He was there at the scrubbed wood table that evening. He had changed a little. He looked older and more solemn.

He took my hand and shook it warmly.

"How nice to see you, Annora."

"And for me to see you, Joe. How are you?"

"Oh, quite well. It seems a long time . . ."

"It is."

"You've been to Australia since."

"Yes."

"I'm very sorry. I heard, of course."

I nodded.

"Are you staying here long?"

"I haven't many plans. I am just spending a little time with Frances and Peterkin."

"They are doing a wonderful job here."

It was obviously trivial conversation. I thought, We are both a little nervous of each other. He is remembering how I caught him coming out of Uncle Peter's study, putting those papers in his pocket. He is embarrassed about that and because I have lost my family and my home.

How different life was for both of us since our first meeting in the Park!

In the candle-lit atmosphere, amongst all the talk, the tension seemed to lessen. Once or twice Joe smiled at me at something which was being said, and I felt pleased to see him again.

One of the helpers—an earnest young woman from a county family—was saying: "I met Reverend Goodson this afternoon. He is a little displeased with us. He says no good can come of what we are doing because so much of the money we are using comes from a tainted source. Those, my dears, were his very words."

I saw Joe flinch and then his mouth hardened. I knew he was thinking of the manner in which Uncle Peter was attempting to rehabilitate himself by giving so generously to charity.

She went on: "I told him how you had rescued Maggie Trent from that savage she was living with and that you had saved her life, for he would surely have killed her. I told him about little Tom, bruised and terrified, who is too big for chimneys now and was still being forced up them. He would have gone mad, poor mite. He was scared out of his wits of being burned to death. And there are others like that, I said to the reverend gentleman. I said, 'If they can save people like that, they are not going to look twice at where the money comes from.'"

"You gave him something to think about perhaps," said Peterkin.

"The trouble with people like him," said Frances, "is that they are not given to thinking. Their minds run in channels laid out for them. It saves a lot of energy to follow the set rules. Happily his opinions are of no importance to us. Joe, you'll see a lot of difference in the houses since you were last here. We've extended, started new projects. We've had luck."

"Thanks," said Joe rather bitterly, "to your generous father-in-law."

Frances looked steadily at her brother. She knew that he hated my Uncle Peter and that he could not forgive him for ruining his father; but she, in her calm commonsensical manner, wanted old hatchets buried. She took the long view. Whatever had happened had brought great prosperity to her world and she had to welcome that. She was doing more good, she reckoned, than any commission for the suppression of vice could have done. Frances believed in action, not talk.

But she was fond of her brother and she did not want to spoil his visits by getting involved in arguments about which they could not agree.

She changed the subject.

"Annora has been working hard since she came here. I was going to suggest she take a day off. Why don't you two take a trip up the river? There's a lovely old-fashioned little inn I've heard a good deal about. They serve whitebait. It really is good, I'm told. I imagine you two have a lot to talk about."

Joe was looking at me expectantly.

I said: "I should like that."

He smiled. "Then let's do it."

Frances seemed satisfied. She then went on to talk about an extension to the kitchen which she was planning.

It was pleasant on the river. We rowed down towards Richmond and found the inn near the grassy bank just past Kew. It was called the Sailor's Rest. It looked charming. There was a garden in front facing the river; tables and chairs were set out.

Joe tied up the boat and we went ashore.

Over the food, which was served by a maid in a mopcap and a Regency-style dress, I asked Joe questions about what he was doing. He was living in the North with his parents, he told me. His father owned a cotton mill up there and that was their main interest now.

"You are finding it satisfying?" I asked.

"Oh, it's quite absorbing . . . in a way. I'm learning a lot about cotton and trade is good. It has increased tremendously in the last years. Hargreaves' spinning jenny and Crompton's mule have speeded up production and kept prices down. We export a great deal to Europe. Oh yes, it is interesting, but . . ."

"I know, Joe, what you really wanted was to go into politics."

He was silent. Then he said: "It's the reason why I don't come to London very much. Every time I pass the Houses of Parliament I feel a terrible longing . . ."

"Why don't you try to get in?"

He looked at me in amazement. "How could I . . . now?"

"That is all in the past."

He shook his head. "As soon as one of us came into prominence it would all be remembered. Annora, I cannot understand Frances taking his money."

"Frances has a very good reason, and she makes the best possible use of it."

"To take money from the man who ruined our father!"

"I wish you could talk to Uncle Peter. I wish you knew him."

"I'd rather know the devil."

"Joe, you have to try to look at this coldly, calmly, without bias. You have to try to understand."

"I understand perfectly. There was an important post almost certainly about to be bestowed on my father—a chance to do good, to wipe the town free of vice. Your uncle looked on it as a stepping-stone to his ambitions. Moreover he himself was trading in vice. How ironical it would have been to have had him on the Commission! But as I say, he saw it as a stepping-stone to his ambitions. And trying to get it . . . he destroyed my father."

"And you tried to destroy him. But it seems he was indestructible."

"I cannot understand you, Annora. I think you are on his side."

"No. That's not true."

"And Frances . . . there she is taking his money and saying, Thank you very much, dear Papa-in-law. I can't understand my sister."

"I can. She takes it because she can make good use of it. And what is she doing with it but bringing help to those who so sorely need it?

If she did not take it, think of how those people would suffer. She is saving *lives*, Joe."

"It is a question of morality."

"What is morality? Uncle Peter takes from those people who spend their money in an immoral way, you would say. But suppose they did not spend this money, it would not be going into the Mission. It might be spent on fine clothes, houses, horses. It's a difficult question to answer, and I think Frances and Peterkin are right to take the money. In fact I think they are wonderful people."

"That money is given by your uncle, not because he wants to do good but because he wishes to be seen as a philanthropist, whose good works will wash away his past."

"That is true. Oh, Joe, we'll never agree about this. But . . . why don't you try to get into Parliament?"

"And face all that scandal being revived?"

"If it were . . . by your opponents . . . it would only be for a short while. After all, it was not even you who were involved. At least, that is what people would think."

"I see that your uncle is setting up Helena's husband now. I suppose he will decide which way the young man is to vote."

"I think Matthew will judge for himself. Uncle Peter spoke for him during the election. Everyone knows he was supporting his son-in-law. That did not spoil Matthew's chances. So why should what happened to your father spoil yours?"

"I couldn't risk it."

"If you don't take risks now and then you can't hope to succeed."

"Annora, I want to be there. It's the life I want. I know I could do it. I could have got in at the last election."

"You should have tried."

"I couldn't face it. All that stuff in the papers. I was afraid it would be revived. I shall never forget it."

"It's past."

"And you and I," he went on. "We were getting on very well, weren't we? And that stopped it. That day you saw me in that room . . ."

"I know."

"You seemed to despise me."

"No. Joe. I understood."

"It was for my father."

"You didn't do *him* any good by your attempt to ruin Uncle Peter."

"And I lost your friendship, I know. You were different afterwards. You couldn't forgive me for using you to get into the house. I was desperate. If it had been *your* father, wouldn't you?"

I thought of the accusation that woman had made against my father. Yes, I would do a great deal to prove her wrong . . . not only for the sake of Cador, but for my father's memory.

I said: "I understand how you felt about your father."

"He is a good man, a man of high morality. Think of that sleazy scandal involving such a man. Think of my mother, the family. I could have killed him when I knew he had set it all up."

"He is ruthless. He brushed people aside to get what he wants. But that is not all of him. People are strange. They are not all bad . . . not all good."

"I think any goodness he may have is lost beneath the weight of evil."

"He is a manipulator, a man who must have power, who must . . ."

"Use people to his own ends."

"Yes, that's true. But, Joe, it's past. Let's forget it. Let's think of you . . . and your future."

"I shall be in the mills. I shall force myself to stop dreaming of what might have been."

"That is no way to live really. Not when there is a way open to you."

"I see no way."

"I do. Pull yourself together. How long will this government last, do you think? Be ready for the next election."

"And face all that slanderous mud?"

"Yes, face it, Joe. They'll soon get tired of throwing it."

"I couldn't do it, Annora."

"Then you must content yourself with the cotton mill. Oh, Joe, forgive me. I sound sententious. Who am I to talk? I am undecided, floundering hopelessly."

"Life has been hard to us both, Annora."

"Uncle Peter says that you cannot help yourself lying down and letting events get the better of you. You have to stand up and fight."

[292]

"And ruin other people's lives as you do so?"

"That is not necessary. But don't you see, Joe, you tried to ruin him just as surely as he tried to ruin your father. But he wouldn't have it. He's fighting his way back."

"I can't bear to hear you talk of him as though he is some sort of glorious warrior. Attila the Hun possibly."

I smiled. "Try to rid yourself of your bitterness. Frances has."

"Frances has taken advantage of the situation."

"Frances knows what she wants and she is not going to let anything stand in her way."

"Frances is doing good to the community. Your uncle is doing good to himself."

"The method is the same."

"We shall never agree on that."

"But, Joe, do get up and fight. You will never be content if you don't try to get into Parliament. All your life you will bear a grudge against fate which robbed you of your chance, and when you are very old and have become mellow you will ask the question: Was it fate which robbed me of my chance, or was it myself?"

"You make it sound easy."

"It certainly isn't that. I know how you feel. But you ought to try. You ought to face up to it. Forgive me, Joe. I'm preaching. It's the last thing I want to do. I know you hate me to mention it but I can't help thinking of Uncle Peter and the way he is overcoming all that scandal. I think there was just as much about him as about your father in the papers. He planned your father's fall and carried it out. You planned his. You were both equally successful. You've had an eye for an eye. Your father gave up. Uncle Peter didn't. So . . . fight on, Joe."

He looked at me steadily. "I don't think I could do it."

"Be bold and see. Oh dear, I'm upsetting you. It was to have been a pleasant trip up the river."

He said: "It has been good to see you again, to talk to you frankly."

"I'm afraid I've said too much. It is not for me to advise you. You have to make up your own mind. I am the last person who should try to tell you what to do."

"You are very unhappy, Annora."

I did not answer.

[293]

"The shock must have been terrible and then that dreadful woman from Australia."

"That's over, Joe. I'm trying not to think of it. But there is so much to remind me of them."

"It makes my affairs seem almost trivial. They do to you, don't they?"

"You have your family, Joe."

"I know. I'm going to think about what you've said. Don't let's lose touch again."

I nodded. Then I said: "Frances was right. This is a very pleasant spot."

Helena's baby was due in a few weeks.

Aunt Amaryllis came down to the Mission and her purpose was to persuade me to come back to be with Helena until her baby was born.

She said: "You were with her at Jonnie's birth and she says what a comfort you were to her. Moreover, Jonnie does miss you. Do come back and be with her, Annora."

So I went.

How different this was from Jonnie's birth. Helena had come a long way since then. This was her husband's child and an astonishing relationship had grown up between them. Helena was proud of Matthew. He had scored a hit with his maiden speech; it was clear that he was going to do well in politics. He was going to be one of those who would be responsible for the abolition of transportation in due course. He was working for it with such enthusiasm and it was inconceivable that he could fail.

Uncle Peter was satisfied with his son-in-law and nothing was going to be spared in sending him forward. I wondered how long it would be before Uncle Peter himself was back in Parliament.

Helena hovered between bliss and apprehension. She was longing for the baby. With great pride she showed me its layette and I wondered whether, like myself, she was comparing this with Jonnie's birth.

Jonnie himself was now at a delightful age. I drew for him with coloured crayons and he showed me what he could do. He was interested in the new arrival and confided to me that he wanted a brother.

[294]

Every morning he would come to my room and ask: "Has he come yet? He's very lazy. He ought to be here by now."

There was great rejoicing when the baby was born, and Jonnie's wishes were granted. It was a boy.

Helena was very proud to see the notices in the paper. "Son for Matthew Hume."

Uncle Peter was delighted. "There is nothing people like better than babies," he said.

The baby flourished. The christening was to be a grand affair and was to be celebrated in Uncle Peter's house—the baby's home was not large enough to accommodate all the guests. Uncle Peter had seen that several important people were invited—many of them politicians.

It was during this celebration that I learned something which made me feel I had touched the very nadir of despair.

It came out quite naturally. The drawing room was crowded. I stood there with a glass of champagne in my hands when a middle-aged man came up and spoke to me.

I had not heard his name, nor had he heard mine.

He just said: "What a crowd. Well, Matthew's baby would attract attention, wouldn't he? Amazing what Matthew has done . . . such a short time he's been in the House."

"You are a Member of Parliament, are you?"

"I hope to be. I'm taking over a constituency in the south west. I have just been making a tour, talking to my prospective supporters, trying to clock up the votes."

"What part of the south west?"

"It's a big constituency. Rather remote and scattered. In Cornwall actually. The people take a bit of knowing. Farmers, fishermen, miners. I've had chats with them on the quays and in their cottages."

He was garrulous which one would expect of a man who hoped to become a Member of Parliament. He was entirely interested in himself and I was glad of that for I did not want him asking me questions.

"They're a superstitious community. One has to get to know about them, how their minds work, how best one can impress them. Have to make their interests yours. You get to know what is happening in these little places and then you talk of little else . . . and slip in the propaganda so that they won't notice. For instance, there was some place where there had recently been quite a big case . . . well, big for them . . . about some property . . ."

"Oh?" I said faintly. "Where was that?"

"Somewhere down there. Somebody had come out from Australia and claimed this estate . . . rather a large one. But that it seems was old news. What they were all talking about was her marriage . . ."

"You mean the marriage of the one who claimed the estate?"

"Yes, that's it. Apparently it was a nice little bit of gossip, and when they've got something like that on their minds they just won't talk about anything else. You have to listen and seem as interested to hear as they are to tell you. It's the only way of winning their votes. So I stand there saying 'Really? Did she then? Well, I never did.' Apparently this woman who'd just got hold of the mansion was marrying some chap from the Manor which was a sort of rival estate. Could have knocked them down with feathers, they kept saying. I didn't get to see the married pair. But that's what I'm telling you. You have to listen and hope to get in what you're really there to . . . I just listened and told them how amazing it was. Well, that's an example of what you have to do."

"Was the name of the place . . . Cador, do you remember?"

"Why, that's it. Do you know it?"

"Yes," I said flatly. "I did."

"Grand sort of place. So was the other one, this Manor. I reckon that was what they were all so excited about . . . linking up the two . . ."

I felt rather dizzy with the shock. I heard myself say, "So you'll be standing at the next election?"

He went on talking but I was not listening.

I was thinking: So Rolf has married that woman. "The chap from the Manor." How could he? But everything was clear now. I had been right. He would do a great deal for Cador.

It had taken this to tell me how much I loved Rolf. In spite of everything, more than anything I wanted to be with him. I might have married him, but fate had conspired to take him from me. No, that was not true. I was the one who had broken it off.

How I wished now that I had married him! Even if he had been in the woods that Midsummer's Eve; even if he wanted Cador. I had made excuses for Uncle Peter and I had seen the good amongst what was deplorable in his character. But I had made no allowances for Rolf from whom I had expected perfection.

I could talk to no one of this. I felt wretchedly empty. I could never be happy again.

For some days Helena did not notice that there was anything wrong with me. Then at last she said: "You look pale, Annora, and very unhappy. Is it because of the children?"

I looked at her in astonishment and she went on: "Oh, I know how you love them, how you've always loved Jonnie. I felt that you often wished he was yours. Now I have two and you have none."

"Oh, Helena," I cried. "What an idea! I am so glad for you. I think all turned out beautifully. And now you have little Geoffrey. You are lucky, Helena."

"I know. I feel it isn't fair. Everything came out so well for me, didn't it? I never told you, but I saw John Milward some time ago. He talked to me. I was never sure how I should feel if I saw him again, and I felt nothing . . . nothing at all. I had to keep reminding myself that he was Jonnie's father. He said how sorry he was that it had turned out the way it had. But I couldn't be sorry. He was very weak really . . . and now it has all worked out with Matthew. Matthew is wonderful. My father says he can be a great politician. It is what he really wants to do. I don't think John Milward would ever have been anything without his family. Matthew is thinking of writing a book about chimney sweeps. He feels very strongly about that and my father thinks it is a good idea."

"I'm so glad it has turned out like this for you."

"I wish it could for you. Perhaps it will. Joe Cresswell is a very nice young man."

"I know."

"And he is very fond of you."

I wanted to shout at her: But I want Rolf. I've always wanted Rolf. I was too stupid to see how important he was to me.

The idea of his living at Cador, which he had always wanted, with that woman, was more than I could bear. It made me angry and then desperately unhappy.

I saw Joe before he went back to the North.

We went again to the Sailor's Rest.

He said: "I'm going back tomorrow, Annora. But I shall come up again. I was thinking you might like to pay us a visit. My parents would like to see you."

"Perhaps I will, Joe."

"It's a different life up there, you know."

"I'm sure of it."

"I've thought a lot about you. I believe you think I am rather weak."

I was silent for a moment, then I said: "What I think is, Joe, that if you want something, you have to take some action; you have to get it. You can't let it slip through your fingers. If you do, you're going to regret it all your life."

I was speaking for myself really. Joe still had a chance. I had lost mine.

He said: "I shall come back, Annora. Think of me . . . and then we'll meet again."

I knew what he was suggesting. There was a bond of friendship between us. We had always had a fondness for each other. Could it grow to something stronger?

I was thinking: Is this a way of escape? Could I go to the North of England among more hardy, down-to-earth folk? It would be a complete breakaway.

I liked Joe. I was not in love with him by any means. Helena had not been in love with Matthew when she married him. But I was not Helena . . . and I loved Rolf.

But she had loved John Milward. But had she really? What was it she had said recently: "I don't think I really loved John so much as what he stood for. He was the only one who had taken notice of me and I loved him for that. He was a symbol to me that I could be attractive too. Perhaps that was what I felt for him and when he deserted me because of his family I thought I was heartbroken because of him . . . but it wasn't really so. It was because of what he stood for. Then there was Matthew. I didn't love him at all but he was so good to me . . . he's such a good man. I can help him. I'm happy with him . . . happier than I ever thought I could be after John had gone."

That might be how it was with her. It was different with me. I wanted Rolf. I always had. I had thought of him constantly. I had compared everyone with Rolf and they had all seemed wanting.

How greatly he had desired Cador . . . always. He loved the place. I could see how much he had wanted Cador, just as Uncle Peter wanted power.

They were the sort of men who set out to get what they wanted, letting nothing stand in their way.

John Milward . . . Joe Cresswell . . . they were different.

Now I had to stop brooding. Rolf was lost to me forever and I had to go on.

How?

Joe? I could be very fond of Joe. I had liked his parents. I was very fond of his sister Frances. I could picture quite a happy life with Joe . . . if I could forget Rolf. I *had* to forget Rolf.

I could devote myself to work in Frances's Mission. That would be satisfying.

I wanted to start afresh. I had to, because all the time I had been really waiting for Rolf. What I had in my heart been hoping he would do was come to London to woo me, to insist on my returning to Cornwall.

I must have been foolish. I had deserted him on the day I was to have married him and I could not have dealt him a more humiliating blow. It was more than a man could endure.

Besides, it had been Cador he wanted; and he had that now.

Let me be sensible, I prayed. I have been telling Joe that he should be. Now let me tell myself.

I had an income from my mother. I was not rich but on the other hand I was not poor. I was in a position to make a decision. I could not go on drifting.

I must sever all links with Cornwall, I told myself. I will sell Croft Cottage, and then there will be no more temptation to return to it.

When I told Uncle Peter and Aunt Amaryllis of my plans, Uncle Peter said: "You should write to Tamblin. He can see to everything."

"No," I said. "I want to arrange the sale myself."

"My dear girl, you'd have to stay there. You wouldn't want to do that . . . not in that little cottage."

"But I should, Uncle Peter."

"Wouldn't you feel unhappy being so close to Cador?" suggested Aunt Amaryllis. "All those memories."

"I do want to do this my way. I don't want to leave it to Mr.

Tamblin. I want to be there once more . . . just to say my final farewell to the old place."

"Well, if you want to do it your way, you must," said Uncle Peter. "But remember it might not be easy to find a buyer."

"I expect you want to go through the things you have stored up there," said Aunt Amaryllis. "And I daresay you'll want to keep some of them."

"Yes, that is so."

"You can't go alone," said Uncle Peter, frowning.

"I've thought of that. There is a young woman at the Mission. Her name is Kitty. I took quite a fancy to her. I thought I would employ her as a maid and take her with me."

"A girl from the Mission!" cried Uncle Peter. "What sort of girl?"

"She's had a hard life. She came up to London from the country. She had a job as maid or something. The master of the house was offensive and the mistress turned her out. Frances is looking for a good situation for her."

"You want to be careful whom you employ," said Uncle Peter.

"I am being very careful. I like Kitty. Frances says she is a good girl."

"Frances is apt to have a rose-coloured view of her inmates."

"I think Frances is very shrewd," said Aunt Amaryllis.

"In any case, I've made up my mind," I told them. "I shall go down to the Mission and put this proposition to Kitty and Frances. And if they are agreeable I shall employ her. I'll get some clothes for her. I think she would like to go to the country for a while."

Aunt Amaryllis nodded, with tears in her eyes.

I went that very day to the Mission and put my proposition first to Frances.

She was delighted with it. "Just what Kitty needs," she said. "She took a great fancy to you from the day she saw you. I'll send for her. She's peeling potatoes in the kitchen."

Kitty arrived and when I told her what I had in mind, her delight was a joy to see.

"It will be very quiet where I'm going," I warned her. "Just a little cottage on the edge of an estate which was once mine. There won't be any other servants."

"When do we leave, Miss Cadorson?" asked Kitty.

Frances embraced us both—a rare demonstration for her.

"You've made a good choice," she said.

And in spite of what lay before me my spirits lifted a little.

Kitty and I travelled part of the way on the railway, which was a novelty to us both. It seemed so wonderful to travel in such an exciting fashion, but of course the railways were encroaching all over the countryside at this time. It was a great innovation, but nothing could be wholly good, it seemed, and many stagecoach drivers were being deprived of their livelihoods. I had heard many a sad story of their fates from Frances and Peterkin.

We stayed at night at an inn at Exeter and there heard from the landlord that the railways would in time be the end of the old coaching inns.

We travelled the rest of the way by coach which dropped us in the town. Mr. and Mrs. Tamblin were there to meet us for they had been warned of my coming. They both greeted me warmly and I introduced Kitty as my maid. She was very demure and I could see how excited she was. She had told me on the night before that she had never had such an exciting adventure in her life and had never thought to travel in a real train. She stood at the window of the inn and inhaled the fresh country air.

I felt very pleased that I had been able to do something to make her so happy. Mrs. Tamblin told me that she had had certain things taken out of store and put into Croft Cottage, so it could be lived in right away. Then I could decide what other things I wanted. She herself would come along with me to the storage warehouse and explain everything to me. But first we were going to spend a night with them. We could start sorting everything out in the morning. She knew how tired and hungry we must be after that long journey.

"And you travelled on the train!" she cried, looking at us with wonder. I think she thought we had taken our lives in our hands to travel in such a strange contraption.

The Tamblins' carriage had been waiting for us and in a short time we arrived at their house. I was ushered into my bedroom and Kitty was to sleep in a little dressing room attached to it.

"Now you wash the journey off you and then come down to eat. I'll go and see that they get it on the table."

So I did.

Kitty was given a meal in the kitchen and I sat down with the Tamblins.

"It is good to see you back," said Mrs. Tamblin. "I was hoping you might come when orders were sent to see about the repairs to Croft Cottage."

"Is it now in good order?"

"In perfect order. It's a pleasant little place," said Mrs. Tamblin.

"Your mother did well to buy it," added her husband.

"Do you think I shall find a buyer quickly?"

"Property is not going all that quickly now and it is rather remote. A lot depends on luck."

"Perhaps you will like it so much you'll change your mind about selling," said Mrs. Tamblin.

I was silent.

"I was wondering," she went on, "how you'd feel about being so close to Cador."

"I don't know . . . yet."

"What a change in that place! Isaacs is very worried about the way things are going. I saw Mrs. Penlock the other day. She was near to tears."

"It's going downhill fast, I think," said Mr. Tamblin. "Even a big estate can't stand up to that sort of thing."

"What sort of thing?"

"I don't exactly know. There are rumors. Mortgages and so on . . . changing things. They're spending money like water. And there's nothing done to the farms nor to the house itself. You have to keep your eye on those sorts of places. People forget how old they are. A little crack . . . and in no time it's a big crack . . . and my goodness, then there's trouble. You've got to be on the watch all the time."

"I should have thought Bob Carter would have seen to things." I wanted to ask what Rolf was doing about it, but could not bring myself to mention his name.

"Bob Carter? Oh, he's not there now."

"Not there? Where is he then?"

"He went over to the Manor."

"Why?"

"After the marriage, of course."

"But I should have thought . . ."

"Apparently he never got on with Luke Tregern."

"Did he have to? Luke was at the Manor, Bob at Cador."

They looked at me in astonishment.

"Oh, I suppose you haven't heard about the marriage."

"I heard something in London."

"So you know then," said Mrs. Tamblin. "You could have knocked me down with a feather. Of course, being as she is, perhaps it fits. My goodness, it was a bad day for Cador when she took over."

"You just can't do it," said Mr. Tamblin. "You have to be brought up to that sort of thing . . . managing a place like that. You can't take everything out and put nothing back."

"But I should have thought Mr. Hanson . . ."

"He's sitting pretty, of course. The difference in those two estates! We used to say that Cador was the giant and the Manor the dwarf. It's a bit different now."

I repeated: "But I should have thought . . ."

Mr. Tamblin said: "It is clear you haven't heard. That woman, Maria Cadorson, as she claims to be, married Luke Tregern."

Understanding dawned in me in a blinding flash. I felt suddenly deliriously happy.

"I thought . . . that it was Mr. Hanson who had married her," I stammered.

"Mr. Hanson! Marry that woman! You must be joking," said Mrs. Tamblin.

"I heard it in London. Someone said it was 'the chap from the Manor' and I immediately thought . . ."

Mrs. Tamblin laughed. "Not in a month of Sundays could I see that coming about. No, it was Luke Tregern for her, from the moment she got here. She just went for him. He knew which side his bread was buttered."

"He was always sly," said Mr. Tamblin. "He always had an eye for the main chance."

"Mr. Hanson always said he was a good manager."

"That was when he was managing someone else's estate. Now he's gone wild. He's mortgaged the place up to the hilt, so I heard. He doesn't work through me. I suppose he doesn't want me to know too much. I'm too near. But these things get round. Oh, it was a sad day when that woman came to Cornwall."

I was not listening. I was savouring the fact that Rolf had not married her.

I lay in bed that night unable to sleep. I was here, where I had begun to feel I belonged. And I had misjudged Rolf. I had thought he would do anything to get possession of Cador.

And all the time it was Luke Tregern!

How happy I was that I had come back.

I longed to see Rolf.

The next day we went to the cottage. It looked charming. The workmen had done a good job and Mrs. Tamblin had arranged some things as she thought I should like them.

There were two bedrooms and she had bought beds and put those in because she had thought I would not come alone. She had selected a few items of furniture from those stored and had put curtains up at the windows.

I thanked her warmly for all she had done.

"At least," she said, "it's habitable. I don't know how long you'll stay, but if you're going to sell the place you want to have it looking like a home. And you can sell the bits and pieces with the place if you want to."

"You think of everything, Mrs. Tamblin."

I felt as though I were walking on air. I thought: I shall see him again and if he really cares for me . . . this time I shall not be foolish.

Kitty worked hard to get the house as I wanted it. Mrs. Tamblin hovered dispensing little scraps of gossip, little realizing how important they were to me.

Mr. Hanson was away, she told me. He was often nowadays. Mrs. Tamblin had an idea that he deplored the changes. There were conflicts between Luke Tregern and Bob Carter about the land, and it made for an uneasy situation. Mr. Hanson left all the haggling to Bob; it was as though he could not bear to deal with his ex-manager.

During the first afternoon Mrs. Penlock called. It was good to see her and she was quite emotional at our meeting.

"Well there you are, Miss Cadorson. My patience me, it is good to

[304]

see 'ee. What we'm been putting up with since you left. I can't tell 'ee all of it. It's 'ud take a book. I've never been in such a place. There be nothing a body can do. I had all them maids under control, I did. I had everything as it should be. The polish on that dining room table . . . well, it would have done for a mirror. But there's no heart in anything now. They're drinking and gambling to past midnight . . . and in the morning there's all the mess to clear up. Mr. Isaacs he'd be gone in a flash if he had another place to go to. But he won't leave the Duchy. Can't say I blame him. Nor would I. Who wants to go off to foreign parts? Well, you have, Miss Cadorson, but I reckon that's different. Neither Isaacs nor me would wish to work for foreigners."

"Oh, Mrs. Penlock," I cried, "it is good to talk to you again."

"Never should have been," she grumbled. "I know in me bones as she's no right to this place. I reckon it's all a put-up job, I do. And that Luke Tregern . . . what right 'as he . . . lording it over us all? King of the castle. Squire of the house. It's ain't right, Miss Cadorson. It don't work."

"You say there is gambling and drinking. Who joins them in this?"

"All the riffraff of the countryside. Come from miles they do. Where they find them I don't know. Villains, all of them. And they quarrel something shocking . . . him and her. You can hear them shouting. Cador quarrels always took place behind closed doors . . . in the way of the gentry. I don't know what we're coming to. Bob Carter comes in to the kitchen now and then. He's always been a friend of Mr. Isaacs. Mind you, he don't want to be seen at Cador. Luke Tregern wouldn't want him around. He sees too much. But Bob reckons it can't go on. There'll be a climax of some sort, he says. That's what worries us all at Cador, for what'll become of us? Oh, it was a sad day when you went, Miss Cadorson . . . and none of us here believe her tale. There's a bit of trickery somewhere."

"The court believed it, Mrs. Penlock."

"Courts is crazy sometimes. Some of them people couldn't see the noses before their own faces."

"It is wonderful to be back."

I introduced Kitty. "Kitty has come with me from London. I shall need only one maid and Kitty takes good care of me."

Mrs. Penlock studied Kitty with the calculating eyes she bestowed on the maids she employed, and I was pleased to see that they took to each other.

"You must come up to the house," she said to Kitty. "Some of the maids will like to meet you . . . so will we all."

"Is that wise, do you think?" I asked. "*My* maid to come to the house?"

"If I didn't have control over me own kitchen I'd walk out tomorrow, that I would," said Mrs. Penlock severely.

"I'd like to come," said Kitty.

"Then that's it. I'll send one of them over to fetch you."

"I hear Mr. Hanson is away," I said.

"Oh yes . . . so we're told. He's away quite a lot. Mind you, he knows what's going on but he does give Bob Carter a free hand. Bob says how lucky he was to have stepped into the Manor estate. There wouldn't have been room for him at Cador with Luke Tregern." She gave me a sly look and went on: "Bob says Mr. Hanson is not a very contented man lately. I reckon it's time he settled down."

I had been at Croft Cottage a week when Rolf returned.

I had been living in a state of euphoria which meant that I was a good deal happier than I had been for a long time. I had thought that being here, where there were so many memories of my family, I should have been desolate; but this was not the case. They were constantly in my thoughts; I felt their presence here; and it was as though they were urging me to make something of my life—which I knew was what they would do if they were here.

I took pride in the cottage. I had not yet put it up for sale and hesitated to do this. I kept telling myself that there was plenty of time. Kitty and I went into the town to buy a few things which we needed. I was greeted almost ecstatically by the people whom I had known. Jack Gort scratched his head and said that things weren't what they used to be; and he was not referring to his catch. Mrs. Pendart shook her head and said that it wasn't natural for some to step into shoes that didn't fit . . . not by a long chalk.

I guessed that they all deplored the change at Cador and, of course, they would all be very much aware of it. My father and his family before him had exerted a benevolent influence over the community; local troubles were brought to them; their role was that of caring parents.

"Things are different now," was the general comment.

Many of them were uneasy. They knew the great estate was in decline. Farmers were complaining at the lack of repairs to their homes; the place was going to rack and ruin, it was said.

Kitty was often in the Cador kitchen, but I supposed the new owners did not concern themselves much with what went on below stairs; and Isaacs and Mrs. Penlock, much as they disliked the lowering of standards, were still despotic rulers in their own domain.

Kitty had made a friendship with Mabel Tucker whom I remembered as a kitchen maid. She used to come to the cottage on a return visit. I was very pleased to see Kitty so contented.

Then Rolf came over to see me.

He looked older, I thought. There were a few lines on his forehead which had not been there before, and he looked rather solemn. But his face lit up with pleasure when he saw me. He took both my hands and held them firmly.

"I heard you were back," he said. "I'm so pleased to see you."

"It's good to see you too, Rolf."

"I hear you have come back to sell the cottage."

"That was my intention."

"That mean you'll be going away . . . permanently."

"I really don't know what I'm going to do. It's hard to say . . . so much depends."

He nodded.

"All this . . ." He waved his hand. "Such changes. Sometimes it seems quite unbelievable."

"Yes, I know. One goes on for years expecting nothing to change and then suddenly it does . . . drastically. Come into the cottage. We're making it quite a pleasant place, Kitty and I. I brought her with me from London. She is out at the moment. I expect she is at Cador. She gets on very well with the maids there and Mrs. Penlock graciously allows her to visit the kitchen."

Rolf looked round the little sitting room.

"Very pleasant," he said and looked at me sadly. "My dear Annora, what you have gone through! I wish . . ."

I looked at him appealingly. I wanted him to hold me tightly. I wanted to say: This time, Rolf, I would not run away. I want to say I'm sorry. I was so foolish. I just couldn't believe you weren't there that night . . . and now I simply don't care if you were.

He said: "It was brave of you to come back."

"One has to go on living. The people here . . . they talk all the time about the change at Cador."

"It's a tragedy. They are ruining the place. I can't understand it. Tregern knows a good deal about management. He always worked well for me. I never quite trusted him, but he was a shrewd manager."

"Why didn't you trust him?"

"I imagined he was not strictly honest. I think certain sums may have found their way into his pocket."

"Didn't you tax him with it?"

"I had to have something I could prove first. And he really did a very good job. It was just vague suspicions."

"What do you think he is doing now?"

"I'm not sure. I know he is raising mortgages on Cador. It seems as though he is short of money. Yet he is doing nothing in repairs. The place is running down at an alarming rate. I can only think it is due to his gambling."

"I can't bear to think of it. My father was always so meticulous. Any sign of decay anywhere and he had it seen to at once."

"It is the only way. There is something odd going on there."

"And what of her . . . Maria?"

"She is besotted by him, I hear. She was from the time they met. In a way they suit each other."

"I was surprised when I heard she was married. For some time I thought it was to you."

He stared at me incredulously.

"Well, I was told by a prospective Member of Parliament who had been here sounding out the population. He said she had married 'the chap from the Manor.' Naturally I thought of you."

"*Un*naturally," he said. "What *were* you thinking of, Annora?"

"I, er . . . just thought you might have found her attractive . . . and I always knew you had a special feeling for Cador."

He looked at me in such puzzlement that I wanted to tell him that I loved him. I wanted to tell him about my doubts and misgivings which had started on that Midsummer's Ever. I wanted to say: Let's forget it forever. It doesn't matter. Whatever happened then I would put aside, because I knew my only chance of being happy again was with him.

He was looking into the past too, I believed. Was he remembering that morning when I had ridden over to the Manor with a note for him? I could see now what a terrible hurt I had inflicted on him. I wondered whether he could ever forget or forgive it.

It was not for me to say, I am ready to take you, Rolf. It was for him to decide whether he wanted me after what I had done to him.

"Cador, yes," he was saying. "It always seemed to me the most wonderful place on Earth. When, as a boy, I rode over with my father, I always gasped at the first glimpse of those towers. I used to wish that I had been born there. I certainly wished it could be mine. But not in that way. Good Heavens, Annora, what an idea!"

"Are you still interested in antiquities?"

"Yes, as enthusiastic as ever. Old customs and that sort of thing. But I couldn't have married that woman for all the castles and stately homes in England."

We laughed and I said: "Would you like some tea? Some coffee?"

"Some coffee, please."

"I shall have to make it myself. But don't worry. I know how. I did quite a lot of cooking in the Mission which is run by Peterkin and his wife."

"Oh yes. I've read about that place in the papers. Your uncle has given a great deal of support to it." He looked at me searchingly. "Such a lot of things happened in a short space of time. I feel I've been living in a backwater while you've been out in the world."

He watched me while I made the coffee.

I said: "Most of what happened was not very pleasant, Rolf."

He nodded.

"All that scandal with my uncle and the Cresswells. But it seemed nothing compared with what happened after."

There was silence while I set out the cups on the tray.

"You have become domesticated," he said with a smile.

He carried the tray into the sitting room and I poured out the coffee.

"I learned from the newspapers about what was happening to you.

It seemed strange that it should be that way after . . . Well, we had been pretty close, hadn't we?"

"Always . . . until . . ."

"Things change."

"Rolf, I'm very sorry for what I did to you."

"You did the right thing."

I was aghast.

"Yes," he said. "It would have been wrong for you. It was better to make the break while there was time, even if it was at the last moment . . . rather than go and make a mistake."

"But . . ."

"Don't worry about it, Annora."

"Have you . . . forgiven me?"

"My dear Annora, there is nothing to forgive really. It seemed right for us then, didn't it? It seemed natural. I think we were carried away by childhood memories. And that, of course, is not a good reason. It wasn't the past we had to think about but the future. It's over now. Let's forget it."

Those words were like a tolling bell telling me of the love which was dead.

"After all," he went on, "we're still good friends . . . the best of friends."

How often had those words been spoken, I wondered, to end a broken love affair. "We're good friends . . . the best of friends."

Friends are good to have, but when one has been hoping for more, how sad those words are!

"What about those Cresswells?" he asked. "There was a big scandal about Joseph, wasn't there? It ruined his career."

"Yes. And then of course there was my uncle."

"That shady business of his. He seems to have shrugged all that aside."

"He would. He knows how to make life go the way he wants it to, and when he comes to obstacles he just treats them as though they are not there. He's very interested in Helena's husband and is giving him his support."

"Oh, yes, Matthew Hume. That was a good book he wrote."

"He was collecting the material when he was with us in Australia. Matthew and Helena are very happy now. They have another child."

"You were very fond of the first one."

"Jonnie is adorable. He did a great deal for me when I was so desolate."

He nodded. "There seems to be quite a friendship between your family and these Cresswells."

"Well, Peterkin married Frances. She is the one who opened the Mission, and of course my Uncle Peter gave a lot of money to that."

"And there was the son."

"Joe Cresswell, yes."

"I gather he is a great friend of yours."

"Yes. He gave up his ambitions to become a Member of Parliament at the time of the scandal. I told him he was wrong to give up. He ought to have been like Uncle Peter. Just shrug it off. After all, it was not his affair. It was his father who was involved. I don't see why it should affect him."

"The sins of the fathers . . ."

"Very unfair. However, I'm trying to persuade Joe to make an effort to get into Parliament. I don't think he will be happy until he does."

"You found parliamentary circles interesting?"

"Oh yes, very. I helped Helena and Matthew during the election."

"It must have been fascinating."

"It was really . . . an entirely new way of life."

"Yes, of course." He looked at his watch. "You make a very good cup of coffee. I must be going. It has been so pleasant to see you, Annora. I hope you are not going to run away too soon. You must come over to the Manor. I have some curios to show you . . . some instruments we have dug up. Bronze Age, I guess. Someone from the Museum is coming to see them."

"I'd love to look at them, Rolf. And I'd love to see you again."

He took my hands and held them for a long time.

A few weeks passed. Mr. Tamblin asked me if I was ready to put the cottage up for sale. I said: "Not yet. I should like to stay here in peace for a little while."

"Sales take a long time to go through," he pointed out.

"I know. But just at the moment I don't want to think about selling."

I saw Rolf now and then. Knowing how fond I was of riding, he told me to use his stables when I wanted to. I took advantage of the offer and often when I was riding, I met him, and we rode as we used to, galloping our horses along the shore. I looked up and saw the towers of Cador and remembered how I used to stand there, looking out through the battlements at the sea. I was overcome with sadness. There were too many memories here. Sometimes I thought I ought to go back. Rolf was fond of me, but it seemed that he had given up all thought of our marrying. I had deceived myself into thinking that we might come together again. Why is it that one thinks if one repents, everything can go on as before? Of course he would never trust me again. If we decided to marry how did he know that I should not reject him again?

He invited me to dine at the Manor. Expectantly I went. But there were other guests and although he was the perfect host, it was just a pleasant evening.

He called at the cottage and I gave him coffee. Usually Kitty made it. She delighted in playing the maid and looking after me. I had rarely seen such a change in a girl. She loved the country; she had her friend Mabel; she was a welcome visitor to the Cador kitchen; her life had changed miraculously. I made up my mind that whatever happened I must keep her with me.

I looked forward to the morning rides. I always hoped that I would meet Rolf. I invariably did, and the thought came to me that he looked for me as I did for him.

We talked a great deal about the old days, and I noticed how often the Cresswells came into the conversation. He was also very interested in Jonnie.

I talked very enthusiastically about the child and about the Cresswells. The weeks I had spent at the Mission, I told him, had done a great deal for me.

I tried to make him realize what a wonderful woman Frances was—so strong, so determined, and so unsentimental for all her desire to do good.

"Like her brother Joe?" asked Rolf.

"Not in the least. Frances is herself and no one is quite like her. She changed Peterkin completely. I used to think he would never do anything, and when we met her and went to the Mission, he found a purpose in life and he fell in love with her."

"Well, she is one of the Cresswells."

"She reminds me of Uncle Peter in a way. She kept her head up when all that was going on. She didn't let it affect her work."

"And now your uncle is climbing out of the slime of scandal with the help of the Cresswell Mission."

"They are such a charming family. I spent a week-end there once . . . long ago, it seems, before all that happened. Mr. and Mrs. Cresswell are so delightful. It was good to be in the heart of such a family."

"Which contained Frances and Joe."

"Yes and all the others. Oh, I do wish Joe would try to get back."

"I've no doubt you will persuade him."

We had come to a field and he broke into a gallop.

They were happy mornings. I did not want to give this up, for always in my heart was the hope that something would happen . . . some little word, some little action, and I would be confessing how I felt and he would tell me that he had never changed.

Then the rumors started.

Kitty had been out with Mabel and she told me that one of the boys from the stables had been in the woods when he had seen a fire.

"It was where the old witch's cottage used to be," said Kitty. "It wasn't an ordinary fire. There was something funny about it."

"Funny?" I asked. "How can a fire be funny?"

"Ghostly. Like it wasn't there . . . and yet it was."

"Do you mean it kept disappearing?"

"I don't know, but young James was so scared he just ran, and he didn't stop running until he was back in the stables. He said it was like having the Devil at his heels."

I told her that there had always been a certain feeling about that particular part of the woods since one Midsummer's Eve when a mob had set fire to the cottage.

"I expect it was just a tramp making a fire," I said. "What else could it have been?"

"Mrs. Penlock thought it might be Mother Ginny come back to haunt the place. Mr. Isaacs even said he wouldn't go near it for a gold watch . . . not even for a farm."

I did not take much notice. But the rumours intensified. Someone saw a figure there. It just appeared among the trees. It wasn't possible to see who it was but it looked like an old woman.

Few people went to the woods and certainly no one did after dark. There was a certain tension everywhere. It reminded me of those days just after that Midsummer's Eve. People looked a little furtive and I wondered how many of them were remembering that night.

I went down to the quay one morning with Kitty to buy some fish. Jack Gort was there with his creels and his tubs.

I said: "Hello, Jack. Had a good catch?"

"So-so, Miss Cadorson," he answered. "Could have been better. Wind's a bit strong. Couldn't stay out as long as I'd have liked to. I dunno. These winds do blow up sudden, like something's behind it all."

"Oh?" I said.

"Well . . . all this going on in the woods. Fires and figures like . . . It don't be healthy if you'm asking me."

"You don't believe Mother Ginny's come back to haunt all those people who sent her to her death?"

"Oh, 'twas her own doing. Her should know that. But they say as some don't rest and I reckon she be one of them."

"Poor Mother Ginny! It was a terrible thing that happened to her, and those who had a hand in it might be conscience-stricken."

"Oh, 'twas her own doing," he insisted. "Her ran right into the fire."

"You were there, Jack. . . ?"

"Aye."

"With half the people in this place."

He nodded. "You be right there, Miss Cadorson."

I thought: They should feel uneasy. Let them remember. That way it may never happen again.

I went back with Kitty.

Mrs. Penlock called to see me.

"Oh, 'tis nice to see 'ee settled in," she said. "I reckon you won't want to be leaving."

"I'm quite comfortable here."

"But for all that, 'tis not the place for you. Up at the big house, that's where you belong to be."

"That's all over, Mrs. Penlock."

" 'Tis a strange life. A bit topsy-turvy it do seem. But you've got that nice girl Kitty to do for you . . . couldn't be a nicer girl. She and Mabel get along like a house on fire. She's got such tales. I reckon that London be a terrible place, and wasn't it wonderful the way she went to that Mrs. Frances? I reckon she's a bit of a saint, that one. Could do with more like her in the world. Kitty just about idolizes her. It's Mrs. Frances this and Mrs. Frances that . . . and she's got a good word to say for you, too. Then she talks about that nice brother . . . a fine, upstanding fellow . . . just the sort of brother she'd expect Mrs. Frances to have."

"I can see she is keeping you well-informed."

"I like to hear about what's going on up there. And I'd like to see you nice and happy. I always had a soft spot for you . . . even more than your brother and I'll say it even though he's gone. I can see you now, sitting on that high stool at the table watching me kneading the dough . . . and every now and then when you thought I wasn't looking that little hand would shoot out and take a raisin or a nut. I saw you. 'I've got eyes in the back of me head,' I used to tell you; and you said, bright as a button, 'Your hair's covering them so you can't see out of them.' Sharp little thing you was. You were the favourite in the kitchen, I can tell you now, and there was a few tears shed when you was pushed out and Madam came to take your place. Nothing will make me believe she has a right and that goes for Mr. Isaacs and the rest of us."

"You've all made me feel so welcome back here," I said.

"Welcome! Why shouldn't 'ee be in your own cottage . . . and what should be your home, too. And would be if I had any say in it. We like to see you about and we like your Kitty, but I suppose you've got to think of the future and what we all want at Cador . . . from our side of the house, that is . . . is your happiness. We was all upset when you turned down Mr. Rolf. But you know what's best, I reckon. We'd like to see you married to someone nice . . . and with babies . . . even if we do have to read about them in the newspapers."

"Why should you read about them in the papers?"

"Well . . . Parliament and all that, you know. If you was to marry one of them . . . they put it in the papers when there's a baby."

I realized that Kitty had talked a great deal. She was devoted to

Frances and that meant Frances's brother; and I expected she had already decided that I was going to marry Joe and was glorifying my relationship with him to such an extent that the Cador staff had decided he was the man for me.

It was no use trying to stop gossip. It had always been and always would be.

I found myself becoming obsessed by that presence in the woods. Very few people went there nowadays and when they did it was usually in twos and threes. They saw nothing. It was only if you were caught alone, they said.

I was overcome by a desire to discover.

I went there one morning. I sat by the river where Digory and I used to throw stones into the water, straining my ears for the sound of a footstep, the crackle of bracken which would tell me that someone was close.

There was nothing but the sounds of the woods, the faint breeze ruffling the leaves on the trees, the gentle murmur of the water.

After a while I rose and went to the clearing. There was the burned-out cottage and beyond it the broken-down shed and the overgrown garden where Mother Ginny used to grow her magical herbs.

And as I stood there thinking of that terrible night, the half-broken door of the old shed creaked and started to open. I felt a shiver of alarm. They were right. There was a presence here. What I expected, I was not sure. The ghost of Mother Ginny as I had last seen her, mud-bespattered, her grey hair wet from the river. . . ?

A man stood there.

I gasped and we stared at each other. Then it struck me that there was something vaguely familiar about him. He seemed to feel the same about me. Then a wild idea came to me. I said: "You . . . you are Digory."

"I know you now you speak," he said. "Miss Cadorson."

"Digory! So you have come back."

"I served me term," he said. "I always intended to come back. There's something I have to do."

"How are you living?"

"Here."

"In that old shed?"

"I'm used to roughing it."

"But what do you live on?"

"There's fish . . . hares . . . rabbits . . . I've got these woods to myself."

"I've thought a lot about you, Digory. I've wondered where you were. We were in Australia . . ."

He nodded. "It was in the papers. Everyone was talking. I'm sorry for you, Miss Cadorson."

"Thank you, Digory. I can't let you stay here like this."

"I be all right."

"What is it you've got to do?"

"I've got to make it up to me granny."

"Make it up to her?"

"Him that killed her," he said.

"It wasn't one. It was the mob."

"It was one who egged 'em on like. They'd have sport with her per'aps. But her could take that. She wasn't afraid of 'em. It was him. I saw him clear. I'm going to kill him or make it so's he won't be as 'andsome as he was."

"This is madness, Digory. I'm going to take you back with me. I'm at Croft Cottage now. I'm not at Cador. It turned out it didn't belong to me after all. It's a long story. Perhaps you've heard."

"I ain't heard nothing," he said. "They'm all frightened of me. Makes me laugh it does. Anyone comes through these woods and I only have to make a little noise and they run for their lives. I'm frightening them, you see, like they frightened me granny . . . and me too. All this time it's been with me. I used to say to myself, I'll go back and frighten 'em all . . . all them that was there that night and none of them doing a hand's turn to save her. But him . . . I'm going to get him because he was the one. He had a covering-up . . . a grey thing he was wearing that come right over his head, so he thought you couldn't see his face. But I did. I saw. It was when they was dragging her to the river. The hood moved and I saw him as clear as I see you now. And he said, 'Come on. She bain't fit to live.' And I said to myself, 'And you bain't fit to live and one day I'll get you.'"

I was trembling. I was not the only one whose life had been dominated by that terrifying night.

I saw murder in Digory's face and I thought, He plans to kill Rolf. He had never forgotten . . . never forgiven.

I said: "Listen to me, Digory. If you carry out this plan you know

[317]

what it will mean. The hangman's noose at worst. At the best sent back for the rest of your life."

"I be past caring."

"It's murder."

"It's what they call justice and since the law won't do it someone must."

"Don't act rashly."

"I've planned this for years."

"Listen to me. You must be half starved."

"No. I have money. I bought things on my way here. I've got a little store. I've got tea and flour. I make a fire. I make dampers. Then I catch fish and rabbits, as I said. I know how to live in the outdoors. I can look after meself. I've planned this . . . for years. When I've done it, I'm going back. I worked me way over on a ship and I'll work me way back. No one will know I've been here but . . ." He looked at me fearfully. "I shouldn't be talking to you. You've made me tell you . . ."

"There was always a special friendship between us, Digory. You remember that night. My brother and I looked after you, and my father did too. He gave you work. Everything would have been all right if you hadn't stolen the pheasant."

"That wasn't ordinary stealing. 'Tweren't meant to be."

"It was stealing whichever way you look at it. I am not going to leave you here. I am going to take you back to my cottage. There's a shed in my garden. You can sleep there. Remember how you used to sleep in the Dogs' Home? I have a maid . . . just one . . . Kitty. She'll know and no one else will, I promise you."

"You're spoiling my plans."

He put his hands in his pocket and drew out a gun.

"Digory! Put that away. Do you want to be caught with that in your possession? Do you want to be sent back to Australia?"

He looked at me through narrowed eyes. "You're spoiling my plans," he repeated. "I don't want nobody to know I'm here. I could do what I've got to do and be away. Nobody would know I'd been here . . . 'cept you."

"I see. So you think you can shoot me, bury my body and nothing will be said?"

"You was always a bold one. I don't think I could shoot you. You was good to me, you was . . . you and your brother . . . so was your father. But if you tell I'm here, it will spoil everything. And what am I doing, telling you what I plan?"

"You are telling me because you are not sure that your plan will work. In fact you know it is very risky. Moreover I'm an old friend. I saved you once . . . and I'll save you again."

"She was me granny," he said. "I hadn't got no one else."

"You stole, Digory. You were a thief. The first time I noticed you you were stealing fish on the quay."

"I wouldn't have gone on being a thief. I didn't mean to steal. The first time was the meat for your Devil Spot." He looked at me sharply. "You've still got it."

I nodded.

"And the second time was the pheasant. It was because of him. I wanted to take something from him because of what he had done to me granny."

"It was a foolish thing to do."

"I didn't know then what I wanted. I'm not a boy any more. I'm a man and life 'as been cruel to me. But there's one or two who 'as been kind and you be one of them."

"Then trust me again. Come to the shed. I promise I won't say anything to anyone about this without telling you first. That place must be draughty at night. My shed has a proper roof. You'll be comfortable there. I'll give you some blankets and hot food. And, Digory, I want to talk to you. You must give up this plan. It can only lead to disaster for you."

"And for him. That's what matters. For me . . . I don't care. But I won't get caught. I've had all those years to plan and I've worked it all out. I'm not a silly boy any more, you know. This is what I've planned for. I'm going to that Manor and I'm going there to wait for him. I've been there at night but he doesn't come out. I've seen Bob Carter there. I don't yet know what he be doing there. But I'll get him one night, that I will, and then I'll rest for I will 'ave avenged me granny."

"Digory," I said, "do you remember how we used to sit on the bank and throw stones into the river?"

"Yes."

"I used to talk to you a lot. You never listened."

"Oh yes I did. I remember the day you showed me your house. It was something I shall never forget . . . all them wonderful things. I used to think a lot about them when I was away. I thought I'd like to go back there. I'd like to work there like I did before."

"Oh, Digory, if only you hadn't gone to the Manor woods that night. If only you had lived honestly."

"He killed me granny," he said. "I knew him . . . and when he caught me with the pheasant, I said to him 'You killed me granny,' I said. 'You was wearing a grey thing hiding your face, but it didn't hide it from me and I saw you, Luke Tregern, and I don't forget.'"

"Luke Tregern!"

"'Twas he. He couldn't fool me. There he was urging them on. 'Finish her off,' he said. 'Her sort shouldn't be allowed to live.' No more should his sort."

The realization hit me so forcibly that I could not listen to what Digory was saying.

So it was Luke Tregern who had been there that night.

Everything was becoming clear. He had been in the house often. He would have seen the robe. Rolf might have shown it to him. He was always showing people things he had discovered and he had had a respect for Luke Tregern's intelligence.

I heard myself say: "So it is Luke Tregern you have come back to kill . . . to take your revenge . . . I thought it was someone else."

"Who else?" he said. I did not answer and he went on: "I took the pheasant because it was his in a manner of speaking. He treated them birds like his own precious pets. So I took one. I was going to make a brew that would be a spell, so that everything would go against him. But he caught me. I said to him, 'Luke Tregern, you killed me granny!' He said, 'Stop that talk or it will be the worse for you. If you as much as mention the old witch I'll see you hanged from a gibbet.' And he gave evidence against me. He said I'd made a habit of stealing his pheasants and he'd lain in wait to catch me and he had, redhanded. And they listened to him and when I tried to speak they wouldn't let me. So he got me sent away for seven years. And then I thought, I'll come back, and I'll make him pay for what he's done to me granny . . . and to me."

It was as though a great burden had been lifted from my mind. I had misjudged Rolf. It was true that he had, as he told me, been in

Bodmin on that night. I wondered how I could have doubted him. The explanation was simple. Rolf was away. Luke Tregern had gone to the drawer and taken out the robe. After that night was over he simply put it back. I had no doubt that wearing the robe had appealed to his sense of the dramatic. Perhaps he had wanted to appear anonymous. He had been deeply conscious of his position as agent and manager of a big estate and felt it undignified to mingle with the fishing and mining community as one of them.

But there was one thought which was singing in my mind. All these years I had misjudged Rolf. My nature was suspicious and distrustful and I deserved so much of what had happened to me.

My immediate concern was Digory.

I had to stop his carrying out this plan for I could see that it would only bring him further trouble.

"Digory, you are coming with me. I have to talk to you. There is so much to say. Promise me you'll take no action until you have talked to me."

"I can't promise that. Suppose I was to come on him . . . and we was alone?"

"It isn't the way. Do you think I don't understand how you feel? A great deal has happened here since you've been away. I told you I was no long at Cador. I want to talk to you. But first I want you to promise me that you will come after dark to Croft Cottage. I shall tell no one except my maid. She will have to know because she is there. But I will impress on her that she must be discreet and I know she will do as I say. Please listen to me. Remember we saved your life once. What would the mob have done to you if we hadn't hidden you?"

"They would have killed me most likely . . . like they did my granny."

I nodded. "Then trust me, Digory. Let me talk to you. Let us reason this out in comfort. You need care. You need food. You may have been able to live here in the woods for a while but . . ."

"It won't be for long. I'll get him soon."

"Promise me you'll come tonight. You'll have the shed. We'll keep you there. It's better than here. Digory, listen to me. My brother and I saved you before. Remember that."

"I do believe you," he said, "but I won't come. I won't have

[321]

anyone else know I'm here. That maid 'ud have to know. I don't trust nobody 'cept you. I'll find him and when I can get him, I'll take him. Then I'll go. But I won't come to you.''

"You mean you'll stay here in the woods? Someone might see you. Some say they have.''

"They've seen ghosts. That's good. It keeps them away. I'm safe here. I wouldn't feel safe anywhere else. This is where I was . . . where she was. I feel she's here sometimes . . . looking after me.''

"Can I bring you anything?'' Are you warm enough at night? I'll bring some food.''

"No, don't. People might see. I couldn't have anyone knowing.''

"I'll help you all I can, but I'm going to try to stop you. I'm going to make you see that you're playing a dangerous game. If you harm him and you're caught that will be the end for you.''

"I wouldn't care as long as I got him.''

"I have to go now,'' I said. "I don't want Kitty wondering where I am. People are getting uneasy about what is going on in the woods. Fires have been seen. They know someone is here.''

"Ghosts,'' he said again.

"That's what some think. Others might not. I came to see for myself, remember.''

"I'll take care. And you'll tell no one.''

"No. I'll tell no one.''

"You've done a lot for me.''

I looked at him sadly and I thought: You have done a lot for me.

I went back to the cottage thinking of my own folly for doubting Rolf.

I wanted to go to him and tell him that that which I had been unable to get out of my mind for years had now been made clear to me. I wanted to try to make him understand about that night before the day when we were to have been married and how I had imagined the grey robe was my wedding dress. But I should have to tell him *how* it had been made clear to me and I had promised Digory that on no account would I tell anyone that he was here.

But I must stop him in his mad design. If he attempted to kill Luke Tregern, the result would no doubt be death for him.

I could imagine how he had cherished thoughts of revenge during those years of servitude. I knew from Matthew's book they they would have been grim, that he would often have been filled with despair. And perhaps what had kept him able to endure his lot was the thought of revenge.

I had to be careful.

I had to save Digory.

I smuggled food out to the woods. It was not easy, as it had been at Cador where there was so much in the larder that a little might not be missed.

"I can't see the remains of the chicken," said Kitty, puzzled.

I thought I should have to be careful. I took a blanket down with the chicken and some bread.

He was glad of them.

"I might have to tell Kitty," I said, "because she is going to miss the food."

"I won't have anyone told," he retorted. "Don't bring food. I'll manage."

"Digory, have you thought any more about what I've said?"

"What?" he asked.

"That if you . . . harmed him . . . you would suffer just as much."

"I wouldn't be caught."

Two days passed. I had not seen Rolf. I did not go to the stables because if I did I should surely see him and I should find it difficult not to tell him that Digory was in the woods. I longed to tell him that I knew the truth about that night now. But how could I explain without betraying Digory?

I was constantly worried about him. I had seen the purpose in his face and I knew that he was plunging to certain disaster.

I bought some cheese in the town.

"I'll tell Kitty you've taken the Cheddar," said Mrs. Glenn who ran the shop.

"Oh, that's all right. I'll tell her."

And I thought how difficult it was to do anything in such a place without being detected.

What would Kitty say if she knew I had bought cheese?

I cut a piece off and put it in the larder, so that I should be prepared.

"Cheddar!" she would say. "Why did you buy that? I thought it wasn't one of your favourites."

But when Kitty came in she was so full of the news that she did not notice the cheese.

"What do you think? Luke Tregern has disappeared."

I felt sick. I stammered: "Disappeared?"

"Yes. He left the house yesterday afternoon and he didn't come back."

"What do they think has happened to him?"

"That's what they don't know. Mrs. Tregern's in a rare state, they say. They say she's well nigh crazy. Annie, the maid there, says she thinks there was a big row."

"And that . . . he's left her?"

Kitty nodded. "You see, they both went out riding together yesterday afternoon . . . and when they come back she heard them shouting. She said . . . and Annie heard this with her own ears . . . 'What are we going to do?' just as though she was desperate like. Then after a while he went out . . . and he didn't come back."

Oh, God help him I thought. He's done it. And I thought I was making him see the folly of it and what it would do to him.

"Do they think he has left her?"

"What else? There was all this trouble when they come in. They say she was white as a sheet . . . half out of her wits. I reckon he's gone off. Of course they said he married her for Cador . . . he being only the manager of the Manor then. Well, I don't know. You do see life in the country, after all."

"So the general feeling is that he has left her?"

"Where'd he go, that's what I wonder. They say he hasn't taken anything with him. Just the clothes he's standing up in. He just walked out . . . just like that . . . and he didn't come back."

I wanted to be alone. I went into my bedroom and shut the door.

Where was Digory now? He wouldn't be in the woods surely. He would have gone by now. He wouldn't hang about. He wouldn't want to be caught. There would be a search for Luke Tregern. They would not suspect murder at first. They would think he had just walked out of the house, left his wife.

Apparently they had quarrelled now and then, and yesterday there had been this big upset. They had been out together riding and when they had come back she had looked white as a sheet and half crazed;

he was clearly disturbed. They had quarrelled and he had walked out. I was going over it as Kitty had told it.

Yes, I thought, he walked out to the woods where Digory was waiting and there he met his death.

I could not rest. I had to go to the woods.

To my amazement Digory was there.

I said: "You've done it then, Digory. You didn't listen to me." He looked bewildered and just stared at me.

"I know," I said. "The whole town knows he has disappeared. Where is he, Digory? What have you done with his body?"

He continued to stare at me. Then he said: "I can't believe it . . . There she was, on her horse. He was with her . . . I couldn't understand. I didn't expect to see her . . . She knew me. She just stared at me. She was so white I thought she was going to fall off her horse. And he was there with her . . . *Him* . . . If I'd had me gun I could have killed him."

"*If* you had your gun . . ." I stammered.

"Then she said my name. She said to me, 'It's you . . .' I could see she thought she was dreaming. The last thing she thought was to see me here. She hadn't seen me for two years. I left when my term was done. I heard someone had been looking for me . . . and I was sorry. I wanted to know who it was. It was a mate of mine who told me. I run across him in Sydney and he said someone had asked him where I was. He'd told him I was at Stillman's. He didn't know I'd gone, he was trying to find me, see how I was. A real gentleman who was going to offer me something back in England. He couldn't remember the name. Sir Something Somebody he said."

I said: "Digory. It was my father."

"It don't matter now . . . It's them . . . But this fellow gave my address to your father or what he thought was my address. But it wasn't, see, 'cos I'd left there two years before."

I was thinking of the entry in the notebook. "Was this address Stillman's Creek?"

"That's it. That's where she was. There was three of us sent there. There was Tom James who gave your father this address and Bill Aske . . . He was educated. He'd been in a lawyer's office. Forging, that was what he was picked up for. The three of us landed up at Stillman's."

"Tell me all about it please, Digory."

"She was there. She worked for her father. She was mad about England. She used to make me talk to her . . . all about it. About the green fields and the rain and the houses, too. She wanted to know all about the *big* houses . . . so I used to tell her. I could stop work and talk to her. Talking was easy. Over and over again she'd make me tell her . . . so I told her all about what you'd showed me in the big house."

"She was Maria Stillman," I said.

"That's her."

"And did you know her mother?"

"'Course. She was old Stillman's missus. Stillman came out to settle and Mrs. Stillman came out on one of the ships . . . a convict. She went to Stillman's to work and he married her. She was an old tartar she was."

"Maria Stillman is living at Cador now, Digory," I said, "because she says she was my father's daughter and that he wasn't really married to my mother."

"She was old Stillman's daughter. She took after her mother, she did. She got Aske to forge her father's signature. Something about money. She used to say one day she was going to England. She was going to live in a grand house like Cador."

I felt dazed. It was much a tangled web of lies and deceit and who would have thought that Digory would be linked to it and should be the one to bring me the truth?

"I'm sorry, Digory," I said. "I can't think clearly. This is such a revelation. Oh, Digory, why did you have to do it? Why couldn't you have seen it was no good? We would have looked after you . . . given you a start."

I heard the sound of horse's hoofs.

I said: "Someone is coming. Perhaps they're looking for you. You'd better hide."

I tried to pull him towards the shelter of the shed, but I was too late.

Maria was there. Deliberately she slipped off her horse and tied it to a bush. We stared at each other.

She said: "They're both here. What luck. It makes it easier."

She seemed as though she were talking to herself.

"You've told her then," she said to Digory.

[326]

"Yes, he has told me," I answered. "I always knew it was false but now I know the truth and how you were able to do what you did."

"You're the only one who knows . . . well, the two of you . . . and that's how it's going to stay."

Calmly she brought out a small pistol.

"What are you doing?" I cried. "Do you think you'll get away with this?"

"Yes," she said, "I do." And quietly: "I have to."

I saw that her hand was shaking. She was a very frightened woman, and that knowledge gave me courage. She does not want to kill, I thought. She is a cheat, a liar, fraud, but she does not want to commit murder.

I said: "They will catch you. They will hang you for murder, hang you on a gibbet."

I saw her lips twitch. "They won't catch me."

"Of course they will."

"No . . ." She shook her head. "There's been a prowler in the woods. Everyone's talking. They'll think . . . And I've got to." It was as though she were speaking to herself. "I can't lose Luke. I can't lose Cador . . ."

She had lifted her hand. Digory moved clumsily towards me as the shot rang out. I felt something touch my shoulder and then there was another shot. The grass was rushing up to meet me and Digory was lying on top of me. I saw flashing lights; something was happening to my shoulder . . . and then there was darkness.

When I regained consciousness I was in an unfamiliar bed. There were people in the room. I could vaguely hear their voices; they moved about me like shadows. Then I slipped once more into darkness.

This was my condition for several days, although I was unaware of the passing of time.

Then I awoke one morning to acute discomfort. I was swathed in bandages and aware of nothing but pain.

A woman came to my bedside. I did not know her.

She touched my forehead. "Go to sleep," she said.

I shut my eyes obediently. It was what I wanted to do.

They gave me something to drink and I was very, very drowsy.

[327]

When I awoke someone was sitting by my bed. A voice: "Annora
. . . *dearest* Annora."

"Hello, Rolf," I said. I felt I was beginning to come back to life.

I was in the Manor. They had brought me there. I had been there
for two weeks and I knew now that I had been close to death.

I could not quite remember what had happened. There were times
when I thought it was something to do with Midsummer's Eve. And
when I thought of it afterwards, I supposed it was.

I heard the story gradually.

One of the maids had found us in the woods. Greatly daring she
had come to the clearing, and she had seen us lying there. She had
run screaming and hysterical back to Cador. Isaacs and Mrs. Penlock
had thought she was being fanciful, she was so hysterical. But when
she said she thought it was Miss Cadorson and there was a man there
and a lot of blood, Isaacs came with several of the men.

They were deeply shocked to find us.

Bob Carter was there and he took the news to Rolf, who immediately came hurrying to the woods.

He told me about it afterwards.

"You were lying there, so still, so white, with your blouse scarlet
with blood. And he was there . . . half covering you. The bullet had
gone into his back. It got his lung. The doctor said that from his
position he would have saved your life."

I could scarcely bear it. I had meant to do so much for him. Poor
Digory, who had never had a chance, and who in the end had given
his life to save mine.

Rolf said I should be taken to the Manor and he would get nurses
to look after me. He wanted me under his roof. The doctor thought it
a good idea, for Croft Cottage was small and lacked certain
amenities.

So I was taken there and Rolf told me that he sat beside my
bedside every day willing me to live.

It seemed that the first bullet had hit me just below the shoulder
and the second had not touched me because Digory had been there to
shield me.

I said: "I am remembering. He moved towards me just as she
fired."

"He saved your life. I wish I could show him what I feel about that," said Rolf. "I wish I had a chance to repay him . . . not that one ever could, but I could have tried."

I said I wanted to know what happened.

Rolf said: "The doctors forbid all that sort of talk."

"But I must know."

"You will. All you have to do now is rest. But you are out of danger. You are with those who love you."

"Those who love me. . . ?"

"Your family is here, Annora. Your uncle and aunt, Helena, Matthew, Jonathan and Tamarisk. Claudine and David . . . all of them."

"I know then that they were expecting me to die," I said.

"Don't speak of it. I could not have borne it."

"Do you mean that, Rolf?"

"You know, don't you?"

"You speak as though you care for me."

"Of course I care for you. I always have. You always knew it."

"I didn't. I thought you did not care for me any more. It was not for myself . . ."

"It was you, remember, who rejected me."

"Foolish creature that I was. Rolf, kiss me . . . please."

He did gently, and very tenderly.

I said: "I have been lying here and yet not here. I was floating off far away from the world . . . and unhappiness. I seemed to have left all that behind."

"Don't . . . please."

"Not now you're here, Rolf. And you look at me as though you love me and you talk to me as though you love me. If that is true I want to get well. I want to be here . . . with you."

I was getting better though I was very weak and still suffering from pains in my shoulder. The wound had yet to heal and that, they told me, would take time.

Gradually I learned what had happened.

I could not help feeling sorry for Maria in spite of everything. I kept thinking of the blank despair in her face when she had fired that shot. I could picture her dreaming her dreams. Digory had made me see that home where she had lived and dreamed of England. Her father was a settler, her mother an ex-convict. I daresay they had both yearned for home at some time and had conveyed that yearning to Maria although she had never seen—at that time—the place they called Home. Cador became a sort of Mecca to her. She made Digory talk of it over and over again. And then when the drowning incident occurred she saw her chance. She had the forger who could provide her with a marriage certificate; and she had come to England full of daring, with him as her solicitor, seeing it all as simple.

Then when Digory had come back and recognized her she was caught. She must have thought the chances of his coming back were very slim. If she had considered that seriously for a moment she would have realized what a dangerous position she could be in.

Luke Tregern had married her. He was the calculating villain. He had seen his great chance; he would get his hands on Cador. But he was less simple than Maria. He saw all sorts of pitfalls. He did not believe that my family would let the matter rest. He guessed that my Uncle Peter—that man of great ability and manipulator of his fellow men—would take some action—and how right he was in that. It must have occurred to him that although Maria was in possession at the time, she might not remain so. So he had decided to syphon off money and invest it abroad. He had mortgaged the property as far as he could and had banked the money in Australia under a false name and he intended to escape there when it was necessary.

That scene in the woods when he and Maria had come face to face with Digory, told him that the moment had come, more quickly than he had thought it would. He had been preparing himself for some time for sudden departure. So he was ready. As soon as he knew that Digory was in the neighbourhood and had seen Maria he prepared for flight.

He was picked up in Southampton where he was waiting for a ship to take him to Australia.

It was ironical that when he was brought up for trial he was sentenced to fourteen years' transportation; and eventually departed for Australia in a very different manner from that which he had planned.

As for Maria, when she learned that I was still alive, before she could be brought to justice, she went down to the shore and walked into the sea.

That was the tragic end of her dreams.

I had visitors every day. Helena brought Jonnie, who looked at me with enquiring eyes and wanted to know why I was all tied up.

I told him I had had an accident and would soon be untied.

He regarded me solemnly and asked me to tell him a story. Rolf came in and found us together.

"This is your house," announced Jonnie.

"Yes," replied Rolf. "Do you like it?"

"Yes."

"Would you like to live here?"

"With you?"

Rolf nodded.

"And Auntie Annora?"

"Ask her."

He looked at me and said: "And Mama and Papa and Geoffrey . . . We could all come. Here I'd have a pony."

Helena came in and took him from the bed. She regarded me with concern. "You mustn't tire yourself," she said anxiously.

Uncle Peter came.

He said: "I've had things checked."

I looked at him enquiringly.

"This Maria," he said. "You didn't think I was going to let them get away with it, did you? If you had left it to me it wouldn't have gone so far. Soon as I heard the verdict I sent a man out to Australia . . . a detective to scent out the truth. It took a bit of time but at last we traced it. She was living on her father's property. He had had convict labour and one of these was Digory. That was how she came to know about the house. Her mother died a few years ago. This Stillman was Maria's father. There was never any question of it. The whole thing was a fabrication. And it ought to have been seen as such right from the start. I always said you should have let me deal with it."

"I know, Uncle Peter."

"Well, there'll be no haggling now. Cador will be back . . . where it belongs."

"Thank you, Uncle," I said.

"You get well . . . quickly."

"I promise to do my best."

[331] .

Rolf sat by my bed.

He said: "You are well enough now to talk."

"What about?" I asked.

"Us. I think we should try again, Annora. And this time, please don't decide right at the last moment to stop the ceremony."

"I won't, Rolf. I'll be there."

"What a lot of time we've wasted. Where did it all go wrong?"

"On Midsummer's Eve . . . years ago . . . when I saw that figure in the grey robe urging on that cruel mob to violence."

"You thought that of me!"

"You had the robe. I couldn't believe it. It bewildered me. It gave me a jaundiced view of the world. I think I stopped believing in anybody from then on."

"But I told you. I was in Bodmin on that night."

"I know you told me. I wanted to believe you, but I couldn't forget. I know now that even if you had been there I should still love you. I shouldn't have allowed my doubts to get in the way. I know now that it was Luke Tregern who was there that night in the robe. Digory saw him."

"He must have taken it from my drawer. I remember showing it to him. He was interested in the old customs. I remember telling him how they went back to pre-historic days. I caught him once wearing a coat and hat of mine. I came in and found him preening before a mirror. I was amused. Tregern was the sort who set great store by bettering himself."

"It wouldn't go, Rolf . . . the memory of that night. It haunted me. On the night before the day when we were to be married I dreamed. I thought I was there and you were in the robe and when I woke up I saw my wedding dress hanging in the cupboard . . . The door had blown open and I thought for a moment that you were in the room, in the robe. It seemed significant . . . an uncanny warning. You see I was afraid I was never going to forget. Now that I know it was Luke Tregern I believe I can stop thinking of that Midsummer's Eve. I don't think I shall have any more nightmares about it."

"I see that you had a poor opinion of me if you thought I was there urging on that mob. What else did you think of me?"

"That you wanted Cador."

He looked at me steadily. "You thought I wanted to marry you because you owned Cador?"

"It was the way I was looking at everything. After that Midsummer's Eve I ceased to trust anyone. Forgive me, Rolf."

"I have not been without my doubts. Why do we doubt the one we love? Why do we look for flaws? Why do we distrust perfection? Annora . . . you and Joe Cresswell . . ."

"Yes?"

"I heard the talk. I believe it came through Kitty to the Cador kitchens and from theirs to mine . . . and that seeps through the house. They seemed to think you were going to marry Joe."

"Oh no, no," I said. "I liked Joe. I wanted to help him. He suffered so much when his father was in trouble. But I never loved him . . . not as I love you."

"I guessed there was something between you. Annora, if you would care for Jonnie to come here . . . to be brought up here . . . I could be fond of him . . . treat him as my own son."

"Jonnie, come here! His mother would never allow that. Helena dotes on him. He's her beloved first-born." I stared at him in astonishment. "Oh no. You couldn't have thought . . ."

"Well," he said. "You went to Australia. He was born there. You were friendly with Joe. There seemed to be some mystery about his birth."

"You thought he was mine! And you were ready to marry me and have him here. Oh, Rolf, I do love you so much. Jonnie is Helena's child. John Milward is his father. Matthew, who scarcely knew her then, nobly married her so that as she was to have a child she should have a husband."

"What a web we wove with our imaginations!"

"You no less than I. I'm glad of that. It makes me feel less guilty. Helena is wonderfully happy. Isn't it marvellous that all that contentment should have come about in a marriage which was so arranged?"

"How much better one should be when the two people concerned have been in love ever since they knew each other. That's true, isn't it?"

"Yes, it's true."

[333]

"There is one little point which needs clearing up. There is still Cador. It will now come back into your possession. How will you know I am not marrying you for Cador?"

"I'll take the risk," I said. "And frankly, I can only rejoice that you may want it so much that you are ready to take me with it."

"That's a fair offer. Now I have something to tell you. Luke Tregern raised money with Cador as security. It's mortgaged up to the hilt. Some of the money which Luke Tregern amassed will be retrieved no doubt. But not all. Cador will not be in the sound financial position which it was before all this happened. I'll tell you something; I secured the greater part of the mortgages. So you could say that instead of your bringing Cador to me I am bringing it to you."

I was astonished. I had been warned that a great deal of harm had been done to the estate during Maria's possession. I knew that Bob Carter was going into the accounts with Rolf, but I had not realized to what extent it had suffered.

Rolf took my hands and said: "There is only one thing for you to do now and that is get well . . . just as quickly as you can."

We were silent for some time.

Then he said: "Annora, there is nothing else, is there? No other misapprehension, no other misunderstanding?"

"No," I said. "Nothing."

"We'll be married in Midsummer. That will exorcise the ghosts."

"Then there will be another Midsummer's Eve to remember," I said.